T0382115

THE
REBEL
WITCH

ALSO BY
KRISTEN CICCARELLI

Edgewood

THE CRIMSON MOTH SERIES
The Crimson Moth

THE ISKARI SERIES
The Last Namsara
The Caged Queen
The Sky Weaver

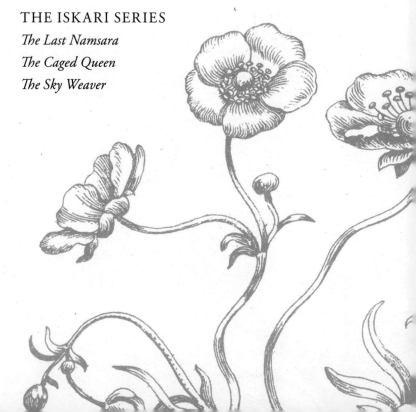

THE REBEL WITCH

KRISTEN CICCARELLI

MAGPIE

Magpie Books
An imprint of
HarperCollins*Publishers* Ltd
1 London Bridge Street
London SE1 9GF

www.harpercollins.co.uk

HarperCollins*Publishers*
Macken House,
39/40 Mayor Street Upper,
Dublin 1
D01 C9W8
Ireland

First published by HarperCollins*Publishers* Ltd 2025
4

A catalogue record for this book is available from the British Library.

ISBN: 978-0-00-865061-2 (HB)
ISBN: 978-0-00-865062-9 (TPB)

This novel is entirely a work of fiction.
The names, characters and incidents portrayed in it are
the work of the author's imagination. Any resemblance to
actual persons, living or dead, events or localities is
entirely coincidental.

Printed and bound in the UK using 100% renewable electricity by CPI Group (UK) Ltd

MIX
Paper | Supporting
responsible forestry
FSC
www.fsc.org FSC™ C007454

This book contains FSC™ certified paper and other controlled sources
to ensure responsible forest management.

For more information visit: www.harpercollins.co.uk/green

FOR THE BRAVE ONES
WHO LIGHT THE WAY

PART ONE

In the beginning, there was darkness. Until the Seven Sisters laughed and a world burst into being. The sisters walked its waves and carved its shorelines. They breathed life into all things and bound the world together with love, goodness, and beauty.

But they couldn't stay forever. Before moving on, they chose a select few to watch over the world in their absence. To help these guardians love and protect their creation, the Seven Sisters gave them a gift.

The gift of magic.

And then, like a flame extinguished, they vanished.

—CREATION MYTH FROM
THE CULT OF THE ANCIENTS

ONE

GIDEON

GIDEON TUGGED AT THE jacket of his stolen uniform. The forest green fabric was stiff, as if it hadn't been broken in.

The poor guard he'd taken it from was currently unconscious and tied up in a supply closet on the third floor of Larkmont Palace. Four other guards hadn't been so lucky. Their bodies were floating in the frigid waters of the fjord.

He'd had no choice.

Gideon was deep in enemy territory. If discovered, he'd be better off dead.

His thoughts were a dark contrast to the bright ballroom he stood in. Musical instruments hummed as they warmed up, preparing for the private recital that was about to start. Chandeliers winked overhead as servants wove between the glittering guests in Prince Soren's ballroom, offering one last round of refreshments before the music started.

As Gideon stood along the wall, watching the room like the other guards, his gaze fixed on his mark: the beautiful girl in the golden dress.

Rune Winters.

Prince Soren stood beside her, his palm pressed to the small of Rune's back. The Umbrian prince wore a tailored suit, his family's silver crest stitched into the cape slung stylishly over one shoulder, and his hungry gaze roamed down the dress Rune wore, inviting his rich friends to do the same.

Gideon's blood burned as he watched them.

It was a beautiful gown—he couldn't deny it. Made by some fancy designer, it likely cost a small fortune. But it wasn't *Rune*. Gold didn't suit her, and the cut was severe. The plunging V neckline ended a few inches above her belly button in front and at the base of her spine in back, sending a powerful message:

Look at her. She's mine.

The prince wanted his guests to admire the beautiful witch on his arm. To Soren, Rune was an exotic creature. A living artifact he was determined to add to his collection.

If Harrow's intel was correct, one week ago, the prince had asked her to marry him. And Rune had accepted, on one condition: if Soren wanted her for a wife, he had to give Cressida an army.

It's why Gideon volunteered for this job.

With an army, Cressida would wage war against the New Republic. If she won, she would reinstate the Reign of Witches and more people would die.

Gideon couldn't let that happen. So long as Rune was the lynchpin in this unholy alliance between Cressida and Soren, he couldn't let her live.

Gideon had kill orders and he was going to see them through. Right here. Tonight.

He'd waited all evening for his chance. Standing against the wall of the ballroom, sweating in this stolen uniform, he watched Rune flirting with her betrothed. Watched Soren flirt back: touching her with hungry hands, devouring her with haughty eyes.

It was driving him to the brink.

Alex was barely in the ground, and Rune was already engaged to another man. A prince, no less.

Is that what she wanted all along—a prince?

He was a fool to think he'd ever had a chance.

Gideon fingered the gun holstered at his hip. He was ready. More than ready. All he needed was the right moment . . .

"Do you miss your home?"

Gideon scanned the circle of party guests surrounding Rune and Soren until his gaze landed on the speaker: a young woman with wheat-gold hair braided into a crown.

Rune laughed. "Can you miss a place where everyone wants you dead?"

Gideon watched her press her champagne glass to her red lips, then tip the last swallow into her mouth.

It was her third drink tonight.

Not that Gideon was counting.

"What was it like before the revolution?"

"We witches once lived as you do," Rune said, motioning to the grand hall they stood in, where chandeliers twinkled and marble columns propped up the painted ceiling. "Our lives were full of music, beauty, art . . ."

Yes, thought Gideon. *And your luxuries came at the expense of our misery.*

The buzz and hum of fiddles grew louder. Gideon glanced across the room, where guests began to fill chairs facing the musicians.

"That way of life was stolen from us the night Gideon Sharpe led a group of revolutionaries into the palace."

At the sound of his name on her lips, his attention shot back to her.

"He murdered two queens in their beds while his comrades cut the rest of us down in the streets. He would have let them murder me, too, if Cressida hadn't saved me."

Gideon bristled. *You're leaving out a lot of the story, sweetheart.*

"It must be heartbreaking," said the prince as his knuckles grazed the bumps of Rune's spine in a slow path downward. "To be so far away, knowing the horrible things taking place there . . . I'm glad you're free of it."

Soren's arms slid around her waist, in what might have been an effort to comfort her, but felt more like a reminder: Rune was *his*.

Gideon rolled his shoulders, forcing himself to relax.

"Witches are still being slaughtered for nothing more than the crime of being what they are," said Rune, studying her empty glass from within Soren's arms. "I'll never be free until every last one of my sisters is free, too."

The hum of instruments fell silent and an announcement sounded: the recital was starting.

One by one, the circle of guests dispersed, moving toward the musicians.

Twining his fingers through Rune's, Soren tugged her toward their seats. They'd barely walked two steps when the first song started, and Rune's footsteps faltered.

Gideon watched her jerk to a stop.

"Everything all right?" asked the prince, turning back to her.

As the music rose, Gideon glanced to the musicians. The song was familiar. But why he recognized it, he didn't know.

"I-I need to powder my nose." Rune seemed to be struggling to compose herself. "I'll be right back . . ."

"Don't be ridiculous," said Soren. "The concert has begun." He lowered his voice. "This recital is for *you*, Rune. To celebrate our engagement. You need to be here."

His fingers white-knuckled around hers.

Gideon's eyes narrowed. His body tightened like a coiled spring as he watched Soren drag her onward. Closer to the music. The very thing she was trying to get away from.

"I need . . ." Rune tried to tug her hand out of his. When Soren appeared to grip harder, refusing to release her, Gideon stepped out of position along the wall. The guards stationed ten paces down glanced his way, reminding Gideon that he was surrounded by enemies. He couldn't draw attention to himself.

Also: Rune didn't need to be rescued. This was made clear as she stepped directly in front of Soren, blocking his path to the chairs.

"I promise not to miss much." Pushing herself onto her toes, she slid her pale arms around the prince's neck and grazed his cheek with her lips, lingering there. When Soren's free hand settled on her hip, admiring its curve, she added: "Later tonight, when the recital is over and the guests are gone, I have something special planned for you."

Gideon's heart dropped at those words. As he watched Soren slide his hand up and run his fingers along Rune's jaw, his entire body turned to stone.

"Something special?" the prince murmured, leaning down to press his mouth to Rune's.

Slipping her hand into his brown hair, Rune kissed Soren back, giving him a taste of what was to come. Soren pulled her in closer, and Gideon knew this wasn't the first time. There had been other kisses. Probably more than kisses.

The realization awoke something in him. Something tremulous and aching. It knotted around his rib cage, threatening to drag him to the bottom of the sea.

Enough.

He reached for his pistol.

But before he could finish this, Rune slipped out of Soren's grasp.

"I think you'll like my surprise." Her cheeks were rosy as

she walked backward. "See if you can guess what it is while I'm gone."

Rune winked. The prince's eyes darkened with lust.

Gideon was going to be sick.

Rune spun on her heel and strode away, leaving Soren and Gideon to stare after her, the dress putting her on full display.

She rushed past guests making their way toward their chairs and guards stationed along the walls. As she hurried to the door, she nearly ran straight into the servant coming through them, halting just before they collided. The young woman balanced a shaking tray of glasses in one hand and held a bottle of whiskey in the other.

Gideon watched Rune exchange a few words with the servant, take the bottle from her, and disappear into the hall.

There it is.

The moment he'd been waiting for.

TWO

RUNE

DON'T CRY DON'T CRY *don't cry.*

Tears burned in Rune's eyes as she fled down the hall, past the stoic guards in their dark green uniforms. She was glad the rims of their hats shielded their faces, preventing her from seeing what they must think of her.

She couldn't let the tears spill. Not here. Not with them all watching.

But no matter how fast she ran, she couldn't outrun the song still playing in the ballroom, each note an arrow through her heart.

Alex's song.

The wistful tune had transported Rune back to Wintersea, to standing in her library's doorway, watching her best friend hunched over the keys of her grand piano, his hands casting a spell over the room.

Alexander Sharpe.

This song—the one chasing her away—was the last he'd ever written.

Rune touched his ring, still on her finger, as a wave of grief swelled inside her. She scrambled for something to protect herself against the terrible wave, that horrible *missing*, and came up empty-handed.

It was why she'd needed out of that ballroom. Before she broke down sobbing in the middle of a party to celebrate her upcoming marriage to a prince.

We would have been married by now.

She would have preferred Alex over Soren. Alex was her best friend. Other than her grandmother, he was the only person in the world who'd ever truly loved her. She might not have been *in love* with him, but given enough time, perhaps she could have been.

But Alex wasn't the only thing she missed.

If Rune was being honest, she missed her home.

Home.

The word seared her.

Back in the ballroom, Soren's friend had asked if she missed the New Republic, and Rune had laughed the question off.

But the truth?

The truth was Rune missed the sight of Nan's gardens, sparkling with dew. She missed riding Lady through the wildest parts of Wintersea. She missed the smell of the sea and the woods and the fields. She missed the winds and storms.

She liked Umbria and its capital, Caelis. She liked the architecture and the art, the culture and fashions and food, the absence of anti-witch sentiment. She liked it for a visit or a holiday. But it wasn't where she belonged.

Rune hadn't realized she'd feel this way when she agreed to marry Alex and leave the New Republic. She didn't know that in leaving the island behind, she was leaving her heart with it.

Could you miss the place where everyone wanted you dead?

Rune squeezed the whiskey bottle's neck. *Apparently yes.*

If there weren't a dozen guards watching her flee, Rune would have guzzled whiskey straight from the bottle. The three glasses of champagne had numbed her a little, warming her insides and blurring the edges of her vision. It was how she got through most evenings now: in a fog of intoxication.

But if she were going to get through *this* evening, she'd need more than three glasses of alcohol. She'd need an entire bathtub full.

As Alex's song built, growing louder, as its melancholic sound sank into her bones, Rune hiked up her dress and ran, glancing back over her shoulder to make sure Soren wasn't following.

Soren. Her fiancé.

Rune shivered, her skin still numb in all the places he'd touched her.

Later tonight, when the recital is over and the guests are gone, I have something special planned for you.

A cold sweat broke out over her skin.

Why did I say that?

Rune had nothing planned. She'd simply needed to flee.

The thought of going to him later, *alone*, made her gut twist. She would rather walk into the sea, her pockets full of heavy stones.

Make him want you.

It was the directive Cressida had given Rune when they first came to Umbria: to make herself irresistible to Soren Nord, an Umbrian prince.

It was what Rune was good at, after all.

Enticing men.

Soren possessed a fleet of warships. As a former admiral in the navy, he was well traveled and had a penchant for collecting beautiful, exotic things. Best of all, though: he was sympathetic to witches and rumored to be on the hunt for a wife.

So after the opera one night, while Cressida watched from the wings, Rune waited for the prince to exit his box and planted herself directly in his path. He'd walked straight into her, spilling wine down the front of her very expensive dress.

The prince was horrified at his clumsiness. And Rune was so gracious and forgiving. To make it up to her, he invited her to the ballet the next night. And the theater two nights after that. Suddenly, they were spending every day together. Going on strolls or carriage rides. Dining alone.

He was smitten, and Rune stoked his affection, playing her part perfectly, until she had what Cressida wanted: a proposal.

But to Soren's surprise, Rune turned him down.

I can't marry you, she told him, reciting her lines. *Not until every last witch is safe.*

More specifically: she *wouldn't* marry him—not unless he gave Cressida an army to wage war on the New Republic.

Rune had no desire to marry Soren, nor was she interested in doing the witch queen's bidding. The very idea of working for Cressida filled Rune with dizzying self-loathing.

But Cressida had saved her life, along with Seraphine's. Cressida didn't want her dead, unlike Gideon and everyone else in the New Republic. Most importantly: Cressida wanted to save the witches they'd left behind. Girls who were being exterminated at this very moment.

Every week, the names of dead witches made their way to Rune's ears. The Blood Guard had captured Aurelia Kantor, a powerful sibyl—a witch who could see into the past, present, and future. And now they were using her to give them the locations of every witch in hiding. It allowed them to hunt down and execute witches with merciless precision. Sometimes as many as three or four a week.

Ancients knew what they were doing to Aurelia to get that information.

Once, the Crimson Moth would have rescued her. But the Moth was here in Larkmont Palace, all the way across the Barrow Strait, half-drunk on champagne.

Look at yourself, Rune thought. *Partying with princes while your sisters are murdered.*

She'd abandoned those girls. And if Gideon Sharpe wasn't stopped, there would be no witches left in the New Republic.

If Rune were still on the island, she would have already broken

Aurelia out of custody and smuggled her to the Continent, protecting other witches in the process. But the only way in was by sea, and every port of entry teemed with witch hunters and their witch-hunting hounds—dogs trained to scent magic. They were even stationed aboard ships traveling to and from the island.

Only one ship—the *Arcadia*—refused to allow the Blood Guard and their beasts to board their vessels. But that just meant the witch hunters traveled undercover. And once the boat entered New Republic waters, it was boarded by hounds who sniffed out every witch before they could set foot on the island.

Even *if* Rune got the sibyl out somehow, the Blood Guard would never stop hunting her kind. The New Republic's spies were searching the continent for Cressida Roseblood and her growing court, and if they had a sibyl in their hands, it was only a matter of time before they found where they were hiding.

They will never stop hunting us.

The only way to keep witches safe was to destroy the Blood Guard and tear down the New Republic.

And the only way to do *that* was to put Cressida back on her throne.

Rune wanted Cressida on a throne like she wanted a hole in her chest. The girl was vile. A cold-blooded murderess. But when compared to the alternative—a society that wanted to tie girls like Rune up by the ankles, slit their throats, and watch the blood drain from their bodies—Cressida Roseblood was the lesser of two evils.

Because under the rule of a witch queen, at least witches would be *safe*.

With Soren's backing, Cressida would ensure no witch was ever hunted again.

Cressida was in the capital, looking for more alliances to forge, but she was due back any day now. The moment she returned, she and Soren would sign the contract his lawyers had drafted, sealing their alliance.

And Rune would be required to marry him.

The powder room came into view. Rune fixed her gaze on the door. Once safely inside, she would let herself fall apart. Just for a minute. And when that minute was up . . .

Rune thrust the door open and stepped inside, letting it swing shut behind her.

Candles lit the dark room, flickering in wall sconces and in candleholders lining the sink's ledge. As she strode to the sink, Rune uncorked the whiskey and took a long sip straight from the bottle. It burned her tongue and throat.

I thought I left all of this behind.

Rune had assumed it would be easy. After all, she was used to playing roles. Playing the part of "smitten fiancée" should have been a piece of cake.

But ever since Alex's death, the flirting and scheming and deceiving was taking a toll. Hence: her near breakdown in front of Soren's friends, and the bottle of whiskey gripped in her fist.

After fleeing the New Republic, Rune had foolishly thought she might finally get to be herself. No longer a silly, shallow socialite but a witch in plain sight. The *real* Rune Winters.

But who is that? she thought. *Who is the real Rune Winters?*

She shoved the question down.

It doesn't matter. Cressida needed an army, and Soren had one. It was up to Rune to secure that army. What mattered was who she *needed* to be: a girl who would put an end to the Blood Guard and finally ensure the safety of all witches.

You can do this. Remember what's at stake.

At the sink, she took another long sip of whiskey, shivering at the taste, and glanced into the mirror. Tears streaked her face.

Her reddened eyes stared back at her, splotches of pink mottling her nose and cheeks.

Her gaze moved downward. The golden dress Soren had given her was not at all her taste. Gold was for accents only; it drew too much attention otherwise. And the cut was, well . . . razor-sharp. It put her entire body on display.

She hated it.

It made her think of another dress. One that suited her like no other ever would. Because the giver knew what her soul required, not just her body.

Rune fought off that thought before its claws burrowed in.

She would *not* think of Gideon Sharpe. She was *done* thinking about him.

Except, apparently, she wasn't.

Like Alex, Gideon had also proposed to Rune. Not marriage, exactly, but a partnership. A future together.

She fisted her hands.

Gideon never really loved you. He loved the girl he thought you were. So it doesn't matter what he proposed.

Gideon could never love a witch.

She wasn't sure what was more upsetting: that Alex had loved her, or that Gideon didn't.

Rune had been so certain the Blood Guard captain would hunt her down—as he'd sworn to do. But two months had passed, and he hadn't come.

Maybe he decided I'm not worth his revenge.

Maybe he's moved on.

Rune clenched her fists.

Who cared what the reason was? He was gone. Out of her life.

Tears burned in her eyes, sharper than the whiskey. Rune took another swig, hoping it would numb her enough to go back to the ballroom. Surely Alex's song was over by now.

But her feet refused to turn around and walk her back.

Rune glanced at the ring on her finger and lowered the bottle.

He's gone. He's never coming back. You've had two months to grieve. It's time to move on.

Alex would understand why she had to do this. Why she needed to marry Soren. He wouldn't like it, but he would understand. He would forgive her.

It was the thought of Alex—kind, good, safe Alex—*forgiving* her that did Rune in.

Instead of rallying, the opposite happened. Something tried to claw its way out of her. She grabbed hold of the sink's ceramic sides, desperately needing to hold it back.

But she couldn't.

The grief erupted.

Rune gripped the sink and broke into silent, quaking sobs as the sadness wrapped around her like chains, pulling her down with its weight. She was so overwhelmed by it, she almost didn't hear the door open behind her.

Though her vision was blurred with tears, she saw forest green flash across the mirror.

Great. Soren has sent one of his guards to fetch me.

Could she not have five minutes alone?

Was this to be the rest of her life?

Palming the tears from her eyes, she reached for the smile she used as a weapon. The one that masked the emptiness inside. She was about to use it on this unsuspecting guard, when another glance into the mirror stopped her. Rune would know that cruel mouth anywhere.

Gideon pushed back his hat and aimed his gun straight at her.

As their gazes met, Rune's heart pounded like a hurricane.

I thought you'd forgotten me.

THREE

GIDEON

*A*S HE RAISED HIS gun to kill, Gideon made his first mistake of the evening.

He looked at Rune before firing.

Those cold gray eyes bored into him. The same eyes that haunted him night after night. The eyes of a girl he wanted to forget.

Why is she crying?

Gideon squeezed the pistol in his hand.

It doesn't matter. I don't care.

But he couldn't unsee the tears streaming down her face. Couldn't *not* notice the whiskey bottle—significantly less full than when she'd grabbed it while fleeing the ballroom.

The sight of her threatened to crack something in him. It was a dangerous, destabilizing feeling. Gideon needed to steel himself against it.

"Some things never change, do they?"

Rune spoke calmly to the mirror, her gaze locked on him. Gideon resisted the urge to skim the lines of her golden dress.

Shoot her, damn it.

"Stalking a girl into the powder room with the intent to murder her is business as usual for you. Isn't it, Gideon Sharpe?"

"Funny how you can't keep my name out of your mouth tonight."

Her gaze hardened to pewter. "What would your brother say if he saw you right now?"

Those words landed like a slap. He shrugged off the sting, forcing himself to remember that this witch was a master of deception. She'd deceived him into thinking she was an innocent girl. A girl who loved him. Meanwhile, she'd been secretly saving witches to build Cressida's army. Not to mention, engaged to Alex.

Alex.

"My brother is dead because of you."

She turned to face him, and Gideon couldn't help himself. His gaze raked down the vicious V cut of her dress, now so close to him. Taking in far too much of her.

He swallowed down a sharp breath. "That dress looks ridiculous on you."

Liar.

Rune rose to the bait, eyes flashing. "Soren would disagree, I think. He can't keep his hands off me."

A poisonous feeling swept through Gideon.

She lifted her chin and smirked.

Gideon remembered her fingers twined through the prince's. How generous she'd been with her kisses. Staying close to him at all times. Letting him show her off to his friends.

She'd never done those things with Gideon.

It was a stern reminder of how out of his league she'd always been. How had Gideon ever let himself believe she'd settle for someone like him?

He'd been a sucker from the start.

"You've raised your expectations considerably," he said. "Aiming for a prince."

Her face hardened into a mask, but not one he was used to. All trace of the frivolous socialite she once pretended to be was gone. This mask was blank as a stone.

"On the contrary. These days, my only requirement for suitors is that they don't want me dead. Most people would call those *low* expectations."

"Whatever you say." His shoulders straightened and he steadied his aim, needing to get this over with. "I'm just glad Alex isn't here to witness how fast you've moved on."

The words visibly struck Rune. Her hands clenched. "If Alex were here, I wouldn't *have* to move on."

"Until he discovered the truth: that you're a conniving little—"

Rune flung the whiskey bottle straight at his head.

Gideon ducked. The wind of its passing ruffled his hair. The glass shattered against the wall behind him, and the spray of alcohol dampened his neck. A blur of gold shot past, and Gideon realized, almost too late, Rune was bolting for the exit.

He'd expected a spell, not a bottle flying at his face.

Gideon grabbed her around the waist and shoved her against the wall. He heard the air whoosh from her lungs. Before she could recover, he pinned her wrists over her head, then shoved his knee between her legs, trapping her there.

Rune gasped, glaring up at him.

Keeping her wrists pinned with one hand, he pressed the barrel of his gun to her temple.

Her smell invaded his senses, like juniper and sea salt. Threatening to weaken him. He swallowed, heart racing. It was dangerous being this close to her.

"I wish Alex never stepped in front of that bullet," she said. "It should be *you* who's dead. I wish it was you!"

The words were like a rusted knife in his gut.

How many times had he wished the same?

He remembered it all too well: Cressida demanding Gideon come with her, then lifting her gun and firing when he refused. Alex taking the bullet intended for him.

He could still hear Rune's scream. Still see her in his mind, covered in his brother's blood, clinging to Alex as he died.

And yet: if Rune had never helped Cressida Roseblood, Alex would be alive. It was Cressida who fired the gun, but Rune had helped conceal her. She'd been in league with Gideon's greatest enemy the whole time. Even now, Rune was trying to put Alex's murderer back on the throne.

This is why you're here.

He'd failed the Republic by falling in love with his mark. He'd suspected Rune was the Crimson Moth—a villainous witch he'd spent two years hunting—and he'd fallen for her anyway.

Rune had never loved Gideon. It had all been an elaborate farce. The entire time she'd pretended to court him, she was in love with his brother.

What had she said near the end?

Alex is twice the man you'll ever be.

Rune made Gideon believe that someone like her could love someone like him. And it was a lie. He was beneath her and always would be.

But Gideon hadn't wanted to see the truth.

He'd wanted Rune.

Because I'm weak.

By falling for her, Gideon had failed the Republic he'd helped build, the friends and soldiers he'd sworn to stand beside, the citizens he'd vowed to protect. Rune had weakened him, and that weakness had gotten people killed. It would continue to if left unchecked.

It's why Gideon was here. To carve out the weakness in his heart by eliminating the source: *her.* And into the hole left behind, he would pour molten steel. Until he was welded back together. Until he was stronger and colder than iron.

He dug the barrel of his gun into Rune's temple.

She didn't wince or look away. Just locked gazes with him. As if she'd been waiting for this moment. Waiting for *him*.

"Go ahead. Pull the trigger."

"I intend to."

"Yeah? *Prove it.*"

He'd forgotten the way her eyes raged when she was angry. Like a storm he wanted to walk straight into.

"We both know what you want to do to me, Gideon. Well, here's your chance."

His gaze slid to her mouth. "You have no idea, the things I want to do to you."

From this close, he noticed everything: the puffy redness of her eyes, the pink splotches on her face, the tears drying on her cheeks.

The alcohol on her breath.

Gideon knew Rune occasionally indulged, but this was something else.

He frowned. "You reek like an alehouse."

"Spoken like a true gentleman." Her voice was a husky growl.

"I've never been a gentleman." He leaned closer. "If you mistook me for one, that's on you."

It was impossible not to be aware of every inch of her. The heat of her thighs on either side of his knee. The fevered beat of her pulse beneath his palm. She was as small and soft as he remembered. Flawless. *Lovely.*

Gideon had a desperate urge to take her face in his hands and ask her what was wrong, to make her tell him why she was so upset.

He shook off the temptation.

This was what she did to him: made him completely irrational.

She's a coldhearted seductress. Don't let her deceive you.

Rune had opened her mouth—probably to insult him further—when the shouts of several guards made them both freeze. Boots thudded in the corridor. They must have heard the bottle shatter and were now in search of its source.

Gideon glanced around the powder room. The only exit was the door behind him, which opened into that same corridor. The moment the gun went off, he'd give his location away. And with no exit, the guards would corner him.

He'd be as good as dead. *Worse* than dead. If they arrested him, he'd be at Cressida's mercy. He couldn't fall prisoner to her again. Gideon would take his own life before it came to that.

The pulse in Rune's wrist quickened beneath his thumb. If she called out, they would find him for sure.

"Scream for help," he whispered as the guards drew closer, his gun still pressed to her temple, "and I'll put a bullet in your brain."

"If I stay silent, you'll kill me anyway."

True. But Rune seemed to want to live a little longer, because she didn't scream.

He cursed himself for hesitating. He should have come in, shot her, and left. No thinking. Just doing.

But he'd always preferred the raw, wild Rune to the one hiding behind a mask of style and poise. If he'd found the latter in this room—a beautiful girl powdering her perfect nose, not a hair out of place nor a crease in her dress—they probably wouldn't be having this conversation. She'd already be dead.

Instead, he'd found *this* Rune.

His Rune.

A total mess.

The basest part of him wanted to tilt her head back and kiss her until she told him why she was crying.

No. He gritted his teeth. *That is the opposite of what I want.*

But now that he'd thought it, Gideon couldn't *un*think it, and his mind pulled him down more dangerous paths. The last time he and Rune were pressed against each other, she'd been beneath him. In his bed. He'd been worshiping her with his mouth. Whispering delicious things into her skin. They'd given themselves to each other in an act that couldn't be undone, and now he was suffering the consequences of that decision.

This girl.

He'd wanted so badly to be worthy of her. He'd dared to hope he could be, stupid fool that he was.

Never again will I fall for her tricks.

"Help me understand," he whispered, listening to the receding footsteps, suddenly needing to know. "You'd put Cressida back in power despite knowing what she's capable of? Do you long for terror and bloodshed?"

"For the people who want to hunt me down and slit my throat?" Rune furrowed her perfect brows. "What else should I want for them?"

He narrowed his eyes. "And when it's all over, and your precious witches are safe, with your tyrant sitting once more on her dark throne, you'll be married to a prince who treats you like a prize. Is that also what you want? To be put on display, like a trophy in a glass case?"

She seemed to hesitate, then tilted her chin in defiance. "Soren will make me happier than *some* men ever could."

To think he'd kissed the mouth those words came out of.

"You might fool the rest of them, but you don't fool me. Look at you, Rune. You're drinking yourself sick to get through an evening with him." It made him think of himself, not so long ago. And he didn't like the reminder. "You'll hate being Soren Nord's wife."

"You have no idea what I hate."

"I have some idea."

Her eyes crackled like lightning. "You don't know me at all."

"I may not know *Rune Winters*," he whispered, his mouth an inch from hers. "But I know the Crimson Moth. And she is no caged thing."

Rune flinched. "Stop it."

"I pity the man who clips her wings."

"Stop talking."

"Say goodbye to your freedom, Rune."

"Shut up!"

She bucked against him, and Gideon nearly lost his grip on her wrists. He'd forgotten how strong she was, despite being half his size. He withdrew his knee to regain control.

His second mistake.

Rune thrust her small knee straight into his groin.

Pain exploded like a bomb, lighting him up. The room went bright white. Gideon doubled over, collapsing to the floor as the unbearable pressure in his balls made the world fade away. He curled his knees to his chest to protect himself, in case she tried again.

Rune picked up his gun. "That's for handing me over to be purged."

Gideon groaned, lying in a puddle of whiskey and broken glass and pain.

The door flew open.

The smell of blood and roses filled the room as someone stepped inside.

"Why, Gideon Sharpe," came a voice that still haunted his nightmares, "what a pleasant surprise."

Her shadow slid over him, turning his blood to ice. Gideon didn't look up. He knew who he'd find there: a witch with birch-white hair and eyes as cold as a frozen sea.

Cressida Roseblood.

Gideon shut his eyes.

Fuck.

He'd always told himself it was better to be dead than in Cressida's clutches. That if he ever fell prisoner to her again, he'd find a way to end it all.

He glanced at his pistol, still in Rune's hands.

Utterly out of reach.

FOUR

GIDEON

G UARDS GRABBED GIDEON'S ARMS and hauled him to his feet, locking his wrists into manacles behind his back.

Cressida approached. Her hair was damp, as if she'd ridden through a storm to get here. And her gaze was a knife plunged into his chest. Gideon's pain vanished, replaced by a numbing fear.

This was his worst nightmare come to life.

Cressida glanced from him to Rune, who held Gideon's gun and was still aiming it at him. A question flared in the young witch queen's eyes, but she didn't voice it. Only held out her hand to the guards, demanding the key to his chains.

"Ava, I need you," Cress told the young woman who'd come in with her. "Everyone else: get out."

Gideon recognized the girl who stepped forward: Ava Saers. A witch and former scar artist to the Rosebloods. During the Sister Queens' reign, wealthy witches employed scar artists— talented artisans adept at cutting casting scars to form beautiful patterns in a witch's skin. The Roseblood sisters liked to carve each other's scars, but would partake of Ava's artistry on special occasions. He remembered watching Ava carve with almost delicate ease into their skin.

She was one of the first witches the Crimson Moth had stolen from his holding cells.

Ava's auburn hair was knotted fashionably to one side of her head, and her sapphire gown shimmered in the candlelight as she walked toward her queen. She must have been a guest at the recital tonight.

How many other witches is Soren giving sanctuary to?

After popping open her sequined clutch, Ava withdrew a small knife.

Cressida unclasped her cloak and let it fall to the floor, giving Gideon an unobstructed view of both arms. Silver scars covered every inch of her skin, each one painfully familiar to Gideon. Like a garden of flowers starting at her wrists and twining upward, growing toward her shoulders.

Ava pressed the knife to Cressida's skin and started to cut, adding petals to a lily in the botanical pattern.

The smell of Cressida's magic bloomed in the air: the coppery tang of blood mingled with the sickly sweet scent of roses.

When Ava finished, Cress dipped her fingers into the blood seeping up. Gideon blanched as the witch queen crouched, smearing bright red spellmarks across the floor before him. Magic thickened the air, making him nauseous as her spell took hold.

Thick, invisible ivy crawled up his legs, securing him to the floor. The magic didn't stop there: it climbed up his arms and chest and shoulders. Immobilizing him.

Gideon strained against the spell. His muscles bunched and his teeth clenched. As if his will alone could break the bonds of her magic. But the more he struggled, the tighter it bound him.

Cressida's spell held him fast.

You deserve this.

If he hadn't hesitated at the sight of Rune's tears, if he'd simply pulled the trigger, he'd be riding back to Caelis right now, his mission accomplished.

Cressida rose to her feet and walked toward Gideon before pausing.

"Rune?" She glanced over her shoulder. "Did you hear what I said?"

Gideon looked past the witch queen to find Rune still in the room, standing a few paces beyond them. She seemed frozen in place, the pistol in her hands trained on him, her gray eyes unreadable.

Their gazes locked. An invisible charge electrified the air.

End this. Put me out of my misery.

She knew what Cress had done to him in the past. She knew what Cress would do to him now.

"Rune." He stared her down, pleading. *"Shoot."*

Her eyes were a raging storm. If she pulled the trigger, it would not be out of pity but something much stronger.

Cressida stepped between them. "Give Ava the pistol."

Like a severed thread, the command snapped Rune out of whatever thoughts ensnared her.

"The *pistol*, Rune."

Rune glanced down at the gun in her hands. And then, like a good little foot soldier, she handed it over to Ava.

She didn't look at Gideon again. Just turned and walked away, shards of glass crunching beneath her shoes. The door swung shut behind her, leaving Gideon alone with Cressida and her scar artist.

Like she didn't care at all.

Ava walked to the sink and set his gun down on its ceramic edge, then stared into the mirror as she fixed her makeup.

"Look at us. Reunited at last."

He tore his gaze from the door Rune had exited, returning his attention to the enemy in the room. Cressida Roseblood was beautiful—in a cold, terrifying way. Like being lost in a blizzard, knowing it was going to kill you.

Blood dripped down her arm and smudged the fingers of her hand. She stopped a foot away from Gideon and drew out her casting knife. Pressing its flat, crescent edge beneath his chin, she forced his gaze to hers.

Running the edge of the blade down his throat, she said: "Did you come to Larkmont alone?"

His mouth went dry. "Yes."

She walked around him, trailing the knife across his shoulders, stopping at his back. He felt her slip the key into his manacles, then twist. The chains rattled to the floor.

He tried to reach for the knife, for *her*, but his freed hands were still bound by her spell.

Cressida continued circling, dragging her blade over his body, until she faced him once more. Hooking her knife into the collar of his stolen jacket, she tugged downward, popping open the top button. Gideon heard the rip of his undershirt beneath.

His heart pounded.

"And your purpose here?"

"To assassinate Rune Winters."

She continued, popping the next jacket button, tearing his undershirt further. "Why?"

Gideon swallowed. "To stop her from securing an alliance between you and Soren Nord."

"And was she happy to see you?"

Gideon paused, not understanding the question.

Cressida sliced swiftly downward, cutting open the jacket and the shirt beneath. The fabric fell open, revealing Gideon's chest.

The corner of her mouth curled as her gaze slid from his throat down. He knew that look. It made him break out in a cold sweat.

"You stole everything from me, Gideon."

"I'm pretty sure it was the other way around."

"I want to forgive you. I do."

Forgive *him*?

"After you murdered my sisters, I wanted you to suffer. I've had a lot of time to think about what I'd do to you, once I had you in my hands again. And I've realized . . . well, I'm *indebted* to you."

He stared at her.

Had she gone mad?

Cressida took his jaw in her grip, forcing him to look at her. Her ice-blue eyes chilled him to his core.

"You made me realize how much I took my sisters for granted. How much I *need* them. Elowyn, Analise, and I are so much stronger together. Which is why"—she bared her teeth in a smile—"I'm going to bring them back."

She'd definitely gone mad.

"Your sisters are nothing but bones in the ground." He didn't know this for certain. Analise and Elowyn's bodies went missing in the chaos of the New Dawn. People had assumed the corpses were stolen and defiled or thrown into the mass graves reserved for witches killed in the revolution.

"Oh, Gideon." Cressida laughed. "You think I'd let my sisters rot?" She shook her head, sending her pale hair scattering like snow. "I hid their bodies somewhere safe. For two years, I've kept them preserved with magic."

"That's not possible."

But this was Cressida Roseblood. He knew exactly what she was capable of.

"A resurrection spell simply requires the sacrifice of a close kin—someone with strong blood ties to the deceased." She tilted her head, narrowing her eyes. "I could do it in my sleep."

"Your entire family is dead," Gideon pointed out. "You don't have any kin."

"Oh, but it turns out I do."

He frowned. *What?*

"A long-lost sibling." She smiled. "Unfortunately, I don't know who or where they are. All the sibyls in my employ can't See them. Someone's concealed them with an ancient spell—for now."

A missing Roseblood heir?

Dread filled his chest like lead. Cressida alone was one thing. She might retake her throne, but she'd struggle to hold it by herself. With the purgings, witch numbers had drastically declined. People remembered the tyranny at the Reign of Witches' end, and they would not welcome its return. She'd have to use force and fear—which was precisely why she needed Soren's army.

Does Rune know about this?

Elowyn and Analise were the more powerful—and the more vicious—Roseblood sisters. They had tortured Gideon's mother and were the reason both his parents were dead. If Cressida resurrected them, it would mean the return of all three witch queens. Together, they would end the New Republic.

"But enough about that." Cressida's hands coasted up the lapels of Gideon's jacket, pushing it and his tattered shirt back over his shoulders and down his arms, staring all the while at the brand seared into his pectoral.

Her brand.

"Let's talk about *us*. I'm doing this for your own good, Gideon."

"Somehow I doubt that," he said, trying to figure out what *this* was.

"In order to forgive you, I need to trust you."

She came closer, until only a sliver of space separated them.

Gideon's entire body tensed against her closeness, her spell holding him fast.

"And in order to trust you, I need to ensure you're mine." She traced her casting knife softly over his exposed collarbones. "Mine *alone*."

He could not revert to past Gideon—the pathetic boy who crawled back to her night after night. Like an abused dog returning to its master, hoping maybe this time, he would get kindness instead of a kick in the ribs.

You're not that Gideon anymore.

That Gideon had no choice but to submit to her. The lives of those he loved were in her hands.

"You can't escape me," she said. "Even when we were apart, I've haunted your every step. Prowled your every dream. Haven't I?"

Gideon gave a tight smile. "In truth, I never think of you."

"Liar." Her mouth snarled. She pressed her knife back to his throat. "A horse once broken can be broken again. By dawn, I'll have you begging for me. Just like the old days."

The thought of it scared him more than anything.

Gideon stared her down, trying to conceal his fear. "Do what you like to me. I won't grovel to you again."

Where had he learned to lie, so boldly, to his enemy's face?

Perhaps he'd learned it from Rune.

"Everyone I love is dead," he said as she pressed the cold steel of her knife to his skin. "You have nothing left to bind me to you."

Cressida's eyes glittered like ice. "If that were true, you'd have shot the Crimson Moth and walked out of Larkmont before anyone noticed her missing."

He frowned. *What?*

"I see the way you look at her, Gideon. You once looked at me the same way."

Gideon nearly laughed. "At *Rune*? You're mistaken."

"Rarely." Her voice flattened. "I'm not blind. Rune is beautiful. I understand why you'd be tempted."

Tempted?

"I'm the opposite of tempted. My feelings for Rune are as dead as my feelings for you."

Cressida smiled. "Fine. I'll play along." She pressed her hands to his bare chest. He couldn't tell if her skin was cold as a corpse, or if that was just the effect she had on him. "Just remember: I don't need you willing, Gideon. I only need you obedient. And I *will* have your obedience . . ."

She pressed her palm to the brand seared into his pectoral.

"I left something here, the day I branded you." She tapped her fingertips against the raised edge of the scar: a rose inside a crescent moon. Her insignia. "A spell I intended to activate long before now, but never got the chance."

She leaned in and pressed her lips against the scar.

Gideon shivered, his body wanting to recoil. But no matter what she did, he couldn't fight back.

"This is going to hurt," she murmured.

Hurt was an understatement.

Pain flooded Gideon like lightning. Scorching hot. Bright white. As if she were branding him all over again. Only this time, there was no red-hot iron pulled from the fire and held to his skin. No burning flesh.

But the pain was just as intense.

One minute, Gideon was trying not to flinch. The next, he was screaming.

It seemed endless, this fire. Burning him from the inside out.

Making him wish for death—or at the very least, the vicious stab of Rune's knee between his legs. That pain was nothing compared to this.

Rune.

He latched onto the memory of her. The defiant tilt of her chin. The lash of her insults. The whiskey bottle sailing toward his head.

It was nonsensical. They hated each other. But the moment Gideon tried to focus on something else, the pain rushed in again, overwhelming him.

So when the pain grew to agony, his mind sharpened on Rune alone. The smell of her skin; the alcohol on her breath; the heat of her pressed between him and the wall.

But soon, not even the memory of her was enough, and the fire spread, devouring Rune, burning her out of him.

Only when Gideon begged for death did it stop.

Cressida pulled her hand away and the pain dissolved. Gideon would have collapsed if not for the spell fixing him in place. Sweat beaded his hairline and dripped down his back. His entire body shook from the pain.

At the sink, Ava still faced the mirror, reapplying her makeup.

Cressida stepped closer.

"Tell me you missed me," she whispered, running the tip of her finger down the center of his chest. "Tell me you never stopped thinking about me."

Gideon tried to slow his racing heartbeat. Tried to remain calm. Whatever happened, whatever pain she inflicted on him, he could not give in to her. He needed to be made of cold hard iron this time, not flesh.

Her eyes flashed like shards of ice. "You can have my love, Gideon. Or you can have my wrath."

Is there a difference?

Sliding her arms around his neck, she pressed herself against him, lifting her mouth to his. "What's it to be, darling?"

Gideon stared at the wall behind her, trying to prepare himself for what was coming. If he hardened himself, if he willed himself to feel nothing—to be as emotionless as the pistol resting on the sink—it wouldn't matter what she did.

"Will you come to me willing, or shall I force you?"

FIVE

RUNE

*I*N THE HALL, RUNE fell back against the powder room door, hands clenched, anger squalling through her.

Whatever she'd once felt for Gideon Sharpe was gone. *Gone.* This feeling coursing through her? It was the opposite of love; it was fiery, insatiable *hate.*

What kind of girl falls for someone who despises her very nature? Who wants her *dead*?

A pathetic, self-hating one.

Rune refused to be that girl any longer.

Forget him.

There were spells for erasing memories. Rune wished she knew some, so she could raze every memory of Gideon Sharpe from her mind. Because even now, he was closer than her very breath. Rune felt the Blood Guard captain as if he still had her pressed to that wall. The scrape of his unshaven cheek. His mouth, inches from hers. The heat of his gaze, burning her up.

Rune wanted to scream. Wanted to push off this door and stride away, putting him behind her forever.

Except Cressida was in that room with him.

Gideon had told Rune what the witch queen had done to him. But there were things Gideon *hadn't* told her, she knew. Sickening things. Things Cressida would do again, if he ever fell back into her clutches.

He's in her clutches now.

Rune squeezed her eyes shut.

It was why he'd begged her to shoot: he'd rather be dead than face what Cressida had in store for him.

He came here to kill you, she reminded herself.

Rune didn't want to care about Gideon—who *definitely* didn't care about her. If he did, he wouldn't have put that gun to her head. He wouldn't have come all the way here intending to end her life.

His agonized scream filled the hall.

The sound lit her up. Like a switch being flicked.

Rune spun to face the powder room door, her heart pounding in her chest.

Gideon's screams grew louder.

Rune clenched her hands so hard, her fingernails dug into the skin of her palms. She might hate him for what he'd done. He might be her worst enemy. But that didn't stop the sound of his agony from tearing her apart.

What is she doing to him?

Rune stepped toward the door. She grabbed the knob, wanting to wrench it open. She wanted to . . .

Do what?

Helping Gideon would require defying Cressida. And while Rune might be valuable to the witch queen, she wasn't *invaluable*. Rune couldn't walk in there and tell her to stop. Cressida would laugh in her face—or worse: hurt him more.

And even if she *could* rescue him, Gideon would only try to kill Rune again—and probably succeed next time.

But if I do nothing?

When Gideon's screams fell silent, the quiet was worse. At least if he was screaming, Rune knew he was alive.

He just tried to murder you! He doesn't deserve your pity, or your help.

But there was something nagging at Rune. Something she couldn't shake.

Gideon had had the upper hand in that room. He could have taken his shot long before she ever looked into the mirror and saw him. Likely, he could have shot her long before she even *entered* the powder room.

So why did he hesitate?

She shouldn't care. Not at all. Not even the tiniest bit.

"Rune!"

She looked back to see Soren running toward her, his cape gone and the tailcoat of his jacket flapping behind him. Four soldiers flanked him. "They said you were attacked . . ."

Rune needed to let the knob go. The prince was her duty, not Gideon.

"I'm taking you to my rooms." Soren grabbed her arm and forced her to face him. His expression was stony as he scanned down the front of Rune, checking to see if she was damaged. "This fiend may not have acted alone. There could be other assassins lurking in my halls."

Rune glanced back to the powder room door. *But I can't leave him.*

"I won't let him harm you." He pulled her away. The sharp smell of his cologne burned her nose. "You'll stay in my quarters. I'll post my personal guards outside the doors."

"But I—"

"I want you to stay there until I tell you it's safe to come out."

Rune stared over her shoulder at the powder room door. Willing it to open. Willing Cressida to bring Gideon out and hand him over to the palace guards, who would march him down to whatever cells lurked beneath Larkmont, where he could rot for all Rune cared.

But the door remained shut. And now it was getting smaller,

and her chest was getting tighter, and when Soren dragged her around a corner, it disappeared from view completely.

Rune felt sick.

I have to do something.

But what?

She had no reason to ask Soren to turn back. And it's not like Cressida would stop hurting Gideon simply because Rune wanted her to. Rune would have to force her—and that was impossible. Cressida was a far more powerful witch, despite Rune's advancements under Seraphine's tutelage these past two months.

And Cressida was their only chance of saving the witches they'd left behind.

Rune couldn't defy her.

"I'm starting to understand the danger you live under," said Soren. Two guards opened his bedroom doors, allowing him to usher Rune inside. "I could *kill* that man."

"Whatever you'd do to him . . ." Rune watched the guards shut the doors behind them. "Cressida will do worse."

The lamps were dimmed. It took a moment for Rune's eyesight to adjust to the dusky light. The heavy smell of incense burned, filling the air with cinnamon and sandalwood. When the room's details became clearer, Rune noted its contents: a canopied bed, a wardrobe, a dressing table.

"I'm going to lock you in," said Soren. "I'll return when I'm certain the palace is safe and you're no longer in danger."

Rune wasn't listening. She was still thinking about how she had no power to stop Cressida from hurting Gideon. No leverage. Nothing to barter for him with.

But Soren does.

The thought flared inside her.

Soren had already turned toward the door. This was his

estate. His father's *kingdom*. And not only that: Cressida desperately needed his army.

Rune couldn't ask him to save the man who'd tried to assassinate her. But she didn't need Soren to save Gideon. She just needed him to get Gideon away from Cressida.

"Doors and guards won't keep me safe," she blurted out.

Soren stopped and glanced back, taking in her disheveled state. Rune knew how she looked: tearstained, roughed up, every bit the victim. Beneath his rage—how dare another man touch *his* fiancée—was the same look she'd seen earlier.

Hunger.

For *her*.

Normally, that hunger made Rune feel like a cornered animal. Tonight, she would use it to her advantage.

She tugged him to the bed. Brushing aside the canopy, Rune took hold of his shoulders and pushed him downward, until he was seated at the bed's edge and his polished boots were planted on the floor.

"I will never be safe until Cressida retakes her throne," she said, holding his gaze. Hiking her dress to her thighs, Rune climbed into his lap, straddling him, then slid her arms behind his neck. "I will always be in danger until Cressida, with the help of *your* army, puts all witch hunters to death."

Rune ignored the sudden bulge in his pants. If she weren't worried about Gideon, it would have repulsed her. But Rune was only half here; the other half of her was in the powder room.

This was what she was good at: Seduction. Deceit. Spinning webs of lies to ensnare her prey.

"I must confess," she whispered against his clean-shaven cheek. "I wasn't sure about this betrothal before tonight. I thought you were only marrying me to show me off, like an interesting piece of art."

Her hands dropped to his, guiding them to her hips.

Soren's gaze slid from the golden dress bunched around her waist to her pale thighs.

"And now?" he breathed.

She eased herself further into his lap. "Now? I think fate intervened at the opera. I think she wanted you to protect me."

"Hmm," he murmured, lowering his mouth to her neck.

Rune tilted her head to give him easy access. Normally, she would have recoiled at his kisses. Now she felt nothing. She'd played this game hundreds of times before. It's how she'd saved so many witches.

Tonight, Rune felt foreign to herself. Like it wasn't really her sitting on Soren's lap, nor was it her hands running through his hair. Like this girl was a ghost, and the real flesh-and-blood Rune was somewhere else.

You've spun the web, she told herself, *now bait it.*

Every minute she wasted was another minute of Gideon at Cressida's mercy.

"Do you remember the surprise I mentioned?" she asked, feigning a small gasp as Soren's teeth scraped her collarbone.

"How could I forget?" he murmured against her skin.

"It's a holiday," she said. "You and I are going to Caelis for the weekend. I've booked everything. The dinners, the ballet, the hotel room . . ."

At the words *hotel room* Soren pulled back. His blue eyes darkened, the pupils dilating. Probably imagining what the two of them alone in a hotel room would mean.

Forcing Rune to imagine it, too.

One day, I'll have to spend every night in his bed.

Soon, it wouldn't just be a weekend. Once they were married, it would be the rest of her life.

Her skin prickled.

Soren's hands roamed freely now. Up her thighs. Under her dress.

I know the Crimson Moth. And she is no caged thing. Gideon's voice brushed her mind like a whisper. *I pity the man who clips her wings.*

Rune grabbed Soren's wrists, halting his progress. "I need you to do something for me."

His breath shuddered out of him. "Yes?"

"Seal the alliance with Cressida *tonight*. And then tomorrow, we can celebrate in Caelis."

Cupping the back of her neck with both hands, Soren angled her face to his. "Fine," he said, moving in for another kiss. "I'll find her as soon as—"

"No." Rune pressed herself flush with him. "Find her *now*. And don't take no for an answer."

"All right, all right." Soren chuckled, mistaking her motives entirely. He gave her thighs a squeeze. "Consider it done, my darling."

Dragging himself away from Rune and the bed, he gave her one last hungry look before ordering his soldiers to stand guard at the door.

And then he locked her in.

SIX

GIDEON

"**W**HO SHOULD I HURT to make you comply?"

Cressida faced Gideon, her willowy frame mere inches from his. Beyond her, Ava stood at the sink, smoothing her hair.

"One of the staff?" said Cressida when Gideon didn't answer. "One of their children?" She trailed off, thinking about it. Her hands slid down his chest, dropping to his trouser buttons. "Or perhaps Rune Winters?"

She must have misunderstood the expression that crossed his face, because she continued: "The things I've done to you can easily be inflicted upon the Crimson Moth. In fact"—she smiled, undoing the first button of his trousers—"you could watch while I do it. Would you like that?"

Every muscle in his body tightened.

"I think it would be *very* entertaining . . ."

She started undoing the second button when a knock interrupted them.

Glancing over her shoulder, Cressida narrowed her eyes on the door. Ava turned away from the sink to go answer it.

"Tell them to go away," Cressida said.

No sooner had she issued the command than the door swung open.

Ava halted as Prince Soren stepped in, looking regal in a navy blue tailcoat, if not a little flustered. Cressida spun to face the intruder, but at the sight of the prince, she reined in her anger.

"My lord." Her voice was cheerfully restrained. "I'm sorry for the trouble we've brought upon Larkmont. As soon as—"

Soren waved his hand, cutting her off. His gaze fixed on Gideon. "Is this the brute who attacked Miss Winters?"

"Indeed," said Cressida. "I've bound him with a spell. He can't harm you unless I remove it."

Soren strode forward, stopping directly in front of Gideon. The prince squared his shoulders and drew both hands behind his back, reminding Gideon he was an admiral, not just a prince. They were the same age, but the sea air had weathered Soren's face, making him appear older.

Gideon was slightly taller, though, forcing Soren to look *up* at him even though Gideon sensed he very much wanted to look down on him.

Staring at the prince, all Gideon could think of were the man's hands all over Rune. Of Rune drunk and crying at the sink.

Gideon's thoughts spiraled to places he'd rather not go.

What does she let him do to her when they aren't in public?

He went hot all over. The beat of his pulse pounded like a drum in the base of his throat.

Soren's lip curled, as if he were inspecting a dead rat. "How dare you touch her."

Gideon knew better than to open his mouth. But he couldn't help himself.

"At least she likes it when I touch her."

Soren's face reddened.

Crack!

The prince's knuckles collided with his jaw and the force of the punch slammed his head to the side. Blood welled in Gideon's mouth. He spat it onto Soren's crisp white cravat.

The man seemed about to throw a second punch—or perhaps wrap his hands around Gideon's neck and choke the life out of him—when Cressida stepped in.

"Let me deal with him, Your Highness. There's no need for you to get your hands dirty."

Seeming to remember himself—he was a prince, he didn't stoop to the level of rats—Soren stepped back, untying his now bloody cravat and dropping it to the floor.

"I'm afraid your plans for him must wait." He turned to Cressida, his face still red. "My lawyers have drafted the contract. All it needs is our signatures."

Cressida's brows lifted in surprise.

"That's wonderful." There was no edge in her voice this time. "But I really should attend to our enemy." She glanced at Gideon. "Why don't we sign over breakfast tomorrow?"

"Rune is impatient to be married," said Soren. "And I know you're impatient to have your throne back. Which is why I must insist we do this now. I'd rather not risk any more"—he glanced at Gideon—"interruptions."

Gideon watched a nerve in Cressida's cheek jump. She clearly loathed the idea of leaving Gideon, but she was outranked. And this was what she wanted: an alliance to help her wage war against the New Republic.

Sliding her casting knife into the folds of her cloak, Cressida glanced at Ava. "Bring him to my chambers."

At those words, a chill crept over Gideon's skin.

"We'll finish this there. I won't be long."

Gideon watched the witch queen follow Soren out of the room, shutting the door behind her. When they were gone, Ava pushed away from the wall.

"Come on, then."

Gideon looked at his pistol, still resting on the sink. There was one bullet left in the chamber—he'd used up the others earlier, getting past Soren's security. To move him to Cressida's chambers, Ava would have to remove his magic bindings.

He needed five seconds at most.

The witch slashed her skin with her casting knife, then touched her fingertips to the blood before smearing a bright red symbol across his chest. Her fingers looped and slashed, dragging across his skin. The stench of her magic filled the air, coppery and cloying.

Another spell?

Ava stepped away, smiling. Turning, she walked to the sink and cupped her hands under the water, then let it drip over the symbols Cressida had drawn onto the floor. She ran her shoe across the marks, looking almost bored as she severed the witch queen's spell.

Gideon's muscles tightened as the tendrils of Cressida's magic loosened their grip on him. Releasing his shoulders and arms first, then his legs and feet.

When the spell vanished entirely, Gideon lunged for the pistol.

"Stop!"

It was like running into an invisible wall. His entire body jerked to a halt on Ava's command, his spine going sword-straight.

"Turn toward the door."

In horror, Gideon found himself doing exactly as she ordered. The spellmark on his chest . . .

It binds me to her words.

Whatever she commanded, he'd be forced to do.

"Drop to your hands and knees, witch hunter."

Against his will, Gideon lowered himself to the floor. Before him, shattered glass glittered across the tiles.

"Now *crawl.*"

Gideon picked his way through the glass, teeth clenching as

shards sliced into his hands and embedded in his knees, leaving a trail of blood in his wake.

He'd been a fool to think he could save himself.

Halfway to the door, he heard footsteps in the hall. He glanced up, watching the handle turn.

Is Cressida back already?

A dread as cold and dark as the sea swept through him.

But when the door swung open, it was an altogether different witch who stepped through.

Her golden dress caught the light, her strawberry blonde hair tumbled in waves down her shoulders, and her gray eyes simmered like a storm.

Rune.

SEVEN

RUNE

GIDEON WAS HALF-CLOTHED, AND a bloody spellmark blazed across his chest.

The sight of him, *shirtless*, made Rune freeze.

Gideon Sharpe had haunted her these past two months, but the memory of him was nothing compared to Gideon in the flesh. Every line and curve of his body spoke of power and strength.

He must have heard the soft hitch of her breath, because his eyes lifted. The room fell away as Gideon's gaze met hers and his stare held her in place like a spell.

When her eyes dropped to his trousers, she found every button undone.

The sight woke something deadly in Rune.

"What are you doing here, Winters?" Ava materialized from the darkness.

"I came to . . ." Rune glanced at the pistol lying on the sink beyond Ava. The same one Gideon had pressed to her temple not twenty minutes ago. ". . . to tell you Cressida has orders for you."

"Cressida already gave me her orders."

"These are new ones." Rune wished she'd had time to come up with a better plan. It wouldn't take Cressida long to sign those papers, and Gideon needed to be gone before her return.

Rune took a small step toward the sink. "She wants you in

the prince's study. To, uh, bear witness to the signing. I'm supposed to watch the witch hunter while you're gone."

Ava locked her gaze on Rune. "*You* couldn't bear witness?"

"She requested you."

Ava's eyes narrowed. "Why would she do that, if you were
already there?"

Rune was better than this. *Smarter* than this. But escaping
the prince's bedroom—she'd had to go over the balcony and
drop to the one below—had taken more time and attention
than expected.

"There was a conflict of interest." Rune took another step
toward the sink. "I'm going to be Soren's wife. I can't be Cressida's witness."

Ava's voice iced over. "I don't believe you."

Knowing she'd lost, Rune lunged for the pistol.

Ava glanced at Gideon. "Restrain her."

Gideon intercepted Rune, seizing both of her wrists and
wrenching her arms behind her back.

What are you doing? she wanted to scream at him. *I came to
help you!*

Pain shot up to her shoulders and made the world flare red.
The words died in her throat.

"Cressida will be so disappointed when she learns of your
sabotage." Ava tutted. To Gideon, she said, "Kill the Crimson
Moth."

Gideon didn't hesitate.

Whipping her around to face him, he locked his hands
around her throat and slammed her against the mirror. Glass
cracked behind her head. Pain flickered through her.

And then he *squeezed*.

Rune's eyes widened in shock.

Her fingers clawed at his hands, trying to force them to loosen. But Gideon had always been stronger than her, and his grip was a vise. Tighter and tighter. Blocking her air. She wasn't sure if he planned to snap her neck, strangle her, or both.

His dark eyes bored into hers.

Rune's mind blazed with panic.

Please . . . I'm trying to save you!

But why would he care?

This was what he came for, remember? You've given him a second chance to see it through.

Ava watched from a safe distance, arms crossed over her chest, unmoved by Rune's struggle. Rune would get no sympathy there.

Which was when she remembered the pistol.

Gideon had shoved her against the mirror directly beside the sink, where his gun still rested. If she could reach it . . .

As her lungs burned, crying out for air, Rune's knuckles knocked against the sink's cold ceramic. She patted the edge, her hand shaking . . . but the gun was on the other side.

The room blurred.

The bright red symbol on Gideon's chest filled her vision.

Rune's lungs were about to burst. Soon, nothing would matter, because she'd be dead.

Her fingertips brushed metal.

Hope flared as her hand gripped the pistol.

One shot. Make it count.

Rune lifted the gun and fired.

EIGHT

RUNE

*T*HE *BANG* RANG IN her ears.

Gideon's hands loosened from around her throat as he stumbled back, staring in horror. Behind him, Ava dropped to the floor. Dead from the bullet in her brain.

The only sound in the room was Rune's and Gideon's uneven breaths.

Rune shook out her hand, which stung from the force of the pistol's release, then lowered her gaze to the spellmark on Gideon's chest. She'd nearly shot him. But at the last second, she had recognized the symbol.

Binder. A spell that bound its victim to a witch's command.

It was a calculated guess, but considering Gideon's hands were no longer locked around her neck, a correct one. Which meant Gideon hadn't necessarily wanted to strangle her; he'd simply had no choice.

If Ava had cast *Everlasting* alongside *Binder*, the spell would have held despite Rune's killing shot, and it would be Rune dead on the floor. But Ava hadn't expected to die. She'd had no need of *Everlasting*—an enchantment that kept a spell intact beyond the death of the witch who cast it.

Seraphine had taught Rune many things since they'd escaped the New Republic, and this was one of them.

"Don't make any sudden moves," she said, gun pointed at Gideon's chest, where the blood-red symbol still blazed. With

Ava dead, Gideon was free to go back to trying to kill Rune. This time of his own free will.

Except . . .

Rune glanced at the sink. Had Gideon intentionally thrust her against the mirror directly beside it? Had he *wanted* her to reach for his pistol, to shoot Ava and sever the spell?

Her mind swarmed with too many thoughts at once.

"Don't think I won't shoot you, too," she said, still aiming the gun at him.

Rune hoped she sounded confident. She'd never fired a gun before today and had hit Ava by sheer luck.

Gideon looked from her to his pistol, his eyes inscrutable. "The barrel's empty. You need to reload."

Is he messing with me?

"Go ahead." He nodded. "Fire away."

"You think I won't?"

He smirked.

Rune narrowed her eyes. Fine. She would call his bluff.

Lowering the gun a few inches so she'd wound him, not kill him—or so she hoped—Rune pulled the trigger.

The pistol clicked but didn't discharge.

She pulled again, but no bullet fired.

Ugh! Who infiltrates a heavily fortified palace with only one bullet in their gun?

Throwing down the pistol, Rune grabbed the casting knife strapped to her thigh and held it out in front of her, making it clear she was still armed and he better not try anything.

Gideon glanced at Ava's body on the floor, unconcerned. "Someone will have heard that."

Rune crossed the room to the door. "Which is only one of *many* reasons we need to get out of here."

Cracking it open, she glanced out into the hall.

The sight of distant guards running straight for them made her quickly pull it shut again.

"They're already on their way."

With no way out, her only option was to use her invisibility spell, *Ghost Walker*. But doing so would leave her Crimson Moth signature behind—letting everyone know Rune was responsible for this.

Unless I conceal it.

Rune scanned the powder room, fixing on the door of a small closet.

Pointing to it, she said, "Get inside."

Gideon, who was at the sink washing the blood off himself, looked to the closet. Then back to Rune. His eyes were doubtful.

"Not the best plan you've ever come up with."

He must have buttoned his trousers when her back was turned.

"I can't cast a spell out in the open." She walked toward the blood pooling around Ava's body. "Cressida will see my signature and know I helped you. I need somewhere to hide it."

He stepped away from the sink, shaking his head. "You're not putting a spell on me."

"It's only a Minora," said Rune, scooping Ava's blood into her cupped palm.

Gideon took another step back. "I've already been subjugated by *two* spells tonight."

Rune rose to face him. "If I don't—"

Shouts from the hall interrupted her.

The guards were almost here.

"Listen," she hissed. "I'm perfectly happy to save myself and abandon you. But if you want to live, I suggest you let me do this."

Gideon glanced toward the door and back to the blood dripping from Rune's fingers. Instead of answering, he walked to the closet, opened the door, and got in.

"There's not enough room in here for two people."

"Then *make* room." Sheathing her knife, she followed him in, careful not to leave a trail of blood in her wake.

Gideon was right. There wasn't enough room for two people.

Shelves lined the tiny closet, each one full of towels, soap, and cleaning supplies. That left only a few feet of space for Rune and Gideon to cram themselves into. Gideon took up most of it, forcing Rune to squeeze in between him and the shelves, leaving less than an inch of air between their two bodies.

Sweet Mercy. She'd forgotten how *large* he was. Like a mountain.

The closet door stood open, letting light from the room beyond flood in. Before she ran out of time, Rune used Ava's blood to draw three symbols across Gideon's freshly cleaned chest.

"Just so we're clear," she whispered, using the last of the blood on the final symbol, "I'm doing this for Alex, not you." Under her breath, she added, "He'd never forgive me if I let her hurt you."

When she glanced up, Gideon was staring at the ring on her finger. The one Alex gave her when he proposed.

"Understood," he said, glancing away.

With the spell finished, magic burned in Rune's throat. It flowed out of her and around him. Gideon shimmered like a mirage and would have vanished from her sight entirely if not for Rune knowing precisely where he was.

Ghost Walker wasn't a true invisibility spell. Instead, it coaxed the gazes of others to bounce off you, allowing you to evade notice. But if someone knew you were there, the spell couldn't hide you.

THUD THUD THUD.

Rune jumped.

"Everything all right in there?"

She glanced toward Ava's body across the room. She still needed to draw the spellmarks on herself, but she'd used all of Ava's blood on Gideon.

THUD! THUD! THUD!

"Who's in there?" demanded the guard.

Gideon grabbed the closet door and shut it, plunging them into darkness. Slivers of light filtered in from the cracks.

"Here." He thrust out his hand. "Use mine."

Rune glanced down to find blood shining on his palm, seeping from what appeared to be dozens of tiny cuts. When he held his hand up to the light filtering in, Rune saw shards of sparkling glass embedded in the skin.

He needed to dig those out before the cuts got infected.

"Better hurry," he whispered, as the door to the powder room burst open and guards flooded in.

Out of time, Rune touched the blood on Gideon's palm and quickly drew the same three symbols on her wrist. Her fingers trembled as she rushed. If she got even one mark wrong, the spell wouldn't work. But if she didn't finish in time . . .

The briny taste of magic prickled her tongue. A second later, Rune's skin tingled as magic flowed out and around her, hiding her the same way it had Gideon.

She glanced up to find two iridescent moths flickering a few feet over their heads. Burning red in the darkness.

She'd barely finished the spell when footsteps headed in their direction. As if on instinct, Gideon's arm slid around her waist, pulling her hips against his, moving her away from the closet door.

Heat poured off him. His scent filled the closet—woodsy,

with a hint of gunpowder. Fire raced through her as old memories surfaced: reverent glances; whispered promises; the feel of his hands and mouth and body on hers, skin to skin.

How what once lay between them was a potent kind of magic . . .

Warning bells chimed in her head.

It was a lie. She fought the memories down, locking them away. *Every second of it.*

The closet door swung open. A soldier poked his head in.

Glancing around, the man looked straight at Rune and Gideon . . . and away. The spell did its job, repelling his gaze away from them.

He didn't bother looking up. Why would he? It was an empty closet.

If he had looked, he'd have sighted the two crimson moths burning like flames in the air overhead.

"Nothing here!" he called out, withdrawing.

Gideon's grip on her relaxed. Rune released a breath, pulling slightly away. Reinstating that inch of space between them.

The closet door hung open.

It's now or never.

Rune needed to get them to the stables, put Gideon on a horse, and send him on his way. Grabbing the belt loop of his trousers, Rune exited the closet, tugging him after her.

"What happened here?" A sharp voice cut through the clamor of the guards.

Rune and Gideon halted.

Cressida strode toward Ava's corpse, her eyes narrowing as she stopped to take in the bullet wound and the blood. Bending down, she picked up Gideon's pistol, staring at it.

Her cool gaze lifted. Fear sparked through Rune, who didn't know if her spells were strong enough to withstand Cressida's detection. They were only Minoras. And Cressida was a far more powerful witch.

Cressida scanned the room, moving past the open closet before pausing at the space where Rune and Gideon stood.

Rune's grip tightened on Gideon's belt loop.

But as Cressida rose to her feet, Soren entered the room. "Dear god." At the sight of Ava, his face went pale. "What happened?"

"Our prisoner escaped," said Cressida, turning toward the prince and away from Rune and Gideon.

Rune relaxed. Cloaked by her spell, she crossed the room with Gideon in tow. When they reached the open powder room door, Cressida walked over to the closet. "You said Rune is locked in your bedroom, yes?"

Gideon stepped into the hall, and Rune glanced back to see Cressida peer inside the closet . . . then glance up.

No.

Soren nodded. "I posted four guards at the door. No one's getting in there."

When Cressida turned back, her eyes were blue flames. "Perhaps we should make sure."

She knows.

Soren shook his head. "I assure you, Rune is—"

Cressida cut him off. "Gideon Sharpe came here to assassinate Rune Winters. He is now roaming the palace. Best to be sure he hasn't found her, don't you think?"

Rune's heart faltered. If they went to Soren's bedroom and found her missing . . .

Cressida strode straight past her, into the hall. The prince followed.

Panic hummed in Rune's blood. Those casting signatures damned her.

Unless . . .

If Rune returned to Soren's locked bedroom before Cressida arrived, it might make her doubt what she'd seen. After all, Rune might have cast a few spells upon first setting foot in the powder room. There were a multitude for enhancing looks. Spells to fix your hair or makeup. Spells to get rid of puffy eyes or splotchy skin from crying. Rune might have gone there precisely to cast such spells. To keep Soren charmed.

How long before they find his bedroom empty?

The prince's chambers were across the palace, on the second floor. Rune and Gideon were on the main floor.

Three minutes. Probably less.

It wasn't enough time. Even if she got to Soren's bedroom before Cressida, there were still a locked door and four guards to contend with. Rune would have to cast another spell to unlock it. And *that* would solidify Cressida's suspicion, sealing Rune's fate.

It was hopeless.

There was no way to get back into that room in time.

NINE

GIDEON

G IDEON COULDN'T HELP BUT notice how different Rune's spell was from Cressida's and Ava's. The latter had used powerful binding spells, meant to force and humiliate him. But Rune's was so subtle, he barely sensed it.

It didn't control him, nor did it control others. It seemed to merely *suggest* that people turn away from him, look past him, or ignore him altogether. It was almost . . . gentle.

"You'll find the stable entrance in the east wing of Lark- mont," said Rune. For some reason, he could still see her. Why the spell didn't affect him, he wasn't sure. "My horse is the chestnut mare. Take her and get far away from here."

He sensed the wrongness in her voice, which was strung tight as a bow.

"Where will you go?"

"I need to be in Soren's bedroom," she said. "Preferably before Cressida gets there. But the door is locked, and four of Soren's men are standing guard, so I can't get back in. If she finds me missing . . ."

She'll know Rune helped him.

Why did she help me?

He recalled her words in the closet.

I'm doing this for Alex, not you. He'd never forgive me if I let her hurt you.

Right. Alex.

The one who would have been Rune's husband by now, if

Cressida hadn't shot him. Alex's ring was on her finger, making one thing perfectly clear:

She's still in love with my brother.

Why else would she save Gideon—a man who'd tried to kill her tonight?

"How did you escape the bedroom?" he asked, to distract himself from this fact.

"I dropped from the balcony."

"Can you climb back up?"

She shook her head, her pace quickening as she turned a corner. The marble statues lining this hall seemed to watch them as they passed, unaffected by Rune's spell.

"The walls are sheer stone." She glanced at him. "Don't worry about me. I'll figure something out. Just get out of Larkmont before Cressida thinks to use a counterspell that will overpower mine."

"Can she do that?"

Rune didn't answer.

Gideon blew out a breath. Raked a hand through his hair. Every moment he lingered here increased his chances of being caught again. But Rune had risked herself for him and was about to suffer the consequences. He couldn't just leave her.

"Is the balcony low enough for me to lift you?"

Her footsteps slowed momentarily. "I . . . don't know."

Gideon would help her—only this once—for Alex. And then he'd get himself to safety, where he would regroup.

This was only a *temporary* setback.

"Show me."

⁘

RUNE LED HIM TO a garden at the heart of Soren's palace. The evening was humid and warm, and the crickets hummed a low, insistent chorus. Stone walls enclosed the garden's four sides, and balconies protruded from the second level.

Gideon guessed these were Soren's private quarters.

"Which one is it?"

Standing in a patch of yellow dahlias, Rune pointed to the balcony overhead. Lamplight flooded out, drenching her in a warm glow. In that golden dress—which Gideon had to remind himself he despised—she looked like a burning flame.

He suddenly noticed her swollen lips.

Gideon frowned. Were they swollen when he first cornered her in the powder room?

No. He'd been so close to her, it would have been impossible not to notice.

Worse than her lips were the bruises on her neck. They weren't bruises from Gideon's hands. These were from a mouth.

Soren's mouth.

Gideon's jaw clenched. He glanced from her to the prince's balcony overhead. "Do you stay in his bedroom often?"

Rune studied the same balcony. "I don't see how that's any of your concern."

She was right. He couldn't care less whose bed she kept warm at night. Gideon was here to pay back a debt, nothing more. If he were delivering her straight into another man's arms, so be it.

She meant nothing to him.

Just as he meant nothing to her.

So why couldn't he keep his stupid mouth shut?

"You've outdone yourself this time. Seducing a prince."

Rune ignored him.

"As his wife, you'll have fancier balls, fancier friends, and fancier wardrobes than you've ever dreamed of."

"Jealous?" said Rune, studying the walls. "If you wanted to marry me, Gideon, you should have said so."

Gideon heard the taunt in her voice.

As if she'd stoop so low.

"Marry *you*?" he said, playing along. "The girl who plans to help Cressida resurrect her sisters and reinstate a Reign of Witches? No, thank you."

Rune's gaze shot to his face. "What?"

"Cressida told me all about it: she intends to raise Analise and Elowyn from the dead. It will be everything you witches want: psychotic murderers back in charge."

"Last time I checked, the psychotic murderers *were* in charge." Rune turned toward him, frowning hard. "Are you saying Cressida told you she's planning a resurrection?"

She seemed genuinely surprised. But Gideon knew Rune to be an expert liar.

"Are you denying any knowledge of it?" He studied her, trying to determine the truth.

"This is the first I've heard of it." She continued scanning the walls. "Anyway, it's not possible. Resurrection spells require an exchange of life for life. The life of a family member must be taken to give life back to the dead. Cressida has no family left. She's the last living Roseblood."

"She seems to think otherwise."

"Then she's mad," said Rune, wading deeper into the dahlias beneath Soren's balcony. Apparently finished with this conversation. "Or she was trying to torment you."

Maybe.

They were running out of time, so Gideon kept his doubts to himself. He scanned the walls, searching for a way up. But she was right: the stones were perfectly smooth. There was nothing to climb.

The balcony, however, *was* low enough for him to lift her.

He strode over to where she stood in the flowers. Crouching, he cupped his hands and held them out.

"Hold on to me."

Rune studied him, as if deciding whether she trusted him to lift her. But soon enough, her hands came down on his shoulders, gripping firmly. Gideon cupped her calf through the silk of her dress, guiding her foot into his waiting palm.

"Let's get one thing clear," she said, as he rose. "If our paths cross again, I won't show you mercy a second time."

Rune's grip tightened on him as she lost, then regained, her balance.

"Good," he said, pushing her higher, muscles straining beneath her weight. "Because the next time my gun is to your head, I *will* pull the trigger."

"*Perfect*," she said, stepping onto his shoulders as she reached for the balcony overhead. "I'm glad we understand each other."

She made a little sound, like a grunt, and the weight of her eased from his shoulders. She'd grabbed hold of an iron bar holding up the balcony's balustrade and was using it to haul herself up.

And then she was gone.

Gideon backed away in time to see the balcony doors close and the lamplight disappear, leaving him alone with the crickets and the dahlias.

What did I deliver her into?

It was none of his business. If Rune had wanted to make a different choice, she would have.

Gideon needed to stop *feeling*. They were at war—or soon would be. Gideon couldn't be flesh and blood; he needed to be gunpowder and steel. Impenetrable. Unyielding.

Turning his back on the doors she'd disappeared through, Gideon strode out of the gardens, and then out of Larkmont.

TEN

RUNE

GOOD RIDDANCE, GIDEON SHARPE.

It was stupid enough saving him once, when he'd come here to end her life. If he tried to kill her again, she would let Cressida have him.

At the sound of voices in the hall, Rune quickly dived into the bed. The sheets were already turned down, waiting for her.

There was no time to strip off her soiled dress and hide it. No time to scrub the blood from her hands.

There was only enough time to smudge the spellmarks on her wrist, dissolving *Ghost Walker*.

Rune had barely pulled up the covers and closed her eyes when the door swung open.

"See?" she heard Soren say, his footsteps padding toward the bed. Rune kept her eyes closed, feigning sleep, as the prince brushed strands of hair off her face. "She's safe."

Soren turned to give his guards orders. "Bar Larkmont's exits. Make sure not a living soul leaves the palace." His voice grew fainter as he walked into the hall. "I want him found."

Thinking it safe, Rune nearly opened her eyes, but the sound of footsteps stopped her.

The air turned chilly as a shadow slid over her. Winter-cold. Rune kept her eyes closed and her body still. She willed her racing heart to slow, fearing Cressida heard every frantic beat.

The witch queen leaned down, her breath rushing against Rune's cheek.

"I know what you did."

Rune's heart pounded faster.

She saw my casting signatures.

Rune could say those signatures were from cosmetic spells. Cressida would have to take her at her word, to keep the peace with Soren. But Cressida had seen Rune deceive and pretend as the Crimson Moth. She knew what Rune was capable of.

Deep down, she knew the truth.

Is she here to take her revenge? Or will she wait?

Even if Rune wanted to open her eyes and run, fear flooded her limbs, turning them to stone.

A predator stood over her. If she moved, that predator would strike.

"Do you really think you can outwit *me*?" Cressida's voice was like a snakebite, flooding Rune with poison. "He's mine, Rune. If you defy me again—"

"Is everything all right?"

Someone had entered the room. Rune felt Cressida straighten and turn, facing the intruder.

"How is she?" Seraphine's voice was like sunshine, thawing Rune's frozen limbs. "I heard about Ava. Horrible. Is Rune all right?"

At the presence of her friend, Rune was tempted to open her eyes. But she remained as she was.

"I'll stay with Rune," said Seraphine. "I promised Prince Soren I'd ward the doors and windows of this room, to ensure she's safe."

"How kind." Cressida's voice was hard as cut glass.

"There's still a chance you can catch your witch hunter." Seraphine's voice was equally hard. "I'm sure you'll want to try."

A tense silence hung in the air. Cressida wanted to punish Rune for her disobedience, but she wanted to catch Gideon more. And the longer she wasted time here, the likelier he was to slip away.

Seconds later, Cressida's shadow receded.

When the door swung shut behind her and her footsteps retreated into the hall, Rune let out a breath, opened her eyes, and sat up.

Seraphine stood across the room, hands planted on her small hips. As Rune flung off the covers and swung her legs out, Seraphine's hands fell to her sides, her gaze sweeping down Rune.

"What have you *done*?"

Rune glanced at herself. The golden dress was ruined, and blood smeared her fingers.

"Ava tried to kill me," she said, putting her feet on the ground. "I had no choice. I had to shoot her."

"*You* shot Ava? I thought the witch hunter killed her." Seraphine shook her head, sending her dark curls bouncing. She blew out an aggravated breath. "Oh, Rune. Why were you even in that room?"

Rune didn't answer. Just stood up and stripped off the blood-stained dress, throwing it into the fire crackling in the hearth. She watched the flames eat the fabric, destroying the evidence of her crime. After searching through Soren's armoire, she found a long-sleeved shirt and pulled it over her head.

Seraphine drew closer. "Where is he?"

"Gideon? I don't know." Rune strode into the adjoining bathroom. *Long gone, I hope.*

"Soren said he came here to kill you," said Seraphine, following her in.

At the sink, Rune turned on the tap and thrust her hands beneath the cold water. "He did."

Seraphine threw up her hands. "Then why save him?"

As Rune scrubbed the blood off herself, her thoughts trailed back to the powder room and the scream she'd heard from behind the closed door. Gideon's torn shirt on the floor. The undone buttons of his trousers.

She might not know exactly what Cressida had done to make him scream, but she knew what the witch queen had been *about* to do.

"No one deserves a fate like that," she whispered, staring at the bloody water swirling down the drain.

Not even her worst enemy.

She intends to raise Analise and Elowyn from the dead. Gideon's voice rumbled through her.

It scared Rune more than she'd let on in the garden.

Queen Raine had outlawed resurrection spells centuries ago. But Cressida wouldn't care about that.

Still, Rune wanted to doubt it was possible; Analise and Elowyn were long dead, and resurrection spells required the sacrifice of someone closely related to the deceased—like a parent, sibling, or child.

Without direct kin to sacrifice, the spell wouldn't work. The only living Roseblood was Cressida herself.

She seems to think otherwise, Gideon had said.

Could it be true? Was there another living Roseblood?

And how could Rune put Cressida on the throne, after tonight? *Knowing* what she would have done to Gideon?

It wasn't the first time she'd asked herself this question.

The answer was always the same: if she didn't, Gideon—or some other witch hunter—would come for her again.

The next time my gun is to your head, I will pull the trigger.

His words were a reminder: *They will never stop hunting us.*

Gideon wouldn't return to the New Republic empty-handed. Not when a bullet in Rune's head would deprive the witch queen of an army. He was probably regrouping at this very moment, waiting for his next chance to assassinate her.

It was why the alternative to Cressida was worse. The alternative to Cressida was witches being slaughtered until there were no witches left. The only way to stop the Blood Guard was to put Cressida on the throne.

Gideon can take care of himself.

If Cressida conquered the New Republic, Gideon was more than capable of fleeing the island and never looking back. Whether he had the good sense to wasn't Rune's concern.

Rune had no reason to care what happened to him or any other patriot once Cressida returned to power. How many of them had informed on girls like her? Cheered as innocent witches were butchered in the street? Had done the butchering themselves?

They deserved what was coming for them.

But isn't that what they said about us?

Rune shook off the question.

"If Cressida suspects you helped him escape," said Seraphine, "it's only a matter of time before she punishes you for it."

Finished washing blood off her hands, Rune turned off the taps, staring into the sink, trying to think.

"You need to get far away from here, Rune."

She glanced up to see Seraphine lift her fingers to a scar near the base of her neck, tracing the raised lines. It was a habit Rune had witnessed dozens of times in their spell casting lessons. It meant she was concentrating hard on something.

Seraphine's clothing normally hid the casting scar's shape. But the thin straps of her evening gown left it exposed tonight. Rune recognized the form of a bird, shining like silver against Seraphine's brown skin.

It was the same bird as in Rune's grandmother's seal. The one Nan used to stamp her letters with.

A kestrel.

"If I run away," said Rune, turning to her, "this alliance will crumble."

Seraphine stopped tracing and dropped her hand. "So?"

So, who would save the witches they'd left behind?

There were still girls being hunted down like animals in the New Republic. There was still a sibyl in Blood Guard custody, being blackmailed into helping them unmask her own kind. Rune couldn't abandon them.

Alex would say that she could. That she *should*. That Rune had done more than enough to save witches from the purge.

But Alex wasn't here.

Rune was adrift without him—the boy who'd cherished her. Alex would never help her with another heist, or protect her with another alibi.

But neither was he here telling her to *stop*; to keep her head down and not risk herself for others.

She was free to be who she wanted.

There was no one holding her back.

If I rescue the sibyl, she told herself, *the Blood Guard can't learn where other witches are hiding.*

She couldn't protect them the way Cressida could—permanently, by seizing power. But she could protect them for now.

If there is a missing Roseblood heir, I can find them before Cressida does and keep them from danger, too.

Rune knew the summoning spell required to find a missing person. It needed to be performed in an ancient location, and the only one she knew of was a ring of summoning stones back on the island.

"Rune," said Seraphine, stepping toward her. "Buy passage aboard a ship and take it to the other side of the world. Hide yourself somewhere she'll never find you. Run and don't look back."

Rune had a better idea.

A plan was forming in her mind. A dangerous one.

"Rune." Seraphine's hands gripped her shoulders. "Promise me you'll run."

"Okay," she said. "I promise. I'll run."

As soon as I complete one last mission . . .

ELEVEN

GIDEON

```
GIDEON SHARPE
THE LARK & CROWN, CAELIS

THE GOOD COMMANDER WANTS TO KNOW IF YOU'VE
ELIMINATED THE TARGET.
                                    HARROW
```

THE TELEGRAM WAS WAITING for Gideon when he arrived back at the Lark & Crown, a hotel in Caelis with rooms so damp, he might as well be sleeping in a bog. The carpets squished unnaturally beneath his boots, and the wallpaper had lifted off the walls. After only a few nights here, Gideon probably had mold growing in his lungs.

The Blood Guard were not welcome in Caelis, and most establishments refused witch hunters service. But the Lark & Crown was desperate for business. So when Gideon showed up, they didn't ask questions. Just took his money and gave him a room.

Gideon shook the rain out of his hair and reread Harrow's telegram.

I've barely been gone a week, he thought. *Give me a little time.*

But he knew the reason for the check-in.

The Crimson Moth had compromised Gideon. He'd been taken in by the very villain he'd spent two years hunting, and in doing so, failed the New Republic. Until he proved his loyalty, the new Commander couldn't fully trust him. None of them could.

Killing the Crimson Moth would not only stop Cressida's alliance; it would prove Gideon was no longer in Rune's thrall.

He wanted to tell Harrow about Cressida's plot to resurrect her sisters but didn't want the information falling into the wrong hands. So, he sent a vague reply.

```
SPYMASTER
OFFICE OF THE GOOD COMMANDER


NEW INFORMATION HAS COME TO LIGHT. THE REPUBLIC
IS IN GREATER DANGER THAN WE IMAGINED. WILL
FILL YOU IN WHEN I RETURN.
                                         GIDEON
```

Within the hour, Harrow sent a telegram back:

```
GIDEON SHARPE
THE LARK & CROWN, CAELIS

SO THE CRIMSON MOTH IS STILL ALIVE?
                                         HARROW
```

Her scathing disapproval radiated off the paper.

```
SPYMASTER
OFFICE OF THE GOOD COMMANDER

I NEED A FEW MORE DAYS.
                                         GIDEON
```

The next morning, her last telegram arrived.

GIDEON SHARPE
THE LARK & CROWN, CAELIS

THE COMMANDER NO LONGER BELIEVES YOU'RE
THE BEST MAN FOR THIS JOB. HE'S SENDING
SOMEONE MORE QUALIFIED TO COMPLETE IT. RE-
TURN TO THE REPUBLIC IMMEDIATELY.

HARROW

Someone more qualified?

Gideon's hands fisted, crumpling the telegram, which he promptly threw in the fire.

He could do this. He simply had to prove it. If the Commander wanted to punish him for his disobedience once he was back on New Republic soil, so be it. Because Cressida Roseblood had to be stopped, no matter the cost. She could not retake her throne, and she could *not* resurrect her sisters.

Cress alone was one thing; she was powerful and cruel. But compared to Elowyn and Analise, she was a novice.

Gideon was seeing this job through to the end. There could be no hesitating this time.

He would find Rune, and he would kill her.

And if a small voice inside him objected, it was only because Gideon was still compromised. Still *weakened* by her. If he thought about how Rune risked herself tonight to help him, he would waver.

Gideon couldn't waver.

If he did, Cressida would rise to power. She'd resurrect her sisters. And together they would destroy the New Republic and usher in a new reign of terror, this one far worse than the last.

Gideon had no choice. Killing Rune was the only way to stop that from happening.

If it broke him, so be it.

TWELVE

GIDEON

PRINCE SOREN TO MARRY HEIRESS-IN-EXILE!

Prince Soren Nord and Lady Rune Winters, a witch recently escaped from the New Republic, wish to announce their engagement. The couple are keeping the wedding's date and location secret, citing privacy concerns, but hinted that the ceremony will occur within the month. The announcement comes hand in hand with Prince Nord's proclamation last night in Caelis, at the Royal Ballet, where he made it clear he supports Queen Cressida's claim to the Roseblood throne and will do whatever is necessary to help her secure it.

So, THE HAPPY COUPLE were in the capital.

If there was one thing Gideon knew about Rune Winters, it was that she loved fashion. As an aristocrat, Rune felt the need to keep up with whatever styles were currently in vogue.

And if there was one thing he knew about Soren Nord, it was that he liked to flaunt his things.

Suspecting the prince would want to indulge his new fiancée—and in doing so, show her off to the upperclasses of Caelis—Gideon headed for Caelis's wealthier shopping district to hunt for them. There, he planted himself against the wall of a tailor shop and waited, scanning the weekend crowds from the shadows.

It didn't take long before Gideon spotted them, and soon he was following the couple at a safe distance. He watched Soren escort Rune into a shop while the prince's bodyguards took their positions outside the door. In the window, faceless mannequins wore wedding dresses edged with lace and pearls.

Should he wait for Rune to exit and take his shot? Or was it better to get her alone? To do this somewhere private and escape undetected?

In the end, Soren chose for him. A few minutes after entering the shop, the prince emerged without Rune. Perhaps he considered it taboo to see her in a wedding dress before the ceremony. Or perhaps he intended to purchase his own matrimonial attire while Rune was trying on hers.

Whatever the reason, the prince stepped out, said something to the bodyguards, and continued down the road, taking one with him. The other stayed to guard Rune, keeping his eyes on the street merchants and their customers.

Gideon relaxed. One guard was easier to deal with than two. *Time to get this over with.*

He headed for the shop. Unsure if the soldiers would recognize him, he swiped a fedora off a hatter's display and pressed it onto his head, hoping it matched the suit he wore.

Tipping the brim forward to shadow his face, he stepped straight past the guard and through the door.

A bell dinged overhead.

The guard briefly glanced at him, then returned to his scan of the street.

"Can I help you?"

The shop matron stepped out from behind the counter, clutching a cane, as the door shut behind him. Her silver hair was done up in an extravagant bun.

"G'day, ma'am." He scanned the shop and found it empty.

Rune must be trying something on. He nodded toward the back, where a mirror stood with fitting rooms on both sides. "I'm looking for my fiancée. She's trying on a dress."

The matron looked Gideon's suit up and down. Her eyes narrowed, deepening her crow's-feet.

The suit had belonged to his father. His parents had been known as the Sharpe Duet, once famous dressmakers employed by the witch queens. Their garments were rare, and therefore priceless—or so Rune had once explained to him.

This shop matron seemed to disagree. Or perhaps she didn't recognize the designer. From the curl of her mouth, she thought Gideon's suit belonged in a discount charity store.

"You must have the wrong shop. Only one young woman is trying on dresses right now." Her tone said: *And she's well above your caliber.*

Gideon flexed his knuckles, trying to rein in his annoyance.

"I'm certain I have the right shop." He started around her.

She stepped to block him, holding out her cane like a scepter. For a woman so advanced in age, she moved unnaturally fast.

"Listen to me, boy. I don't put up with thieves."

A nerve in Gideon's jaw ticked. *A thief, am I?*

"If you don't leave at once, I'll call for the brute standing outside the door."

Gideon glanced across the shop. The fitting room curtains were all drawn back except one—where Rune was trying on dresses. Beyond the fitting area, there was bound to be a door. These buildings all had access to the back alleyways.

He considered retreating to the alley, finding the door, and using it to sneak back in. Except it was likely locked from the outside.

"Did you hear me, son?"

The bell over the door dinged again and a crowd of fashionable young women surged in, speaking in excited tones, their silk gloves fluttering as they spoke. The matron released Gideon from her hawklike gaze and drew her cane away, leaning on it once more.

She greeted the girls with a cheerful smile. She wouldn't want to be seen arguing with Gideon. Riffraff was bad for business.

The girls flocked toward the dresses on display.

Out, she mouthed to Gideon.

He tipped his fedora to her, stepping backward, and headed for the front door until the *clack clack clack* of her cane retreated to the other side of the shop.

"What I can help you with, dearies?" he heard her say.

He opened the door. The bell dinged again. But instead of stepping out, with the matron's attention fixed on her new customers, Gideon quickly doubled back. Heading straight for the only occupied fitting room. He touched the pistol in his jacket but didn't draw it. It was too soon.

Don't think, this time. Just shoot.

As soon as he did, he'd bolt for the back door and use it to escape into the alley. Grabbing the fitting room curtain, he threw it back.

Rune was inside, wearing a white lace dress. Gideon didn't have time to pull his gun on her, because she already had one of her own.

It was aimed straight at his forehead.

THIRTEEN

GIDEON

"GET IN," SAID RUNE, her finger pressed to the trigger. "And keep your hands where I can see them."

She'd been expecting him.

Rune wore a wedding dress with tapered lace sleeves that covered her arms from shoulder to wrist. The sight of it was a perfect reminder: she was meant to be someone else's bride.

Gideon swallowed.

Not wanting to get shot—or seen by the shop matron—he did as Rune said. Stepping into the cramped fitting room, he pulled the curtain across the entrance behind him, shielding them from view. Then faced Rune with his hands in the air.

Her strawberry blonde hair was in ringlets. Gideon had never seen it like that. It made her look doll-like.

A lethal doll.

He glanced at the gun in her hands. It was a gentleman's revolver. Used for dueling and little else.

"You sure it's loaded this time?"

Rune took off the safety. "Soren loaded it for me."

Gideon bristled. What kind of man gave a girl a loaded gun without teaching her how to use it?

Unless he did teach her.

The girl in front of you isn't a girl, he reminded himself. *She's a manipulative witch.*

And the prince caught in her spell was clearly in on this

scheme. Soren and a handful of guards were probably waiting at both exits.

Gideon had walked himself into a trap.

"You've gotten rusty," said Rune. "You thought I'd parade myself through the streets of Caelis *knowing* you were here, waiting to kill me?"

"Could we skip the gloating," said Gideon, "and move on to the part where you put me out of my misery?"

"I'm not going to kill you."

"No, you're going to call your fiancé's bodyguard to do it for you."

To his surprise, Rune lowered her gun. "I'm here to propose a truce."

"A *what*?" Gideon lowered his hands.

Was this a trick?

"A *temporary* truce," she amended. "If you help me, I'll break off my engagement to Soren, nullifying his alliance with Cressida. That's what you want, right? It's why you came to kill me."

She'd snagged a hook in his chest and was reeling him in. Because yes, that *was* why he came to kill her.

"Why would you break off your engagement?"

She glanced away. "You were right. I don't want to be his wife."

The real Rune would never admit to Gideon being right. Was she lying?

Two nights ago, she was fully committed to her role in Cressida's alliance. Clearly, she had some surprise up her sleeve.

He studied her, wary. "What kind of *help* do you want from me?"

Rune sat on a small bench leaning against the wall. Setting the gun down beside her within easy reach, she grabbed a set of shoes off the floor and pulled the first one on. By keeping her hands occupied, she demonstrated the risk she was willing to take for this truce.

After all, Gideon also had a gun.

But he was intrigued, and she knew it.

"I want you to get me safely into the New Republic, and I want you to give me the sibyl you're holding hostage." She glanced up at him, pulling on the second shoe. "If you kill me, Soren will simply wage a war against the Republic to avenge me. So it's in your best interest to help me."

She's bluffing.

Unless she wasn't.

Gideon ran a hand through his hair, thinking. Soren was an Umbrian prince: possessive, entitled, used to getting his way. Men like him didn't take their losses lightly. If Gideon executed Rune, Soren might do exactly as she said: give Cressida an army anyway, to avenge his fiancée—and his wounded pride.

Gideon would prove his loyalty by killing the Crimson Moth. But if Rune wasn't bluffing, her death wouldn't prevent a war; it would *incite* one.

He couldn't risk that.

But a truce with the very witch who betrayed me?

He couldn't risk that, either.

Unless I betray her first.

An idea sparked in Gideon's mind.

What if there's a way to use her to my advantage?

"I need some assurance that you won't betray me again," he said.

"*I* betrayed *you*?" On her feet now, Rune scowled at him. "It was the other way around."

"We'll have to agree to disagree."

Her nostrils flared. "Can you give *me* assurances? I'm risking

my safety. Cressida already suspects I helped you escape! What
are you risking?"

"By helping you get into the Republic? My job. My dignity.
Possibly my life."

Sympathizing with witches was now an offense punished by
death in the Republic. She must have known that, because she
glanced away, biting her lip.

Gideon couldn't trust her. Not ever. But once they were on
the island, he wouldn't have to. It wouldn't even matter if Rune
was lying to him.

She can't betray me if I betray her first.

Gideon knew what he had to do.

He would accept Rune's terms. He'd smuggle her into the
New Republic. And the moment they made port, he'd arrest
her himself.

Once Rune was in Blood Guard custody, alive and unharmed, Gideon could barter with Soren. *He* would define the
terms: Soren could have his precious fiancée back—if and when
Cressida was eliminated.

Gideon didn't care how Soren accomplished it, so long as
Cressida and her witch army were all dead before she tore the
New Republic apart. Once Soren complied, Gideon would
hand Rune over. The Blood Guard wouldn't have to lift a finger.
All they'd have to do was hold Rune hostage until their terms
were met.

If he pulled this off, Gideon would crush two threats at once.
He'd get everything he wanted: Cressida dead, his reputation
restored, and peace reestablished on the island.

The only wild card was Rune.

This could be an elaborate plot to bring him—and the
Republic—down. But if she was lying, all he had to do was get
ahead of her.

"Once I get you onto the island, what will you do?" he asked, playing along now.

Rune raised her gun to his chest.

"If you think I'm going to tell you my exact plans so you can sabotage them, you're dumber than you look."

He glanced at the revolver, noticing the hammer wasn't drawn back. He considered staying silent. Waiting to see how far she'd take this, if she'd really pull the trigger, and then overcome her when she realized her error.

But he couldn't resist.

"You need to cock it before you fire."

Her cheeks reddened. "Curse you," she muttered, then cocked the gun and kept aiming.

But her form was still wrong. It was obvious she had little to no experience with firearms. He marveled at Soren's lack of prudence. If she'd been *his* fiancée, the first thing Gideon would have done would've been to teach her how to properly hold, aim, and shoot a gun.

And then she'd kill me with it.

But she hadn't killed him yet.

He studied her.

Not only was her hair perfect, but so was her makeup. Kohl lined her eyes. Rouge reddened her lips and cheeks. Even her lashes looked darker than usual.

He wanted to smear it all off. To unravel those curls. To strip her down to the Rune underneath.

"What really changed your mind?" he asked. "Because I don't think it's Soren."

Her eyes flashed with some turbulent emotion, like a ship on a stormy sea. It made him even more curious.

"I'm done answering questions. Do you accept my terms or not?"

"You're asking me to go against my orders. What's to stop you from cutting and running the moment I deliver on my end of the bargain? You've betrayed me before, remember?"

"You're not exactly the most trustworthy person, either," she shot back. "You handed me over to be killed the moment you found out what I was."

And I'll do it again.

"*You* made me believe you were in love with me." He stepped so close, the barrel of her gun pushed into the center of his chest. "*You* used me for intel. The entire time you were toying with me, you were recruiting witches for Cress's army!"

"I didn't know she was Cressida!"

Rune winced, probably realizing how loud she'd spoken. She glanced at the curtain hiding them from the rest of the shop.

"I thought she was Verity," she said, quietly. "I thought she was my friend. I didn't *know.*"

This girl was so damn hard to read.

"I can't tell the truth from a lie with you," he said.

Rune said nothing. Just lowered her gun to her side.

Trusting her was impossible. What she was asking of him would require going against everything he'd committed himself to, everyone who *trusted* him. He would be betraying them all if he made this deal with Rune.

Unless I betray her first, he reminded himself.

Rune was certainly plotting the same. He didn't for a second think she would be loyal to this truce. Of course she had some trick up her sleeve. Once he came through on his part of this deal, she would disappear without delivering what she promised—or betray him in some worse way.

I need to be three steps ahead of her this time.

"Well?" asked Rune.

"Fine," he said. "I agree to a *temporary* truce."

She lowered the gun, her shoulders relaxing. As if she'd been tense this whole time, certain he'd refuse. She put the safety back on her pistol. "Good. Here's the plan: there's a back door past the fitting area. If—"

"Darling?" Soren's voice called from outside the fitting room. "How are you faring?"

Gideon froze. Rune's eyes widened.

Clearly she hadn't expected her fiancé to return so soon.

She pushed past Gideon. With her pistol hidden behind her back, she peeked out from behind the fitting room curtain. "I'm not dressed yet, my love. Why don't you wait outside? I'll meet you in a minute."

"There's no need to be shy." Soren sounded much closer. Less than five paces away. "I'll see you undressed soon enough . . ."

Gideon didn't like the way Rune tensed at those words.

In a few seconds, Soren would pull back this curtain, hoping to sneak inside. And when he did, he'd find Gideon already in here.

"Soren," Rune tried again. "You know it's bad luck to—"

The prince grabbed the curtain.

Gideon seized Rune's pistol and pressed it to her head. She stiffened against him.

Soren flung back the curtain. At the sight inside the fitting room, the cocky smile on his face melted into shock.

"Do exactly as I say," Gideon snarled. "Or I'll put a bullet in your *darling's* tiny head."

FOURTEEN

GIDEON

"*Y*OU." SOREN'S LIP CURLED at the sight of Gideon. But he was all teeth and no bite. Gideon had what Soren wanted; Gideon, therefore, was the one with all the power here.

"That's right." Gideon slid his arm around Rune's waist, pulling her tight against him. An eerie calmness settled like a blanket over him. "Unless you'd like your bride-to-be's brains splattered against the wall, you'll do as I say."

The stunned prince looked from Gideon to Rune to the gun.

"Lock the front door," said Gideon.

The words sank in. Soren snapped out of his shock and did as Gideon commanded, striding toward the front door and locking it. Making no move to alert the guards out front.

Gideon nudged Rune from the fitting room, keeping the revolver pressed to her head.

"All of you." He nodded to Soren, the shop matron, and the gaggle of customers—who now looked like a flock of frightened birds. "Get behind the front counter."

As they obeyed, Gideon backed toward the rear of the shop, taking Rune with him.

Under her breath, Rune whispered: "*Left.* The door is to your *left.*"

She hadn't struggled when he took her hostage. As if she sensed his plan the moment he put it in motion. As if she were handing him the reins, letting him steer them out of this.

Gideon found the door. He pressed his shoulders against it.

"If you come after us," he called to Soren, "I'll kill her."

Pushing the door open, Gideon dragged Rune out. It slammed shut behind them.

The sun beat down, blinding him for a second.

"I have a hotel room," he said, letting Rune go. Pulling the fedora off his head, he chucked it in the nearby refuse bin. "We can go there until I figure out a plan."

"I already have a plan."

Rune pulled out of his grip and turned toward the bin. Two suitcases were hidden behind it.

"Give me my gun back," she said. "You'll need both hands to carry these."

Gideon frowned as she dragged them out. Had she packed these and planted them here? But that would mean . . .

"*Now*, Gideon. They'll be on us in seconds."

"Is that the *prince's* luggage?"

"I'll explain everything on the way."

Rune swiped the gun out of his hand and tucked it down her bodice. How there was room for it in there, he had no idea. Next, she pulled out a dove gray cloak and threw it over her shoulders, concealing the bright white wedding dress. After drawing the hood over her head to hide her rose-gold hair, she started to run.

"Come on!"

A high-pitched whistle sounded. One used by the Caelisian police to signify an imminent arrest.

There was no time to think. Gideon grabbed the suitcases— hoisting one under each arm—and ran after Rune.

Perhaps it was the suitcases weighing him down, but Rune was surprisingly swift, even in a cumbersome gown. It took him a minute to catch up with her as they wove through the back alleys and away from the shopping district. Heading toward the water.

Almost as if she'd mapped out and memorized this route beforehand.

"Pick up the pace!" she called. "Or we'll be late!"

"If you hadn't made me your pack mule," Gideon panted, his grip on the suitcases tightening, "I'd be—"

Wait.

"Late for what?"

A sudden shot rang out. They both ducked. Gideon glanced behind them, sighting a soldier two streets back who was taking aim again. With both arms full, he couldn't draw his gun. He was about to drop the suitcases when a shot rang out. Loud and very close to his head.

He ducked out of the way, but the heat of the blast was warm on his face. When he looked up, he saw Rune aiming her revolver at the officers behind them.

Grabbing her gun, he pushed it down, aiming it at the ground.

"You nearly shot me," he hissed.

"Sorry." Her tone suggested she was sorrier she'd missed him.

More shots rang out behind them, followed by threatening shouts. This time, they both ducked behind a refuse bin.

"We need to find a crowded street," he said, listening to the bullets bounce off metal and brick.

They could more easily lose their pursuers in a crowd.

Rune nodded her agreement. "This way."

She led them further toward the water. Fire burned in Gideon's biceps as he tried not to drop Rune's luggage while also trying to keep pace with her.

Soon the alley opened into the harbor front, where the

entertainment district drew locals and tourists alike. On the busy sidewalk, passing art galleries and cafés, Rune slowed, blending in with the crowd. Gideon set down the luggage to give his arms a reprieve, then lifted each bag by its handles.

Now he and Rune looked like any other tourists newly arrived in the city and searching for their hotel.

"Where are we going?" he asked, scanning the crowd. Looking for uniforms.

"The *Arcadia*."

Gideon knew it by reputation: the only passenger ship that barred witch hunters and their hounds from boarding.

"I bought us passage. It departs at one o'clock."

Gideon spluttered. "One o'clock?"

That was *right now*.

"Otherwise, we'll have to wait until it returns next week. The entire Caelisian police force—not to mention Cressida—will be looking for us by nightfall. We can't afford to wait that long."

Mercy. *She* was three steps ahead of *him*.

She predicted I would agree to this before I even showed up.

Gideon *was* rusty.

"That's a three-day voyage." Not far behind them, he saw police officers pushing through the crowd. "All of my things are back at the hotel."

"I've taken care of everything." Rune nodded toward the lighter suitcase. "That's Soren's. You'll have to make do with his wardrobe."

He'd have to wear the prince's clothes? For the next three days?

"Absolutely not."

"Oh, are silk and brocade too fancy for you?" Beneath her gray hood, Rune rolled her eyes.

"They won't fit me!" he spluttered.

"Men with guns are chasing us, Gideon. Well-fitting clothes are the least of your concerns."

She was right.

His mood darkened.

Caught behind a group of tourists gawking at the architecture, Gideon dodged around them and into the street so he and Rune didn't lose ground to the police behind them. Up ahead, the *Arcadia* loomed. It was a passenger steamship, and its long gangplank rose from the quay to the upper deck, where a few stragglers stood waiting in line to board.

Beyond the *Arcadia*, out in the harbor, a fleet of Soren's warships were emerging through the morning mist. Gray plumes from the vessels' smokestacks choked the sky.

The prince's navy must be getting ready to sail for the New Republic.

"You better be right about this," Gideon said as he glanced behind them. Officers were searching civilians only twenty paces away, asking questions.

His body was a coiled spring. How was Rune so calm?

"What if someone recognizes your name? Or your face?"

"The tickets are in your name," she said as they reached the gangplank and started up it. A group of four stood in line ahead of them. From their fashionable clothing, Gideon guessed they were in Caelis as tourists, or here on business. "And I plan to change my face."

Gideon didn't like the sound of that.

"Next!" a loud voice called, piercing the silence.

They both glanced up as the passengers ahead stepped off the gangway and onto the ship. The ticket taker stood in a crisp navy uniform. When his bored gaze fell on them, he paused, glancing from Rune's dress to Gideon's suit.

"Well, isn't this a sight. It's so refreshing to see a young couple settling down instead of sowing their wild oats all over the place! Congratulations on your nuptials."

Gideon was about to correct the mistake when Rune slipped her arm through his and stepped in closer. The press of her body surprised him.

"It was a lovely ceremony," she said to the ticket taker, beaming up at him. "We eloped."

Oh. No.

No no no.

Gideon glanced from Rune's lace wedding dress to his vintage suit, realizing this was *exactly* how it looked: like they had just been married.

"I've dreamed of a wedding in the Umbrian Mountains ever since I was a little girl." Rune smiled sweetly up at Gideon. So sweet, it was making his stomach ache.

What have I agreed to?

This wasn't the plan. It couldn't be. But the Caelisian police were down below, looking to arrest the witch hunter who'd kidnapped Prince Soren's fiancée. One wrong move and it was all over. If they spotted Gideon, if they cornered him and Rune, she would throw him to the wolves. She'd walk free while they hauled him off to prison, and then find another way to smuggle herself into the New Republic.

Gideon needed to avoid arrest. The Caelisian authorities would not be sympathetic to a witch hunter. And once they put him in a cell, Cressida would know exactly where to find him.

"Welcome aboard the *Arcadia*, Mr. and Mrs. Sharpe."

The words were like a lightning strike, zapping Gideon to alertness. Rune flinched beside him, equally jolted.

"Thanks," they whispered.

Handing over their ticket stubs, Rune stepped onto the ship.

Gideon followed behind, hauling their luggage across the promenade deck.

"This is not what I agreed to," he said under his breath, scanning the deck for any familiar faces. Staff scurried back and forth, readying to set sail, while passengers strolled or waved to their loved ones.

He'd recognized no one on his voyage here. He hoped the same would hold true on the voyage back.

"You promised to get me safely into the New Republic," said Rune, untucking her arm from his. "You should be thanking me for helping you make that happen."

"*Thanking* you?"

The gall.

As he followed her to the stairs leading down to the lower levels, Gideon glanced back to the quay, where police were still stopping and searching civilians. At least they'd made it onto the ship. He hoped the *Arcadia* left port before they thought to search it, too.

"We need to find our cabin," said Rune, stepping into the stairwell, a few steps ahead of him.

Gideon slowed.

"Cabin?" His hands tightened on the suitcases' leather handles as he dodged other passengers and their luggage, many of them smiling at the sight of Rune's gown and congratulating Gideon. "As in *one* cabin? Shared between the two of us?"

"I bought our tickets at the last minute," she called over her shoulder. "There was only one left, in third class."

Gideon halted in the stairwell doorway, lightheaded.

Third-class cabins were tiny, cramped things. They barely fit one small bed.

He doubted Rune knew this. She'd likely never traveled third class in her life.

And their charade was fully entrenched. Having declared themselves newly married, they had to act the part. For three straight days.

"Hurry!" Rune's voice echoed up to him. "You're falling behind!"

An understatement if he'd ever heard one.

Had he forgotten how clever she was? Not only was Gideon woefully unprepared—at this rate, he'd never catch up to her.

FIFTEEN

RUNE

WHEN RUNE OPENED THE door to their cabin, she wondered if she'd made a grave error.

The room was as small as a dog's kennel. Wedged between the walls was a bed barely big enough to fit two people. Between the door and the bed frame was space to set down their suitcases, and little else.

There was no closet or dresser, and the only light came from a small window over the bed.

"I've died and gone to hell," said Gideon from behind her.

He dropped their luggage on the floor and shut the door. With two people in such a small space, the temperature was already rising. Standing, Rune untied the tassels of her cloak and tossed it onto the bed.

"It could be worse," she said, defensive.

Though what *worse* looked like, she couldn't imagine.

Rune almost heard Gideon's growled thoughts as he scanned the room they'd be confined to for the next two nights.

Resigning himself, he peeled off his jacket—she'd immediately recognized the Sharpe Duet style when he showed up in her fitting room—and tossed it onto the bed. As he unbuttoned the cuffs of his shirt, Rune noticed how smart he looked in his father's suit. He'd tailored it to fit himself, and its classic look unexpectedly complemented her vintage-inspired dress.

We do pass as newlyweds.

Her stomach dipped. But before she could banish the odd

feeling, a knocking came from down the hall. Gideon glanced toward the door, rolling up his second sleeve. At the urgent voices, Rune opened it and peeked out.

Uniformed officers walked the corridor, knocking on cabin doors and questioning the inhabitants.

Her pulse kicked.

"The police are here."

There was only one way out of this corridor—the stairwell— and it was on the other side of the officers.

We're cornered.

Before they spotted her, Rune shut the door and turned to Gideon. "Take off your clothes."

He raised an eyebrow.

"A vintage suit would be easy for the shop matron to describe to the police," she explained.

Seeming to agree, Gideon unbuttoned his shirt and nodded to her dress. "Won't they also be looking for a girl in a stolen wedding gown?"

Rune glanced down at the dress she wore. It would give her away in an instant.

As Gideon shucked off his shirt, Rune reached for the laces at the back of the dress. The shop matron had helped her into it and tied the laces tight. Now, the harder she tugged on them, the tighter they knotted.

The knocking got louder.

Closer.

Rune glanced at Gideon, who was shirtless and working at the buttons of his pants. "Um . . . Gideon?"

He turned to face her, giving her a view of his very defined abdomen.

Rune spun, pointing to the laces at the back of her dress.

"You've got to be kidding me," he said.

Gideon stalked toward her. Which, with three feet of space to move in, only required half a step.

"Trust me," she said through gritted teeth. "I'd rather not have to ask you for help."

"Trust me," he growled back, "I'd rather not have to give it."

Gideon picked at the knots until one came loose. Then he *yanked*, jerking Rune with him. She had to press her hands flat against the clapboard wall and lean into them to stop herself from flopping around like a rag doll as he tugged and pulled.

"Next time," he said, hauling at the laces, "you're going to tell me the entire plan *up front*."

Rune scowled at the wall. "If I'd told you the entire plan up front, you wouldn't have agreed to it."

"Exactly," he said, his growing irritation evident in his roughness.

"That's why I didn't tell you."

The laces loosened as he moved downward, baring her skin to him. Exposing her back to his gaze, from her shoulders to her hips.

Realizing it, Rune went hot all over.

"If you'd told me, we wouldn't be in this—"

Before he could tug the dress off, the knocking arrived at their door.

"What do you want?" he roared, transferring his anger from Rune to whoever was knocking.

"Police! Open up!"

They both froze.

Rune nodded for him to answer it. He hesitated, then finally went as she wriggled free from the dress. Dropping it and his jacket on the ground, she kicked both pieces of clothing under the bed.

Rune needed to illusion herself, and fast.

Gideon swung the door open, angling it to hide Rune, who now stood in her underwear.

Unsheathing the knife at her thigh, she pressed its honed edge to her calf, where a multitude of silvery casting scars shone, carefully fashioned into the image of moths in flight. The moths started at her ankle and fluttered up the back of her leg.

Rune added a cut to the newest half-formed moth.

"Yes?" Unfettered annoyance dripped from Gideon's voice.

Rune pressed her fingers to the blood welling up.

"S-sorry to disturb you, sir," came a woman's voice.

Rune didn't envy her. The sight of Gideon shirtless was enough to stun any woman.

She drew the Mirage's spellmark on her ankle in blood.

"Are you the Sharpes?"

The name clanged like a discordant bell in Rune's ears. *The Sharpes.* It's who she and Alex would have been. To hear it referring to her and Gideon . . .

"That's right," said Gideon. "What do you want?"

Finally, the tang of magic burst on her tongue as the illusion took hold. She hoped it was enough.

"We have some questions for you."

Knowing she needed to make an appearance, Rune called out: "Who's there, pumpkin?"

She could almost feel Gideon wither beneath the pet name.

"No one important, *sugarplum.*" There was an edge to his voice. Like a wolf's warning growl. He turned his attention back to the police. "As you can see, we're a little busy. I'm sure you understand."

He started to close the door, but an officer stepped forward, stopping it from shutting.

"This will only take a minute."

Standing in only her underwear, Rune glanced at her

suitcase. Was there enough time to find something to throw on? She was about to try when the officer pushed the door open wider, searching for Mrs. Sharpe.

Drat.

Her crimson moth signature flared in the air, directly in front of her.

Double drat.

She quickly stepped in front of it, hiding evidence of the spell.

Through the open door, her eyes met the officer's. She watched his gaze drop, running slowly down her body. As if he had every right to look.

White-hot anger flared in her chest. But there was nothing Rune could do. In this moment, she was at his mercy. They both were.

Suddenly, Gideon stepped between them, blocking Rune from the officer's gaze. Grabbing the shirt he'd discarded a few minutes ago, he gently pulled it down over her head. Startled, Rune pushed her arms through the sleeves as the hem fell to the tops of her thighs, covering everything but her legs.

She glanced up to find a fire raging in Gideon's eyes.

He was shielding her from them.

Or, more likely, shielding the proof of her witchy-ness: the blood dripping down her calf, the spellmark on her ankle, the signature floating behind her.

If the change in her appearance surprised him, he didn't show it.

"Can we hurry this up?" Gideon's voice held a warning as he turned back to the officers. He stepped toward the door, forcing them into the hall. "My wife and I were just married and would like to be alone."

"Of course," said the officer. "We, um, were wondering if you've seen this girl?"

There was a short pause, then: "No."

"And your wife? Mrs. Sharpe, have you seen this girl?"

Gideon stepped aside, but only barely, allowing Rune to answer. In the doorway, one officer held out a locket. It hung from a golden chain and was instantly familiar.

Rune had gifted it to Soren two weeks ago. It was an exact twin of a locket he'd given her.

And *her* face was painted inside.

"I've never seen that girl in my life," said Rune, glad she'd had the chance to illusion herself.

"There. Are we good?" Gideon's rough voice made his role of impatient new husband all too convincing. Before they answered, he said, "Great. Goodbye."

He slammed the door in their faces.

The room seemed to have shrunk since they first entered it. Still facing the door, Gideon heaved a sigh. Rune stared at his bare back, unable to stop her eyes from tracing the corded muscles in his shoulders and arms.

"Thank you," she whispered.

"Under any other circumstances"—he turned to look at her, his gaze dropping to his massive shirt hanging off her small frame—"I would have thrown him out."

Unable to find her voice, Rune simply nodded.

The foot of space between them felt like a sliver as they stood half-dressed in front of each other.

She tried to hold his gaze and failed, her eyes dropping to take him in. She heard the breath he let loose, as if they'd unknowingly been playing a game called *Who can hold off the longest?* and now that Rune had lost, Gideon could let himself lose, too. His eyes trailed down her form as he allowed himself to look at her the way she was looking at him.

The air felt strained. Rune was afraid to move, suddenly all too aware of the bed behind her.

"Are you—"

"I should—"

Their voices cut the tension.

Gideon stepped away. Toward the luggage. Turning to Soren's suitcase, he unzipped it, reached inside, and pulled out the first thing he found: a gray knit sweater. Pulling it on, he said, "I'll go see if they have any other available cabins."

He stepped out into the hall.

The door swung shut behind him.

Rune sank onto the bed, her breath rushing out of her. There would be no other cabins. They'd already been reluctant to give her this one, which was normally reserved for staff. She could have told Gideon this, but in truth, she wanted him gone so she could get her thundering heart under control.

Two nights, she told herself. *It's only two nights.*

Two nights in bed with Gideon Sharpe.

Rune squeezed her eyes shut, trying not to think of all the ways this could go horribly, disastrously wrong.

SIXTEEN

GIDEON

*T*HERE WERE NO EXTRA cabins.

They offered Gideon a bunk in the staff quarters, but taking it would ruin the newlywed image that was now firmly in place.

Gideon would just have to gird his loins and continue down the path Rune had forced him onto.

You've pretended to be in love with her before. You can do it again.

But there was that voice inside him again, small and insistent, begging to differ:

How much did you really pretend?

If Gideon were honest, Rune had always enchanted him. He was fifteen the day he met her and his heart first jumped into his throat. Ever since, he'd spent his time insisting he *wasn't* drawn to her, for his brother's sake, and for the sake of his pride—because someone like him could never deserve someone like Rune. She had said as much herself two months ago, when he exposed her as the Crimson Moth.

Standing at the railing on the upper deck, watching the Continent disappear in the distance, Gideon blew out a ragged breath. It was only two more days before they reached port. He could keep up this charade for two more days.

After that, Rune would be at his mercy. The moment they docked, he would arrest the Crimson Moth and hand her over.

It would restore his standing as a patriot, prove his loyalty.

It would burn this weakness out of him.

The salt wind stung his cheeks as he thought back to the cabin. To that officer drinking in the sight of Rune's nearly naked form. Despite the cold air, the rage it ignited still simmered inside him.

After everything Rune had put him through, his first instinct was to protect her. She was like a magnet sending the arrows on his moral compass spinning. Making him forget who he was and everything he'd committed himself to.

But it was worse than that.

As he'd unlaced her dress, Gideon had tried not to admire the swoop of her shoulder blades, or the ridges of her spine. He'd tried to ignore the urge to touch her porcelain-smooth skin, to slide the dress off her shoulders and down her arms. To let the whole thing drop to the floor.

Gideon clenched his hands into fists.

No.

He wouldn't fall prey to her again. He needed to be impenetrable if he was going to stay ahead of her. He needed to keep his distance. The further apart they were, the clearer his head got. And the clearer his head, the better he could focus on his plan.

But how was he supposed to keep his distance in that tiny bed?

The thought of it—of lying next to her—made Gideon feel things he didn't want to feel. Things he'd tried so hard to forget.

He scrubbed his hands over his cold face.

Mercy. What a mess he was in.

The sun was setting on the horizon. It would only get colder from here on out. With a shiver, he turned to make his way belowdecks, but familiar voices stopped him in his tracks.

"If Miss Winters is on the *Arcadia*, they won't simply arrest her."

Further up the deck, leaning over the railing side by side as they stared out to sea, were the officers who'd questioned him and Rune. Gideon angled himself closer to a nearby post, keeping himself concealed.

"You think they'll kill her?"

"Witches are executed on sight in the New Republic. This spy will have the same orders."

There's a spy on the Arcadia?

Gideon remembered Harrow's telegram. *THE COMMANDER NO LONGER BELIEVES YOU'RE THE BEST MAN FOR THIS JOB. HE'S SENDING SOMEONE MORE QUALIFIED TO COMPLETE IT.*

Of course Harrow would plant a spy onboard the one ship barring working Blood Guard soldiers and their witch-hunting hounds. He should have suspected as much.

Under every other circumstance, he would have approved the measure. But if there was a spy in his midst, he couldn't let them discover Rune, never mind assassinate her. He needed her alive to barter with.

Worse: if the spy on board was Harrow's, there was a good chance they'd recognize Gideon. It would look highly suspicious if a report was sent back to the Good Commander's spymaster saying Gideon was returning with a secret wife after failing to assassinate the Crimson Moth. Harrow would assume the worst: Gideon had fallen prey to Rune *again*.

He couldn't—*wouldn't*—let that happen.

Once Gideon figured out who this spy was, he'd stop their interference by telling them his plan. But if they discovered Rune first and killed her, he'd not only be left empty-handed, he'd look like he teamed up with a criminal. He'd be seen as a traitor.

Gideon needed to stop that from happening at all costs.

And Rune . . .

Rune.

His chest knotted. What if this spy had already found her?

SEVENTEEN

RUNE

B Y SUNDOWN, THE BOAT was out at sea and
Gideon still hadn't returned. Hungry and tired of being confined to their cramped cabin, Rune donned a pastel green
evening gown and a pair of cream-colored gloves, then set out to
find dinner.

The *Arcadia* had six decks, and after asking for directions
from the staff, Rune eventually found her way to the third-class
dining saloon on the lower deck. Through the portholes, the
sea churned beneath a blackening sky. Caelis's harbor was long
gone on the horizon.

The saloon was abuzz with the sound of conversation
and the clink of silverware. The narrow room was dimly lit
by candles burning in sconces on the wall, and there was no
reception desk, forcing Rune to choose a seat herself. But
diners crammed every table, most of them shooting glances
her way.

I'm overdressed, she realized.

Overdressed and drawing unwanted attention to herself.

She found a vacant booth across the room and slid into it.

Two menus lay on the table. Picking one up, she pretended
to skim it while simultaneously scanning the saloon.

At least this is the Arcadia.

The *Arcadia* was governed by Caelisian laws. That's why
she'd chosen it. The safety it provided, along with the illusion
disguising her features, gave her enough cover to relax, at least

temporarily. The spell would wear off later tonight and need to be recast tomorrow morning.

But once Rune stepped into the New Republic, she would be unprotected. As soon as they arrived in port, witch hunters and their hounds would board and check every cabin. Only after everyone was accounted for and thoroughly searched would they let passengers disembark.

Rune would never get past the dogs, who would sniff out her magic immediately. If Gideon couldn't circumvent them, this would all be over.

She was completely at his mercy.

What have I done?

"Why is a pretty girl like yourself dining alone?"

Looking up, Rune found a young man standing over her. His mouth curved in a friendly smile, and his eyes sparkled in the candlelight. His hair reminded her of Alex's—a tawny gold—and in one hand he held a wine bottle; in the other, two glasses.

"My . . . um . . . husband is seasick," she lied.

He didn't wear the staff uniform, suggesting he was a passenger.

"Pity." He set both glasses down and began pouring wine. "Would you like some company to help pass the time?"

"She already has company."

The familiar voice was like an earthquake's tremor, reverberating through Rune.

The young man glanced up midpour. Rune reluctantly followed his gaze.

Gideon had changed into a dark green suit from Soren's luggage. The jacket was too tight, the seams stretched to their limit. But the ill fit only made Gideon look more impressive, drawing attention to his well-defined shoulders and the strength in his arms.

"You're the seasick husband, I take it?"

Gideon glanced at Rune, who smiled weakly up at him.

"The very one." His attention returned to the young man. "And *you* were just leaving."

Sensing he couldn't win this fight, the man quietly withdrew, leaving the wine and the glasses. Gideon slid into the booth across from Rune and set the glass of water he'd brought with him down on the table.

It was too small a space for someone as big as Gideon. Beneath the table, his legs crowded hers, forcing Rune to tuck her knees between his.

"Do you have to be so rude?" she said, watching her wine benefactor retreat.

"You're naive if you think all he wanted from you was some company."

Rune rolled her eyes. "Not everyone has ulterior motives, Gideon. Some people are just *nice*. You could try it sometime."

"Trust me." Gideon watched the would-be suitor search for another table. "I'm a man. I know what he wants."

She scoffed. "You're ridiculous. All men have built-in radar telling them the thoughts of other men?"

"Something like that."

His gaze lifted to her. For a moment, that sparkling silence from the cabin returned. Rune became aware of the candle burning low in the sconce on the wall beside them. Of how small and dark and far away their booth was from the other diners. Of how she and Gideon looked to everyone else in the room: like a couple having dinner together.

This was a game they hadn't played before.

She cleared her throat and changed the subject. "Any luck finding a second cabin?"

He shook his head. "They're all full."

Just like she'd told him when they boarded. She circled the
rim of her wineglass with the tip of her gloved finger. "You were
gone so long, I thought maybe you'd jumped overboard and
swam back to shore."

"And why would I do that?" He lifted his glass to his mouth.
"The Barrow Strait is freezing this time of year."

"But perhaps less daunting than sharing a bed with me."

Gideon choked on his water. His eyes lifted to hers as he set
down the glass.

"Why should I be daunted?" He lowered his voice. "I've survived the beds of witches before."

Is he referring to Cressida? Or to me?

Both, she realized.

For some stupid reason, being lumped in with Cressida, as
if they were one and the same, hurt fiercely. Ordinarily, Rune
tried not to think about the night she'd spent in Gideon's bed.
But she was thinking about it now.

"Is that what it was between us?" She lowered her gaze to her
wine. "Something for you to survive?"

"That's rich, coming from you." Gideon leaned back, crossing his arms. An agitated energy rolled off him. "The entire
time you were seducing me, you were in love with my brother.
So don't pretend like your feelings are hurt."

Rune glanced up.

What?

"Oh, come on. You're going to play coy with *me*?" His mouth
curled like he'd eaten something rotten. "There's no need to
pretend anymore. I see you clearly, even with that illusion."
He lowered his voice and nodded to her altered face. "Seeing
you with Soren made your skill at seduction abundantly clear.
Watching him so utterly convinced of your affection was like
watching myself, two months ago." She heard the disgust in his

voice. "You might have deceived me once, but you won't do it again."

Rune glanced away.

Had she feigned feelings for Gideon at first? *Yes.* Had she tried to seduce him to obtain valuable intel? *Of course.* It was the only way to rescue Seraphine.

But at some point, she'd stopped pretending.

At some point, the lie became real.

Gideon had no reason to believe Rune's feelings had been sincere. So it shouldn't have surprised her that he believed she was in love with Alex. She was still wearing his brother's engagement ring, after all.

There's no point explaining it to him.

He'd never believe her. Even if he did, it wouldn't change anything. She was a witch. Nothing Rune did could ever change his mind; her inherent, unalterable *essence* revolted him.

She finished her wine in one gulp.

"Poor, innocent Gideon. Deceived by a witch." On an empty stomach, the alcohol hit fast. Her face grew warm, and the chatter dimmed around them. "What a victim you are."

Her anger flared and she reached for the wine bottle, pouring herself another glass.

"Of *course* I deceived you. If you'd known the truth from the beginning, you would've had me executed!"

Gideon glanced around the saloon. "Keep your voice down."

Rune winced. He was right. She'd spoken too loudly.

Following his gaze, Rune looked out over the room but found no one watching them. Hopefully the roar of conversation, combined with their distance from the other diners, would make eavesdropping difficult.

Still, Rune and Gideon were supposed to be newlyweds on their honeymoon. They should look disgustingly infatuated with each other. Instead, they looked more like rivals in a verbal shoot-out.

Gideon must have had the same thought, because he reached across the table and laced her gloved fingers through his.

Startled, Rune stared at their hands.

It's fake, she reminded herself. *He's playing the role of doting husband.*

Pulling her hand closer, Gideon turned it over so her palm faced him. Slowly, delicately, he traced her gloved hand, feigning affection, trailing his fingertips over her palm.

She remembered the way his hands had adored her that night in his bed. Before he knew what she was.

She wanted to take off her gloves. To feel his skin against hers again.

No. That's the last thing you want.

She needed to keep her wits about her. She could never, ever trust this boy. No matter what, she mustn't let down her guard.

"How could I possibly have been myself with you?" she whispered, letting the rancor in her voice give her true feelings away as he gently stroked her hand. "You *hunt* people like me. You would have hung me up for the crime of my existence and cheered while my enemies cut open my throat."

His fingers stopped tracing as some dark emotion flooded his eyes. But it was there and gone before she deciphered it.

"So yes: I lied to you. I lied to *everyone.*"

"Not Alex," he said, as he touched the place where a ring still rested on her finger, hidden beneath the glove.

"No," she whispered, withdrawing her hand and curling it in her lap. "Not Alex. Your brother didn't hate what I was."

"And for that, he's dead."

The words made Rune's eyes burn.

"You know what? Let's not do this." She looked out over the

dimly lit room crammed full of diners. "We have to tolerate each other for a few more days. But once we both get what we want, we never have to speak again. So let's just . . . stick to the plan."

"Fine by me," said Gideon, crossing his arms over his chest again and leaning back in the booth.

"Speaking of plans." Rune took another swallow of wine, getting down to business. "What is yours, exactly? How are we going to get past the hunting hounds once we make port?"

He avoided her gaze as he spun the water glass between his thumb and forefinger.

"Sometimes the dogs make mistakes," he said.

Rune squinted at him. "What do you mean?"

"They can smell magic on someone who's unknowingly come into contact with a witch or a spell, but who isn't a witch themself." He ran his hand over his jaw, as if still thinking it through. "Once they board, the dogs will smell your magic—there's nothing you can do about that. But before the Guard can arrest you, they'll have to take you aside for questioning and check you for scars. Since you're an exceptional liar, and you don't have any scars, they'll assume it was a mistake."

Rune winced. "Actually . . ."

He glanced up at her as he took another sip of water. "Actually what?"

A storm of emotions swept through her. Shame, anger, fear.

"I do have scars."

He slowly set down his glass. "You're joking."

Rune lifted her chin in defiance. *Does that repulse you?* she wanted to ask. When she'd had none, at least he could pretend she wasn't the thing he hated most.

"Where are they?"

"I'm not showing you."

"You might have to."

"You're a captain. Surely you can make them—"

"A *disgraced* captain."

"You outrank every Blood Guard officer waiting in every New Republic port."

"Outrank them, perhaps. But I can't refuse to let them search you."

"No?" She leaned in, holding his gaze, keeping her voice low. "If I were truly your wife, you would let their filthy hands strip me naked while their gazes wolfed me down?"

The look that crossed his face was primal. *Raw.* Like she'd let a prowling animal escape inside him.

"Of course not," he said, wrangling it. "I'd never let them strip a girl I loved and search her body for scars—but we're not talking about that. We're talking about *you*." His eyes had gone cold as the sea. "You're not a girl. You're a witch."

The words stung worse than a slap. Rune looked away to hide the hurt.

"I have a better idea," he continued. "Once we arrive on the island, I'll arrest you, put you in manacles, and tell the Blood Guard officers waiting in port that I have orders to bring you to the Good Commander alive."

"And then you'll refuse to unlock the manacles and *actually* hand me over." Rune sipped her wine, avoiding his gaze. "No, thank you."

Her attention suddenly collided with the police officer from Caelis. The one who'd shamelessly ogled her in their cabin. He was taking his seat at a table portside, staring at Rune while he lowered himself into a chair.

Goose bumps erupted over her skin.

Why is he still on the ship?

Before she panicked, Gideon pressed his knees against hers beneath the table. She glanced up to find him glowering at the officer. Gideon didn't seem surprised to see him, almost as if he knew the man had remained onboard after they disembarked.

"Speaking of trusting each other . . ." Gideon reached for a loose strand of Rune's hair. Twirling it around his finger, he tucked it securely behind her ear. It was so gentle, so sweet, Rune almost forgot how dangerous he was. Almost forgot they were being watched.

She had the strangest urge to lean her cheek into his palm.

Blaming it on the wine, Rune dragged her eyes back to his.

"If I'm going to defy my orders," he said, "and smuggle a condemned criminal into the Republic, I need to be sure you're not helping Cressida from the inside. Tell me what your plans are."

Rune shook her head. "That wasn't our deal."

"Neither was this," he said, placing his hand on her knee beneath the table. "I didn't sign up to be your pretend husband."

"No," she said bitterly. "We both know how much you loathe that prospect."

Again, something dark flooded Gideon's face. As if taking her words as a challenge, he reached his other hand beneath the table and hooked them both under her knees, pulling her toward him, stopping only when she was nestled securely between his legs. Rune gripped the edge of her seat to stop from being pulled under completely.

What is he doing?

His hands were so big, he could almost close one around each leg. A reminder of how easily he could overcome her.

"How about a trade?" he said. "I'll get you past the witch-hunting hounds *if* you tell me your plans."

"You already promised to get me past the hounds."

"That was before your little newlywed trick. I'm rethinking my offer."

Before Rune could rail against the injustice, he cupped her

legs above the knees. The warmth of his palms penetrated her dress, seeping into her skin. Rune's grip tightened on her seat as his thumbs stroked her. Tenderly, and a little possessively.

Her heart sped up.

This is fake, she told herself. *He's trying to lower my defenses.*

He made no move to release her, and Rune made no move to force him.

Instead, she studied the stern lines of his face. He was inscrutable, this man. Probably plotting her downfall.

But if he was, what would make him change his mind?

Rune knew his suspicion of her was fair. Gideon had no reason to trust her. Not after she'd deceived him. Not after she'd aided Cressida, both wittingly and unwittingly.

Keeping her plans secret would deepen his suspicions.

Could she tell him just enough to make him trust her?

If he trusted her, he'd have no reason to betray her.

"You told me there's a missing Roseblood heir," she said, a little breathless from his stroking hands. "If that's true, I . . . I'm going to find them. All I want is a chance to warn them of Cressida's plans." *And get them as far away from her as possible.*

He narrowed his eyes.

"According to Cressida, this person is concealed by a powerful spell," he said. "No sibyl can See them."

Interesting.

He hadn't mentioned that.

Gideon's legs still pressed against hers, pinning her like a moth to a board. "It will take months, if not years, to track them down."

"For you, maybe. But I know a spell that will summon them to a specific location."

His stroking stopped. "Which location?"

"You think I'd tell you?" She shot him a haughty glance and took another sip of wine. The familiar fog of intoxication was creeping in, blurring everything beyond their booth and muddying her thoughts. "If I give you the location, you'll have your witch hunters lying in wait to ambush us."

Rune wasn't naive: if Gideon found this missing Roseblood first, he'd kill them. There would be no hesitation. Killing them would put a permanent stop to Cressida's resurrection plans.

"Why should I believe you?" he said. "You could summon this person and hand them over to Cressida."

"I'm trying to *escape* Cressida, not help her."

"I thought you were trying to escape Soren."

Rune flinched. *Right.* Soren was the reason she'd given Gideon for making this truce.

"I'm escaping them both," she said, finishing the second glass of wine. The warmth of it flooded her thighs.

She really needed to eat something.

"How do I know you're not lying?" he said. "To convince me to get you past the hounds?"

Annoyed, Rune reached into the pocket of her dress and pulled out a gold locket. It was identical to the one the officers had brought to their room. Only inside this one was a portrait of Soren.

And something else.

Cupping it in her hands to hide it from prying eyes, she popped the locket open.

Gideon peered down. "What is that?"

Rune picked up the lock of white hair and held it to the light. "Cressida's hair. To summon the missing Roseblood, I needed hair, blood, or nail clippings from someone directly related."

Hair was the easiest to obtain. Rune had used *Ghost Walker* to creep into Cressida's room the night before last and snipped it while she slept.

Dropping the hair back into the locket, she snapped it shut.

Gideon's eyes lifted to her face, and Rune thought she saw admiration there.

Must be a trick of the light.

"Once I have the sibyl," she said, "once I've found and warned this missing heir, you'll never see me again. I'm done with all of this. I'm going to run as far away as I can get."

"You could use the sibyl to find the remaining witches on the island and recruit them to Cressida's war. To attack from within *and* without. It's what I would do."

"But I'm *not* doing that."

They stared each other down. His gaze was a heavy weight, his eyes full of calculations.

He was trying to decide if he believed her.

"At some point," she said, "you're just going to have to trust me."

"Yes," he murmured. "That's the problem. Isn't it?"

Movement nearby made them glance toward the police officer. His partner had joined him, taking a seat at his table. The officer motioned in Rune and Gideon's direction.

"I'm not sure he's convinced by our charade," said Rune.

"No," said Gideon. "I don't think he is."

So far, Gideon was doing all the work in their game of seduction. Perhaps it was time for Rune to join in.

She turned back to find him watching the officers, his brow furrowed and his mouth stern. What would it take to make that mouth smile—even just a little?

Leaning across the table, Rune pressed the pad of her thumb

against his lower lip. Gideon's gaze returned to hers as she dragged her thumb slowly across.

Instead of smiling, Gideon shivered.

It sobered her. Rune remembered the day he learned she was a witch. When he made it perfectly clear how sickened by her he was.

I'm not sure what disgusts me more, he'd said. *What you* are, *or that I fell for your act.*

Gideon was only pretending he couldn't keep his hands off her to throw their watching audience off their scent. Deep down, he couldn't stand the thought of touching her.

It made Rune go cold.

How far could he take this before his disgust overrode everything else?

She met his dark gaze, wanting to know.

Pouring a third glass of wine, she took a long swallow, then slid her gloved hand beneath the table, placing it over one of his. The wine hummed loudly in her blood now, stripping away her inhibitions as she dragged his palm further up her thigh.

Gideon drew in a sharp breath. "Rune . . ."

See? thought Rune. *I can play this game, too.*

He made no move to withdraw. "What are you doing?"

"Performing. Same as you." Her cheeks were warm from the wine. "We're newlyweds, right? Let's make them believe it."

His hand tightened around her thigh. "Is this how you'd behave with a real husband?"

She looked up at him through her lashes. "I suppose that would depend on the husband."

The shadows in his eyes darkened. *With disgust?*

No. Not exactly.

In fact, Rune thought she saw desire there.

An echoing desire howled through her.

"Rune . . ."

She liked how he said her name. Half-desperate. A little crazed.

"Yes, Gideon?"

He leaned in so close, he could kiss her if he wanted to. His lips parted, as if he was about to tell her some secret, when a feminine voice interrupted them.

"Captain Sharpe? Is that you?"

EIGHTEEN

GIDEON

IT TOOK A MOMENT for Gideon to pull himself out of Rune's intoxicating spell and look up.

A familiar young woman stood before their booth. Her auburn curls were pulled back into a tidy bun, and her cheeks dimpled as she smiled down at him. The last time he'd seen her, she'd been wearing a red uniform with a gun at her hip.

Abigail Redfern.

Abbie was a patriot Gideon had met at revolutionary meetings. They'd learned how to load and shoot a gun together. They'd fought alongside each other at the New Dawn. Abbie believed in the New Republic as much as Gideon did.

Maybe more.

After the revolution, they grew closer still. Like two people stumbling out of the darkness together, reaching for each other to make sure they were, in fact, alive. It had been easy with Abbie. *Nice.* Falling into her bed after a long shift, or bringing her back to his. Soothing each other's wounds with kisses. Holding each other to fend off the nightmares.

But it wasn't meant to last. And when Abbie went to work for the Tribunal—a job that came with much higher pay—Gideon fell out of touch with her. He hadn't seen or spoken to her since.

"Abbie? What . . . what are you doing here?"

She'd traded in her Tribunal uniform for the navy outfit worn by the *Arcadia*'s staff, and in her hand were a paper pad and a pen. Which gave him some idea.

He slid out of the booth and stood up.

"I work here," said Abbie, throwing her arms around him and squeezing him in a hug. "In the kitchens, mostly. But sometimes I help wait tables."

Gideon hugged her back. She smelled like cinnamon and bread.

"I can't believe it's you!" Abbie pulled away, then grabbed his shoulders. Unlike with Rune, he didn't have to bend to look into her eyes. "I haven't seen you in . . . what? Over a year?" When her gaze dropped to the rest of him, she stepped back, cocking her head. "You got fancy."

Gideon glanced down at Soren's suit.

"Trust me, I feel like a peacock."

Abbie laughed. "Yeah. Emerald is *not* your color."

"I agree. He looks best in red or black."

Gideon froze at Rune's voice. Abbie turned to face her, then glanced quickly back at him.

He rubbed the nape of his neck. "This is . . ." For some reason, he couldn't get the words out. "Abbie, meet . . ."

"I'm Kestrel," said Rune, smiling brightly up at Abbie.

A little too brightly.

He recalled the three glasses of wine she'd had.

"Kestrel Sharpe."

Gideon winced at the sound of his last name attached to her fake one.

Abbie's smile faltered. "Oh. Oh, you two are . . ." She looked at Gideon, who was staring at a dark knot in the table's grain.

"Married," said Rune. "Just recently, in fact."

Is she slurring her words?

"Oh! Well. Congratulations." Abbie's smile returned, but it was no longer so enthusiastic. She turned to Gideon. "Are you busy at sundown tomorrow? Some friends are playing a few rounds of Poor Man's Trap on Deck C. You should join us. There's . . . a lot to catch up on." She looked to Rune. "Apparently."

Catching up with Abbie, a girl he'd once courted, while playing husband to Rune?

No, thank you.

"I don't think—"

"We'd be delighted," said Rune.

Gideon frowned at his fake wife, who was *definitely* slurring her words.

"Is Poor Man's Trap a card game?" asked Rune. "I've never played it."

Abbie arched an eyebrow at Gideon, then patted his chest. "I'll let you explain it to her."

Someone called her name, and Abbie glanced across the saloon. "I should get back to work." She backed away, her brown eyes on Gideon. "Six o'clock. Deck C. Don't forget." The corner of her mouth curved. "Hope you've been practicing."

And then she was gone.

"She seems nice."

Gideon glared at Rune as he slid into the booth. "What are you doing?"

"*Being friendly*," she said. "I know it's difficult for you." She turned to watch Abbie wade back into the diners. "Who is she?"

"An old friend," he said.

Rune threw him a skeptical look. "Old friends don't give hugs like that."

Gideon frowned. "What are you talking about?"

With her elbows on the table, Rune dropped her cheeks into her hands. "She barely kept her hands off you."

He shook his head. "You're drunk."

Gideon glanced at Abbie's retreating form.

Why is she working on the Arcadia?

The money couldn't be *that* good.

Gideon recalled the conversation he'd overheard above deck, and the pieces clicked into place.

Is she the spy?

He glanced from Abbie, who stood at the bar giving the bartender an order, to Rune, who was in the middle of pouring her fourth glass of wine.

"Whoa," he said, stopping the bottle and grabbing the glass.

He'd watched her gulp down three glasses already. And Rune was *tiny*. They were walking a very fine line as it was. Gideon couldn't let her drunkenly say or do something that would give them away.

"Hey!" She reached for the glass. "That's mine."

Gideon held it and the bottle out of reach. "I think you've had enough."

She wrinkled her nose at him.

He'd only seen Rune tipsy once before—when she first tried, and failed, to seduce him in her bedroom. But this second time only proved what he'd thought then: Rune was horribly cute under the influence of alcohol.

"You don't want to do something you'll regret," he told her.

She narrowed her eyes. "Like *what*?"

Like give our entire pretense away, he wanted to say.

"We're sharing a bed, remember?"

A blush swept up her throat. "If you think I'd try to take advantage of you—"

Gideon barked a laugh.

Oh, Rune. If you had any idea . . .

Her face got redder. "What's so funny?"

"You. Taking advantage of me."

She crossed her arms over her chest. "Because I'm so repulsive, you wouldn't even be tempted?"

Gideon laughed harder. "You *are* drunk. Come on, sugarplum. We're leaving."

Reaching for her gloved wrist, he slid from the booth and pulled her after him.

"But I haven't ordered dinner . . ."

"I'll have them deliver it to our cabin."

Threading her fingers through his, he glanced over at the police officers seated near the windows, only to find their seats empty. Gideon scanned the dining saloon, but they were nowhere in sight. Hoping he and Rune had thrown them off with that display of wanton lust, Gideon led her away, glancing back only once to find Abbie watching them.

He waved to her, remembering what Rune had gotten them into. The last thing he wanted was to fully commit to this charade under the watchful eyes of Abbie. *Especially* if she was a spy. But it would seem suspicious to back out now.

Once they were inside their cabin, Gideon locked the door behind them. Rune sat down on the bed. The moon was full and shining through the window, casting a glow over her.

"Everything is spinning," she whispered.

"You need to drink some water." He crouched in front of her and pulled off her shoes. "Food will also help."

Rune lay back on the comforter. "Too bad you whisked us away from the food."

"Yes. Too bad we didn't stay longer so you could out us to everyone on board."

"Gideon?" She propped herself up onto her elbows and scrunched her eyebrows together. "What are you doing?"

Gideon, who'd pushed up her dress and was pulling down her stockings, stopped in his tracks.

What *was* he doing?

Helping her undress. Like he would if she were his actual inebriated wife. So he could put her to bed.

He shot to his feet and stepped back.

Snap out of it.

This was *Rune*. The Crimson Moth. The witch who was plotting to betray him as certainly as he was plotting to betray her.

He reached for the door. "I'll get you some water."

"And food!" said Rune, flopping back down. "I'm starving."

FIFTEEN MINUTES LATER, GIDEON had a pitcher of water and an empty glass. Their food was being prepared and would be delivered within the hour.

"Bad news," he said, stepping into their cabin. "Dinner won't be . . ."

The sound of soft snoring made him fall quiet.

Rune was asleep on top of the covers, bathed in white moonlight. Her illusion had worn off, giving him a perfect view of her rust-gold hair spilling across the pillow. Her dress lay in a heap on the floor, and covering everything but her legs was his shirt, which she was wearing.

The sight made his chest squeeze.

Didn't she have a proper nightgown?

Rune's mouth lay partly open, and her breath stirred a strand of hair stuck to her cheek. She seemed like just a girl, lying there. Innocent. Vulnerable.

His gaze slid down her pale legs, snagging on the silvery scars etched into her calf. Drawn like a magnet, he set down the water he'd brought and sat on the small bed's edge. The scars formed a pattern of moths in flight. The delicate things started at the base of her ankle and fluttered up her calf, stopping below the back of her knee.

He wanted to hate them.

But he didn't.

Instead, he had the strangest urge to take her leg in his hands and trace the silver lines. Memorize them with his fingers.

Or his mouth.

Gideon shut his eyes. *What is wrong with me?*

This girl had betrayed him in the worst way. And she'd betray him again—he'd be a fool to think she wouldn't.

And she's still wearing Alex's ring.

Guilt stabbed at him.

He hated himself for the thoughts in his head, for flirting with her at dinner, for *touching* her like he had. As if she belonged to him. He vividly recalled Rune pulling his hand up her leg, and the molten desire that had flooded him. This was the girl his brother had loved. The girl who'd be married to Alex right now if Gideon hadn't failed to protect him.

It should be Alex sharing her bed. Now Alex was gone, and Gideon, who'd always tried to be a good older brother, had moved right in. Even if it was pretend.

Gideon let out a ragged sigh. Stepping back. Watching her sleep. Forcing himself to remember she wasn't some innocent girl.

She was the Crimson Moth.

A rebel witch.

Gideon remembered their conversation in the saloon.

You told me there's a missing Roseblood heir. If that's true, I'm going to find them. All I want is a chance to warn them of Cressida's plans.

She might be lying to him. She might secretly be planning to aid Cressida from inside the Republic.

But Gideon didn't care about that so much. He cared that she'd thrown a wrench into his plans. Now he needed to decide between arresting Rune once the *Arcadia* made port—or waiting for something better.

It was Rune who'd given him the idea.

If I give you the location, you'll have your witch hunters lying in wait to ambush us.

If Gideon did as he'd promised—smuggling Rune past the Blood Guard and their hounds, handing the sibyl over—there might be a way to eradicate not only Cressida and her army, but this missing Roseblood heir. Because even if Cressida was destroyed, there would still be other witches ready to take up her cause.

Her sisters could still be resurrected by someone else.

Rune didn't need to give him the location. She just needed to unwittingly lead him to it. And once she summoned the missing Roseblood and Gideon eliminated them, he'd resume his plan of taking Rune hostage and using her to barter with Soren.

There was just one problem:

The witch-hunting hounds.

Gideon had no idea how he was going to get her past them.

NINETEEN

RUNE

THEY WERE IN THE boiler room.

Heat steamed the air, curling her hair and making it stick to her sweaty skin. And *he* was there in front of her.

They were arguing. Something about a cravat. She wanted him to wear it, and he was refusing.

The mist swirled around them. He walked her backward, angry. Her shoulders hit the wall, cornered. She shoved him. He grabbed her wrists. They glared at each other. His eyes dropped to her mouth. Hers followed suit.

They were arguing again—only not with words. His mouth was on hers, hot and insistent; hers was hungry, insatiable, devouring.

I don't want to hunt you anymore, he growled in her ear.

What do you want to do to me?

Her hands tugged his hair.

His fingers unbuttoned her shirt.

This. He pinned her to the wall and murmured her name into her skin. *Rune, Rune . . .*

"Wake up."

Rune's head pounded. Her mouth was dry. And the room was rocking.

"Rune, *wake up.*"

She opened her eyes, squinting in the darkness.

"Are you all right?"

She looked up into Gideon's face. Real Gideon, not dream

Gideon. He was leaning over her, shirtless. His skin gleamed with sweat. Behind him was the cabin's oak-paneled ceiling.

"You kept thrashing. I didn't know what else to do."

Rune sat up and looked down at herself. The sheets were twisted around her legs, and his white cotton shirt stuck to her sweaty skin. Even her hair was damp and sticky.

She glanced back to Gideon, sitting in a pool of moonlight. A hint of stubble shadowed his jaw, and sleep had mussed his dark hair.

Ancients help me.

She'd been having a sex dream about Gideon Sharpe. *While lying right next to him.*

Mortified, she scooted away, pressing her back up against the wall and pulling her knees to her chest. She tugged the hem of his shirt down to her toes to hide herself from view.

The only sleepwear she'd packed was lingerie. Lingerie chosen for a romantic getaway with Soren. There was no way in hell she was going to wear it while lying next to Gideon.

Hence his shirt. On her body.

"Why is it so hot in here?"

"I tried to open the window, but it's sealed shut."

She thought of her dream. Of the heat and the sweat and the . . .

"Did I . . . say anything?" Her voice sounded strained in her ears. "Or . . . do anything?"

She winced at the thought.

Please tell me I didn't embarrass myself!

For the merest beat of a heart, Gideon hesitated. Then shook his head. He pushed himself to the bed's edge, where she heard him pour something.

"Here." He handed her a glass of water. "For your headache."

Rune took it.

"I'm going back to sleep."

She watched him move back to his side and lie down, facing away from her. The mattress was so small, if he sprawled on his back, he'd take up the whole bed.

Rune sipped at the water, head throbbing, not trusting herself to lie down. Or close her eyes.

When he'd fallen back to sleep, she got dressed and slipped from the room.

No more wine, she told herself. *You're officially done with alcohol. Forever.*

TWENTY

RUNE

*R*UNE SNUCK INTO THE first-class library, where the armchairs were plusher and more comfortable. She curled up in one and slept there until late morning, when the librarian arrived.

Afterward, Rune avoided their cabin, hoping that in doing so, she'd avoid Gideon, too. Instead, she explored the ship. Since the *Arcadia* was friendly to witches and Rune needed a seaworthy vessel to smuggle the sibyl, herself, and potentially the Roseblood heir out of the New Republic, she wanted to know if the *Arcadia* could be used for such a purpose.

They couldn't board as passengers; they'd never get past the witch hunters and the hounds in port. But a ship as big as this one was bound to have multiple cargo holds, and if Rune managed to find one, or at least find out how and when they were loaded, it might be a way off the island.

She tried several times to get down to the ship's lower levels. But dressed as she was, she couldn't pass for staff, and every time she got beyond a door, a staff member would spot her and lead her back out again, thinking she was lost.

Rune considered using spells to unlock the doors, but that meant leaving a trail of bloody spellmarks and crimson moth signatures in her wake. Which would lead those two police officers straight to her.

By evening, she was no closer to her objective than she'd been that morning.

She needed someone to get her past the doors. Someone who belonged on the other side, and would therefore help her blend in.

"I PROPOSE A NO-DRINKING policy this evening," said Gideon as they made their way to Deck C to meet Abbie and her friends. He wore Soren's most casual suit and had left the jacket buttons undone.

"I'm never touching a drink again," muttered Rune, shivering in the brisk air.

I should have brought a shawl.

Tomorrow, they would dock in the New Republic's largest harbor. Which meant Rune had only tonight left to find a way down to the cargo holds. Her best chance was to endear herself to Abbie's friends, who she assumed worked aboard the *Arcadia*, and convince them to give her a tour of the lowest decks.

The moment they emerged into the open air, Rune heard the crack of a gun firing. Startled, she was reaching for Gideon's arm, unsure what they were walking into, when the sound of shattering porcelain, followed by laughter, stopped her.

Huh?

As they turned the deck's corner, she found the source of the shooting—and the laughter.

"Sharpe!" a young man in a red cap with his sleeves rolled to his elbows yelled across the deck. "I confess: I didn't believe Abbie when she said you were aboard. Come to show her up?"

Beside the young man stood Abbie, her curls freed from their bun. She held a rifle aloft while another young woman across the deck threw a bone-white plate into the air.

BANG!

The plate shattered, its pieces dropping into the ocean.

"She's kicking everyone's ass."

"As usual," said Abbie, lowering the rifle and grinning at Gideon. "You're welcome to try beating my record."

Rune suddenly realized what Poor Man's Trap was.

"We're . . . trapshooting?" asked Rune, shivering again as a gust of icy wind hit.

Gideon didn't hear her. "I doubt I'll have to try very hard," he called to Abbie as he tugged off his jacket, dropping it over Rune's shoulders. The warmth of him settled into her skin, and Rune couldn't help snuggling into the fabric, thankful.

The eyes of Abbie's friends followed Gideon's jacket, landing on Rune.

"Whoa. Who's the aristo?"

"His wife," said Abbie, who'd stopped grinning as she handed the rifle to Gideon.

Someone whistled in appreciation.

It was then that Rune realized she was in unfamiliar territory. Give her a ballroom, an evening gown, and a four-piece band playing a waltz, and Rune knew exactly who she was and how she was supposed to behave. But here, on the lower deck of a ship, with people who broke china for fun and whistled at girls they found pretty . . . Rune was at a loss.

"Clearly it pays to be the hero of a revolution."

"Enough," growled Gideon, cocking the gun.

The catcalls quieted.

Rune came as close to the group as she dared, remaining a few steps away as Gideon took three shots in a row, shattering all three plates. In the distance, the sun hung low in a red sky.

"Isn't this a little . . . wasteful?" she said.

Abbie threw her a look that said Rune was the silliest thing she'd ever encountered.

"We only use the broken china," said a voice at her ear. "When the sea gets fierce, and the ship rocks enough to send the furniture tipping, it's hard to keep the dishware secure. A lot of it ends up chipped from sliding around or broken from crashing on the floor."

Rune looked up to find the young man who'd kindly brought her wine before being scared away by Gideon. He wore the navy *Arcadia* staff uniform now, and the sea breeze blew his golden hair back from his face as he studied her with an amused smile.

"I'm William, by the way."

"Kestrel," she said, holding out her hand to him. "Sorry about Gideon's behavior last night."

He took her gloved fingers in his. "No offense taken. I get grouchy when I'm seasick, too."

Right.

"So," said the boy in the red cap, who'd first called out to them. Like Gideon, he was built like a soldier. "How did a classy girl like you sully herself with a man like Gideon?"

Sully herself.

The phrasing brought to mind Rune's illicit dream from last night. She could almost feel the heat of the boilers and Gideon's hands on her skin.

Gideon lifted the rifle and fired another shot, bringing her back to reality.

Five for five.

"Love doesn't sully you," she said. "Love purifies you."

Real love, anyway.

Gideon paused as if to glance her way, but reloaded instead.

"That so?" The young man grinned. As if he was *very* amused.

"*Singh*," Gideon growled, already aiming again. "Lay off her."

"You seem to know my husband," she said, watching Gideon. "Did you fight alongside him at the New Dawn?"

The boy Gideon referred to as Singh took off his cap. "Yes, ma'am. Abbie and I both did."

This was new information. Rune tried to absorb it while studying Abbie, who looked fierce in the wind, her reddish-brown curls blowing across her face, her shirt partially unbuttoned with the sleeves half-rolled as she watched Gideon fire.

"How did you end up on the *Arcadia*?" asked Rune. "I thought they didn't let witch hunters aboard."

"Oh, we're no witch hunters," he said. "In my opinion, the revolution went too far. Something needed to change—don't get me wrong. No one should cower beneath their government's boots. But the Republic has become what it meant to correct: a nation ruled by fear. It's the Reign of Witches without the witches." He glanced at Gideon. "No offense, Sharpe."

Gideon said nothing. Just took another shot, shattering a plate into the wind.

Rune liked this boy.

"No politics," said Abbie. "You know the rules."

He shrugged, but shot Rune an easy smile. "I'm Ash, by the way. Ash Singh."

"Kestrel," she said. "Kestrel Sharpe."

Gideon missed his next shot. He handed the rifle to Abbie. "Nine in a row. What's your record?"

"Eleven." Reloading the gun, Abbie turned to Rune. "Wanna give it a go?"

"*That*"—Gideon intercepted the gun—"is a terrible idea. Unless you want to get shot. Kestrel shoots like a . . ."

Rune arched a brow. "Like a what?"

Gideon shut his mouth.

Smart boy.

Rune shrugged off his jacket, grabbed the rifle—which was a

lot heavier than she'd expected—and hoisted it. She'd watched him shoot several times now. How difficult could it be?

"I'm ready!" she called to the girl throwing dishware.

A white dessert plate shot up into the air. Rune closed one eye, aimed the gun at it, then pulled the trigger.

The shot went wide. The girl throwing plates ducked, covering her head, as the plate dropped into the sea.

"Good effort," said Abbie, patting her shoulder.

Was that derision in her voice?

Instead of giving the gun back to Gideon, Rune kept trying.

Abbie's friends all gave her advice. Ash and William cheered her on. She was starting to relax when, after her sixth miss, she noticed neither Gideon nor Abbie was nearby.

Lowering the gun, she spotted them several yards away, at the railing. Abbie leaned her hip against it, staring up at Gideon, while Gideon bent toward her, fully absorbed by whatever she was saying. Abbie brightened beneath his attention, the way a sunflower soaks up the sun.

An old friend, Gideon had called her last night.

Rune doubted it.

She took another shot. Again, it went wide. Ash and William were losing their enthusiasm. The others wandered away, in search of more interesting sport. But Rune was determined to hit a plate. Just one plate. As she took aim again, she saw Gideon and Abbie moving further up the deck, out of hearing distance. Into her line of sight.

Abbie teasingly punched his arm. Gideon laughed.

What are they talking about?

They had an easy way about them. No tension or friction or argument simmering beneath the surface.

Was that the kind of girl Gideon wanted?

Is that who he ends up with?

Something twinged in her chest as Abbie slid her hand into the crook of Gideon's elbow, pulling him closer, biting her lip as she stared at him through her eyelashes—all tricks Rune herself had used to seduce men.

Rune pulled the trigger without looking where she was aiming. *BANG!*

Gideon grabbed Abbie, pulling her out of the line of fire and into his chest.

Whoops.

Rune lowered the gun. Gideon glared straight at her.

"Sorry!" she yelled. "I'm so sorry!"

"I warned you," he said loudly to Abbie, leaving her behind as he stalked toward Rune. He was a dark force, like a thunderstorm spreading across the deck.

Rune took a step back.

He grabbed the rifle. No longer having the higher ground, she let him take it.

"I could kill that prince for giving you a weapon without teaching you how to use it."

What?

Instead of storming off and taking the rifle with him, he took Rune's arm. "Come here," he said, positioning her in front of him.

"Wh-what are you doing?" she whispered as his hand dropped to her waist, pulling her against him.

His breath warmed her neck. "Teaching you how to handle a gun."

"You don't have to do that," she said, feeling hot despite the cold air.

"For the safety of everyone on deck, I do." He placed her hand on the barrel. "You want to grip the stock firmly. Like this." He squeezed lightly to demonstrate. "Next, you want to steady the butt against your shoulder." He drew the gun back until it pressed securely against her shoulder, between her arm and collarbone.

"Now, put your finger on the trigger." He guided her hand so the end of her gloved finger—right in the center of her fingertip and the first joint—rested on the trigger.

"Keep your elbows down and in." His lips brushed her ear. "And try to relax."

Relax. Yes, easily done when he was *everywhere*. Forcing her to remember how big and warm and strong he was. How was she supposed to relax when his arm coiled around her waist and the heat of his chest seeped into her back?

Her heart started to pound. She closed her left eye, trying to focus.

"*Don't* close your eyes," he said. "Pay attention to your breathing instead." He pressed his free hand high on her torso, just below her breasts. "Breathe from here. You want to inhale, and only when you exhale do you squeeze the trigger."

Her body was on fire in all the places he was touching her.

"That's . . . a lot of things to remember."

"You don't have to get it right the first time."

"Okay," she said, sucking in a lungful of air.

And then she fired.

The plate fell into the sea, perfectly intact.

His voice softened. "Very good."

"I missed."

"Yes, but your aim improved. Try again."

Rune did. She missed all the shots she took, but not wildly so. They fell into an easy rhythm. Rune shooting. Gideon correcting her form. Reminding her to breathe, or to follow through when pulling the trigger.

When she finally relaxed, his rough cheek brushed hers. "What were you dreaming about last night?" His voice was low, near her ear. "When you called out for me."

Rune's shot went wide.

What?

She'd called out for him?

Humiliation flooded her.

She kept her gaze fixed on the girl with the plate, trying to focus. But feverish images from last night kept flashing through her mind. "It was nothing. Just a dream."

His arm tightened around her, anchoring her to him. "It didn't sound like nothing."

Rune lost control of her breathing. Lowering the rifle a little, she turned her face toward his. Their breath mingled in the space between. "Trust me," she said, her gaze dropping to his mouth, "you don't want to know what it was about."

"Oh?" His eyebrows shot upward. "Now you *have* to tell me."

She shook her head and lifted the rifle anew, mentally running through each piece of advice: Relax. Breathe. Both eyes open. Elbows down and . . .

"*Rune.*"

"You're distracting me."

"Am I?" He dragged her closer against him.

Rune swallowed. "We were arguing. About a cravat."

"You're lying."

Only partially.

"Tell me the truth."

The girl across the deck flung the next plate into the air. Rune fired. This time, the china exploded.

Rune watched the white shards plunge into the sea like falling stars.

"I hit it," she whispered in disbelief, lowering the gun to her side. "Gideon! Did you see? I hit it!"

Pride surged, ballooning her chest. She turned to face him.

"Sharpe!" Abbie interrupted. "We're moving inside where it's warmer. Fancy a game of cards?"

"Always," said Gideon, letting Rune go. Just like that.

He moved to Abbie like metal to a magnet. The cold rushed in, making Rune hug herself. Ash and the others were already filing into the stairwell. As Abbie turned Gideon in the direction of her friends, Gideon smiled at something she said, forgetting Rune.

They looked so natural together.

It was a reminder: Gideon needed Abbie and her friends to believe his fake marriage was real. What better way to do that than to flirt with his fake wife while teaching her how to handle a gun?

"Is he always like that?"

Rune dragged her eyes away from Gideon and Abbie to find the golden-haired William standing beside her, frowning at the pair.

"What do you mean?"

"Attentive to other women, at your expense."

"What? Oh . . . no. It's not like that. He and Abbie are old friends."

William said nothing. Only studied Rune with something like pity.

If William saw what Rune saw when she watched them together, maybe her gut feeling was right. Abbie was infatuated.

Was Gideon?

It doesn't matter. I don't care.

Even if Rune *did* care—hypothetically speaking—there was

no way to compete. Abbie wasn't a witch, but a normal girl. Something Rune could never be.

A heaviness sank inside her. Like a boulder weighing her down.

Above them, the sky was darkening. Rune shivered in the chilly breeze. She glanced at Gideon's jacket, still lying on the deck at her feet.

"I know a good place to warm up." William held out his arm. "If you want to join me."

His eyes sparkled as he smiled at her.

Rune's gaze dropped to the white name tag on his uniform, declaring him part of the *Arcadia*'s crew. Recalling the doors she couldn't get past and the cargo holds she needed to find, Rune said, "I'd love that. Thank you."

She took his arm and they followed the others inside, leaving Gideon's jacket in a crumpled heap behind them.

TWENTY-ONE

GIDEON

"*T*ELL US, SHARPE: HOW'D you convince that poor, sweet girl to marry you?"

They were below deck, in the Crew Alleyway—a long hallway meant for employee use, in the ship's second-lowest level. Around them, stewards, servers, and restaurant staff rushed past.

Poor and *sweet* were not words Gideon would have chosen to describe Rune.

"Actually," he said, thinking of the pistol pointed at his head while Rune dictated her terms in the wedding shop's fitting room. "She convinced me."

"Ha!" laughed Ash. "Good one."

They were so close to the engine here, Gideon felt the vibrations beneath his feet. The sound of its thumping echoed through the Alleyway like a giant heartbeat.

"I swear it's true." *She coerced me.*

Gideon was still thinking about the way Rune fit against his chest: soft and warm and small. He didn't know why he'd asked about her dream, because the way she'd called his name in the dark last night was best forgotten. She'd never said it like that before—half cry, half moan.

What exactly had they been doing in her dream?

He glanced back to where Rune trailed far behind, with William at her side.

Gideon had been reluctant to leave her with that boy—whose

hungry look betrayed him, even if Rune was determined not to see it. But he needed to know if Abbie was Harrow's spy. Even if she wasn't, she might know who was. The only way to find out was to engage her.

He needed to be careful, though. If Abbie was a New Republic spy, and there were witch sympathizers among them—Ash had all but admitted to being one earlier—Gideon didn't want to get her reported.

"You used to despise aristos," said Abbie from beside him. "You used to reject their invitations and avoid their parties."

Gideon still did that. He'd rather get his ribs broken in the boxing ring than make polite conversation in a ballroom.

"She's not your type in other ways, too."

He raised a brow. For someone he hadn't seen in a year, she was being very forward.

"I didn't realize I had a type."

"The Gideon I knew liked to be challenged." Her brown eyes met his, as if daring him to contradict her. "He enjoyed being kept on his toes. The Gideon I knew had stared into the darkness, and carried it with him."

Two crew members rushed by, forcing Abbie out of their way and closer to Gideon.

She lowered her voice so only he would hear her. "He would never be happy with someone who couldn't stare into the darkness, too."

"And Kestrel can't?"

She shot him a look. "She's sweet. But she's not your equal. She's the kind of girl who cares more about a muddy hem than whether she can hit a moving target."

Gideon coughed to disguise a laugh, trying to imagine the Crimson Moth worrying about dirt on her clothes.

"I used to think that, too." He knew better now. There were depths to Rune he might never reach.

He glanced back again to find Rune's eyes on him. Their gazes snagged. What was William telling her?

He didn't like leaving her alone with that guy. He should go retrieve her.

Except this was why he'd come: to suss out Abbie and tell her what he was planning, so if she was Harrow's spy, he could convince her not to report him.

"The last time we spoke, you were working for the Tribunal. What happened? How did you end up"—he glanced around at the Crew Alleyway's cramped quarters—"here?"

A different beat echoed through the hall now, competing with the engine's sound. Something more melodic and wild.

Music.

"I got annoyed with the bureaucracy."

As they drew closer to the sounds of revelry, Abbie led him through a door and into a dark, warm, boisterous room full of people. Some stood at the edges sipping drinks, others played cards at tables, and still others danced in the center. Abbie had to shout to be heard over the music.

"It was Harrow who suggested working on ships. If you get on the right ship, you can wake up in a different port every morning. I started on the *Arcadia*, to get experience. But at the end of this week, my contract will be up, and I can transfer to a bigger ship."

Gideon studied her. Had she intentionally dropped Harrow's name? Or was that coincidence?

"When was the last time you and Harrow spoke?" he asked as their group descended on an empty card table.

"The last time we docked in the capital." Which would have been roughly a week ago.

Are you working for her? he wanted to ask, but he didn't dare in such mixed company. *Are you her spy?*

Abbie took a seat at the table. If he joined her, he wouldn't be able to ask. And he needed to, because if she *was* the spy, he needed to tell her what he was planning before she reported him, or—if she had kill orders—before she hurt Rune.

Gideon looked to the whirling, stomping dancers.

"Abbie?"

She turned back around.

He held out his hand to her. "Dance with me?"

The corner of her mouth turned up as she took his hand.

As he led her into the dancers, Gideon looked to make sure Rune was still in view. She and William weren't at the card table with the rest of Abbie's friends. Gideon scanned the room, but there was no sign of her. Realizing he didn't even know if Rune had followed them in, he stopped walking.

"Is everything all right?" asked Abbie.

"I . . ." He turned in a circle, scanning the walls, the tables, the dancers. "Have you seen my wife?"

"She seemed friendly with William," said Abbie. "I'm sure he's taking care of her."

There was an edge in her voice. Like she meant something else.

Gideon frowned, remembering the way William had tried to insert himself in Rune's booth last night, plying her with wine. She was a beautiful girl, sitting alone. Gideon had been under no illusions about what he wanted, even if Rune had.

But Rune was a master of seduction herself. Surely she could see his game.

Right?

Gideon hesitated.

If he was wrong, if Abbie wasn't working for Harrow, then

the spy was still at large while Rune wandered through the ship, oblivious to the danger.

He let go of Abbie's hand.

"I'm sorry. I need to find her . . ."

Before someone else does.

TWENTY-TWO

RUNE

"*I* TOLD YOU IT WAS warm down here!" William yelled to be heard above the engine's noise. He stepped off the steel catwalk and descended the spiral staircase, leading Rune deeper into the boiler room. The steam from the boilers wafted up to them, moistening Rune's skin as the *SHUNK SHUNK SHUNK* of the engine beat loudly. "Careful not to slip!"

Rune gripped the rail, wanting to put as much distance between herself and Gideon as possible. She and William had left the room where the ship's staff were having an after-work party, and where she had found Gideon taking Abbie's hand and leading her into the dancers.

The sight was like a fist squeezing her heart.

Gideon had called Abbie *an old friend*. So why did it seem like more?

And why did it bother Rune so much?

And why hadn't he asked *her* to dance?

A girl like you wouldn't be caught dead dancing with riffraff, he'd once told her.

How can he know if he never asks me?

Sighing, she turned her attention to William.

"Did you fight alongside them at the New Dawn?" She raised her voice to be heard as they descended. "Ash and Abbie and Gideon, I mean."

He shook his head, helping her down the steps. "I grew up on the Continent. I only met Ash and Abbie here, aboard the

Arcadia. Though, from all the stories they tell, I sometimes feel like I *was* there."

Another question hung from the tip of her tongue, though Rune was afraid to ask it.

She forced it out: "Gideon and Abbie weren't just friends back then, were they."

William paused for a second, halfway down, and glanced up into her face. He shook his head.

Rune nodded, lowering her gaze to the next stair, and continued down.

Why would he lie?

But Gideon had lied from the start: pretending to be in love with her to catch the Crimson Moth.

At the bottom, Rune stepped off the staircase to find herself facing a row of black boilers, their glowing red mouths opening and closing as stokers shoveled coal into them.

"Try to stay out of the way," William said as he pressed his hand to the small of Rune's back, guiding her past the sweaty, coal-stained men keeping the fires aglow.

The alley between the bulkhead and the boilers was piled with coal at the edges, and overhead ran the steel catwalk they'd walked down only moments ago.

How many levels down are we? she wondered, staring up through the maze of ladders and pipework.

Rune was no stranger to ships—she'd inherited her grandmother's shipping business. But Nan's ships were wind powered. Nothing compared to this.

For a moment, she forgot about Gideon and Abbie and the knot in her chest, marveling instead at the activity teeming around her. Here she was, walking through the heart of a massive machine kept afloat by hundreds of thousands of parts, all of which were kept running by people who worked around the clock.

She'd never felt so small and insignificant.

"Incredible, isn't it?" William yelled as they walked.

She gave him a smile, even as she began to worry. Because beneath her silk gloves, Rune's hands had started to sweat.

She needed to be careful. There was a spellmark drawn in blood on her thigh, keeping her disguised. If her skin grew too damp, the mark could smudge and the illusion would evaporate, leaving her exposed.

Rune couldn't stay down here long.

"What else is down here?" she asked.

"There's a cargo hold on this level," said William, ducking out of the way of the fire stokers. "It's on the far side of the boilers."

A cargo hold.

Rune tried to contain her excitement.

It was exactly what she was hoping for. If she could look inside—a long shot, since the ship's holds were likely locked—she could determine if there was room to smuggle a few witches.

"Is it the only one? Or are there others?" Worried that her questions might arouse suspicion, she added: "My grandmother used to own a shipping company. I'm *fascinated* by ships."

He smiled, indulging her. "There are other holds, but they can only be accessed from outside."

At the end of the row of boilers, they turned to enter a small walkway leading to the next stokehold.

A trickle of sweat ran down Rune's spine. She needed to get out of here, and soon.

"When do they load them?" It was one thing she'd need to know: when staff entered and exited the holds.

"A few hours before departure. They seal them after the witch-hunting hounds check the luggage."

Rune frowned. "Seal them as in . . . lock them? With a key?"

"Seal them with hatches," he said. "Which are bolted and caulked."

Well. *That* was unfortunate. Rune could unlock a door with magic, but she couldn't unbolt a hatch without people noticing.

"The hold on this level is only used for coal and ship supplies, though. So it isn't bolted." To Rune's surprise, he took her hand and tucked it into the crook of his elbow. "Should we investigate? Or would you rather return to your husband?"

His thumb grazed her knuckles. Surprised by the intimate gesture, Rune glanced up to find his eyes asking a wordless question.

Trust me. Gideon's voice echoed in her mind. *I'm a man. I know what he wants.*

Was Gideon right? Had William brought her down here to seduce her?

Rune stared at his hand on hers, feeling uneasy.

But if it got her into the cargo hold . . .

I might not get another chance to investigate.

What other choice did she have? If she wanted to smuggle witches aboard the *Arcadia*, she needed to see inside that cargo hold. To do that, she needed to play along.

It wouldn't be hard; this was a game she excelled at.

Rune looked up at him through her eyelashes. "I'm sure my husband doesn't even know I'm gone."

The corner of William's mouth lifted. "Then let's—"

Behind them, a voice roared like thunder. Louder than the engine's noise.

"What the *hell* do you think you're doing with my wife?"

William flinched.

Rune spun to find Gideon materializing from the steam,

storming toward them. His massive frame filled the narrow alley, and his eyes were black with rage.

Gideon lunged for William, grabbing the lapels of his jacket and shoving him up against the bulkhead wall. William winced at the impact.

"Stop!" Rune grabbed Gideon's arm before he did further damage. "He was only—"

"And *you*." Without letting go of William, Gideon threw her a dark look. "What were you thinking? Coming down here alone? With *him*?"

I warned you about this guy was the furious accusation.

But what right did he have to be angry? Rune wasn't his actual wife. He'd made it clear the very idea of being married to her appalled him.

And he'd been flirting with Abbie all evening.

The latter made her hands clench.

"Do you have to be such a brute?" Rune took William's arm and pulled him from Gideon's grasp. "What's wrong with you? He's just giving me a tour."

"It's true," said William, innocently lifting his hands. "I'll bring her right back when we're done. I promise."

"You're not bringing her anywhere." Gideon's hands were fists at his sides, mirroring Rune's. "She's coming back with me."

Rune crossed her arms. "I'm not going anywhere with a man who behaves as abhorrently as you do."

"As your *husband*, I insist." He prowled toward her, reaching for her.

"Insist all you like," said Rune, twirling out of his grip. "I'm refusing."

He was standing over her now. Head bent. Inches away. His

gaze bored into hers as they seethed at each other. "Listen, you demon: I will carry you out of here if I have to, and you know it."

"That's precisely my point!"

William cleared his throat. "I really don't think this is—"

Gideon tore his gaze from Rune to glare at the man beside them. "Get the fuck out of here. Before I throw you into something worse than a wall."

Rune rolled her eyes.

But she looked to William. "Go. I'll be up in a minute."

Gideon watched him leave. Only when William disappeared into the steam did he turn his rage back on Rune.

The heat of it burned her.

"Are you out of your magic-addled mind? What are you doing down here?" He glanced around them, taking in their surroundings as if for the first time. "I told you not to trust that . . ."

His eyes narrowed as some realization dawned on him.

"Merciful Ancients. This is part of your plan, isn't it? You're going to use the *Arcadia* to smuggle your witches out of the Republic. *That's* why you're down here."

Rune's heart fell. Was she so transparent?

To him? Apparently yes.

"You're unbelievable." Gideon stepped back, running a hand roughly through his hair. "Here I was, thinking he was trying to take advantage of you. But it's the other way around, isn't it? *You* lured him here to use for your own purposes."

Okay, *that* was too far.

Rune hugged herself, trying to shield herself from his anger. "Yes, Gideon. That's me: *a grand seductress.*"

She'd had quite enough of this conversation. Moving to go around him, Rune started to follow William back to the party.

He stepped in front of her, blocking her way through the narrow alley. "You say that as if it isn't true."

A wave of anger swept through her. She wanted to shove him, but any amount of force she used wouldn't budge him. It would only make her look pathetic.

"Let me pass!"

This time when he reached for her, Rune wasn't fast enough to evade. He pulled her in close, his grip firm on her wrist. "I was *worried* about you. Afraid you were falling prey to some cad, when I should have known better." His gaze flickered over her face. "The Crimson Moth only ever pretends to be prey. In truth, she's the predator."

The words stung. But of course this was how he viewed her. Rune wasn't someone doing whatever she needed to do to survive people like him. To Gideon, Rune was a cruel witch. A dangerous temptress. A master manipulator.

Just like Cressida.

His voice was low. Rough. "You've made a fool of me yet again."

Caught in his grip, Rune gave up trying to pull free and glanced away, no longer able to meet his gaze. It didn't matter that it wasn't true—that it was William who brought her down here. Gideon would see what he wanted to see.

He stepped closer, taking up all the air. Raising her already sweltering temperature.

"Do you have nothing to say for yourself, Rune?"

Why did something so simple—him saying her name—threaten to shatter her into a million pieces? She hated his effect on her. She wished she could reverse it. Wished he felt half as agonized as she did.

"Did I wound your pride, Captain Sharpe?" she said, hoping to sting him the way he had stung her. "It wasn't personal. As you said: I use everyone."

She tried to tug her wrist free. But his grip held her fast.

"Sometimes I think I could forgive you for that—using me, to save your precious witches. I could understand it. But the thing I can't forgive, the thing I will never understand, is how you could make me fall for you when all along you were in love with my brother."

Rune glanced up into his eyes. His gaze was intense. A tempest of feeling. It wasn't the first time he'd accused her of such a thing. This time, trapped as she was with him, Rune couldn't let it go unchallenged.

"It wasn't like that."

"You're still wearing his ring!"

The anger radiated off him. It surprised Rune, who felt him holding the worst of it back. And deeper than the anger: hurt. *Real* hurt.

Rune frowned, confused by it. You couldn't hurt someone who didn't care about you . . . right? And Gideon didn't care about Rune—not the real Rune. Not the witch.

His free hand lifted, as if to touch her, then clenched instead, returning to his side. "I hate your damned lies."

Her lies? What about *his* lies?

"You want the truth?" Her own hurt bubbled up, like steam from a volcano ready to erupt. "*This* is the truth: I would have married you in a heartbeat, had you asked me. I would have married you *knowing* you would hand me over to my killers—or kill me yourself—the moment you found out what I was. That's how pathetic I am, Gideon! That's how desperately I wanted to be yours!"

His brow creased as his eyes searched her face. "Then why say yes to my brother?"

"Because he loved me! Because he didn't want me dead! It was the best offer I was ever going to get!"

This time, when she tried to yank herself free, Gideon let go.

She stumbled back several steps, glancing down at her gloved hand. The one bearing Alex's ring.

She'd been afraid to take it off. As if removing it would dishonor him.

I wish it was yours, she wanted to say to Gideon. *I wish you'd given it to me.*

But saying so would be a profound betrayal of Alex.

"I loved your brother," she said instead. "But only as a friend. A dear friend. Maybe it could have become more, eventually. And maybe that wasn't fair to him. But . . ."

She felt guilty for thinking it, but sometimes she wondered if Alex had been in love with a version of Rune that didn't exist.

I know the Crimson Moth. And she is no caged thing.

That's what Alex had gotten wrong: he wanted to give Rune a quiet, comfortable life. And for a moment, Rune had thought she wanted that. But deep down, she knew the peaceful future she might have had with Alex would never have satisfied. Not completely.

There was a part of Rune's soul—most of it, maybe—that yearned for adventure. That craved a challenge. That liked a little danger.

For better or worse, Rune needed these things to feel alive. In wanting her to live a safe, easy life, Alex was—without realizing it—wanting Rune to be *less herself.*

She tugged off her glove. Sliding the ring from her finger, she walked toward Gideon, grabbed his hand, and pressed the silver band into his palm. The moment his fingers closed around it, relief flooded her. Like a burden lifted.

"I was just a girl to Alex." She stepped away, pulling her glove back on. "Someone to be loved and cherished and fought for. That's why I said yes to him."

The nerve in Gideon's jaw ticked.

"I'm not a girl to you, am I? I'm a witch, and always will be. Something to be hated and hunted down. Not cherished or protected. Not *loved*."

Rune waited for him to deny it. To contradict her.

But he only stood there, silent and stoic. Confirming what she already knew.

I am such a fool.

Stepping around him, Rune ran for the stairs.

TWENTY-THREE

GIDEON

*R*UNE WAS RIGHT ABOUT one thing: she wasn't just a girl. Not to him.

She was so much more than that.

Rune was a sparring partner. Someone to fight with, and admire. Someone to *match*.

Rune was a force. One Gideon could barely keep up with.

He wanted to go after her and tell her as much. The problem was . . . well. There were a lot of problems.

Gideon lifted his fist, opening it to reveal the ring lying on his palm. His mother's wedding band.

I would have married you in a heartbeat, had you asked me.

Ancients help him.

He wanted it to be true, but it didn't make sense. Even if he weren't a witch hunter, even if they weren't sworn enemies, Gideon had nothing to offer Rune. He was a soldier; she was an heiress. She was *nobility*.

And she's deceived me in the past.

Rune could easily be deceiving him now. The last time he'd believed her, her lies had burned him badly.

And if she isn't lying?

He ran a hand across his forehead.

Did it change anything?

Did it change *everything*?

In the heat of the boilers, Gideon loosened his collar and

rolled back his sleeves, trying to think. Going through all the reasons he had to mistrust her. Hate her, even.

She deceived me by hiding her identity as the Crimson Moth.

But Gideon could hardly fault her for it. He would have done the same, if their positions were reversed.

And Gideon had deceived her right back.

She betrothed herself to Alex.

Because Alex didn't hate what she was. Because being with Gideon would have been a death sentence. He had made that clear the moment he handed her over to be purged.

She helped Cressida rise.

Except, according to Rune, she hadn't known her friend Verity was really the witch queen in disguise. Was she lying? Possibly. But Gideon knew Cressida all too well—and she was certainly more than capable of this.

The evidence he'd held against her was toppling like a house of cards.

So, what was left?

Even if Rune loathes Cressida, she has reasons for supporting her.

Cressida would restore a world where witches like Rune would no longer be hunted. She had every reason to want a new Reign of Witches. She could be secretly working for Cressida and lying to Gideon through her teeth.

What if Rune and Cress had struck a deal? What if, once Cressida had her throne, her resurrected sisters, and the island under her control, she disposed of Soren, eliminating Rune's need to marry him? This whole thing might be an elaborate ruse.

I would have married you in a heartbeat, had you asked me. That's how desperately I wanted to be yours.

He thought of Rune in the steam, eyes bright, face flushed, hair coming undone. He'd wanted nothing more than to take her in his arms and kiss her. To tell her with his mouth and hands what he couldn't say with his words.

Gideon gritted his teeth. Pressed his fists against the wall.

No.

Loving Rune was what had allowed her to dupe him the first time. If he didn't eradicate this naive desire to believe her—to believe she loved him, to believe he could ever be worthy of her—he would never stop Cressida from bringing evil back to power in the New Republic.

He and Rune were enemies at war. Rune was the key to destroying Cressida, and Cressida had to be destroyed. He needed her as a hostage, to bargain with. He needed to stick to his plan. Nothing more.

He couldn't let Rune weaken him again.

Even if he wanted her to.

ANNOYANCE PRICKLED GIDEON AS he neared the party. The fiddlers' joyful, driving beat and the rowdy, grinning dancers were at odds with his dark mood. They made his teeth clench. For a second, Gideon contemplated returning to their cabin instead of rejoining the revelry.

But there was still a spy running loose. And he needed to find them before they found him—or, worse, Rune.

So he stepped into the room.

Gideon saw her immediately. Like a compass that would always find north. The moment his eyes landed on Rune, she glanced up from the center of the crowd, where she danced with a young man in suspenders.

In a flash, Gideon remembered her drunk and weeping in the powder room, a hollow look haunting her gray eyes. She was neither drunk nor weeping now, yet the look in her eyes was the same.

Gideon was caught in the snare of her gaze. Rune's eyes always reminded him of a storm. Like thunder and lightning, mingled together.

Except . . .

Wait.

A moment ago, her eyes had been blue, her hair the color of wheat.

Now her eyes were gray, and her hair was returning to its natural strawberry blonde.

Her spell was wearing off. And she had no idea.

Gideon recalled the police officers knocking on doors, showing every passenger aboard this ship a locket with Rune's likeness.

Anyone in this room could recognize her.

Gideon surged toward her, cutting through the dancers, getting jostled and bumped and sworn at.

"Excuse me," he said when he arrived, cutting in. "I need to borrow my girl."

The young man started to protest, took one look at Gideon, and stepped away with a gesture that said, *All yours.*

"What are you doing?" said Rune.

Gideon ran his fingers through her hair.

"Your illusion . . ."

Rune glanced at his hand, where the rose-gold strands sifted across his palm. Her face paled.

He slid his fingers through her gloved ones. They needed to get her out of here before someone noticed.

Unless someone already has . . .

Gideon glanced around the room, spotting Ash and William and the rest of Abbie's friends engrossed in a game around a card table. Abbie wasn't with them.

Where is she?

He kept scanning, tugging Rune toward the exit. But when his attention fixed on the door, his steps halted.

Rune froze behind him.

The same officers who'd interrogated every passenger on the ship, asking if they recognized Rune's face, were currently stepping into the room.

Shit.

Gideon turned to Rune, cutting her off from their view.

"I can't recast it with so many people around." Rune's grip tightened on his hand as she pulled him back into the chaos of whirling dancers.

He nodded, his thoughts buzzing, trying to come up with a plan. He scanned the room again, searching for a different exit and finding none.

"They've split up," said Rune, staring over his shoulder.

Not good.

Gideon couldn't keep himself positioned between them both and Rune. His gaze snagged on a dark corner across the room. If he could get her to it, she could recast the spell there.

The song ended.

Breathless and laughing, the dancers stopped dancing and their swirling skirts came to a standstill. They began to scatter and disperse, leaving Rune and Gideon exposed.

They had seconds before she was seen and recognized by the officers. Once that happened, Gideon would be arrested. The ship would turn around. He'd be delivered straight to a Caelisian prison—or, more likely, to Cressida.

More importantly, Rune would be exposed to the spy sent to kill her. A spy she didn't even know was hunting her.

Somehow, Gideon needed to make everyone in this room believe they weren't seeing Rune Winters, the kidnapped witch from Caelis, and her captor—a witch hunter who wanted her dead. He needed to make them see nothing but a couple of newlyweds.

Rune's head turned, her gaze flickering between the officers. "Gideon . . ."

Fuck it.

Taking Rune's face in his hands, drawing her gaze to his, Gideon did what he'd wanted to do for days now. Ever since he found her crying in that powder room.

He slid his hands into her hair and kissed her.

Rune tensed, like a deer in a hunter's crosshairs.

Don't fight me, baby.

He ran his thumb along her jaw to soothe her. He needed her to help him make this look real. At least until the next song started and they could escape to the shadows.

Either his stroking worked, or Rune figured it out, because she relaxed. Then kissed back, her lips parting beneath his.

It was as if the betrayal of the past few months never happened.

Gideon suddenly couldn't understand why they'd stopped doing this.

He missed her hair in his hands. Missed her warm, sweet mouth. Missed the way she melted like butter beneath his touch. His entire being ached for her. Every touch of her lips, every press of her body, sent him closer to a deadly fire. One that had burned him before, and, he suspected, would burn him again.

Hooking her arms around his neck, Rune arched against him. Telling him how very mutual this feeling was. That he wasn't alone in his wanting.

If this was weakness, he wanted to be weak.

If this was sin, let him be damned to hell.

Kissing Rune was like a realignment. There was before, when everything was off its axis. And there was after, when everything was steady and *right*.

When the next song started, Gideon used the crowd as cover to guide her backward, kissing her as he moved through the dancers, toward that dark corner, and pressing her up against the wall.

She was hidden here, in the darkness. He needed to step away and let her recast the spell.

Instead, he tipped her head back and kissed her harder.

Is this real? his mouth asked. *Can I trust you?*

But if Rune's mouth had an answer, he couldn't decipher it.

Their fervent hands slid over each other, as if they'd both completely lost control. The things that he wanted to do with her . . .

He wanted to take her back to their cabin.

Wanted to lay her down in their bed.

Wanted to . . .

PAIN exploded inside him. Hot and sharp and excruciating. Starting in his scar, it ricocheted outward like a detonated bomb.

Gideon gasped for air.

I need to ensure you're mine. Cressida's voice echoed, like a nightmare shattering a dream. *Mine alone.*

TWENTY-FOUR

GIDEON

*T*HE SCENT OF CRESSIDA'S magic burned in the air. Vividly, he remembered her pulling the brand from the fire and searing his flesh with it; remembered her activating the curse hidden inside his skin.

Gideon's eyes flew open.

It wasn't Rune pushed up against the wall beneath his palms; it was Cressida. Cressida's lips swollen from his kisses; Cressida's hair a mess from his hands.

He recoiled, yanking himself away from her. His heart pounded in his throat as he shuddered. He nearly reached for the gun tucked into his belt but stopped himself just in time.

Because the moment he severed contact, the pain receded, and with it, the girl who'd abused him.

He blinked, and it was Rune standing before him again, her illusion entirely gone. Her lips parted in shock. Her gray eyes filled with hurt.

But was it true? For a second, he didn't know. *Could* it be Cressida standing before him? It wouldn't be the first time she'd stolen a girl's identity.

Rune pushed past him, disappearing into the crowd.

No. He ran a shaky hand through his hair, coming to his senses. Cressida and Rune were impossible to confuse. They were as different as poison and its antidote.

Gideon would *know*. Of that, he was certain.

Remembering the spy in their midst, he went after Rune,

but quickly lost her in the fray. When he came out the other side, he scanned the room. The only sign of her was the faintest whiff of magic. It was a scent he recognized now: like a breeze rolling in off the sea.

Rune's magic.

He made for the hall, but it was empty.

His brand throbbed. His whole body trembled from the shock of pain. He rubbed at the aching scar through his shirt, trying to remember Cressida's words.

I left something here, the day I branded you. A spell I intended to activate long before now, but never got the chance.

Gideon recalled the times he'd touched Rune since then. Grabbing her gloved hand. Unlacing her dress. Taking off her shoes.

It was never skin-to-skin contact . . . until tonight.

Tonight, he'd cupped her face. Run his fingers over her jaw. Kissed her mouth.

Suddenly he knew what Cressida's curse did.

And he'd never hated her more.

TWENTY-FIVE

RUNE

RUNE CROUCHED UNDER AN abandoned card table across the room, her heart pounding wildly, her face glowing with heat. A crimson moth signature fluttered in the air next to her head, the only trace of her *Ghost Walker* spell.

She watched Gideon push through dancers and card players, searching for her. She couldn't see the police officers but assumed they were still in the room. So long as no one looked under the tables, she was safe. She only hoped her spell wouldn't fade before the staff put them away at the end of the night.

That kiss . . .

It had started as a way to shore up their facade, but quickly descended into more. Rune had lost control of herself, overcome.

The things he did to her, just by touching her . . .

Briefly, she'd thought it was the same for Gideon. That he craved her the way she craved him. But then something changed. While Rune softened, Gideon stiffened. It was unmistakable. *Undeniable.* Gideon had pulled away in disgust—she'd seen it plain on his face.

Because I'm a witch.

And though he might be attracted to her, the moment he'd remembered what she was, he couldn't override his revulsion. It didn't matter how much he might like kissing her; she repulsed him.

Of all the boys in the world, why did she have to fall in love with the one who could never, ever love her back?

Why couldn't she shoot these feelings dead?

From her hiding spot, she watched Gideon stride into the hall. The moment he was gone, she breathed a little easier.

Until Abbie followed him out.

Rune's eyes tracked the girl. Knowing now the two old friends had been anything but, her chest tightened. From their inability to stay away from each other, she concluded that one or both wanted to be more than friends again.

Rune closed her eyes. She might not be able to kill off these feelings. But she could run from them.

So that's what she did.

Crawling out from beneath the card table, she crept through the boisterous room, unseen. She would head for the boiler rooms and finish what she'd started. This time without Gideon stopping her.

TWENTY-SIX

GIDEON

*R*UNE WASN'T IN THEIR cabin. Gideon could only assume she'd used her invisibility spell to elude him. If she didn't want to be found, he wouldn't find her.

He turned to the mirror on the clapboard wall, its surface cloudy with age. Pulling off his shirt, he stared at the brand on his chest. The scar still flared ember-red and was hot to the touch.

Gideon remembered the tiny sound Rune had made when his fingers stroked down her throat. Every muscle in his body tightened at the thought of that sound. Of her throat. Of *her*.

He could never be with Rune, even if he wanted to be.

Cressida had made sure of it.

He wanted to put his fist through the glass. To take a jagged piece and cut the brand out of his skin. He was about to search the room for Rune's casting knife to do just that when a knock on the door stopped him.

Hoping it might be Rune, he swung it open.

It was Abbie.

Her auburn curls were loose around her shoulders, and her white blouse was half tucked into her pants.

This wasn't great timing. But it had been Abbie he'd initially gone to find after the argument with Rune. Now that she was here, he might as well use the opportunity to ask if she was Harrow's spy.

Abbie stepped into the room, shutting the door behind her, forcing Gideon to back up a step.

"We need to talk," she said.

He nodded, wishing—not for the first time—that the room was far bigger. "Agreed."

"This must be more than a coincidence, right? You and me. On the *Arcadia*. The last week before I transfer out of here, and *you* show up. Isn't that strange?"

This was good. They could finally be clear with each other. But before he could ask her if she was working for Harrow, Abbie continued: "There are things I need to say, Gideon. And if I don't say them now, I'll always regret it."

He frowned. "Huh?"

"I don't care what your reasons were for marrying her—to get out of trouble, to rectify some scandal—I can help you. I'll get you out of it. I've been saving up for years now, and . . . I have means. I can settle whatever debts got you into this mess."

Gideon's frown deepened. *Debts?* "What are you talking about?"

Abbie closed the space between them and took his hand. "You don't have to pretend with me."

He glanced down to find her fingers interlaced with his. "Abbie, what—"

Suddenly, she was pushing up on her toes.

And pressing her lips to his.

Whoa. Okay. This was *not* where Gideon had thought this was going.

He was about to pull away and apologize for whatever he'd done to lead her on—but there was a question burning in the back of his mind.

Would the curse activate?

Is it only Rune who triggers it? Or can anyone?

He cupped Abbie's neck and kissed her back.

The seconds ticked by. Old memories from after the revolt

seeped up. The two of them, together. But the images were hazy. Like a book he'd once read and all but forgotten.

Gideon felt nothing: no flaring scar; no excruciating pain.

It should have brought relief, but it didn't. Because neither did he feel anything else. No unquenchable thirst. No fusing of two souls. Kissing Abbie was nothing like kissing Rune. The former only made him want the latter.

Is this how it's going to be?

Had Rune utterly ruined him?

Enough.

Gideon took hold of Abbie's arms and thrust her back a step. She opened her eyes, looking dazed.

"Are you the spy Harrow planted on this ship?"

Abbie's brows knit. "What?"

"There's a spy on board, searching for a witch named Rune Winters. They're working for Harrow."

"I . . ." She shook her head. "I told you: I ran away from all that."

She seemed too stunned to be lying. But if it wasn't her, who else could it be?

"Do you have any idea who the spy is? You said you spoke with Harrow the last time the *Arcadia* was in port."

"She and I didn't talk about work." Abbie stepped away from him. "Did you not hear anything I just said? About you and me?"

Gideon pulled in a breath. He was being rude.

"Abbie. Whatever you and I once had, it's in the past."

"Then why kiss me back?"

Gideon touched his scar. "I'm sorry. I needed to answer a question."

Her voice trembled. "But . . . why would you marry her, unless you had to?"

It's not a real marriage.

It's what he should have said. But he was thinking of Rune in the boiler room, pouring out her heart to him.

"Why indeed," he murmured.

Stricken, she took another step back before turning and fleeing the room.

Gideon ran both hands over his face. *Merciful Ancients.* How had he gotten himself into this mess?

Oh, right.

Rune.

Rune had gotten him into this mess. Rune, who was still missing. So long as her invisibility spell hid her, she'd be safe. But her earlier illusion had worn off. This one might, too. And if her crimson moth signature was found . . .

He paced the limited floor space in their cramped cabin, the floorboards creaking beneath his weight. If he were a spy closing in on a witch, would he keep his distance, waiting to strike? Or would he get in close, perhaps be friendly, and lower her defenses?

He halted, recalling the young man who'd been circling Rune like a hawk ever since they boarded.

William.

What if Gideon was wrong about him?

It might not have been Rune who lured William down to the boilers. It might have been the other way around. Gideon hadn't asked her; he'd assumed.

What if William was circling her not because he was a cad who wanted her in his bed, but because he was an assassin who wanted her in a grave?

TWENTY-SEVEN

RUNE

R UNE FINISHED HER *PICKLOCK* spell and pulled open the door to the cargo hold. The engine's thumping quieted as she stepped into the darkness within. After fumbling around, she found the chain for the nearest gaslight and tugged.

The room illuminated.

Black coal was piled high along two walls and in the middle of the room. Like small mountains. The other wall was packed with wooden crates—likely containing supplies for the ship.

There was no luggage in this hold. And if there was no luggage, there was no reason for the hunting hounds to check it before departure.

It was exactly what she needed to get a few witches out.

The gaslight flickered as Rune walked around the piles of coal and across the room, trying to estimate how long they'd need to hide themselves here. With the *Arcadia* sympathetic to their cause, it wouldn't matter if they were found after disembarking from the New Republic. It was when the ship was still in Republic waters that they were in danger. If they could conceal themselves until the ship was out at sea, they'd be safe.

The door shut behind Rune, making her jump.

"I had a feeling I'd find you here."

She spun to discover William standing in the hold with her, unbuttoning his jacket. Her heart pounded. Could he see her because *Ghost Walker* had faded? Rune's skin was sticky with sweat from the boiler room's heat. Combined with the steam, the spellmarks for *Ghost Walker* may have already faded.

Or could he see her because he expected her to be here?

"William!" With her pulse racing, Rune managed to smile. "You startled me."

"Did I?" The corner of his mouth curled as he shrugged out of his jacket and set it down on a crate.

Unease churned in her stomach.

"I should get back," she said, starting toward the exit. "Before Gideon comes looking for me."

William blocked her path. "Oh, don't worry about that. Your husband has his hands full. He and Abbie are in your cabin. I'm sure they'll be a while."

Rune halted, her heart sinking like a stone.

He took a slow step toward her. "You deserve someone who sees you, darling. A man who reciprocates your adoration."

Rune took a step back, trying to keep some distance between them. "I think you have the wrong impression."

"Oh?" he said, coming closer.

"I'm . . . in love with my husband."

The backs of Rune's legs hit something hard. She glanced over her shoulder to find a crate behind her, and several more stacked behind it. When she turned to him again, William was directly in front of her.

"That's the sad thing, isn't it?" William lifted his hand. Ran the backs of his fingers across her cheekbone.

Rune stiffened beneath his touch.

"It's obvious to anyone with eyes that you pine for a man who doesn't want you." He tucked a lock of stray hair behind her ear. "Unlike your husband, I knew from the moment I saw you that you were special."

Through the cloth of her dress, Rune checked the knife she kept strapped to her thigh. She would use it if she had to.

But only if she had to.

"I'm flattered," she said. "Truly. But I've had too many men in my life lately. I'm trying to pare back . . ."

She ducked under his arm, whirling to face his back as she moved toward the door. She'd gotten what she came here for. This room was big enough to hide three witches—herself, the sibyl, and the missing heir—though it might be tight.

"Do you like cards?" she asked.

William didn't bother following. Only pivoted to watch her with a look that made her skin prickle. When she'd finally put enough space between them, she turned toward the door, her back to him. "We could go upstairs and play a round of—"

"I was hoping for something more intimate."

The click of a cocked pistol made Rune freeze.

"Turn around, Crimson Moth."

The breath shuddered out of her.

He knows who I am.

Rune stared at the door, contemplating making a run for it. William had left it open a crack.

His clothes rustled as he moved toward her.

"Turn around, *witch*, or I'll shoot."

Rune let out a slow breath and did as he said.

The barrel of his gun was pointed at her head.

This was it, then. Her flirtatious games had finally caught up to her.

Except I never flirted with him.

He'd lavished his attention on her without provocation. Now she knew why.

"Gideon Sharpe doesn't act like a husband because he *isn't* one, is he? Can you explain to me why a Blood Guard captain is smuggling a fugitive witch back into the New Republic?"

Rune's gaze darted to either side, looking for something to defend herself with. There was nothing but coal and oversized crates. And by the time she grabbed her knife from underneath her dress, he'd have put three bullets in her.

This was the end. And Gideon didn't even know where she was.

Nor does he care.

The gaslight flickered again, changing the shadows behind William.

"I'll make you a deal, Rune Winters." William stepped closer. "If you come back with me to my room, I won't shoot you."

The insinuation of what he would do to her in that room was unmistakably clear.

Rune lifted her chin, staring him down. "I'd rather be shot."

"And if I don't give you a choice?"

The shadows moved again. Only this time, it wasn't because of flickering lights.

A few paces beyond William, someone stepped out from behind a tower of crates, silent as a wolf. Gun drawn. Rune's pulse hummed as his furious gaze met hers over William's shoulder.

Gideon.

The sight of him lit a flame inside her.

When had he entered the room?

William took another step toward Rune, oblivious to the man behind him.

Before he came an inch closer, Gideon said, "She said no, *William*. Didn't your parents teach you that when a girl says no, she means it?"

His voice was like a barrel full of gunpowder, ready to be lit.

William went still as a statue.

"You're not her type," Gideon continued. "That's what she's been trying to tell you. You should have taken the loss and left her alone."

William licked his lips, staring at the door over Rune's shoulder. "And what *is* her type, Captain Sharpe?"

Rune studied the witch hunter in the shadows. *Stupid brutes, apparently.*

"Drop the gun," said Gideon.

William narrowed his eyes, pointing it more firmly in Rune's direction.

"*Drop. The. Gun.*"

His voice was a dangerous growl.

The pistol clattered to the floor at William's feet.

"Kick it toward Rune."

The pistol came skidding toward her. Rune bent to pick it up. The metal was still warm from his grip.

"Go back to the cabin, Rune. I'll finish this."

Rune frowned. "What are you going to do?"

Gideon's angry gaze flickered to hers. "Send him to the bottom of the sea. It won't take long. I'll meet you in our room."

TWENTY-EIGHT

GIDEON

GIDEON WANTED NOTHING MORE than to send this insect of a man overboard. The way he spoke to Rune, *looked* at Rune, made Gideon's skin crawl.

Unfortunately, he needed William alive.

"With respect, Captain Sharpe," said William, his back to Gideon, his hands in the air. "You had orders to kill the Crimson Moth. So why is she alive, pretending to be your wife?"

"You can lower your hands," said Gideon, who kept his gun trained on the spy. With Rune gone, he needed to convince William of his plan. And he wasn't likely to have much success if he continued to torment him.

William's arms dropped.

"Harrow knew you weren't able to go through with it." He slowly turned to face Gideon. "That's why she sent me to do your job for you. But now you're interfering with *my* kill orders. How many times are you planning to betray the Republic?"

"The only person I'm planning to betray is Rune." Gideon lowered his gun, but kept it cocked. "Which is why I need your help."

William's forehead creased.

"I need to bring the Crimson Moth in alive."

William crossed his arms, studying Gideon. "I'm listening."

"We were wrong to think killing her would stop this war from coming—it won't even delay it. Soren will give Cress an army anyway, as revenge for his dead fiancée. It was the wrong plan from the start."

"And you have the right one?"

"Cressida isn't only plotting a war. She's plotting to raise her sisters from the dead."

William's eyes widened.

"Our main goal," Gideon continued, "should be destroying her before she can set all her plans in motion. And the best way to destroy Cressida is to use Rune as a bargaining chip. To do that, I need to deliver Rune into the New Republic so I can set a trap for her and the long-lost Roseblood heir she's going to summon."

Gideon had William's full attention now.

"And this is where you come in: I need you to convince Harrow to trust me."

"You're not exactly in a position to ask for trust."

"Nevertheless, I'm asking you to report this back to her. All I need is one week. If, in a week, the Roseblood heir isn't dead and I haven't delivered the Crimson Moth into Blood Guard hands, Harrow can kill me herself."

William fell silent, thinking it over. "All right. I'll report what you've told me."

"One more thing."

"Pushing our luck now, are we?"

Gideon lifted his pistol, aiming it directly at the center of William's forehead. Reminding him who exactly was lucky here—lucky to still be alive. "I need to get Rune past the witch hunters and their hounds when we make port. If I manage to do everything I'm planning, I'll make sure the Good Commander knows you helped me. It'll mean a promotion, and a pay raise. But first you have to do me this one favor and make sure no hunting hounds set foot on this ship or anywhere near it before we deboard tomorrow. Can you do that?"

"I think so. Yes."

"Good." Gideon lowered the gun and put the safety back on. "Stay out of sight. I need Rune to think you're dead."

"Fine," said William, turning to leave.

Gideon called out: "And tell Harrow the next time one of her spies gets in the way of a job, I won't be so gentle with them."

William paused before the door, which hung open, revealing a steamy boiler room beyond. "For someone running out of chances, you make a lot of threats. Don't forget what the punishment is for sympathizing with witches. They don't carve a letter into your forehead anymore and send you on your way."

No. With Cressida on the loose, they couldn't afford to be so lenient. Now, sympathizers were taken out back and shot.

"Screw this up," said William, "and it'll be over for you. When it is, I'm coming for your little Moth."

It took everything in Gideon not to raise his gun and fire.

TWENTY-NINE

RUNE

CLOUDS OF STEAM PRESSED in on Rune as she listened to William's footsteps thud away from the cargo hold. The metal wall was hot against her back, but the rage in her heart was hotter.

Gideon's words rang in her mind: *The only person I'm planning to betray is Rune.*

She'd suspected as much. Of course she had. She'd simply hoped for something else.

Hope is for fools.

How many times did she need to learn that lesson?

Rune's heart pounded as Gideon stepped past her, following William out. The steam mostly concealed her, but if he wanted to find her, he could. All he had to do was turn around and *look*.

But Gideon didn't look. Just followed William through the boilers and up to the level above. Their feet thudded on the metal catwalk overhead while Rune waited for her heart to calm.

This is good, she told herself. *It's a reminder.*

Gideon was her most dangerous enemy. He would only ever hand her over to those who wanted her dead. Everything she'd admitted to him tonight didn't matter. He didn't care. All that mattered to Gideon was stopping Cressida.

His plan was like a bucket of ice water, waking her up.

She couldn't lower her guard with him again. If she wanted to stay alive, to do what she intended, she needed to cut out these deadly feelings at the root. If Gideon was plotting to be-tray her, she needed to betray him first.

Rune pushed away from the wall. Steam swirled around her as she made her way back through the boiler rooms. Trying to come up with a way to outwit the Blood Guard captain.

When she returned to their cabin, she found it empty and remembered what William had said about Gideon and Abbie.

Did he go to her room instead?

She shoved the thought away.

Abbie can have him.

She didn't want to sleep in Gideon's shirt again, but neither could she put on the silky thing she'd packed for a weekend getaway with Soren. So she climbed into bed in her shift.

When the door finally opened—minutes or hours later, Rune couldn't tell—Gideon stepped into the room, closing the door behind him.

Where were you? she wanted to ask, but she pretended to sleep instead. Because did she really want to know?

She felt his attention fix on her, steady and intense. Beneath it, Rune's throat went dry as sand. She desperately wanted to swallow, to moisten her mouth, but feared that small sound would give her away.

She kept her eyes shut and her body still, but she couldn't stop her pulse from racing at the clinking sound of his belt un-buckling and the rustle of his clothes coming off, piece by piece, then dropping to the floor.

When he pulled back the sheet she slept under, Rune tried to think of something else—anything else—than a mostly naked Gideon getting into bed with her. Not so long ago, Gideon and Abbie had been alone in this room, doing Ancients knew what. The mattress dipped beneath his weight. Rune stiffened to stop herself from sinking with it and dipping toward him.

The room fell silent.

"Rune?"

She swallowed.

With less than three inches of space between them, his heat curled toward her. His familiar smell infused the air. Every nerve in her body sparked at his proximity.

Rune clung to her side of the bed.

He loathes you.

"That kiss . . ."

The memory flashed in her mind: his hands in her hair, his mouth against hers, the heat of his body pressing her to the wall.

"Please," she whispered. "Let's forget it ever happened."

Gideon drew in a breath. He was silent for a long moment.

"If that's what you want," he finally said.

"It is."

Silence descended again. Soon, the sound of his breathing came slow and even.

How was she supposed to sleep with him lying right next to her? When all she could think about was his plot against her, and how he and Abbie would celebrate together when the Crimson Moth finally got what she deserved?

Several hours later she gave up trying.

Quietly, she got dressed and left Gideon behind, escaping for a walk along the upper deck's promenade, trying to clear her head. The sun peeked up from the horizon, turning the sky pink and silhouetting the island in the distance.

When the Sister Queens ruled, the island country had been called *Cascadia*. Rune remembered the old map that once hung in Wintersea House, *CASCADIA* printed in bold letters at the top, greeting visitors when they arrived.

But once Nicolas Creed, the late Good Commander, rose to power, he renamed it. The maps now read: *The Republic of the Red Peace.* Everything bearing the former name was considered contraband and destroyed in the revolution. Even the coins, which bore the old name, were melted down and recast into new ones.

Rune had kept Nan's old map as an act of rebellion and hid it away in the cellars of Wintersea.

"Did you miss it?"

Rune straightened, her body recognizing a predator.

But there was no threat in his words. A few seconds later, Gideon stepped up next to her, dressed in Soren's shirt and pants, the seams nearly bursting as they tried to contain his muscled form. He leaned over the railing, staring toward the island ahead.

From the dark smudges under his eyes, he looked like he'd gotten about as much sleep as she had.

Rune stared at him for a long moment, letting her eyes trace over the planes of his face before tearing her gaze away and looking toward their home.

"Yes," she whispered. "With my whole heart."

PART TWO

We witches were given a precious gift, and with that gift comes a sacred task. The Ancients bestowed magic on us for one purpose: to use for the good, the true, and the beautiful.

My cousin intends to twist this purpose with vicious lies. I feel them spreading through my court like poison, a little more every day, infecting even my closest advisors.

I fear I can no longer stop her. The worst is imminent. Tonight, I will go to the stones and ask for Wisdom's help.

—FROM THE DIARY OF
QUEEN ALTHEA THE GOOD

THIRTY

RUNE

"**H**OW DID YOU MANAGE it?" Rune tried not to slip as they made their way down the rain-slick gangway. "There isn't a single witch-hunting hound in sight."

She knew how he'd done it, of course. She just didn't want to give him a reason to think she'd overheard his scheming with William.

The sky was moody overhead. Black clouds sat on a gray horizon, letting them know it had recently stormed, and might storm again, if it felt like it.

"I had someone take care of it," Gideon said, carrying their luggage beside her.

Right, thought Rune. *Just like you'll take care of me, soon enough.*

But the moment she stepped off the dock and onto the busy wharf, her dark thoughts scattered. Rune felt like a ship dropping anchor after months adrift on an ocean of tempestuous waves. The island beneath her was steady. Secure.

She breathed in, and with the salty air came the smell of sea and rain. Of lichen and juniper forests.

Tears pricked the corners of her eyes.

Of home.

But for Rune, home meant danger. This was witch-hunting territory, and here her life was forfeit. She couldn't walk the New Republic's streets as herself. Not to mention: Gideon's plan was now set in motion.

She needed to be especially careful.

Rune had cast *Ghost Walker* before disembarking, in case they were walking into a trap. It had been Gideon's idea, oddly enough. As if he half expected one.

But if they were walking into a trap, it was yet to be sprung.

"Can I borrow your horse?" Rune asked.

She needed to get to Wintersea House. Needed it like she needed air to breathe and water to drink.

Wintersea was safe. Wintersea was *hers*.

If Gideon didn't lend her his horse, she'd have to rent one from the city stables. Rune had packed enough money to get her through the next week or so. She didn't want to be here any longer than that.

"Where are you planning to go?" he asked.

"Home," she said as she walked across the wharf, toward the city streets. "To Wintersea. Once you have the sibyl, bring her to me. In the meantime—"

"Rune . . . you can't."

Can't? Rune scoffed. If he thought she was going to stay here in the city with him—

"Wintersea House is the residence of Noah Creed now."

Rune stopped in her tracks.

What?

"He claimed it after you left."

Left. Like she'd had a choice in the matter. Rune hadn't *left*. She'd been forced to flee for her life.

Her hands curled into fists. All her things now belonged to the Good Commander's son? Her books and clothes and casting room; Lady, her beloved horse; Nan's gardens and the pine needle path through the woods to the beach . . .

All Noah's.

"Where am I going to go?" she whispered.

"My apartment," said Gideon, turning onto the street and heading toward Old Town.

Rune stared at his back, feeling like she might burst into tears. But what choice did she have?

THE LAST TIME SHE was inside this tenement building, Gideon handed her over to the Blood Guard.

The time before that, she gave herself to him, body and soul, when they made love in his bed.

When she stepped through the door, flashes of memory hit like a gale-force wind—his mouth grazing her thigh, his cold voice ordering his soldiers to arrest her.

A war of emotions raged within her. She felt dizzy with them all.

Though she'd been to his parents' tailor shop downstairs a few times, she'd only been to his apartment once—on the night she spent in his bed. It had been dark then, with only the moon shining through the windows to illuminate things.

Now, daylight laid everything bare.

The main room was sparsely furnished. On one side stood a small kitchen with a woodstove; on the other, a sitting area with a sofa and shelves. The sofa was worn, but not threadbare. The floorboards beneath her feet were warped and scuffed, yet sturdy. And she even spotted books on the shelves.

As she made her way over to read their titles, a wooden figurine no bigger than her palm grabbed Rune's attention. Someone had carved the pale wood into the shape of a deer. Its smooth curves called to Rune, and she picked it up.

"It was Tessa's," said Gideon, shutting the door behind them. "My father made it for her."

Rune knew almost nothing about Alex and Gideon's little sister, except that she'd died young. Killed by Cressida.

Rune ran her fingers over the deer, which exuded a kind of warmth despite being made of nothing but wood.

Nan had bought Rune dozens of toys as a child. Too many, probably. But no one had ever *made* Rune a toy. She found fragments of Levi Sharpe in the chiseled surface, where the man had skillfully shaved away wood to expose the form beneath. He'd left his marks; something to say he'd been here, that he loved his daughter.

Realizing her knuckles were turning white, Rune loosened her grip on the deer.

"I'm going to shower," Gideon said from behind her. "And then I need to report to the Commander. Are you hungry? I don't have much food, just some apples and hardtack under the sink. But there's a day market a few streets over where you can buy food to cook."

Cook?

Her?

Rune lowered the deer and stared at Gideon.

"Right." He ran his hand over the back of his neck, glancing at the ceiling. "You don't know how to cook."

"I have servants for that," said Rune, defensive.

Or rather, she'd *had* servants for that. Now she had nothing.

He sighed. "Never mind. I don't want you burning the building down. Wait until I get back, and I'll make us dinner."

Rune watched him disappear down the hall. Who'd taught him to cook? His mother? His father?

She glanced down to the deer figurine in her hand, wondering what that would be like: Having a mother and father. Being taught to cook.

Rune wouldn't have traded Nan for anything in the world,

but that didn't mean she wasn't curious. What was it like, growing up in a family like Gideon's? Parents. Siblings. A house full of people, teeming with life. The loneliness nipping at her heels for years suddenly caught up, sinking its teeth into Rune.

BOOM! BOOM! BOOM!

The pounding scattered her thoughts.

Rune went to the window and glanced out.

Half a dozen soldiers in red uniforms stood outside the door below. She drew back, keeping out of sight and sucking in a breath.

Had Gideon summoned the Blood Guard? Had they come to arrest her?

It made no sense. If he wanted her arrested, he should have let them discover her on the *Arcadia*. They could have taken her straight to prison from there.

"What . . ." Gideon emerged from the hall, his shirt half-unbuttoned, his feet bare. He glanced at Rune, heading for the window.

His mouth thinned into a grim line. "Damn it."

The pounding increased.

"How do they know I'm here?" Rune backed away, nearly tripping over the coffee table.

"They're not here for you," he said, re-buttoning his shirt and striding across the room to check the windows on the other side. "They're here for me."

"Why? What did you do?"

"It's what I *didn't* do." Gideon unlocked the pane, then swung it out. "They'll want to search the apartment."

Rune joined him at the open window, peering down into an empty alleyway below.

"I'll help you up."

She frowned at him. "Up *where*?"

"Onto the roof." He took her hips in his hands and lifted her into the pane. With no other options, Rune got her feet under her, then gripped the pane. The roof was directly overhead, a little slanted, but not enough to be steep. "Here. Take this up, too."

Gideon left and came back with her suitcase as the pounding on the door down below grew more insistent. Grabbing the leather handles, Rune hefted it onto the tiles overhead, then crawled up after it.

"Stay there until I return."

"And if you don't return?"

"Then you're on your own," he said, before swinging the pane shut.

Wonderful.

A moment later, muffled voices entered the apartment below. Rune took off her shoes to ensure she didn't slip, then kept low to the rooftop tiles as she scurried toward the roof's peak, lined with chimneys. Keeping herself hidden, she peered down to the street below, watching as two Blood Guard soldiers brought Gideon out, his hands bound in front of him.

They forced him onto a horse, and then rode toward the palace.

She heard booted footsteps inside as the remaining soldiers searched his apartment. Only when they, too, left, taking their horses with them, did Rune relax. Pressing her back to a chimney, she sank to the sun-warmed tiles and let out a breath.

Feeling a sudden roughness beneath her palm, she lifted her hand. Three names were scratched into the tiles: *Tessa. Alex. Gideon.* The Sharpe siblings must have played up here as children.

That's how Gideon knew where to hide me.

Nan would have killed Rune if she'd ever tried to climb onto a roof.

Her fingers traced the names, lingering on his. Wondering what trouble he was in, and if he would return—or if she'd be forced to find her way down and rescue him.

THIRTY-ONE

GIDEON

*I*T WAS ALWAYS A shock these days, stepping into the Good Commander's gaslit study. The room itself hadn't changed. Familiar leather-bound books lined the walls, and a solid mahogany desk stood on the carpet with a wingback chair behind it.

The sight was almost comforting.

It was the man seated behind the desk who was not.

It should have been Nicolas Creed in that chair. A father figure, mentor, and friend. Gideon still recalled Nicolas's calloused hand pressing a pistol into his palm before they took the palace by force at the New Dawn. It was Nicolas who'd first believed in Gideon. Who'd taught Gideon how to believe in himself.

But Nicolas was dead. Yet another victim of Cressida Rose-blood. Gideon had dug the man's grave himself, right after digging his brother's.

And the person sitting at the desk was his son, Noah.

The new Good Commander.

Noah wore his father's black uniform, with a scarlet cloak pinned over one shoulder. He propped his elbows on the desktop and steepled his fingers while listening to the young woman already inside the room, standing before the desk, giving an account.

Even from behind, the Good Commander's master of spies was easy to recognize. Her black hair was pulled up into a top-knot. The bottom half of her head was shaved close to the scalp, drawing attention to her missing ear—taken from her by witches she'd been indentured to under the Sister Queens' reign.

At the sight of Gideon stepping through the door, the Good Commander's jaw tightened—a movement so slight, Gideon wondered if he'd imagined it.

Noah held up his hand, halting his spymaster's words.

"Impeccable timing, Sharpe. Harrow was informing me of trouble on the Continent. And here you are: the source of it." He nodded for the soldiers to bring Gideon forward.

With his hands shackled, Gideon let himself be nudged toward the Commander. When he stopped beside Harrow, her bright gold eyes locked on his. Not so long ago, Harrow had been Gideon's informant, freely bringing him information to aid in his witch hunts.

Now Harrow reported to the Good Commander, who disseminated her intel as he saw fit. Gideon couldn't blame her for the shift in loyalty. He'd failed her—failed all of them. Which was precisely why he needed to convince them to support his new plan. He had to fix what he'd broken.

"Start over, Harrow." Noah looked Gideon up and down, as if inspecting every crease of his shirt and fleck of dirt on his pants. "I'll deal with you in a minute, Sharpe."

Glancing back to Gideon, Harrow said, "I have a contact who's infiltrated the witch queen's ranks."

Gideon frowned, interrupting her. "To infiltrate Cressida's ranks, this contact would have to be a witch."

"That's correct."

"You're sure she can be trusted?"

"That's why we're bringing in the sibyl," said Noah. "To verify." He nodded for Harrow to go on.

"My contact says Soren has given Cressida an army and will sail with her to lay siege to the New Republic in a matter of days."

"I could have told you that if you'd simply waited for my report," said Gideon.

Harrow cut him a look. "Soren has also *doubled* his initial war chest because of his fiancée's kidnapping."

"It doesn't matter," said Gideon. "There's a way to circumvent this war *and* destroy Cressida. But it requires keeping the Crimson Moth alive."

Harrow narrowed her eyes, turning her full attention on him. "You're compromised, Comrade."

Gideon brushed this off. "*You* aren't thinking strategically. None of you are." He looked around the room, which, other than the soldiers, contained a handful of Noah's ministers. "If we kill the Moth, it will only enrage the prince. You think it's bad now that he's doubled his war chest? If his fiancée is dead, he'll hold nothing back. You will make things worse."

Harrow crossed her arms. But she was listening.

It wasn't Harrow he needed to convince, though. It was the new Commander.

He turned toward Noah, who was staring Gideon down from behind his father's desk, his eyes cold as glittering ice.

"Cressida believes she has a long-lost sibling. A missing Roseblood heir, who she can use to resurrect her sisters."

Startled murmurs rippled around the room.

"Resurrection is a myth," said Noah.

"You certain of that? Because we can't afford to be wrong."

Gideon ignored the intense dislike radiating at him from across the desk and forged ahead. "Rune is hunting for this Roseblood heir. Once she finds them, she intends to smuggle them back to the Continent. My plan is twofold. First: we ambush them. I'll learn when and where Rune is planning to launch her escape and ensure the Blood Guard are lying in wait.

"Second: once we have them surrounded, we execute the

Roseblood heir and arrest Rune, who we use to negotiate with Soren. All the prince has to do if he wants his precious bride back is cooperate with us. And all we'll require of him is this: once we prove to him that we have Rune in custody, he must order his soldiers to turn on an unsuspecting Cressida, killing her and every witch in her army. If he doesn't comply, Rune dies. If he *does* comply, we return Rune to him, unharmed."

Gideon glanced around the room, meeting the eyes of every official and soldier, one after another.

"We will prevent a war we're not sure we can win, *and* we'll rid ourselves of Cressida, along with any possibility of resurrecting her or her sisters."

The room fell quiet.

"And if you fail to deliver?"

Gideon turned to Noah.

"If I fail, we'll go to war and lose." He glanced at Harrow. "If I fail, Cressida will not only reclaim her throne, but resurrect Elowyn and Analise and usher in a new Reign of Witches—"

Gideon broke off as palace guards escorted a shackled young woman into the room. Iron cylinders encased her hands, preventing her from casting spells, and her copper hair hung in greasy strings down her back.

The woman was Aurelia Kantor: a witch they'd been using to track down others of her kind. As a sibyl, Aurelia saw into the past, present, and future. This Sight allowed her to know the exact locations of every witch on the island—which the Blood Guard had been forcing her to tell them, one by one.

"I want to see my daughter." Aurelia's voice scratched, as if she'd gone too many days without water. "It's been two weeks. I don't even know if she's still alive."

The daughter in question was a two-year-old child in the

care of a guardian halfway across town. Her name was Meadow. Kept under lock and key, Meadow was the only thing securing Aurelia's obedience.

"Ask her," said Gideon. "Let her verify everything I've said."

The sibyl's head turned, hawklike, to face Gideon. Her emerald eyes thinned as she took in his restraints, a question in them.

"Is Cressida Roseblood planning to resurrect her sisters?" said Noah.

Her eyes shuttered and she looked away, pressing her thin lips together.

"Is it possible?" he asked.

Still she didn't answer. Gideon was preparing to barter with her. Better rations, increased visits with her daughter—these things usually worked. But before he could, Noah spoke from behind his desk.

"Bring in the child."

Gideon hadn't seen the kid since the two were captured together. The unspoken threat to Meadow's safety had always been enough to make the sibyl comply.

A soldier brought the toddler into the room and set her down on an armchair that dwarfed her tiny frame. It was clear she'd been taken far better care of than her mother. White ribbons tied her wispy red hair into pigtails, and the clean dress she wore looked more expensive than anything in Gideon's closet.

But her eyes were wide and terrified.

"Mumma?" Her chin trembled at the sight of her mother, in chains and kneeling on the floor several paces away. The girl held out her tiny hands to Aurelia, whispering: "Mumma, Mumma. I want to go home."

Gideon watched the witch struggle to control the emotion in

her voice as the tears ran down her daughter's cheeks. "I know, baby. Soon. We'll go home soon."

It was a lie. Aurelia knew perfectly well that neither she nor her child was ever going home.

Noah rose from his chair. "Is Cressida Roseblood planning to raise her sisters from the dead?"

"I don't know," said Aurelia.

"Bring the child here," said Noah. "And hold its hand down on the desk."

What?

Gideon spun to watch Noah lift his dead father's sword down from the wall. A dark dread coiled in his stomach.

This was not how he would have done it.

Because you are soft, said a voice inside him. *And your softness gets people killed.*

The Good Commander was demonstrating what a strong leader looked like.

But this . . .

"No! Please!" The witch's voice shook as she looked to Gideon. "Don't let him hurt her!"

"He won't," he said, hoping this was true. "If you answer the question."

As Noah gripped the sword in two hands, the child tried to back away. One guard grabbed her arms while the other seized her wrist, pinning her little hand to the desk.

Meadow started wailing.

No mother should be put in this position. No *child* should be put in this position.

Gideon stepped forward. But what could he do? His hands were bound. He was as much a prisoner here as the witch and her child.

Noah lifted the sword into the air. The blade glinted in the lamplight.

"Stop!" Aurelia stumbled forward, chains clinking. "I'll tell you what you want to know. Just don't hurt her! Please!"

"Then answer the question: is Cressida the last living Rose-blood?"

The witch's shoulders slumped as she realized the choice before her: the witch queen—who would kill her for her treachery—or her daughter. Tears flowed down her cheeks as she stared at her terrified child.

"Forgive me, my queen . . ."

Gideon watched as her green eyes clouded over, turning milky white. Her breathing slowed as her body went still as marble. More statue than flesh.

"Cressida's mother, Queen Winoa, had a fourth child with her second husband," she said finally. "But the sickly thing died in childbirth. The queen never fully recovered from her grief. For years, she heard it crying at night, and would wander the palace halls in search of it."

Gideon knew the story. Cress had told it to him more than once. Cressida's mother had remarried when her first husband died. Cress and her sisters hated their stepfather—who, by all accounts, was an unspeakably cruel man—and blamed him for turning their mother against them after the stillbirth.

"Everyone thought she'd gone mad," he said.

Even Cressida.

"But the child didn't die," said Aurelia. "It was stolen away in the night."

Gideon frowned. "Why?"

"To save it from the royal family's dysfunction? To fulfill a prophecy—or stop one from coming true?" She shook her head. "It's unclear."

"And this person—are they alive? If so, who are they? And where can I find them?"

Aurelia's eyes went whiter still. Her brow creased as she concentrated hard.

"They're alive, but . . ."

It was several minutes before the clouds retreated from her eyes. When they did, she drew in a sharp breath and collapsed to the floor.

"I can't See them." Aurelia bent over like a dog while the guards kept her daughter's hand pinned to the desk. "Something's blocking my Sight."

Noah raised the sword again.

"She's telling the truth," said Gideon, stepping forward to intervene. "Cressida said the same thing, that a spell is blocking sibyls from seeing this person. As if someone wants to keep them hidden."

Reluctantly, Noah lowered the sword. He glanced at the sibyl. "This missing Roseblood—can they be used to resurrect Elowyn and Analise?"

Aurelia released a breath. "Yes."

"If this person were found and killed," said Gideon, "could Cressida use her own blood to cast the spell?"

Aurelia shook her head. "It's an Arcana spell—it requires the blood of a close family member. A parent, child, or sibling. But it isn't just blood that's demanded, it's *life*. The spell requires the kin's life be sacrificed in exchange for the resurrection of the dead."

"So if Cressida used herself as the blood sacrifice, she'd die in the process."

Aurelia nodded.

"In other words: if this missing Roseblood were disposed of before Cressida found her, Cress wouldn't be able to cast the resurrection spell."

"That's correct."

Gideon looked to Noah. Aurelia had just made it clear

Gideon's plan was the best one they'd come up with. Noah had no choice but to concede.

The Good Commander nodded to the guards still pinning Meadow. The moment they let go, the girl ran for her mother, locking her little arms around the witch's neck. Despite her chains, Aurelia hugged her child tight, forming a protective shell around her.

Harrow stepped forward, walking a slow circle around the chained witch. "We know Soren has given Cressida an army. What we need are numbers. How many ships, soldiers, and artillery does she have at her disposal?"

Gideon remembered the steamships sailing into Caelis's harbor.

"Eleven ironclads, nine gunboats, and seven troopships," said Aurelia. "Plus thousands of well-armed soldiers."

It would be more than enough to take the capital by force.

Harrow glanced at the Commander and nodded, as if the sibyl was indeed verifying the information delivered from her contact.

"And the terms of the alliance?" asked Noah.

"Once Soren's army helps Cressida take the capital, the prince will marry Rune Winters. If the wedding does not take place as promised, Soren will retract his men, artillery, and ships, leaving Cressida to fend for herself."

Gideon watched as Aurelia hummed a familiar lullaby against her child's cheek, trying to calm her. It was the same lullaby his mother once sang to him and his siblings, frightening away their nightmares, soothing them when they were sick.

He shook the thought away.

This witch was nothing like his mother.

A soldier crouched in front of Aurelia, whose arms tightened around her child. The song in her throat quieted and her lips curled in a snarl, like a she-wolf ready to tear out his throat if he came any closer.

"Captain Sharpe." Noah's voice pierced the silence, forcing Gideon's gaze to the Commander. "Soren's ships may have already disembarked from the Continent. If so, they will be here in three days. In order for your plan to work, we need to get a message to the prince, and have the Crimson Moth ready to hand over when he arrives. I'm therefore giving you two days to come through on your promises. If the Crimson Moth slips through your fingers once again, I'll have to assume it's intentional. *Two days.* Understood? If you fail, you'll be accused of sympathizing with witches and put in a cell to await execution."

Execution.

The word rang through him like a gunshot.

But could he do it in two days?

Did he have a choice?

Gideon steeled himself. "You must let me work unhindered. I need your complete trust, even if it looks like I'm compromised. To get the information we need, I must convince Rune I'm on her side. No sending soldiers to search my apartment or arrest me. No interference whatsoever."

The Crimson Moth could not expect an ambush, or she would outmaneuver them.

Noah slit his eyes. "Fine. Agreed."

"Great," said Gideon, flatly. "Now, if someone wouldn't mind releasing me"—he held out his manacled fists—"I'll escort the sibyl back. I have a few more questions for her."

"THIS ISN'T THE WAY to my cell," said Aurelia. They'd taken her child away, and ever since, her eyes had gone dark.

Gideon led her through the palace's gaslit halls, boots thudding on the marble floors. "I'm not taking you to your cell."

She glanced up at him. "Then where are you taking me?"

Gideon couldn't help but compare the feral-looking thing beside him to the aristocratic woman he'd originally brought in. Two months in the palace prison could drastically change a person.

"That depends on your answers to my questions."

She narrowed her eyes.

"Where is Cressida keeping the bodies of Elowyn and Analise?"

Aurelia glanced away, pretending to study the marble walls as if they were made of complicated tapestries rather than blank stone.

He stopped, forcing her to halt. "Tell me where they are, and I'll get you out of here."

She cocked her head, studying him carefully. "Why should I trust you?"

Gideon shrugged. "You can't." He glanced behind them, then up ahead. The hallway was empty; a corridor of white. "But you can barter with me: the answers I need in exchange for your freedom."

She sharpened like a freshly honed knife. Her green eyes blazed at him.

"I'm not going anywhere without Meadow. And I'm not telling you anything more until she's safely in my arms."

Turning on her heel, she headed toward the palace prison.

"You want answers? Free my daughter first. Then, we'll talk."

THIRTY-TWO

RUNE

*R*UNE WAITED FOR GIDEON on the crest of his tenement's roof, perched between two chimney stacks, the sunbaked tiles warming her bare feet as she stared over Old Town. Smoke plumed from the factory district into the blue sky overhead, while the smell of coal mingled with the salt of the nearby sea.

Rune watched the comings and goings of people in the street, some pushing carts, others pulling livestock, others running messages or out on errands.

Before the revolution, Nan forbade Rune from ever visiting this side of town. It was dirty and rough, she said. Not for people like *them.*

Rune drew her knees up and rested her chin on her arms, watching the city below. What would it have been like to grow up in a place like this, instead of Wintersea? Would she have become someone different, or would she be the exact same Rune?

And who is that?

Who was she, deep down? Beneath the witch. Beneath the aristocrat. What made her *her?*

Did a person change depending on their circumstances? Or was there something permanent about everyone? Something steadfast and true, *despite* their circumstances?

Rune didn't know the answer, and it bothered her.

Her stomach growled, reminding her she'd eaten nothing since yesterday.

There's a day market a few streets over where you can buy food to cook, Gideon had told her. Rune looked for it from where she sat.

She could learn to cook. How difficult could it be?

Rune reached for her shoes and was about to make her way down to the roof's edge when she turned to find a Blood Guard soldier climbing up from the window below.

Rune sucked in a breath.

The young man looked up.

"Gideon," she said, her breath rushing out. She'd been so busy daydreaming, she hadn't seen him come up the street.

Rune looked him over as he clambered up to the perch where she sat. He'd traded Soren's clothes for his scarlet uniform, and the shackles they'd taken him away in were gone.

In fact, he seemed completely unharmed—not to mention unfazed.

What did they want?

And what did he give them in exchange for being released?

But Rune already knew. She'd overheard every word of his plan down in that cargo hold.

Beneath his arm was a folded Blood Guard uniform. He held it out to her.

"What's this?" she asked, taking the jacket and pants.

"For you." He came to sit on her perch. Their hips touched as he sat down, but he didn't move away. "I need your help."

Rune cocked a brow. "Yeah?"

"The sibyl has a child. A little girl named Meadow. We've been using her as leverage to make the witch talk."

Rune's stomach clenched. A *child.*

She had assumed the Blood Guard must be doing something horrible to Aurelia Kantor to get information. Otherwise, why would a witch give away the location of other witches, knowing they'd be hunted down?

This was why.

They had her child.

"She refuses to leave the prison unless I free Meadow first."

A heist?

Gideon wanted to do a heist. With *Rune*.

It shouldn't have, but it thrilled her.

"I suppose I could help." She ran her hands down her dress, trying not to sound pleased about being needed.

"Good," he said, already rising and making his way to the roof's edge. "Then put on that uniform and let's go. I have boots for you inside."

"Wait . . . *now?*" said Rune, grabbing her shoes and following him down on bare feet, the stolen uniform tucked under her arm. "Could we at least eat something first? I'm starving."

GIDEON BOUGHT THEM DINNER from a street vendor. It would have scandalized Nan to see Rune gobbling up chicken pie with her fingers and licking off the grease. But Rune was so hungry, she didn't care.

Gideon tried not to laugh as he offered her the rest of his.

Afterward they fetched his horse, Comrade, from the stable and rode to the city's east side, where most of the aristocracy lived in residential neighborhoods along the water, away from downtown's hustle and bustle.

Rune illusioned herself before coming, because she knew the area well. Many of Nan's friends had lived there before the Blood Guard purged them and redistributed their homes to revolutionaries. The neighborhood butted up against a quiet port where the wealthy docked their boats. Alex had kept one here before he died.

As Gideon went to tie up Comrade, Rune waited. The house

they needed to infiltrate backed onto the promenade, and Rune wanted to inspect it before they went in.

She looked out over the calm water, where several sailboats were anchored. Nan had taught Rune how to sail when she was a child. Since her birth parents had died at sea, Nan was determined that Rune would never be afraid of it. Rune had even sailed Alex's two-person sailboat on occasion.

As she waited for Gideon to return, she read the names painted on each boat, until one that was painfully familiar made her breath catch.

Dawn's Aria.

What was Alex's sailboat still doing here?

"Here," said Gideon, interrupting her thoughts.

Rune tore her gaze away from the boat to find him holding out two ice cream cones. "What's this?"

"I didn't know what flavor you'd like. All of them are good, honestly."

"You bought them . . . for me?"

"One's for you. The other's mine. I'll take whichever one you don't want."

Rune eyed the ice cream cones—one chocolate, the other vanilla—then glanced to Gideon in his blood-red uniform. She'd gotten used to him in regular clothes—if you could call a prince's clothes *regular*. In uniform, it was harder to forget what he was.

A soldier.

A witch hunter.

Her enemy.

Yet here he was, buying her ice cream.

Is he trying to lower my guard again?

Rune reached for the chocolate ice cream. He relinquished it.

"What were you staring at out there?" He nodded toward the water. "You seemed deep in thought."

"Oh, um . . ." She looked back to *Dawn's Aria*. "Is that Alex's boat?"

Now that Gideon knew she planned to smuggle witches aboard the *Arcadia*—and intended to stop her—Rune needed a new escape plan.

Would a sailboat work?

It wasn't her first choice. The Barrow Strait was known for its rough waters, and Rune alone could only handle a small boat. Something easily tossed about—or capsized—in a bad storm.

But if she didn't have another option . . .

Gideon followed her gaze to the water.

"It's Alex's boat, yes." His voice softened. "I couldn't part with it after . . ." He trailed off, shaking his head. "I suppose it can't sit out there forever. I'll have to sell it eventually. Ancients know *I* can't sail it."

Rune, who was plotting out her new escape plan, distractedly said, "I could teach you."

Gideon glanced at her. "Teach me to sail?"

Their gazes met.

Why had she said that? They weren't friends. If she managed to pull this off and escape with her life, she'd never see him again.

And that was the *best-case* scenario.

"Forget it. It's silly." Desperate to change the subject, she motioned to her ice cream. "Thank you for the treat."

Gideon hesitated, as if he wasn't ready to let the topic go.

Not wanting to linger on Alex's boat, in case it made him suspicious, Rune forced a change of subject: "So, is this your standard romance routine? You take whatever girl you're courting for ice cream and a promenade?"

His mouth quirked. "Are we courting? I wasn't aware."

What? Heat rushed into Rune's cheeks. "That's not . . . no. I didn't mean—"

He glanced back over his shoulder, toward the ice cream parlor.

"Actually," he said, interrupting her spluttering. "I come here whenever I miss my family."

Oh.

"My parents first took us here for Tessa's tenth birthday," he said, nodding at her to walk with him, leaving the view of Alex's boat in the distance. "It was the first time we had ever eaten ice cream. My mother's designs were getting popular, and there was suddenly extra money to splurge on things we didn't absolutely need."

They walked side by side along the waterfront path, eating their ice cream. When groups of women or other couples strolled past, taking in the sea air and sunlight, Gideon would step off the path to give them room, then rejoin Rune.

"Tessa loved chocolate best, and Alex loved vanilla. My mother's favorite was pistachio."

"And your father?"

"He didn't like sugar."

Didn't like sugar? Rune licked her cone. Cold and sweet. *Mmm.* "I can't imagine not liking sugar. Or spending my childhood without eating ice cream . . ."

The words were out of her mouth before she could stop them.

Why had she said that?

What an insensitive thing to say!

But Gideon didn't notice—or, if he did, he didn't seem to mind. Only glanced at the row of houses ahead, each one facing the waterfront. Which one was keeping the sibyl's child captive?

"It never bothered me, how we lived. I had nothing better to compare it to. Not until . . ." He glanced at her. A small smile tugged at his mouth. "You have ice cream on your face."

Mortified, Rune swiped at her chin.

Gideon shook his head. "No, it's . . ."

Pulling off his riding glove, he brushed his thumb across her lip. When he drew his hand away, the pad of his thumb was smeared with chocolate. Gideon studied it, as if he didn't know what to do.

He offered it back to her.

Rune didn't hesitate. It was chocolate, after all.

She took his thumb in her mouth, sucking off the ice cream. As her teeth grazed his skin, she heard Gideon swallow. The sound made her glance up to find him staring at her, eyes going dark. The last time he'd looked at her like that was right before he kissed her on the *Arcadia*.

Right before he remembered that what she was repulsed him.

Rune pulled away, releasing his thumb. Her heart thundered in her ears as she quickly turned and kept walking. "Which house is it?"

Her voice sounded shaky.

Gideon cleared his throat. "The yellow one." Up ahead stood a lemony three-story house. It was gated on all sides, and dark green ivy climbed the iron bars, obscuring their view of the yard.

Rune slowed her pace, taking it in. With the gate leading to the waterfront locked, they couldn't get in or out this way. Which left the front door as their only entrance and exit.

Through the ivy, Rune counted four uniformed guards in the back gardens. There would be more security out front and inside.

She glanced at the pistol at Gideon's hip, her hand going to the revolver Soren had given her, holstered at her own. Two guns would run out of bullets fast if they ran into trouble.

"I'll need your jacket," she told Gideon, turning away from the house and starting back in the direction they'd come.

"What for?"

"You'll see."

THIRTY-THREE

RUNE

"**Y**OU CAN NEVER BE too prepared," said Rune as they emerged from the wooded park. Gideon had kept watch while she hid in the trees, enchanting their jackets with a reversal spell called *Witch's Armor*.

It's for repelling harm, she'd told him, quoting the spell book she'd learned it from. *Like armor, the spellmarks will deflect a knife aimed at your chest, or make bullets bounce off you.*

What Gideon *didn't* know was that Rune had also drawn the marks for a beguiling spell on the inside of her wrist, hidden by the sleeve of her uniform.

Beguile wasn't as coercive as *Truth Teller*. It was a simple Mirage spell, one Cressida had shown her when Rune still believed her to be Verity. According to Seraphine, Nan had used *Beguile*, too, often during business dealings to help with persuasion. It couldn't force someone to do what she asked, but it nudged them in that direction. Essentially: it made the wearer difficult to resist, though not impossible.

It wouldn't work on someone like Gideon, for example, who delighted in opposing Rune. But young guards wanting to impress a pretty girl? It might work on them.

They approached the yellow house. The front gates were open, revealing statues of two Ancients flanking the front steps: Patience and Justice. Patience held an hourglass in her hands; Justice bore a bandolier across her chest.

Only a single guard stood outside the front door. Rune

guessed him to be about nineteen or twenty. It was dinnertime, and Gideon knew that half the staff were on their breaks. This was part of their strategy: the amount of security would be diminished for the next half hour or so, increasing their odds of not just getting in but getting out.

At the sight of Rune and Gideon, the guard stood straighter. Possibly because of their red uniforms, or because he recognized the Blood Guard captain.

Gideon nodded a silent greeting.

"Hi," said Rune, turning up the brightness of her smile like the flame in a lamp.

The guard was tall and broad, though not as tall and broad as Gideon, and his light brown hair shone with hints of red where the sunlight hit.

His gaze fixed on Rune, running down her uniform. It fit her perfectly, because Gideon knew her measurements. He'd taken them himself, not so long ago.

"Can I help you with something?" asked the guard, his attention still wandering over Rune.

"We're here to collect the witch's child," Gideon said, interrupting the guard's perusal. "The Commander needs her at the palace."

The guard tore his gaze from Rune and straightened at Gideon's commanding tone. "The child was already at the palace this morning. Do you have papers?"

Rune shot Gideon a look. *Papers?* He might have mentioned needing papers.

"There wasn't time to draft them," she said. "It's a last-minute request from the Commander's office."

"I'm afraid I need to see papers before I can let you in."

Time to improvise.

"I told you this would happen, Captain." Rune pivoted, as

if to leave. "We should have insisted on—Ow!" Rune winced, grabbing her ankle as if it pained her. "I think I—" Pretending to lose her balance, she stumbled backward and fell right into the guard. "Oof!"

He caught her around the waist, steadying her. "Are you all right?"

From this close, she could smell the shaving soap on his skin. Rune leaned into him, still holding her ankle as she balanced on one leg. "I'm so sorry . . . it's my bad ankle. It acts up sometimes."

She glanced at Gideon, whose eyes were narrowing.

Well, it's not like you were getting us anywhere helpful.

"Don't put any weight on it," said the soldier, who scooped an arm under both her legs, lifting her. "I'll take you to the parlor. You can rest there while I find someone to call for a physician."

She looped her arms around his neck. "That's so kind of you, but I don't want to be a bother . . ."

The *Beguile* spellmark grew warm against her wrist as Rune ran a finger along the collar of his jacket. The guard watched her movements, entranced.

Swallowing, he said, "It's no bother."

Rune gazed up at him through her eyelashes. "What's your name?"

He carried her through the doors and into a small parlor room. "Ed." He shook his head. "I mean, *Edmund*. My friends call me Ed."

"Edmund," she purred.

Over the guard's shoulder, Gideon glowered at her.

"I'll ask the housekeeper to fetch the physician." Edmund put her down on the settee. "Stay here."

"Of course." Rune turned her glowing smile on him again. "I won't budge from this spot."

The moment he was gone, Rune rose from the settee. Gideon stood like a thundercloud by the door, still glaring at her.

Ignoring him, she peeked her head out into the hall, watching Edmund disappear around a corner. "Let's find the nursery before he realizes we're missing."

When all was clear, Rune stepped into the empty hall.

Gideon followed.

Even the walls here were yellow. Like butter melting in the sun.

They passed household staff going about their duties: a woman hauling a basket full of laundry; a man bringing in fresh-cut wood from outside. Rune smiled at each one, acting like she belonged here. Hoping *Beguile* would work on them, too.

When they were finally alone, Gideon growled: "Was that really necessary?"

"Was what necessary?"

She found a set of stairs and climbed them. The nursery was on the third floor. Rune had noticed it from the boardwalk: an open window facing the harbor front, where a mobile of twirling clouds hung above a crib.

That room was their destination.

"You didn't need to flirt with him."

Rune bristled. *Really?* "My flirting got us inside. You should be thanking me."

But Gideon was the opposite of thankful. He was surlier than ever.

"That guy doesn't have a chance with you," he said as they hit the second floor, where the stairs ended. "You know it. And I know it. But *he* doesn't know it. Encouraging him to think otherwise is cruel."

"Cruel?" Rune threw him a look, prickling as she strode down

a hall with freshly washed floors and daffodil wallpaper. She looked around, searching for the stairs to the third level. "That's rich, coming from you—a boy who hunts girls for a living."

"*Witches*," he corrected. "I hunt witches."

A door opened further down. At the voice issuing out, they hesitated, glancing toward it.

"I left her in the front parlor," said Edmund, the soldier she'd duped, as he stepped into the hall. "She couldn't walk. I think it may be broken . . ."

Edmund was about to turn and spot them when Gideon grabbed the sleeve of Rune's uniform and yanked her into an empty room, shutting the door behind them.

Rune blew out a breath, grateful despite herself for his quick thinking.

She glanced around. They were in some kind of personal library, with shelves full of books, a writing desk, and windows overlooking the water.

Luckily, the room was empty.

Rune cracked the door open to peer out. Edmund still stood at the end of the hall, speaking with the other staff member. Blocking their way forward.

They were stuck here until he left.

Gideon leaned against the wall, listening to the muffled conversation. His words from a moment ago needled at her.

"This may be hard for you to believe," she whispered, watching the guard outside, "but not everyone is repulsed by me."

Gideon glanced at her. "What?"

"Just because you're disgusted at the thought of me doesn't mean everyone else is," she said, keeping her voice down. "Some people *like* it when I flirt with them."

"What are you talking about?"

Annoyed that Edmund was still speaking to the staff, she shut the door and turned to Gideon, who stood facing her. "That night on the ship, when we kissed. You pulled away like I was . . ."

She glanced away, remembering the appalled look in his eyes. As if he couldn't believe what he'd done.

Rune wished she didn't care. But she did.

"Like you were *what*?" he growled, keeping his voice down.

She fixed her gaze on the polished floorboards beneath her feet. "Like I was a horrifying monster."

He ran a hand through his hair. "That's not . . ."

Gideon fell silent, watching her. As if considering something.

He unbuttoned his jacket.

She stared as he tugged it off, then untucked his shirt. "What are you doing?"

"Putting this to rest. Right now."

Watching him undress was making her temperature rise.

"Putting *what* to rest?"

"This ludicrous idea that you repulse me."

"I *do* repulse you." Her eyes met his dark ones. "You said so yourself."

"*What?*" His fingers paused at the uppermost button of his shirt. "When?"

Rune cracked the door open and peered out. Edmund was heading back in their direction.

She shut the door.

Grabbing Gideon's arm, she tugged him through the bookshelves and across the library, where their conversation was less likely to reach the hall.

"The day you handed me over to be purged," she whispered as she pulled him down the aisle between shelves. "You said you weren't sure what disgusted you more—the fact that I was a witch, or that you fell for my act."

"*Rune.*"

He halted, forcing her to stop walking. She glanced back to find him staring at the ceiling, as if praying for patience.

She let go of his arm.

"You'd betrayed me in the worst possible way." His gaze dropped to her face. "I'd just discovered you were the criminal I'd spent two years hunting—not to mention secretly betrothed to my brother. I was heartbroken! You told me Alex was twice the man I'd ever be!"

"Because you were handing me over to die!" she whisper-hissed, turning fully toward him.

Gideon ran a palm over his face and sighed. "Fair enough." Dropping his hand, he fell silent, considering her. "Since we're airing our grievances: it kills me watching you seduce other men."

"Because it's cruel. Got it." She turned away, heading toward the writing desk, which was the furthest point away from the hall.

He grabbed her wrist, stopping her. "Not because of that."

Rune glanced back at him.

"Watching you flirt with them makes me . . ." He made a sound low in his throat. "It makes want to go to the shooting range and fire off a hundred rounds, imagining I'm firing at *them.*"

Rune stared at him. What was he saying? That he was *jealous?*

"I hated watching you flirt with Abbie." The words were out of her mouth before she could stop them. "I hate that you lied to me about her."

He let go of her and drew back.

"*I* lied?"

Voices in the hall made them both go quiet, glancing to the

door. When it didn't open and the voices passed, she dropped her voice to a whisper again. "You told me Abbie was an old friend. But she's not. She's more than that."

His entire demeanor darkened. Like a coming storm.

"Did William tell you this?"

William the spy? she wanted to shout. But Gideon didn't know she'd overheard his conversation, and she intended to keep it that way.

"William saw you and Abbie go to our cabin together. *Alone.* Why would you do that, unless it was to . . ." She bit down on the rest of that sentence.

Why was she asking him this? Did she really want to know?

"To do *what*?" he growled.

She fisted her hands and glared up at him. *"You tell me."*

He stepped toward her. Rune stepped back.

"To kiss her?" His voice rumbled through the aisle as he continued walking, and she continued backing away. "To rekindle some old romance? Is *that* what you want to hear?" This seemed to enrage him. Why it would, she had no idea. Why did he get to be angry about her romantic entanglements, but she couldn't question his?

Rune bumped into the desk directly behind her. He'd backed her right up against it.

"You want to know? Fine." He moved in close, taking up all her air. "Yes. *I kissed her.*"

The thought of it—his mouth on Abbie's—felt like a bullet in her heart.

Which made no sense.

He was planning to kill every single witch she'd come here to save. He was plotting against her even now. He was a coldhearted brute. Abbie could have him!

But Rune's heart and her head refused to align. They were two ships on different courses.

Her heart had gone rogue a long time ago.

Gideon seemed to be waiting for her next barb. As if they were in a boxing ring, and he wanted her to throw another punch. But any response was pointless. He'd won the match by admitting to that kiss.

She nodded curtly, letting him know she wanted out of the ring. She was done with this conversation. Rune tried to step out from between him and the desk. If Edmund was finally gone, they needed to look for the child.

"We are *not* finished." Gideon pressed his hands flat on the desk, one on either side of her, preventing her from leaving. "I had to watch you kiss that stupid prince. Do you think that was fun for me?"

Soren?

That wasn't at all the same!

Rune didn't even bother trying to break the cage of his arms. "You think I enjoyed kissing *Soren?*"

He towered over her, his face inches from hers. "It's hard to tell, with you."

Did he think Soren Nord was what she wanted?

Fool.

"I hated it." The words were ash in her mouth. "I kissed him because I had to."

Wasn't that obvious?

But no. To Gideon, Rune wasn't a girl fighting to stay alive. She was an aristocrat used to getting what she wanted. She was a witch who bent people to her will.

"You have no idea the kinds of things I've had to do to stay alive," she said.

His eyes hardened. "I have some idea."

Because of Cressida, she realized. Gideon had been at the witch queen's mercy for a long time. He too had done things he didn't want to in order to survive.

"I know a lie lived over and over will destroy a person," he said.

Rune's eyes burned. She glanced away, but evidently not before he saw the tears in them. Because he lifted his gloved hands to her cheeks, turning her face back to him. It took all of her willpower not to lean into his touch.

His thumb brushed across her jaw, tracing the line of it. It was so unfair, the way a single touch from him made her ache for more.

"Rune, the truth is—" He swallowed. "—the entire time I was kissing Abbie . . . I wanted her to be you."

What?

Rune frowned up at him.

"Then why were you so horrified when you *did* kiss me?"

He dropped his hand to her belt and curled a finger through one of the loops. As he pulled her closer and leaned in, his breath feathered against her throat. "Mind if I demonstrate?"

Rune's pulse kicked. She glanced at the door across the room. *I should check the hall.*

But she didn't.

This was the truly terrible thing about Gideon: he made her feel invincible. Like there was no danger she couldn't get out of. Rune first felt it as the Crimson Moth, spending her nights outwitting him. She felt it again now, in a brand new way.

Soon enough, Edmund would discover the parlor room empty and come looking for them. But it didn't matter, because so long as Gideon was on her side, so long as they were a team, there was nothing she couldn't do.

It was irrational. Mad, even.

It scared her as much as it thrilled her.

She glanced at his mouth. "Show me."

Suddenly, Gideon's lips were seeking hers, and hers were answering. Their mouths clashed. Her blood heated. His hand pressed against her lower back, pulling her closer. Burning a hungry fire through her. He captured her mouth again and again, making it clear how *not* repulsed he was.

Their kisses turned desperate. Like their lives depended on never coming up for air. Rune's pulse hammered as his palms settled firmly around her waist and he lifted her onto the desk. When he stepped between her legs, pulling her flush against him, Rune hummed deep in her throat.

She was prepared to give this boy whatever he wanted so long as he promised to *never stop*.

I'm doomed, she realized. *Gideon Sharpe will be the end of me.*

With his mouth still devouring her, he drew her hand under his untucked shirt. Sliding her palm up his chest, he pressed it to his scar. Rune felt the raised skin beneath hers. Cressida had branded him years ago, like he was nothing more than an animal, and now the brand was warm beneath her palm and growing warmer.

Hot.

The hotter it grew, the more Gideon stiffened, his muscles growing taut. Just like when he'd kissed her on the *Arcadia*.

Only this time, Rune recognized it for what it was.

Pain.

Rune tried to pull away, but he had her pinned to the desk. And even though something was wrong—that was clear to her—Gideon wrapped his hands around her thighs and pulled her closer, tighter, as if he didn't want to let her go.

Or perhaps he didn't want *her* to let *him* go.

"Rune . . ." He leaned her back, lowering her down to the desk. Rune wanted nothing more than for them to continue this horizontally. Except his whole body was trembling, as if he was trying to hold off something excruciating.

"Gideon. Wait." She pressed both hands to his chest. "What's wrong? I feel like I'm . . . hurting you?"

Her words seemed to break the spell. Either that, or he couldn't take the pain any longer. Gideon wrenched himself out of her embrace and stumbled back, his brand glowing ember-red through the white of his shirt. As if a scorching-hot iron were searing his skin.

Rune's breath trembled out of her.

What had Cressida *done*?

Gideon bumped into the end of a bookshelf. He grabbed hold of it, using it to steady himself while his whole body shook.

Rune pushed herself down from the desk. Wanting to go to him; unsure if she should.

"It's a curse," he said. "It's why I kissed Abbie. To find out if anyone can trigger it or just . . . you."

Rune's lips parted, but no words came out. *Me.*

"It happens when I touch you. Skin to skin."

Her blood roared in her ears. "Just me?"

He nodded.

Feeling lightheaded, she pressed a hand to the desk, letting it bear her up. "So you and I, we could never . . ."

He shook his head.

Never.

The word was like an echo in an empty cavern.

Rune pushed off the desk. Pacing. Her hands tightened into fists as a tempest welled inside her.

Gideon watched her, a conflicted expression creasing his brow.

She wanted to kill Cressida with her bare hands. How could she do this? It was so *cruel*.

More selfishly: it meant Rune could never have him.

Not that she could have him anyway. Being with Gideon was an impossibility.

But I don't repulse him.

And he hated her flirting with other people.

And he'd clung to her just now like she was a life raft in a maelstrom.

Rune stopped pacing. Lifting her chin, she drew in a deep, steady breath. Resolved.

If there's a way to break his curse, I'll find it.

THIRTY-FOUR

RUNE

"**A**RE YOU ALL RIGHT?**"** Gideon's voice echoed behind her.

All right?

She was livid.

They were on the third floor, glancing into open doorways, looking for the nursery. Edmund was long gone, and had likely found them missing by now. They needed to hurry.

Gideon caught up to her, his long strides keeping pace with her furious ones.

"Does it upset you?" he asked.

"Does what upset me?"

"That a curse makes it impossible for us to be together?"

Be together.

As if, just maybe, he wanted that.

The thought was a spark. One flaring into a fire, warming Rune from the inside out.

"Why should it upset me?" She kept her gaze straight ahead, not wanting him to see the truth in her eyes. "We could never have been together even if you weren't cursed." She kept walking. There were only three more doorways before this hall ended. "You hunt my kind, remember?"

You're hunting us even now. You're only pretending to help me so you can kill Cressida, her army, and the Roseblood heir.

Gideon reached for her arm, coaxing her to a stop and turning her to face him. "On the *Arcadia*," he said, watching her closely, "you said you would have married me, had I asked."

She saw the unspoken question in his eyes: *Is that still true?*

Rune clenched her fists. She never should have admitted that. The only thing saving her from the humiliation of that admission was that he didn't seem to believe her.

Do not tell him the truth. Do the opposite of that. The truth will only get you killed.

Rune had already made the mistake of letting down her guard with Gideon—and as a result, she'd ended up on the purging platform. She couldn't do it again. Just because she didn't repulse Gideon didn't mean he loved her.

He might be in *lust* with her, but that wasn't love. People who loved you didn't plot to betray you. Didn't try to hunt you down or wipe out your kind.

She removed his hand from her arm.

"I think we should focus on—"

Somewhere down the hall, a child started crying. Rune and Gideon glanced toward the sound: the last door on the right. Rune doubled her pace, with Gideon close behind her. When she found the door open, she stepped into the room.

A young woman stood near the window overlooking the harbor. She swayed back and forth, trying to calm the red-haired toddler in her arms. *Meadow*, Gideon had told her.

The moment the nursemaid sighted Rune, she stopped swaying.

"Who are you?" The woman drew the child closer. The crying increased.

"This is Captain Sharpe." Rune began to close the distance between them. "And I'm . . . it doesn't matter. We have orders to bring the child to the palace."

The nursemaid stepped back, increasing the distance between herself and Rune. "You'll have to take that up with my mistress. She's the child's legal guardian."

Rune cocked her head. *Legal guardian?*

It was a practice started after the revolution: taking children away from witches and giving them to non-witches to raise. Usually forever, in cases where the mothers were dead or in hiding.

Rune had burned with anger when it was first put into effect.

She burned with that same anger now.

"Our orders come from the Commander himself," said Rune, continuing forward.

The woman backed up again, straight into the windowsill. The crib stood beside her, its cloud mobile dancing softly in the breeze.

"I-I can't give her to you without permission."

Rune, who knew they were running out of time, drew her gun. "That child doesn't belong to you."

She almost heard Gideon's scowl. She was totally blowing their cover.

Rune didn't care.

"Your mistress is a thief, and that child belongs with her mother."

The servant's eyes widened at the gun, then flicked to Gideon as he moved to Rune's side.

"Better do as she says." Gideon held out his hands, stepping forward to take the child, who was watching them all with fearful blue eyes, her cries getting louder. "She's unpredictable with that thing."

Rune threw him a glare before cocking the gun, her gaze returning to the woman.

"You have three seconds before I shoot," said Rune.

Reluctantly, she handed Meadow to Gideon, who tucked her

inside his coat so *Witch's Armor* could protect her. As he retreated behind Rune, she heard him make small shushing noises.

The moment Rune followed him into the hall, the servant screamed for help.

"Intruders!" Her voice shattered the silence. "Help! HELP!"

Rune winced.

Soon, this floor would be swarming with guards.

Instead of returning the way they came, Gideon made for the servants' stairs. Rune followed, glancing over her shoulder before they descended.

Men in uniforms were heading straight for them.

"Go!" she said, pushing him faster.

He flew down the steps. The stairwell ended in the basement, near the kitchens—or so Rune assumed, judging by the sound of clattering pots and the smell of cooking onions.

Hoping Gideon knew where he was going, Rune ran after him, passing startled staff while guards thundered down the steps behind them. Gideon burst through a set of doors and together they stumbled into a massive dining room. Sunlight streamed in through the tall windows, illuminating dozens of tables set with white tablecloths. Two servants pushing dish-laden carts halted at the sight of them.

"There," said Rune, nodding to a door that led toward the front of the house.

But as they raced toward it, ignoring the servants, the doors ahead opened and several guards flooded in. Gideon halted. Rune turned back only to find more pursuers entering the doors they'd just come through.

Gideon and Rune looked to the windows. But even if they reached them, opened them, they'd be picked off before they climbed out. Already, bullets were flying. Whizzing past their heads.

One hit her shoulder. The force of it knocked her back a step. The bullet bounced off, leaving only a sting—and likely a bruise—where it hit.

At least *Witch's Armor* was holding.

Rune fired back, but couldn't tell if she hit them. She was too busy following Gideon toward the windows.

While cradling the child hidden inside his jacket with one hand, he used the other to flip a table on its side, sending a glass vase full of flowers shattering to the floor and shielding them from the guards on one side. He did the same with a second table, angling it toward the other set of guards.

Grabbing Rune's arm, he pulled her down to the floor, protecting her from the gunfire. They were safe, temporarily. But trapped. With armed guards at both exits, they couldn't run for the windows.

"Here," he said calmly, untucking Meadow from his coat and giving her to Rune. "Give me your gun."

Rune handed him her revolver and pulled the child into her lap, holding her close and softly shushing her the way Gideon had beneath the flying bullets.

When the gunfire stopped, Gideon got up from his knees to look, then raised his gun and fired in both directions, ducking down immediately after.

The return fire came fast and furious. Frightened, Meadow trembled. Rune hugged her tightly, humming a song—one of Alex's—while Gideon used his body to shield them. Rune shut her eyes, listening to the sounds of bullets splintering wood and ricocheting off walls. Trying to think of a spell to get them out of this.

But her mind was a sheet of ice. Blank with fear.

With the arrival of reinforcements, the gunfire intensified. Gideon's gloved hand cupped Rune's head, pressing her face into his shoulder. He kept her head down and out of danger as they sheltered the child between their two bodies.

"You'll be with your mother soon," he told Meadow, whose little arms were locked around Rune's neck. Gideon's voice was warm and steady despite everything falling apart around them. As if he knew precisely how to soothe frightened children even if he was also frightened. As the eldest of three, he probably did. "I won't let you get hurt. That's a promise."

But how could he promise such a thing? They were sitting ducks. If they got out of here at all, it would be in shackles.

But the warmth of his voice, the *certainty* of his words, thawed Rune's fear.

Why does he have to be so damn heroic?

It made her wonder, just for a second, what he would be like with his own children.

At that thought, a strange thing happened. An image flared before her eyes, like a waking dream. She saw a much older Gideon, playing with children. She saw it so clearly, it stole her breath.

In her vision, Gideon was maybe ten years older and chasing three children. She knew the children were his, because two had his eyes, and the third his stern mouth. The children fled through a field full of wildflowers, shrieking and laughing, trying to evade him, while Gideon pretended to let them.

The way this future Gideon beamed made Rune's heart ache. The infectious sound of his laugh made her throat prickle. She'd seen him this happy only once before, for the briefest of moments, on the night they spent together in his bed.

Whether the vision was her own imagining or she was seeing into the future the way some witches could, she didn't know. It had never happened before.

Who was he married to? Who was the mother of those children?

If there was a wife, Rune didn't see her.

The vision vanished like a sudden gale moving on to fill the sails of other ships, leaving Rune disoriented and stranded in the dining hall, the *bang! bang! bang!* of bullets hurting her ears, the acrid smell of gunpowder burning her nose as enemy shouts surrounded them on both sides.

"This is what it would be like," she realized aloud, her fist clutching the lapel of Gideon's jacket as her forehead pressed against his shoulder.

He tilted his head toward her. "What?"

"You and me. A witch and a witch hunter." She pulled away to search his face, still holding Meadow tight. "If you and I were together, they'd hunt us to the ends of the earth." She glanced down at the defenseless child in her lap. More quietly, she said, "Along with any children we might have."

As the bullets whizzed overhead, Gideon fell silent, staring at her. His hand still cupped the back of her head.

"Do you want children?" His voice was strangely quiet, at odds with the ruckus.

Rune's stomach tumbled over itself.

Why did I say that?

In truth, she'd never given much thought to her future. Never really believed she would have one. Rune had always expected to be caught and purged, if not today, then tomorrow. And if not tomorrow, at some point thereafter.

She still expected it.

But his question clanged through her.

What kind of future *did* she want? Would it involve children? A family?

It seemed preposterous to consider. She was too young. Not

to mention hunted at every turn. The world was too deadly a place.

But if it wasn't?

If she were older, and the world was different?

"I—"

Gideon reached for her chin suddenly, drawing her gaze to his. He frowned, searching her eyes. "Rune . . . did you See something?"

"What?"

"Your eyes—"

A bullet whizzed past and sank into the wooden table behind them. Gideon pulled away as if he'd been hit, hissing in pain.

Rune looked up to find blood seeping through his shirt near his shoulder.

"Gideon!"

He touched the blood with his glove, his jaw clenching. "It's just a graze. I'll be fine."

Rune was about to say it didn't look like a graze when movement made her glance over his shoulder. Edmund—the soldier she'd flirted with earlier—stood a few paces behind Gideon, his gun raised.

Rune lifted her pistol and fired first, sending a bullet into Edmund's leg. He grunted and grabbed for the wound. She fired again, forcing him out of sight.

"There's too many of them."

Gideon nodded. "Can you use that invisibility spell to get Meadow out of here?"

"What about you?" Rune frowned at the blood spreading across his shirt, hoping he was telling the truth: that it wasn't serious.

"I'll hold them off while you escape. If we all disappear, they'll know we're still in the room and shoot widely. But if I don't let them get close enough to see I'm alone, they'll think my gunfire is covering you. They'll focus their aim on me while you escape out the windows."

He was telling her to go without him.

"But how will you get out?"

He pulled a small leather satchel out of his pocket. "Don't worry about that." After digging his hand into it, his fist emerged full of bullets. They clinked and rolled as he dumped them on the floor, making them easier to grab and load. "Take Comrade and ride for Old Town. Wait for me there."

"But—"

"The key to my tenement is in my breast pocket," he said, loading his gun as enemy fire whizzed past overhead.

There was no way he'd be able to get past all those guards alone.

"I can't just leave you here!"

"Rune." Her name pulled her gaze to his. "For once in your damn life, don't fight me."

The steely look in his eyes brooked no argument. Rune glared back, knowing he was right—this was the only way to get Meadow out.

But . . .

Rune threw her arms around his neck, hugging him hard. "Promise me you'll stay alive."

When she released him, Gideon blinked in surprise.

"I'll be fine."

It was the best she was going to get. So Rune retrieved the key from his pocket and dropped it into her own. She'd have to trust him. He was a Blood Guard captain. They wouldn't kill him.

Right?

The sound of splintering wood burst in her ears. Soon the bullets would be coming through the tables shielding them.

Balancing Meadow against her chest, Rune grabbed her casting knife and made two small cuts near the back of her ankle. Using the blood beading on her skin, she drew the symbols for *Ghost Walker*, first on the back of Meadow's neck, then on her own wrist.

"*Go*," said Gideon when the spell took effect.

He stood up and started shooting with both guns.

Rune hugged Meadow close as she moved for the windows, staying low to the ground. Arriving at the nearest one, she waited for Gideon to reload and start firing before unlatching and swinging it open.

With all attention in the room fixed on the Blood Guard captain, she lifted Meadow into the window frame, then followed her up.

After dropping down into the gardens below, Rune carried Meadow right through the front gates, slipping unseen past the house guards now on high alert as the sound of gunfire echoed in the house beyond them.

She headed for the water, where Gideon's horse waited, glancing back only once at the yellow house.

You better know what you're doing.

Untying Comrade from his post, she mounted, then kicked the horse into a canter, leaving her heart behind in that dining room, with the boy risking his life so she and a child could escape.

THIRTY-FIVE

GIDEON

GIDEON FIRED, RELOADED, AND fired again. Over and over. Trying to buy Rune as much time as she needed while he dodged enemy bullets.

The air was clouded with smoke from the gunfire, choking out the smell of Rune's magic.

Before knowing she was a witch, Gideon hadn't been able to detect the scent. Unlike Cressida's magic—which smelled strongly of blood and roses—the scent of Rune's blended into the island. It smelled like sea salt and woodsmoke and fresh-cut juniper.

For some reason, the thought of Rune's magic made Gideon think of her mouth. The way it yielded to his in that library. The things it nearly admitted.

He was thinking about how, now that he wasn't allowed to have her, she was all he wanted. Maybe he was destined to want things forever out of his reach.

And her eyes just now . . .

When she'd looked up at him a moment ago, her eyes had reminded him of Aurelia's after she'd just had a vision. Clouded and pale.

But that can't be right. Can it?

He was still thinking about Rune as he ran out of bullets. With no more ammunition, Gideon threw down the guns and raised his hands high, rising from the barricade he'd made.

"I surrender," he called into the smoke-filled room.

The gunfire stopped. He heard someone give an order, and seconds later, several guards emerged from the gloom.

"Where's your comrade?" one asked, keeping his gun trained on Gideon as he glanced behind the barricade. "And the child?"

Gideon shrugged. "No idea."

He didn't struggle as they arrested him.

THEY BROUGHT HIM STRAIGHT to Blood Guard headquarters, which had been relocated after Cressida blew up the original building two months ago. They were now situated in an old stone citadel on the cliffs overlooking the harbor.

As the guards led Gideon through the darkened walkways, the torch flames flickered, fighting against the wind and the damp from the sea.

They marched him into the old war room, with its stained-glass windows running down the length of both sides. A young woman in uniform stood across the long stone table.

Laila Creed.

She was acting captain in Gideon's absence.

Harrow stood beside her. The spymaster planted her hands on the table, staring down at whatever Laila was looking at.

At Gideon's entrance, they glanced up.

"Sharpe?" Seeing Gideon's shackled hands, Laila's dark brows creased. She looked at the guard who escorted him in. "What is this?"

"He was caught trespassing, kidnapping, and firing on security. A second Blood Guard officer was with him. She escaped with the hostage."

Even from halfway across the room, Gideon saw the nerve in Laila's jaw jump.

"What hostage?"

"Meadow Kantor. The sibyl's child."

"Thank you," said Laila, her face darkening.

"Do you want us to take him to—"

"No. Leave him, along with the keys to those manacles. Then you may go."

One guard stepped forward, sliding the keys down the stone table to Laila. She waited until their footsteps disappeared down the hall before turning her full attention to Gideon.

"What the hell, Sharpe. *Again?*"

"I need to speak with Noah."

"Noah's at Wintersea. You'll have to deal with me."

An awkward tension filled the room. It had always been Gideon who gave the orders, and Laila who obeyed them. Now things were reversed, and her stiff posture said she felt weirder about it than he did.

"Then I need you to take these off," he said, lifting his shackled wrists, "and let me go."

"*Gideon*," Laila said through gritted teeth. "They said you broke into someone's house! And helped steal a baby! Who was with you? Or do I even need to ask?"

Gideon evaded the question. "What you need to do is trust me."

She pressed her lips together and crossed her arms. "Why should any of us trust you ever again?"

Gideon flinched. It was because of him that Laila's father, the previous Good Commander, had been killed by Cressida. He was the reason the witch queen was back and threatening them with war. The reason they were all in danger. If he hadn't let Rune trick him, if he hadn't let himself fall for her, he could have eliminated Cressida long before now.

"I bear the blame for it all," he said. "And that's why I have to make it right. But I can't do that in chains—or with you set against me."

"The Crimson Moth was with you, wasn't she?"

This came from Harrow. Gideon forced himself to look at her. If trust was strained between him and Laila, it was nonexistent between him and Harrow.

"The soldier who escaped with the hostage," she pressed. "It was Rune, wasn't it?"

He looked away.

After a moment, Laila said: "Answer the question, Sharpe."

"Yes," he breathed. "It was Rune."

Laila pressed the heels of her palms to her eyes. "*Gideon.* Why do you have such a weakness for that girl? Rune Winters is bad news! If she manipulated you once, you can bet—"

"I'm well aware."

No matter how badly he wanted to, he'd be a fool to trust Rune again, just as she'd be a fool to trust him. "I was using her to get the child."

Laila glared at him from across the stone table, clearly skeptical. But she said nothing. So Gideon continued.

"Noah promised not to interfere with my plans."

"Yes, well, Noah didn't watch you fall for the charms of a manipulative witch only a few months ago. He doesn't realize—"

"I promised the Commander I would deliver Rune to the Blood Guard," he said, interrupting, "*after* I kill the Roseblood heir. The only way to do that is to learn Rune's plans. I need Rune to believe I'm on her side. I need her to trust me."

"And if you're playing right into her hands?" This came from Harrow, who stood with her fists on her hips, looking utterly unconvinced. "She's the one who told you she's here to find the heir. What if it's a lie? What if Cressida sent her to recruit more witches to their cause and attack us from the inside?"

Laila glanced at Gideon, awaiting his answer. But Gideon had none. He himself had wondered this.

"If you have a better plan," said Gideon, "I'd love to hear it."

Judging by their silence, they didn't.

"Cressida killed my entire family," he said. "I have no sympathy for her cause. I want her stopped. I want her *dead*." He strained against his manacles. "By standing here arguing with me, you're only preventing me from accomplishing that. I promised Noah I'd deliver the dead heir *and* Rune Winters into Blood Guard hands. Now release me, so I can make good on that promise."

Laila chewed her lip. "And if Harrow's right, and Rune's playing you? If you get caught in her trap?"

"If I'm caught," he said, smiling at her, "you'll rescue me."

She slit her eyes at him. For several moments, they stared each other down.

Laila glanced away first. Sighing, she grabbed the keys off the table.

"*Fine.* But keep me abreast of your plans. You want out of those manacles? Tell us what you're planning, so we can assist you—or at the very least, prevent you from getting arrested next time."

So Gideon did.

THIRTY-SIX

RUNE

RUNE WAITED THREE HOURS for Gideon to show up. When the sun set and there was still no sign of him, she rocked Meadow to sleep and put her in his bed. Then she found the closet where Gideon kept several spare weapons and boxes full of bullets. She loaded two guns and set them down on the table, in easy reach. In case the Blood Guard showed up.

This was a terrible idea. She drummed her fingers against her leg as she paced. *What was he thinking?*

What was *she* thinking?

I shouldn't have left him.

What if he didn't make it out alive?

When another half hour passed and the apartment grew dark, Rune lit several candles to see by. She considered leaving the sleeping Meadow with a neighbor so she could find out what happened to Gideon and rescue him if need be.

Footsteps on the stairs made her freeze. Rune picked up one of the loaded pistols and aimed it at the door, her body buzzing as she listened to the sound of a key turning in the latch.

Rune's grip tightened on the gun.

But when the door swung open, Gideon stood in the frame.

The sight of him undid every knot in her body. She let out a breath, glancing to the dried blood on his jacket.

Gideon's gaze swept down her, pausing at the pistol lowered to her side. "Are you all right?"

"Am *I* all right?" Rune started for him, drawn like a magnet.

Wanting to fling her arms around him and hug him tight. "Are you hurt? How—"

A woman stepped out from behind him.

Rune halted.

The woman's clothes hung off her thin frame, as if she hadn't eaten in weeks, and her hair hung in limp strings down her back and shoulders. Beneath the grime, Rune guessed her hair was a deep shade of coppery red. Her sunken eyes frantically scanned the room.

"Where's Meadow?"

Oh.

This was Aurelia Kantor.

"She's sleeping," said Rune. "In the bedroom."

She pointed to Gideon's room. The sibyl swept past her, disappearing through the doorway beyond.

As Gideon shut the door, Rune went to him.

"How did you get out?"

"I surrendered to the guards." He studied the long skirt and blouse she'd changed into—fit for riding long distances. In her anxious state, she'd forgotten to button the cuffs of her sleeves. Noticing, he tugged off his riding gloves, tucked them into his pocket, and buttoned them for her—first one wrist, then the other. "They brought me to Laila. After that, it was simply a matter of talking my way out."

That's it? But of course it was probably all part of his plan to betray her. Before she could press him, the floorboards creaked behind them.

Rune turned to find Aurelia cradling Meadow as she emerged from the bedroom.

"The captain says you wanted to see me," said Aurelia.

Realizing how close she and Gideon stood, Rune quickly stepped back, turning away from him. But it was too late. The expression on the sibyl's face said she'd noticed precisely what Rune hadn't wanted her to.

Rune cleared her throat. "That's right." She set her pistol down on the table and paused. Hadn't she loaded two? She scanned the room, looking for the second gun.

"Who are you?"

"My name is Rune Winters. Our enemies"—Rune glanced at Gideon—"call me the Crimson Moth."

"*The Crimson Moth?*" Aurelia's eyebrows arched. "Well, if we're playing games, then I'm the witch queen herself."

She didn't believe Rune.

It wouldn't have mattered, except Rune needed her trust. And her help. So she slid her casting knife from its sheath at her thigh beneath her skirt. Nicking her skin, Rune drew the symbol for *Torch* on her open palm. A flame ignited several inches above it, and a few seconds later, over Rune's head, a casting mark appeared in the air, shaped like a blood-red moth.

"Proof enough for you?"

The skeptical look on Aurelia's face vanished.

Rune fisted her hand, smudging the mark, and the flame extinguished.

"What do you want from me?" said Aurelia, glancing between her and Gideon.

"I need your help with a summoning spell."

The spell was a Majora, which meant Rune needed the blood of someone else—given willingly—to cast it. Hers alone wouldn't suffice.

"And why should I help you?" asked Aurelia, kissing Meadow's cheek, holding on tight as the child clung to her.

"To make amends for all the deaths you're responsible for?" suggested Rune.

The sibyl's eyes flashed.

"And because if you help me, I can get you and Meadow safely off this island."

She saw Aurelia silently making the calculation. It was too good an offer to refuse, and they both knew it.

"How soon?"

"That depends on you, I suppose. The spell can only be cast from one location, and it will take several hours to ride there."

"I'm ready when you are," said Aurelia.

Rune nodded. "Then let's go."

But as Aurelia turned for the door, clutching Meadow to her, Gideon stepped in front of it. His attention fixed on the sibyl. "You're forgetting something."

Aurelia glared at him. "And what's that?"

"I promised to deliver your child safely to you. You promised me answers."

"Don't you think you've tormented me enough?" she said, trying to go around him.

Gideon crossed his arms over his chest, blocking her way. "We had a deal, Aurelia."

Rune glanced from one to the other. *This* was why he had helped rescued Meadow? Not because it was the right thing to do, but because he'd been promised something in exchange?

Her mouth soured.

"If you think I owe you *anything*—"

"What deal?" interrupted Rune.

Gideon glanced at her. That's all it took—a second's distraction—for Aurelia to act. The witch drew the missing gun and pressed the barrel under Gideon's chin.

He froze as she cocked it. Which was when Rune realized he was unarmed. All Aurelia had to do was pull the trigger—and from the look on her face, she would do it with relish.

"I'll give you one minute to say your goodbyes, Captain."

With the gun's barrel still pressed beneath his chin, Gideon held Rune's gaze, his jaw clenched.

Aurelia's next move was plain on her face. She was going to shoot Gideon and leave him for dead. It was safest that way. If he was dead, he couldn't follow them.

Rune agreed with Aurelia's logic. And if it were any other witch hunter barring the door, she might have done it herself.

But it was Gideon.

Even though he was plotting to betray her, even though he would try to follow them—she knew he would—Rune couldn't let him die.

He was Alex's brother.

He'd been tortured and cursed by a cruel witch queen.

More importantly: she loved him, despite a million reasons not to.

So before Aurelia fired, Rune reached for the second gun, still on the table, and aimed it straight at the witch.

Aurelia shot her a startled look. "Stupid girl!" Her eyes burned like green fire. "Whatever he's made you believe, it isn't true." Aurelia cradled Meadow with one arm, still holding the gun beneath Gideon's chin. "He's going to betray you. He has no other choice. If he lets you go, they'll execute him."

Execute him?

The words rippled through Rune.

She knew the laws had changed. There was no longer leniency for sympathizing with witches. But *execution*?

Aurelia pressed the gun harder, forcing Gideon's chin upward.

Rune lifted her second hand to her own gun, gripping it tightly. Keeping it trained on Aurelia. To Gideon, she said: "Step away from the door."

With his hands in the air, Gideon glanced at Aurelia, as if he suspected she'd shoot him anyway. But her child was in the line of fire; she wouldn't risk it. Or so Rune hoped.

Slowly he backed away from her.

To Aurelia, Rune said: "Take Meadow downstairs and wait for me outside."

Aurelia scowled her disapproval, pushed open the door with her hip, then stepped out, leaving Rune and Gideon alone.

Rune lowered the gun.

"I heard your conversation with William in the cargo hold," she said. "I know what you're planning. You're going to follow me, kill the Roseblood heir, then arrest me so you can barter with Soren. Do you deny it?"

Gideon dragged his hands through his hair, turning it into a ragged mess.

"No," he said, heaving a sigh. "I don't deny it."

"Is that still your plan?" she asked him. *After everything?*

He dropped his hands to his sides. "What would you have me do, Rune? Let you escape? If our positions were reversed, you'd be planning the same."

She shook her head. "That's not true."

"No?" He stepped toward her. At his proximity, a tiny bell rang in alarm: *danger, danger.* "Then tell me, what *would* you do?"

Rune stepped back. "I already told you. I'm going to find the last living Roseblood and get them away from Cressida. Then I'm going to break off the engagement with Soren and sever the alliance."

"And if it doesn't work? If Soren decides he has a taste for war despite your broken promises? If Cressida hunts you and this Roseblood down and drags you both back?"

"I . . ."

His presence scrambled her thoughts.

"I . . . don't know."

"Because you don't *have* to know," he growled at her. "All three witch queens back on their thrones would be a boon to you—not horror and misery. If it's a Reign of Terror for everyone else, what's that to you . . . right, Rune?"

That wasn't true or fair.

"What am I supposed to do? Side with *you*?" She raised the gun again, keeping it cocked and ready to fire. The way he'd shown her. "You want me dead, just like every other Blood Guard soldier."

He opened his mouth to respond, but she cut him off.

"Not every witch is a monster, Gideon. Most of us aren't."

He took another step. Rune narrowed her eyes. If he came much closer, she'd be forced to shoot.

"And yet," he growled, "you did nothing while people suffered under witches like Cressida. None of you did."

Rune swallowed. This was true. She might not have known the kinds of cruelty suffered by people like Gideon and countless others at the hands of powerful witches. But her grandmother surely had, as had Nan's friends, all of whom Rune had admired.

Too many witches had done nothing when they should have stood against it.

"Should I hand myself over in penance?" she asked him. "Give you the honor of marching me to the purging platform?"

Gideon looked away, as if remembering he'd done exactly that.

Aurelia was right. She still couldn't trust him. He was still planning to betray her.

He was in too deep not to.

If Gideon let Rune save the witches she'd come here to save, if he let Rune escape, he would betray everything he believed in—his friends and fellow soldiers, the citizens he'd sworn to protect, the Republic he'd fought so hard for.

Rune wasn't a fool. He wouldn't choose *her* over all of that. If he did, they would kill him.

It didn't matter what he'd admitted in the yellow house. None of it mattered. Rune knew he would never choose her. He *couldn't*. Not even if he wanted to.

The thought sobered her. *Sharpened* her.

This is almost over.

All she needed to do was stay a few steps ahead. For a few hours longer.

Rune kept her gun aimed at his chest.

This is where we part ways.

"Don't try to follow me," she said.

Gideon said nothing. But Rune read him as easily as he read her, and the look in his eyes said: *I wish I could say that I won't.*

THIRTY-SEVEN

RUNE

WHEN THEY ARRIVED AT the towering circle of stones, it was shortly after midnight.

Rune and Aurelia had stolen two horses from the city stables and cloaked them all in Rune's *Ghost Walker* spell, hoping to make it impossible for Gideon to follow.

The look in his eyes when she left haunted her the whole way.

The eerie stone silhouettes loomed over Rune like giants, blacking out the stars. The air here smelled like magic. Deep and primal. It made Rune's skin tingle. As if the Ancients had been here mere moments before. As if *this* was the doorway they'd used to exit the world.

Not that Rune believed such things.

But some people did. The Cult of the Ancients, for example—a group of religious fanatics—believed this summoning circle was once used to draw the Ancients forth, back when they *could* be summoned. According to them, the Ancients—or the Seven Sisters, as the cult sometimes referred to them—had been gone too long now, slumbering too deeply, to answer anyone's call.

It was a nice story to tell children at bedtime. But if the Ancients were real, if they'd ever walked in this world they'd created, Rune would have seen proof of their existence by now.

No. If these old stones made her feel things, it was because regular witches had been casting their powerful spells here for centuries. What Rune sensed in this place was merely the echo of their magic, not the lingering presence of deities.

On a nearby hill sat the ruins of a once magnificent temple belonging to the Cult of the Ancients. The temple had been destroyed during the revolution, and its priestesses and acolytes killed or chased into hiding. From where she stood among the summoning stones, all Rune could see of the temple ruins was a half-crumbled wall.

Rune and Aurelia wasted no time. They cast the summoning spell beneath the moonlight while Meadow slept on a bed of moss. Rune had learned the spell while studying under Seraphine, but had never put it to use.

Rune opened her locket and took out the bit of Cressida's hair, placing it in the circle's center. Aurelia took her casting knife and made a small cut in her shoulder, adding to the silvery pattern of casting scars there. Using the blood she supplied, Rune drew the symbols.

"Now what?" Aurelia asked afterward, scanning the deep shadows surrounding them.

Rune looked skyward, to the stars shining overhead.

"Now we wait."

It could take up to twelve hours for the summoned to arrive. And since there was nothing left to do except wait, they slept.

THIRTY-EIGHT

GIDEON

GIDEON CROUCHED AGAINST THE ruined temple wall, trying not to get drenched by the rain. From here, he had a clear view of the valley below. Or he would have, if the storm hadn't moved in. Now, to see anything inside the summoning stones, he had to squint through the gloom.

Yonder, the hunting hound who'd led him to this desecrated place, lay in the dirt nearby, lifting his head every once in a while to stare into the shadows, making Gideon hope this wasn't a trap set for *him*.

Yonder had tracked Rune to this valley using the scent of her blood, which was still smeared on Gideon's jacket from her protective spell.

Gideon had watched Aurelia and Rune cast the spell a few hours ago, then retreat to a small cave to wait. Ever since, the summoning circle had remained empty—except for the tiny crimson moth glowing at its center, declaring Rune's spell active.

A headache was starting in Gideon's temples, either from the storm's pressure or from straining so hard to see. He was just leaning back to give his eyes a rest when movement at the circle's edge jolted him forward.

If not for the white glow, he might have missed her.

Rune stepped into the circle. From her slow, lumbering steps, she seemed to be sleepwalking—or perhaps in some kind of trance. And all around her, in a protective, luminous circle, hundreds of white lights glowed like fireflies.

Gideon frowned, watching as she climbed onto the flat stone at the center of the summoning circle and lay down on its mossy surface. There, she curled onto her side and fell still, her hair fanning out around her.

One by one, the glimmering lights settled all over her body, glowing brighter and brighter. Until she was more glow than girl.

Her signature—the blood-red moth fluttering above her—flared like a simmering coal, and abruptly went out. Declaring the spell finished.

The white glow vanished, leaving Rune alone in the dark and rain.

All at once, a horrifying realization struck.

"Merciful Ancients," Gideon whispered, his heart squeezing painfully.

Rune was the missing heir.

THIRTY-NINE

RUNE

*R*UNE WAS DREAMING OF Gideon again.

This dream, though, couldn't have been more different from the first. Instead of in a hot, steamy boiler room, Rune stood in the rain, the damp cold seeping through her clothes.

Across from her stood Gideon. Water glistened in his dark hair and trickled down his face.

Rune was overcome with an urge to go to him. To press her cheek against his chest and listen to the beat of his heart while he held her.

Before she could, Gideon raised his gun.

Rune froze, her pulse pounding.

Surely he wouldn't. Not after everything they'd admitted to each other.

He cocked the gun, aiming it at her chest.

I'm sorry, his eyes seemed to say. *I wish it didn't have to end like this.*

But hadn't she always known it would?

There was nowhere to run. There was no escape. Nothing to do but accept this.

BANG!

RUNE GASPED, BOLTING UPRIGHT. Her chest heaved as she gulped down air. She glanced at her chest, pressing her hand to her thundering heart, where she'd felt the dream bullet go in.

There was nothing there. No blood. No pain.

She was fine.

Just . . . soaking wet.

Glancing around, Rune found herself lying on a smooth, flat stone inside the summoning circle, the other stones towering around her. At some point, a storm had come through and drenched everything, but it was gone now, taking the night with it.

The sun was high in the sky.

Rune's shoulders sagged with relief.

It was only a dream.

She still saw his face, though. Full of apology. The *bang* still rang in her ears, and a strange heat burned in her chest where the bullet had lodged.

It felt like her vision of Gideon and the three children. Like a glimpse into the future.

Rune shivered.

Aurelia walked across the circle toward her. Only the hem of her skirt was wet; the rest of her was dry. From the sleepy look in her eyes, she'd just woken up.

Before falling asleep, they had all taken shelter in a dugout beneath some broken stones beyond the summoning circle. So what was Rune doing here, *inside* the circle?

"Bad dreams?" asked Aurelia, studying Rune's eyes, as if recognizing something in them.

"Something like that."

Rune wiped the rain off her face and got to her knees. How much time had passed? She glanced up, searching for her spell's signature overhead.

But the once bright-red moth had vanished.

Rune frowned.

"Looks like your spell faded," said Aurelia.

"Maybe I didn't cast it right?"

Should she have collected some of Cressida's blood, instead? Would that have made for a stronger spell?

"It's possible," said Aurelia. "It's also possible the ancient magic protecting this Roseblood from my Sight protects them from being summoned."

They waited a few more hours.

When Meadow woke and started to cry, Aurelia tried to soothe her, pacing and rocking the girl in her arms.

"She's hungry."

But they had no food to give her.

We need to get back to the capital.

Rune glanced around the empty circle, trying to swallow her disappointment.

Why hadn't anyone come?

Aurelia's probably right, she thought, trying to console herself. *And if I can't summon the Roseblood heir, neither can Cressida.*

Or so she hoped.

Right now, Rune needed to focus on the tasks at hand: finding Meadow some food and getting them all off the island.

"Gideon is expecting us to escape aboard the *Arcadia*," explained Rune as she went to fetch their horses. "Which means the Blood Guard will be watching the main harbor—and the *Arcadia* in particular."

"What's your plan, then?"

"They won't be looking for a smaller vessel. If there's only three of us, a sailboat will work just fine."

Aurelia looked skeptical. "It'll take a week to cross the Barrow Strait in a sailboat."

"Five days, actually," Rune corrected her. "If the wind is with us."

"And you have a boat?"

"Sort of." *Dawn's Aria* was sitting unused in the harbor. "It belongs to . . . to a friend of mine. He won't miss it." She glanced at Meadow, yowling with hunger. "We'll need to stock it with provisions first."

FORTY

GIDEON

*R*UNE IS THE MISSING *heir.*
     The adopted granddaughter of Kestrel Winters was a Roseblood princess. Daughter to Queen Winoa. Half sister to Cressida.

Heir to the Roseblood throne.

And no one knew.

Gideon's mind was a tempest as Comrade's hooves thundered down dirt roads, racing back to the capital.

If Cressida learns of this . . .

But Gideon had a bigger problem.

I'm giving you two days to come through on your promises. Noah's voice echoed through his head. *If the Crimson Moth slips through your fingers once again, I'll have to assume it's intentional.*

Tomorrow was the deadline. Gideon had promised to hand over Rune *and* the heir. If he didn't come through . . .

If you fail, you'll be accused of sympathizing with witches and put in a cell to await execution.

There was still time to arrest Rune before she left. He could tell Noah the truth: Rune and the Roseblood heir were the same person.

He could come through on every promise.

But if I tell the truth, Noah will kill her.

It's what Gideon himself had planned to do.

And if I don't tell the truth?

If he handed Rune over to Noah and kept her secret to himself . . . would Noah kill *him*?

Gideon might still be able to talk himself out of a death sentence. Rune's arrest could be enough to satisfy the Commander. Especially if Soren eliminated Cressida and her witches in exchange for the safe delivery of his fiancée.

Laila would back him up, he was certain.

But Rune would never forgive him. Not for handing her back to Soren. Not for bartering with her to get more witches killed. It was betrayal, pure and simple.

And if I don't betray her?

The unthinkable would occur: Cressida would wage a war, win back her throne, and usher in a new reign of terror. One Gideon wouldn't even live to see, because Noah would execute him first.

And if Cressida ever learns who Rune is . . . if she casts that summoning spell herself . . .

Gideon's heels dug into Comrade, urging the horse to go faster.

There was only one choice he could possibly make.

Before he did, there was someone he needed to talk to.

FORTY-ONE

RUNE

WHEN RUNE AND AURELIA arrived at the small harbor where Alex's sailboat was anchored, the harbor front was swarming with Blood Guard soldiers. So Aurelia and Meadow hid nearby while Rune went to check the boat.

Rune slipped into the cold water, careful to keep out of sight as she swam to *Dawn's Aria*. After pulling herself over the boat's side, Rune realized she'd forgotten to leave Gideon's pistol behind and had lost it somewhere in the water.

She'd never find it now. It was at the bottom of the sea.

Cursing her carelessness, Rune went belowdecks, careful not to slip on the wood plank floors with her wet feet. Inside, she found a barrel full of water and blew out a relieved breath, silently thanking Alex for keeping his boat stocked. If they had enough water for the voyage, all they needed was a bit of food—for Meadow, especially.

But where will I find food at this hour?

It was after dusk. No grocers or markets were open.

I don't have much food. Gideon's voice rushed through her head. *Just some apples and hardtack under the sink.*

The key to his tenement building was in her skirt pocket.

Fear flickered through her at the thought of sneaking into his apartment and stealing his food. But if they rationed it, apples and hardtack would be enough to sustain them for the five-day voyage.

Rune didn't have any better options.

Even if he's there, he won't turn me in. He'll wait. He'll want to capture as many witches as possible.

It did little to reassure her. But Rune had an obligation to Aurelia and Meadow. She needed to get them out *tonight*.

Steeling herself, Rune dove back into the sea.

If I'm lucky, she thought as she swam for the wharf, *he won't even be home.*

FORTY-TWO

GIDEON

*T*HE MOON WAS RISING as Gideon strode through the cemetery, its pale light making the gravestones around him gleam. Four white stones stood in a line, a little away from the rest, beckoning him.

Sun Sharpe. Beloved wife and mother.

Levi Sharpe. Doting husband and father.

Tessa Sharpe. A bright light extinguished too soon.

His fingers trailed the stones until he came to the fourth.

Alexander Sharpe. Dearest brother and friend.

Everyone he'd ever loved was right here. Several feet underground.

Dropping to his knees in the upturned soil, Gideon pressed his hand to the cold stone of Alex's grave. Despite having dug this grave himself only two months ago, it was still a shock finding his brother here.

"I know you're not happy with me," he said. "And I'm sorry about that. Everything I've done, I did because I thought it was the right choice."

Well, except for Rune. He'd been utterly selfish when it came to Rune.

Which was why he was here.

Gideon ran his free hand roughly over his stubbled jaw. His breath shuddered out of him. "I know you loved her, Alex."

Gideon closed his eyes.

"I hope you'll forgive me."

Behind him, the crunch of boots on pine needles broke the silence. Gideon tensed, listening. As his hand reached for his pistol—the last one left in his apartment after Rune and Aurelia stole the others—a voice spoke from behind him.

"Sorry to interrupt, Comrade."

Harrow.

He stood and turned to face her. Light and shadow flickered across her as the wind blew through the graveyard, shaking the trees and scattering moonlight everywhere. "I got your telegram. Laila gave the order to double security along the waterfront. Nothing is getting out of Republic waters tonight."

Gideon nodded. "Good. And the soldiers?"

"They're waiting for you at the Crow's Nest, per your request."

"Perfect."

He waited for her to leave so he could return to paying his respects, but Harrow only stood there. Her face was hard to read on any given day, but tonight, the shadows made her impenetrable.

Gideon arched a brow. "Is there something else?"

She kept silent a moment, as if deliberating.

"The Commander has, let's say, a lack of affection for you, Comrade. He will happily kill you if she escapes again."

He was well aware of Noah's resentment. "Those were the terms I agreed to."

More silence filled the gap between them. But still, she didn't turn to leave.

Gideon studied her more closely until he figured out the problem.

Harrow—who barely spoke to him these days unless it was

to snap, who barely looked at him unless it was to scowl—was *worried* about him.

"There was a slight hitch in my plans," he told her. "But everything is on track. I'll handle this. Don't worry."

Despite not looking reassured, she gave a quick nod and moved to leave, heading for the path. As she turned, the moonlight spotlighted the side of her head, illuminating the scar from her missing ear.

"Harrow? You've never told me your story."

She glanced back. He nodded toward her missing ear.

"What happened?" he asked. "Before the revolution."

"Maybe I'll tell you one day."

"You should tell me tonight, in case your fears come true and Noah has the reason he needs to dispose of me."

This made her pause. Instead of walking away, she pulled herself up onto a bigger gravestone, perching there and letting her legs hang down, obscuring the name of the deceased.

"My parents were poor as dirt," she said, gripping the edge. "They had too many debts, and too many children to feed. I was the youngest and most useless of seven, so they sold me."

Gideon frowned, wanting to contradict this: Harrow was nothing if not resourceful. He stayed quiet, though, coming to lean against the gravestone next to her.

"They indentured me to a wealthy witch family, who treated me fine, I suppose. At least, at first."

Harrow's voice, which was only ever biting and sarcastic, suddenly softened.

"Their daughter, Juniper, taught me to read and write. She even shared her favorite books with me: novels, operas, plays. The more fanciful, the better." A strange glow lit up her face as she spoke. Gideon had never seen her look like that. "She would read to me in the evenings, and sometimes in the afternoons, if the weather was nice and if I could abandon my chores without being noticed. We would sit in the trees and recite poetry and plays to each other."

Isn't that the point of art—to tame the monsters in us?

It was something Harrow said to him not so long ago. He'd assumed she was quoting some book at him, to mock him, and hadn't given it a second thought.

"You loved her," he realized.

Harrow flinched, ashamed to be caught out. As if loving a witch was a criminal offense.

"When her family realized, they did *this*." She pointed to the spot where an ear should be. "They hoped to make me unpalatable to her. Maybe I should be thankful they didn't have the stomach to take my eyes, or my nose. That probably would have done the trick."

Her jaw clenched, but she continued.

"They threw me in the cellar and locked the door. They probably hoped I'd bleed to death." Her hands fidgeted in her lap as she picked at her fingernails, already bitten to the quick. "I thought Juniper would rescue me. She'd never spoken her feelings outright. Hadn't made any declarations of love. But I'd *hoped* . . ."

She fisted her hands.

"I kept waiting for her to come, but the door never opened. I stayed alive by catching drops of water from a leaking pipe, waiting to die of starvation." She squeezed her eyes shut. "When the door finally opened, I thought I was hallucinating. It wasn't my mistress; it was a soldier in a red uniform. He said the Sister Queens were dead, and the Reign of Witches was over. He said I was free."

Uncurling her fists, she stared down at her open palms. "Strange thing was, I didn't feel free."

Gideon touched her shoulder. "Harrow. I'm sorry."

She shrugged, and his hand fell back to his side. "We all have our scars, Comrade." Glancing up at him, she held his gaze. "But I don't have to tell you that, do I?"

She slipped down from the gravestone and returned to the path.

"Don't forget whose side you're on tonight." Her voice echoed back to him. "Or there will be worse scars to come."

FORTY-THREE

RUNE

GIDEON WASN'T HOME WHEN she arrived at his apartment. So Rune moved quickly. She needed to be long gone before he returned. The sooner she rejoined Aurelia and Meadow, the better.

Rune was still wet from her swim. Her ice-cold hands shook as she rummaged through his cupboards, stopping only when she found the sack of apples and the bag of hardtack. She'd hauled them out and was about to sling them over her shoulder when a creaking floorboard made her freeze.

"First, you steal my gun. Now, I find you breaking into my apartment and taking my food."

Rune shot to her feet, spinning to face him.

Gideon leaned against the door frame, still in uniform. Watching her. "Were you going to leave without saying goodbye?"

Her heart galloped in her chest.

Is this it? Would he arrest her now? Or would he wait to betray her, expecting a cargo hold full of witches, including the Roseblood heir?

Rune drew her casting knife, gripping it in front of her. Gideon's gaze flickered to the blade and back to her face.

Realizing her stolen gun was gone, he moved like a predator, descending on her. She slashed the air with her knife in warning. But he only grabbed her wrist, holding it away from himself.

"*You* are far worse than a thorn in my side," he said, his dark eyes gleaming at her. "You are a knife in my heart."

His voice was low and dangerous, making the hair on her arms rise. But at odds with his voice were his gloved fingers, which lifted to her throat. Rune let out a soft gasp as he gently traced the arc of her neck.

"And you're a wolf I can't outrun," she whispered, closing her eyes against his touch. "Not even in my sleep."

His hand went still, prompting her eyes to open.

"Dreaming about me again?" He cocked an eyebrow, as if this pleased him. With his grip still tight on her wrist, he leaned in, his breath warm against her cold lips, making her heart beat in triple time. "How often do you dream of me, Rune?"

The look in his eyes made her ache with longing.

More often than I'd like.

Seeing how she shivered, Gideon let go of her wrist. When Rune didn't lash out with her knife, he tugged off his jacket and dropped it over her shoulders.

Rune glared at him. How *dare* he be kind on the eve of his betrayal.

After pulling it snug around her, he tugged her toward him, doing up the top few buttons. Ensnaring her further.

Her fingers tightened around the hilt of her knife.

Are reinforcements on the way? Is that why he's delaying me?

Was his plan to seduce her until they arrived?

Rune was trapped. She couldn't get past him—not if he didn't want her to. The only way to escape was to lower his defenses. And to do that, she needed to play the same game he was playing. One last time.

Rune ran her free hand up his chest, resting her palm against the scar beneath his shirt. Gideon glanced down, watching her. To Rune's surprise, his gloved hand slid over hers, linking their fingers together and keeping her palm pressed to his heart.

Their intertwined fingers filled Rune with a strange and terrible yearning.

"Will you miss me, Crimson Moth?"

She swallowed. "How can you ask me that?"

"Is that a yes?"

Normally, Rune could tell when he was plotting something. Tonight, he was impossible to read.

"Where will you go?"

He was a fool if he expected her to answer that.

"Somewhere you'll never find me."

Gideon stepped closer, until there was less than an inch of space between them. The heat of him called to Rune's cold and trembling body. How easy it would be to step into his arms and let him warm her completely.

Rune mentally shook herself.

No.

If she walked down this path, she wouldn't be able to walk herself back. She'd walk herself straight into another one of his traps.

"I'll miss you the way a fox misses the wolf's snapping jaws," she said.

His mouth curved at her words. "I can't tell if you're insulting me, or flirting with me." He slid a gloved hand behind her neck, tipping her chin upward with his thumb so her mouth tilted to his.

She knew what he was about to do.

The worst thing was, she *wanted* him to do it.

Rune lifted her knife to his throat. Trying to stand firm against the snare of him. "Don't you dare."

Gideon leaned in anyway, calling her bluff as his mouth descended on hers. His free hand slid into her hair, pulling her closer, lips parting hers.

His kiss made her ache in all the usual places. But it also made her ache somewhere new.

What if this is really goodbye?

She dropped her knife and kissed him back.

Gideon's mouth turned devouring. Rune untucked his shirt from his trousers and slid her hands up his bare chest. She pressed a palm to his scar, which was already heating against her touch. He shivered and grabbed hold of her thighs, lifting her onto his hips, pulling her securely against him.

Rune's blood hummed.

This is a trick, she reminded herself, *meant to keep me here until the Blood Guard show up.*

She forced herself to remember Aurelia and Meadow down at the harbor. The two people she'd sworn to get safely across the Barrow Strait. They were waiting for her. She couldn't fail them. Not when she was so close.

He's trying to delay me. This is a distraction. The prelude to a trap waiting to spring closed.

But not even this was enough to snap her out of her madness.

It was Gideon who did that. Trembling a little from the pain of his curse, he lowered her from his hips. Taking her hand in his, he drew the pistol from his holster and pressed it against her palm.

"Promise me you won't lose this one," he whispered, his cheek rough against hers.

Rune glanced up at him.

What?

But he was already stepping away. Leaving his gun in her hand.

"And if someone tries to hurt you," he said, "and there's no other way to stop them, don't think twice. Just shoot. Got it?"

She frowned, watching him pick up her casting knife from the floor, then sheath it in his belt. As if they'd made a trade.

He didn't close the gap again. Just stood to the side, leaving her path to the door wide open.

He wasn't even trying to stop her.

Because he has soldiers on the way. They're probably already here.

"I'll give you a twenty-minute head start." His expression was inscrutable. But his unspoken words were clear: *And then I'm coming for you.*

Twenty minutes. Rune wouldn't even get to the harbor in twenty minutes.

Still, it was something.

She grabbed the bag of food she'd stolen from his cupboards and strode toward the open door of his apartment. She needed to get as far away from him as she could. Needed to start over somewhere he would never find her.

What would that be like—a life apart from him?

Her footsteps slowed, pausing in the door frame. She turned to glance back at him.

"Gideon?"

The sight of him blurred.

"I wish—"

"Don't." His voice was ragged. "Just go, Rune."

She nodded, swallowing back tears. The only safe thing to do was run.

So that's what she did.

FORTY-FOUR

RUNE

SHE EXPECTED A LEGION of soldiers to ambush her from the shadows. But no one was waiting for Rune in the darkness. The clouds had moved on, leaving the stars burning brightly overhead.

Rune kept glancing behind her, searching the streets for any sign of Gideon on her trail. But there was no trace of him. So Rune pulled his jacket closer around her and rode her stolen horse faster.

When she arrived, she found Blood Guard soldiers encircling the waterfront. Quietly, she loosed the horse and entered the wooded park where she'd left Aurelia and Meadow.

"They doubled the security after you left," Aurelia whispered when Rune found her hiding place in the trees. "There are hounds everywhere."

The dogs would smell Rune and Aurelia long before they even got to the wharf.

But that wasn't their most pressing problem: Meadow was crying.

"Hush," Aurelia whispered, hugging the child. "Shhhh, my love. We need to be very quiet."

But it was too late. Before Rune could pull one of Gideon's apples out to soothe her, a shout came from nearby, followed by footsteps. Rune dragged Aurelia deeper into the trees.

If there were witch-hunting hounds, they were done for.

Three soldiers entered the park. Rune glanced at Meadow, whose cries had quieted to a whimper.

"Over here," said one, stepping into a patch of moonlight three paces from Rune. "Do you hear that? Sounds like—"

Something *clicked* beside her. Rune looked to see that Aurelia had drawn her pistol. Hearing the *click*, the soldier turned, squinting into the darkness.

If she fired, the sound would draw every Blood Guard soldier in hearing distance right to them.

And if she didn't, in a few seconds, the soldier would find them.

Aurelia raised her gun.

Rune held her breath, her hand going to Gideon's gun, tucked into her belt.

"Wheatley!"

Rune backed up a step as a puffing soldier ran into view, stopping to catch his breath. "We're needed on the other side of town. Captain's orders. All hands. Make haste!"

The soldiers looked at each other and ran.

Silence flooded the park.

Rune looked to the waterfront, and further out, to Alex's boat waiting patiently in the water.

The way was clear.

FORTY-FIVE

GIDEON

ALF AN HOUR AFTER Rune left his apartment, Gideon stood in the supply room of the new Blood Guard headquarters. He'd ridden straight here and given the order to move most soldiers to the main harbor, where the Crimson Moth would make her escape.

Or so he'd led them to believe.

But Rune wouldn't be smuggling witches aboard the *Arcadia* tonight. The moment Gideon had first accused her of it, she would have abandoned the idea. No, Rune would avoid the main harbor, expecting Gideon to double the security.

But his soldiers didn't know that.

And Gideon intended to buy Rune as much time as possible.

Grabbing an old, rolled-up map of Cascadia—from before the revolution, when this fort had been abandoned—he spread it out across the table. To lay it flat, he pinned one edge with his lamp and the other with Rune's knife, lodging the tip into the wood beneath.

"If I were Cressida," he murmured, scanning its lines in the lamplight, "where would I hide my sisters?" Close to the capital, where she could easily replenish the spell preserving them? Or as far from the Blood Guard as she could get?

It was only a matter of time before Cressida figured out who Rune was. So long as Elowyn and Analise's corpses were out there, fully preserved, Rune's life was in danger. No matter where she ran, she would be hunted.

But if he found the bodies and destroyed them?

Rune would be safe.

Gideon's gaze traced the map, following the roads leaving the capital and pausing at Thornwood Hall, Cressida's former summer home.

Would she hide them inside Thornwood?

After growing up there, Cress would know the house and its grounds intimately.

It was a place to start. If he found no trace, he'd move outward from there.

Leaving the map, Gideon went to the supply room. Grabbing an empty rucksack, he started filling it with sticks of dynamite. He couldn't disable whatever spells preserved the sister queens, but with any luck, the spells would have weakened considerably in Cressida's absence. A few sticks of dynamite might be enough to blow them to bits.

He had no idea if it would work, but he had to try.

And if he couldn't destroy them, he would hide them somewhere else. Somewhere Cress would never find them.

Gideon looked to the windows, where the moonlight poured in. The sea was a black expanse in the distance.

He hoped Rune was on it. Hoped she was safely away.

Slinging the pack over his shoulder, Gideon grabbed the lamp and Rune's knife—the only remnant of her he had left—and turned for the door.

A silhouette stood in the frame, blocking his way.

Gideon frowned into the shadows, trying to make out who it was.

"I *trusted* you."

The voice sparked like a fuse.

Laila.

"You said you knew her exact plans. That it would be to-night. That she would use the *Arcadia*!"

She stepped into the room and the orange glow of his lamp.

Gideon stepped back. "Laila, I—"

"The hounds couldn't pick up a scent," she said, staring at him like he was a stranger. "We checked every cargo hold on every ship in the harbor. There's no trace of any witch."

Here, at the end, this was all he was sorry for: the look on Laila's face.

She was his friend, and he'd betrayed her trust.

"Why would you lie to me?"

Gideon remembered Rune's knife pressed to his throat. Remembered the tears in her eyes as she fled.

Because I love her.

Gideon dropped his sack full of dynamite to the floor.

"Laila, listen—"

"No, Gideon. I will *never* listen to you again."

"If you let me explain . . ."

Several soldiers filed in behind her. With them came Harrow. Even from the shadows, he felt the fury of her gaze burning him up.

No explanation would convince them, and he knew it.

Harrow stepped into the light. "All Rune has ever done is deceive you, Comrade. Witches are all the same. You should have learned this lesson by now."

Looking at Harrow was like looking into a mirror. They both had been hurt by the witches they loved, and had let those wounds poison them.

"Aren't you tired of this bitterness?" he asked her. "Aren't you sick of the hate? Those are easy, Harrow. What's difficult is refusing to harden your heart despite having every reason to. Despite knowing the odds are against you."

Rune had taught him that.

"Live in the darkness too long, and eventually you won't recognize the light," he told her. "You'll become like the monsters you hate."

She scowled, her face shuttering. Closing herself off. "You're lost, Comrade."

No. Gideon was the opposite of lost.

"You and I are free, Harrow. We've always been free. They can torture us, lock us up, leave us to rot—but our souls are still our own. *We* decide what we become. Not them."

Harrow's gaze darkened. As if she couldn't stand to be in Gideon's presence a second longer, she turned and strode from the room.

When she was gone, Laila said, "You know where Rune is, don't you?"

Gideon said nothing.

"You can still turn this around. You can tell me, and we can stop her. Before Noah finds out."

He studied his friend, whose eyes pleaded with him. Laila had a good, brave heart. He loved her like a sister. He didn't want to force her hand.

But neither would he give Rune up.

"I'm sorry," he said. "Truly, I am."

He watched her face fall. Watched her glance away and call for the soldiers behind her. Seconds later, half a dozen officers surrounded Gideon. When Laila gave the command, the men looked at each other, clearly reluctant to arrest their captain.

"Do as she says," Gideon told them. "I intentionally deceived you to help a fugitive escape. Take me into custody."

So they locked his wrists in irons and marched him to the palace.

PAIN EXPLODED IN GIDEON'S cheek. It was the third time Noah hit him across the face with the butt of a revolver, and his ears rang from the pain of the blows.

In his black uniform, the Good Commander towered over Gideon, who knelt on the floor before him.

"You deceived your soldiers to aid the Crimson Moth's escape. I therefore convict you of sympathizing with witches." Noah set the revolver on his desk. "As a revolution hero, it's only fitting to execute you publicly. I'll make an official announcement tomorrow. We'll use you as an example."

He stared down at Gideon, the derision plain on his face.

There had always been friction between them. Gideon guessed it was because of his close relationship with Nicolas Creed, Noah's father. Gideon had always suspected Noah was jealous, but the suspicion had never been confirmed.

"I almost feel bad for you. Abandoned to your death by the girl you love."

Noah nodded for two soldiers to take him to a cell. As they shoved Gideon forward, the Commander's voice echoed behind him: "She was always out of your league, Sharpe."

"I'm well aware," he whispered as they led him away.

FORTY-SIX

RUNE

*R*UNE LICKED THE SEA salt from her lips as the unfurled sails of Alex's boat ballooned overhead. Her *Ghost Walker* spell kept the craft concealed as they headed out to open sea. The wind was against them at first, making them easy prey for bigger, faster ships. So Rune cast *Tempest*—a spell from Seraphine's repertoire of elemental castings.

It was designed for sailing, and when combined with a compass showing which direction a witch wished to go, the spell summoned a strong wind to fill a boat's sails, propelling the craft much more quickly toward its destination.

Rune kept expecting to see a ship in pursuit. To find Gideon at the stern, giving the order to subdue her.

But there was only the sea, rising and falling, everywhere around her.

Aurelia didn't look back once. She sat with her face in the wind, holding Meadow close, shivering in the cold night air. At one point, Rune slid Gideon's jacket off and handed it to Aurelia, who used it as a blanket to wrap the child in.

The island shrank behind them. As the fear of being caught ebbed, Rune ran her hands along the *Aria*'s polished wood, thinking of Alex. How he was saving her once again. She glanced at the stars, sending out a silent thank-you, wondering if it could reach him beyond the grave.

When they left New Republic waters, Rune finally settled in, glancing back one last time as her home disappeared for good.

If she made it to the Continent, the first thing she'd do was find Seraphine and tell her she was running away. Somewhere neither Cressida nor the Republic's witch hunters would find her. Perhaps Seraphine would come with her. If not, Rune would get a message to her once she was safe.

The salt spray dampened her hair. The wind stung her cheeks.

Will you miss me, Crimson Moth?

Rune shut her eyes against the memory of his voice.

She should be happy his plot had failed. She'd eluded him; she should be celebrating.

But instead, a chasm had opened inside her.

You are a knife in my heart.

They sailed on.

FORTY-SEVEN

RUNE

*T*HEY SAILED INTO UMBRIAN waters five days later, assisted by Rune's enchanted wind. While at sea, Rune taught Aurelia how to sail so they could take turns sleeping. It was morning when she navigated them up the fjord's dark waters leading to Larkmont, where she dropped anchor near Soren's estate, keeping out of sight.

Alex's boat had proved a sturdy escape craft, and Rune intended to use it to take them further south. Right now, though, she needed to sneak inside Larkmont, grab supplies for the rest of the journey, and find Seraphine.

She hoped to do all of this without being seen.

Cressida couldn't know she was back. The witch queen would expect her to make good on her promise to marry Soren, and Rune didn't want to think about what Cressida would do to force her hand. Especially after Rune's last act of defiance.

Before she jumped into the waves, Rune took off her boots so they wouldn't fill with water and weigh her down.

"You'll be all right here?" she asked Aurelia. Dropping her boots in the boat, Rune glanced back. Aurelia's long hair was stiff with sea salt. She wore Gideon's jacket to keep out the cold and looked like she hadn't slept in days.

I'll stay with the boat, Aurelia had told her when they entered the fjord. *I have no desire to run into Cressida.*

Aurelia, it turned out, vividly remembered Roseblood cruelty and wanted to keep Meadow far away from it.

"We'll be fine," Aurelia said, her hand on her daughter's head as the girl played with the compass she'd found belowdecks.

Rune looked on with a small smile before diving into the dark water.

The icy cold stunned her. It took several moments for her body to recover from the shock. When it did, she swam for the shore.

She was halfway there when the *crack* of flapping sails made her pause.

To keep the boat hidden, Rune had lowered the sails. But when she looked, not only did she find them hoisted, but she saw Aurelia drawing up the anchor.

"What are you doing?" she called, treading water.

Aurelia reached into the pocket of Gideon's jacket. "I found this on the boat shortly after we left the island." Pulling out some small object, she threw it in Rune's direction.

It plopped into the water.

A jewelry box.

"If I showed you, you would have gone back for him. And I couldn't let you do that." Aurelia pulled the anchor over the side, dropping it in the boat's interior. "I can't let them catch us again."

The tiny box bobbed on the waves before starting to sink.

"What are you talking about?" Rune grabbed the box before it descended too deep and couldn't be retrieved.

"I'm sorry." Aurelia sat down at the rudder. From the way her voice trembled, she sounded truly remorseful. "I have a child to think of. I need to get Meadow somewhere safe."

And before Rune could think of how to stop her, Aurelia turned the boat around and started sailing out of the fjord. Abandoning Rune.

She watched, dumbfounded, as Alex's boat—her escape

craft—disappeared into the distance. She'd risked her life to get Aurelia and her child to freedom, and *this* was how the sibyl repaid her?

What am I going to do?

She could steal a horse and ride for Caelis. Or perhaps commandeer one of Soren's boats. But the prince's sailboats were large, sophisticated crafts requiring whole crews to manage. Rune doubted she could handle one by herself.

The sea's chill was seeping into Rune's bones, and her teeth began to chatter. She needed to get out before hypothermia set in. She could figure out the rest once she was on dry land.

So, with the jewelry box clasped in her fist, she turned and swam for shore.

Wading out of the water and onto the rocks, Rune pushed back her sopping hair, held up the tiny box, and opened it.

A folded, waterlogged note sat inside. As Rune unfolded it, a small coin dropped into the sand, catching the light.

She picked up the coin, holding it up to the sunlight. A hole was punched in the silver, and a thin chain was fastened on.

A penny. But not just any penny.

A word stamped into its surface warmed Rune's shivering body.

Cascadia.

She flipped it over. Queen Althea's face stared out at her, pressed into the silver.

Althea had ruled over Cascadia for a quarter century, during a period of peace and stability. She was the last queen to commune with the Ancients—or so some believed—and legend had it that Wisdom could often be seen walking with her in the royal gardens.

After the revolution, coins like this one had all been melted down. Like the old maps that had to be burned, there were to be no reminders that witches once reigned in the New Republic. The Good Commander wanted history erased.

Someone must have kept this contraband, or found it—at the back of a drawer, perhaps, or between the cracks in some floorboards—and turned it into a necklace.

But why?

She glanced at the note in her other hand. The wet paper was translucent, and Rune had to squint to make out the words written in washed-out ink.

Rune—

I hope you find the freedom you're looking for.

Yours, Gideon

Rune stared at the note. She couldn't make sense of it. It was Gideon's handwriting. But the words . . . the coin . . .

I found this on the boat shortly after we left the island.

But what was a gift from Gideon doing on Alex's boat?

Unless . . .

Rune's heart plummeted into her stomach.

He put it there for me to find.

Which meant he knew she would use Alex's sailboat to escape.

If he knew, why didn't he stop me?

Rune recalled the guards swarming the waterfront, descending on her and Aurelia's hiding place. The only reason they hadn't found and seized them was because . . .

He called them off.

Rune thought back to that night. To the hammer of her heart as Aurelia cocked her gun, ready to shoot. To the relief that flooded her at the soldier's shouted command.

We're needed on the other side of town. Captain's orders. All hands. Make haste!

Gideon had drawn the Blood Guard away, allowing Rune to escape.

She hadn't outwitted him.

Not at all.

And now he'll be accused of sympathizing with witches.

He likely already had been.

If the Good Commander knew Gideon had let Rune go, Gideon was as good as dead.

Rune glanced up from the note, staring across the sea, feeling like she'd made a terrible mistake. Like she'd abandoned half her soul behind in hell.

Did he have a change of heart at the eleventh hour, or had Gideon been deceiving them all for a while now? And if so, when did he decide to let her go?

If she'd paid attention, she might have figured it out. But now Gideon's life was forfeit, and there was nothing she could do. An ocean sat between them, and Rune had no way to cross it.

An urge to leap into the sea and *swim* back overcame her.

Would he have come with me, had I asked?

But even if she had, where would they go? She and Gideon could never be together.

Not in the New Republic, perhaps. But the world is a vast place.

Why hadn't she asked him?

Aurelia was right. Rune couldn't let Gideon die. Not after he'd saved her life.

And if they've already executed him?

Rune had to believe he was alive—that he would find a way to skirt death long enough for Rune to save him. Slipping the necklace over her head, she rose to her feet.

I have to go back.

She walked barefoot on the sand, following the shoreline until Larkmont came into view. Her gaze lingered on Soren's private wharf, where several sailboats were docked, all too big for one girl to manage alone.

But a witch?

With the right spells, a strong enough witch could sail one.

Rune's gaze lifted to Larkmont. Cressida was in there. Cressida, who kept dozens of spell books in the room she was staying in.

All Rune had to do was sneak inside and find the right one.

FORTY-EIGHT

RUNE

*T*HE PRISTINE HALLS OF Larkmont were quiet and still. As Rune crept through them, veiled by *Ghost Walker*, she overheard two guards talking about Soren's trip to the capital, saying his fleet was ready to sail for the New Republic.

Had Cressida and the other witches he'd given sanctuary to joined him there? It would explain the empty palace.

If Cressida was in Caelis, her spell books would likely be with her.

Am I too late?

Rune quickened her pace. Arriving in Larkmont's guest quarters, she walked up to the witch queen's suite and pressed her ear to the door. She heard no voices or movement within, so she opened the door and slipped inside.

Marble columns held up the bedroom's high ceilings, and the lavish furnishings announced that only privileged guests ever slept here.

No breakfast tray sat on the terrace, waiting to be collected. No clothing was strung about. Nothing was out of place.

Is she already gone?

A breeze from the next room brought a whiff of old magic. Rune followed the scent, hurrying through the archway, passing the private bath, and entered the parlor meant for retiring in the evenings.

The open windows let in a breeze. It ruffled the curtains,

sending sunlight flickering through the quiet room. The air smelled strongly of blood and roses—a telltale sign Cressida had used this room for casting. Rune's gaze snagged on a packed suitcase lying on the sofa as if waiting for someone to collect it. Next to the suitcase sat a leather book bag.

Hope flared in her.

Cressida must have left her things to be packed and brought to the capital for her.

Rune opened the bag, pulling out the spell books to look for sailing spells strong enough to help her guide a large ship on her own. The first book consisted of elemental spells, and while some might be helpful—changing the current or tide; calming a strong wind or changing its direction—they weren't what she needed.

Rune pulled out the next and skimmed its pages, recognizing several love spells. She tried flipping past them, only to end up in a section on love *curses*. None of which were useful to her.

Rune was about to toss the entire book aside when the memory of Gideon stopped her. His brand burning beneath her palm, growing hotter by the second. The way he tore away from her, trembling with pain.

It happens when I touch you.

Fury curled like smoke inside Rune.

She stared down at the book on her lap. Instead of setting it aside, Rune flipped back, searching for the spell Cressida had used to hurt Gideon.

She found it soon enough:

TRUE LOVE'S CURSE is an Arcana spell. It prevents a victim from being with his true love by inflicting pain whenever he touches her skin to skin.

The words made Rune dizzy.

They'd both assumed the spell kept Gideon away from Rune, specifically. But this was something else. This was intended to keep Gideon away from his true love. Which meant . . .

It happens when I touch you.

Swallowing the strange lump in her throat, Rune kept reading.

Once cast, TRUE LOVE'S CURSE cannot wear off. Only the blood of the victim's true love, spilled in a sacrificial act, can break it.

What kind of sacrificial act?

Rune scanned down the page and found spellmarks for the counterspell at the bottom. There were three in total. She stared at them.

Those three spellmarks were all it would take to break the curse?

And the blood spilled in a sacrificial act.

The sound of a creaking door made Rune freeze.

"Make haste." Cressida's voice floated through the archway. "In order to sail at dawn tomorrow, we must arrive in Caelis *tonight.*"

The witch queen's footsteps grew louder. Rune's pulse thumped wildly as she shut the spell book and quickly rose to her feet, heading for the windows. *Ghost Walker* concealed her, but the last time she'd used her invisibility spell to hide from Cressida, she was sure the witch queen had still sensed her in the room.

Not wanting to chance it, Rune stepped behind the curtains, clutching the book of spells.

The footsteps stopped.

"What's—"

"*Hush,*" Cressida hissed, silencing whoever was in the room with her. Probably eyeing the open satchel and the spell books scattered across the sofa. There hadn't been enough time to put them away.

Rune held her breath.

A slight breeze at her back told her the window behind her was open. She could turn and climb out. Cressida would never know it was Rune who'd been in here, only that someone had been rifling through her things.

But her mind was on *True Love's Curse.*

On the instructions for breaking it.

Namely: *the blood spilled in a sacrificial act.*

Cressida's shoes clicked on the tiles as she drew closer to the curtains.

If Rune wanted to escape, she had to go *now.*

But she suddenly knew what was required to break the curse. The terrifying thought of it made her stomach clench.

What if I'm wrong? What if it doesn't work?

Cressida stood directly before her now, on the other side of the curtain. Rune heard the breaths she took. Felt the chill of her presence.

Was Gideon worth the risk?

Rune touched the coin hanging around her neck.

Yes.

Gideon had endured unimaginable things under the Reign of Witches. And yet, somehow, he'd emerged with his soul intact. The proof: he'd forfeited his life so Rune—a *witch*—could go free.

Cressida yanked aside the curtain. Clutching the stolen spell book to her chest, Rune looked up, meeting her queen's furious gaze.

"*You.*"

Rune had never been more terrified.

As Cressida's eyes dropped to the book of love spells, her mouth twisted in a mocking smile. "Oh, Rune. Unlucky in love?"

Rune's anger ignited. She lifted her chin. "I suppose I should thank you. If not for your curse, I wouldn't have irrefutable proof that he loves me."

Cressida's nostrils flared. Grabbing Rune's jaw, she slammed her head hard against the window, cracking the glass and sending a stab of pain through her skull.

Despite the shock of it, despite Cressida's ferocious grip tightening on her jaw, Rune stared the queen down. "Touch Gideon again, and I'll make you wish you were dead."

Cressida leaned in, whispering close to her ear. "Do you know what I do to those who threaten me?"

Oh, Rune knew.

Do your worst.

FORTY-NINE

RUNE

CRESSIDA DRAGGED RUNE INTO the bedroom. Juniper—the witch who'd accompanied her into the suite—held Rune in place while Cressida drew a ring of bloody symbols on the floor encircling her.

"Step back, Juniper."

The witch stepped away, her eyes full of pity.

The spellmarks ignited, glowing bright white and forming a complete circle around Rune, like a prison cell. Only instead of steel bars closing her in, it was magic. Rune had seen Cressida use this binding before. Once inside the ring, you couldn't exit.

Rune looked up and saw Cressida circling her, an ensorcelled whip looped at her side. It looked like lightning in her hands, white and crackling.

Releasing the whip from its coil, Cressida narrowed her eyes.

"You think you can protect him from me?"

She lashed the whip. It struck Rune's back, ripping her skin from shoulder to hip. The pain lit her up.

In shock, Rune dropped to her knees.

"Once I have my throne . . ." Cressida's footsteps echoed as she walked around the circle. ". . . the first thing I intend to do is hunt Gideon down."

Another lash struck. Tearing fabric and flesh. Splitting Rune open.

Rune cried out—a raw, animal sound she didn't recognize. It frightened her almost as much as Cressida's whip.

There was nowhere to run. She was completely at the mercy of a corrupted witch who wanted her dead.

"If you kill me, Soren won't give you his army," Rune gasped, desperate to remind Cressida of why her life was valuable.

"Soren is in Caelis. As far as he's concerned, you're still kidnapped in the New Republic."

An icy dread spread through Rune.

"Once he learns your kidnappers killed you, he'll hand me the rest of his army in a rage, to do with as I want."

Another lash caught Rune across the shoulder. She clenched her teeth to stop the agonized sounds escaping her. As fresh blood gushed from the wounds, soaking her shirt, two more lashes sliced open her back.

Rune kept her knees tucked beneath her. She pressed her forehead against the floor, struggling to breathe, using her arms to protect her head while leaving her back exposed. An easy target, her back took the brunt of the lashes, sparing her softer, more vulnerable parts.

Cressida whipped her mercilessly. Ceaselessly. Until Rune's blood soaked her shirt and pooled on the floor.

Her skin was ablaze. The room bled to red. She no longer held back her screams.

Too soon, the soothing numbness of unconsciousness called to her, and Rune slipped toward it.

No. Not yet.

Cressida's whip didn't stop, slicing Rune's back to ribbons. Her entire body shook as she huddled in a puddle of her own blood.

Blood.

The thing that made Rune a witch. The source of her power.

There's something I still have to do.

As the lashes rained down, she thought of Gideon's curse.

Only the blood of the victim's true love, spilled in a sacrificial act, can break it.

This was what she'd been waiting for.

The lashing ceased as Cressida paused to catch her breath, gathering her strength before finishing Rune off.

Barely conscious, Rune recalled the unnamed spellmarks required to break *True Love's Curse*. Pushing herself up on trembling forearms, Rune dipped a finger in the sticky red blood and started to draw.

She hadn't gotten the chance to tell Gideon she loved him.

Perhaps this will suffice.

Weakened, it took her longer than it should have. Before she finished the second symbol, Cressida readied her weapon.

Forcing her mind to clear, gritting her teeth to hold off the pain and stay conscious, Rune completed the second and third symbols.

It should have been a relief. But even as the magic swelled, making her skin tingle and her ears roar, Rune knew she wasn't finished.

"What are you doing?"

Rune's moth signature must have materialized in the air.

Touch Gideon again and I'll make you wish you were dead.

She couldn't kill Cressida. But maybe she could do the next best thing.

"You think *you* can stop *me* with a counterspell?" Cressida threw back her head and laughed. "Oh, Rune . . ."

Before Cressida's final round of lashes began, Rune drew two more symbols, altering the first spell. Hoping it would work. Hoping her sacrifice would be enough.

Magic surged again, swirling around her. Binding the new spell to the first.

The whip came down, catching her off guard and engulfing

her in pain. Rune's forearms refused to hold her upright and she collapsed. Her cheekbone hit the tiles. What little strength she had left fled her body.

Rune lay on her side in a pool of blood.

Get up.

The room went dark at the edges.

Get . . . up . . .

Cressida's shadow slid over her.

Metal scraped against leather as Cressida drew her knife.

Rune closed her eyes, waiting for the killing blow.

"It pains me to do this, Rune. But I know incurable defiance when I see it. Such a pity. You had so much potential—"

BANG.

The door burst open.

Rune's vision blurred; the darkness dragging her under.

"That's enough!"

Someone stepped in front of Rune. Shielding her from Cressida.

Seraphine?

"You will heed me."

Her voice was like a clap of thunder.

"Heed you?" Cressida cackled. "For all I know, you're in league with her."

The voices seemed a world away.

Just before the darkness claimed her, she heard Seraphine say:

"You will heed me, my queen, because Rune is your sister."

FIFTY

RUNE

WHEN RUNE WOKE, THE room was rocking. Tipping from side to side. Creaking loudly as it did.

She opened her eyes, but everything was hazy. There was a bed, and sheets tucked around her. The scent of magic hung in the air, stale and faded. Mingling with the smell of the sea.

Somewhere nearby, glass clinked. She heard water being poured. Turning her face toward it, Rune found a figure silhouetted by the light.

"Where am I?" The croak of her voice surprised her. Rune swallowed to moisten her throat.

"Entering New Republic waters," said a feminine voice.

Rune frowned. That couldn't be right. She was supposed to be at Larkmont.

"You've been in and out of consciousness for several days. You lost a lot of blood."

We're on a ship, Rune realized as her vision cleared and cabin walls solidified around her.

And the witch tending to her was Juniper.

Rune tried to sit up and immediately regretted it: fiery pain blazed up her back. She gritted her teeth and went still.

"Here." Juniper sat down on a chair beside the bed, holding out a glass of water. "Drink."

Rune eyed it carefully. But even if she was being drugged, her thirst won out, and she let the girl press it to her lips.

Rune gulped the water down.

"My spells slowed the bleeding and mended the torn muscles and tendons," said Juniper, rising to replenish the empty glass. "I sped up the healing, but it will hurt for some time."

Rune remembered the lashes raining down; the whip slicing across her back. She remembered the warm, sticky blood on the floor.

I'm her sister.

The horror of it sank into Rune, chilling her all over. She was a Roseblood. Heir to a cruel witch dynasty. Sister to a terrifying murderer.

That's why Juniper was here: to keep Rune alive. Cressida had likely ordered the girl—who was known for her knack with healing spells—to stay by Rune's side.

She needed Rune alive to cast the resurrection spell.

Why didn't Nan tell me?

Juniper poured more water from the pitcher, then returned to Rune's side, holding out the glass.

Rune shook her head, refusing the water. "Can you help me up?"

Juniper looked reluctant, but did as Rune asked, carefully taking hold of her arms and pulling her to a seated position.

Rune's back screamed in protest.

She clenched her teeth, enduring the pain, and sat up. The room spun. Not only had she lost a lot of blood, she hadn't eaten in days. Her weakness made that clear.

Feeling lightheaded, she pushed herself to the bed's edge and stood up slowly. With every inch she moved, the pain became more bearable, until finally she was at the porthole, looking out.

A fleet of ships surrounded them, their stacks pumping smoke into the sky. Rune recognized Soren's insignia emblazoned on their sides.

A familiar island loomed in the distance, silhouetted against the setting sun.

Cascadia.

Was this it, then? Were witches at war with the New Republic?

Rune was about to turn away from the porthole when she caught sight of her reflection in the glass. Her face was sickly pale, and bruise-like shadows hung under her eyes. She looked like a ghost.

If this is what the front of me looks like, how much worse is the back?

Rune glanced at the tarnished mirror hanging on the cabin wall. While Juniper looked on with pity in her eyes, Rune took hold of her shirt's hem and dragged it up over her head. Scorching pain flared up her back, bringing tears to her eyes. Rune clenched her teeth, determined to see the damage.

Lowering the shirt to her side, she turned, glancing into the mirror. Dozens of thick, red lines stood out against her white skin. Covering her back like a web.

It looked hideous.

Rune shut her eyes against the sight of her ruined body.

The sound of footsteps in the hall made her fumble with her shirt, trying to pull it back over her head without passing out from the pain.

She'd barely gotten it on when the door opened.

"What are you doing?" Seraphine stepped inside, her worried gaze falling on Rune. "You should be resting."

Promise me you'll find Seraphine Oakes, my darling. She'll tell you everything I couldn't.

It was the last note Nan ever wrote her.

Seraphine had known who Rune was this whole time. And she'd chosen to keep the truth from her.

"Why?" Rune demanded, emotions flickering through her: anger, betrayal, grief.

Seraphine shut the door behind her and came toward the bed, which stood between them.

"How could you keep such a secret from me?"

Rune felt unmoored. Everything that could be taken from her had been. Nan. Wintersea. Alex. Her position in society. And now this: everything she'd believed about her own history.

Rune was the orphaned daughter of two people who'd died in a tragic accident at sea—that's what she'd been told. But it was a lie. One Nan herself perpetuated.

Why?

"Kestrel and I believed the less people who knew, the safer you were."

"Yes, but you kept the secret from *me*! I'm perfectly capable of keeping secrets, and I deserved to know."

Seraphine glanced at Juniper, who silently excused herself from the room.

"You have every right to be angry," said Seraphine, sitting down on the bed. Her movements reminded Rune of a dove settling down in its nest: gentle, graceful.

She held out her hand for Rune to take.

Rune ignored it, crossing her arms, wincing as the raw skin of her shoulder pulled. "I have a right to know the truth."

"Yes. You do." Seraphine dropped her hand. "You're the daughter of Queen Winoa and her second consort. On the night you were born, the midwife had difficulty turning you around, so she called for me. I managed to turn you, and less than an hour later, there you were, in my hands. But the moment we touched, something . . . woke up inside me." Her gaze dropped to the bed. "I cast an illusion, making the midwives believe you were stillborn. I lied to the queen, saying you were dead. And then I delivered you to Kestrel Winters to raise."

"What do you mean, something *woke up* inside you?"

"The Roseblood family was dysfunctional and depraved," said Seraphine, but she didn't meet Rune's eyes as she said it. "I couldn't let an innocent child grow up in that environment."

Presumably, Cressida and her sisters had been innocent once, too. So why didn't Seraphine take *them* away?

"I don't believe you," said Rune.

She wasn't being told the whole story. She could sense it. And there was still the matter of Seraphine's age . . .

"Nan told me the two of you grew up together. She used to wear a locket around her neck, and inside were two images: one of her at eighteen, and one of you, not much older."

Seraphine nodded. "I remember it."

"You look the same now as you did in that portrait painted forty years ago. How is that possible, unless you're under some kind of spell? Are you cursed?"

Seraphine drew in a deep breath. It shook as she let it out.

"It's *like* a curse, I suppose. Certainly, it feels like one." Seraphine stared toward the porthole, which showed a patch of blue sky. "I have a task to complete, and until it's done, I can't . . . move on."

Rune frowned harder. *Move on?*

Was she some kind of spirit? Trapped here after her death due to unfinished business?

There were stories of such things, but Rune had never believed them. And the woman on the bed was clearly made of flesh and bone. As solid as Rune herself.

Seraphine patted the mattress beside her, inviting Rune to join her.

Reluctantly, she sat.

"It feels like yesterday you were this tiny creature swaddled against my breast as I rode for Wintersea House. And here you are, all grown up." Seraphine's expression softened as she studied Rune. "I keep looking for her in you—which is absurd, I know. You share no blood. And yet, I glimpse her sometimes. As if you carry her with you."

Seraphine touched the bird-shaped scar on her neck.

"The night I brought you to Kestrel, she was so angry with me. She'd never wanted children, and at first refused to take you. She said if I were going to steal a royal baby, the least I could do was raise it myself.

"But I couldn't keep you in the capital to be raised under Winoa's nose. It was too dangerous. The queen was already suspicious of me by then. I was the only witch on her council who didn't hide my disgust for her cruelty. I didn't loathe her in private and flatter her in public, like the others. She knew exactly what I thought: that she was a plague on Cascadia.

"Three days after I brought you to Wintersea, as if sensing my deception—Winoa exiled me. She wouldn't tolerate me undermining her authority anymore. If I didn't leave, she warned, I'd be dead by morning. I rode straight to Wintersea, where I convinced Kestrel to keep you until it was safe for me to return. I didn't trust the queen not to send her spies after me.

"Years later, after Winoa's death, I came back to get you. But by then, Kestrel was in love. You were the best thing to ever happen to her." Seraphine smiled, remembering. "She told me if I tried to take you, she'd skewer me with a letter opener."

Tears clogged Rune's throat. She swallowed them down.

"I miss her," they whispered in unison.

Seraphine seemed about to say something more, about to

reach for Rune, when a sudden *BOOM* echoed from outside the ship. They looked to the porthole.

Cannon fire?

Seraphine rose to her feet and went to look. Rune moved much more slowly, joining her at the porthole.

The ships outside were firing on the harbor.

Rune pressed her hand to the cabin wall, watching the explosions in the distance. The pine boards were rough beneath her palm.

That was her *home* they were sieging.

"So it begins," murmured Seraphine.

FIFTY-ONE

GIDEON

*T*ODAY, GIDEON WOULD DIE.

It's what they told him when they woke him up.

Gideon sat on the floor with his back pressed to the cold stone wall, the prison cell pitch-black around him. He didn't know how much time had passed since the guard came at dawn to say he'd be executed in a matter of hours. It was hard to tell the passing of time in this place. Gideon had been here a week, and had learned to count days by the opening of his cell door, when the guards brought water and bread—first at dawn and then at dusk. But minutes? Hours? It was impossible to keep track of those.

All he knew was that he wouldn't be in here much longer. A firing squad awaited him.

Gideon was that abominable thing the Republic could not abide: a witch sympathizer. No, it was worse: he was a witch *lover*.

Soon, he'd pay the price for it.

When a key turned in the lock, Gideon's heart jumped into his throat.

This is it.

The door opened and light flooded in, temporarily blinding him. Before he could see which guard it was, a hood came down over his head.

"Time to go."

Gideon reminded himself that his entire family was dead, and that he was simply joining them.

I'm not afraid to die.

But if that was true, why was his heart hammering like a war drum?

He didn't struggle. Didn't try to fight off the guard. Ten more would only rush in to replace this one. They would overcome him, one way or another.

Gideon let himself be hauled to his feet.

The guard led him from his cell in manacles. With the hood over his head, Gideon couldn't see a thing. Fear pitted his stomach, growing more intense with every step.

As the prison gates rattled open, he tried to distract himself from thoughts of his impending death. The crowd outside—how big would it be? Would the entire city come to witness the execution of a revolution hero? How many people would cheer as Gideon Sharpe, defender of the Republic, died at that Republic's hands?

Most of all: Was this worth it?

Was *Rune* worth it?

The thought of her only brought resolve.

Rune is worth everything.

BOOM!

The ground shook beneath Gideon's feet.

He paused, steadying himself.

BOOM!

BOOM!

BOOM!

What the . . .

The entire prison trembled around him.

"What was that?"

No one answered. His guard quickened their steps, dragging him forward amidst shouts of rising alarm and rushing footsteps.

Outside, the guard turned him down what seemed like a

quiet alleyway and shoved him against a wall. As Gideon's back hit the bricks, he realized there was no public demonstration.

This would be a quick back-alley execution.

His pulse pounded in his ears as he waited for the gun to fire.

But no gunshot rang out. Instead, the hood came up over his head and sunlight flooded his eyes. Gideon blinked, trying to clear it.

"Laila?"

She was in uniform, looking like she hadn't slept—or changed—in days. In her hand was a ring of iron keys.

"What's going on?"

"You owe me one." She stepped closer and slid a key into the lock of his manacles. After a quick turn and a *click*, the chains dropped to the ground.

BOOM!

They both jumped and looked to the street. Laila had led them away from the palace, where a large crowd was now dispersing amidst the chaos. Soldiers ran back and forth, panicked, as the blasts continued.

"What *is* that?"

"Cannon fire." Laila pressed a pistol into his hand. "We're under attack."

"From who?" Gideon checked the gun and found it loaded. "Soren?"

Laila glanced over her shoulder, toward the mayhem. "We don't know. It just started."

Rune was supposed to break the alliance. If Soren was here, and those were his cannons firing on the city, it meant Rune hadn't come through on her part of their bargain.

She hadn't called off her engagement to the prince.

As more tremors shook the buildings around them, Gideon

headed toward the cannon fire, grip tightening on the gun Laila had given him. "Let's go find out."

The cannons boomed, growing louder the closer they came to the harbor. Soon, gunfire joined them. When Gideon and Laila drew near enough to see the fray, they found the wharf on fire, smoke choking the sky, and buildings crushed by cannon-balls.

Instead of heading toward the harbor front, the Republic's soldiers were running away from it.

Gideon grabbed one. "What are you doing?" He hauled the man in front of him by his jacket. "Your duty is to defend the city."

"It-it's a ghost army, sir." The man's face was white with shock as he fought against Gideon's grip. "Th-they're slaughtering us!"

He ripped himself free and kept running.

Laila stopped another man in uniform. "What's happening? How outnumbered are we?"

The soldier gripped his arm where blood soaked through his coat. He'd clearly been shot. "Hard to say." His breathing came in shallow gasps. "You can't see them. You only feel their bullets. They're cloaked by witches' spells. We don't even know where to shoot."

He too stumbled away, calling back to them: "You should run. We were all told to retreat."

Laila glanced at Gideon.

Where did you retreat if your enemy was invisible?

"We need to tell Noah."

Gideon scowled. "*You* warn your brother. I'm going to get a closer look."

He needed to see this for himself.

"Gideon, I don't think—"

Another round of gunfire drowned out Laila's voice. Reluctantly, she followed.

Soon they were in the thick of it, weaving through back alleys where the city's edge met the harbor. The air was smoky, and the smell of ash mingled with magic and gunpowder. Some soldiers had stayed behind and were still firing. But they seemed to be firing on empty air.

And the air was firing in return, felling them one by one.

Fall back, you idiots.

Using the wall of a fish merchant's shop as cover, Gideon shifted to look further out. Beside him, Laila drew her gun.

He now had a wider view of the burning wharf. Through the smoke, a massive fleet of ships appeared offshore, each one bearing Soren Nord's emblem. In between those ships and the harbor front were hundreds of rowboats full of soldiers, each one carrying a witch.

With the Republic's army in retreat, it seemed there was no longer a need to keep them veiled beneath spells of invisibility. Instead, magical shields protected them, repelling their enemies' bullets.

Gideon's gaze snagged on one boat in particular. Cressida seemed to hold court even there, in that scuffed little dory. She wore a black lace dress, and a circlet of roses crowned her pale head. Her eyes stared hungrily at the city. As if she were about to swallow it whole.

How is this possible?

Rune was supposed to break the alliance by refusing to marry the prince.

"Gideon . . . we need to go." Laila grabbed his arm, tugging. But Gideon couldn't tear his eyes away from Soren's army advancing on them, with Cressida at its helm.

Rune was supposed to stop this from happening. She'd

promised him. This alliance was predicated on Soren marrying Rune. If Soren's army was here, blitzing the hell out of them, Rune hadn't called off the wedding after all.

Or worse: she's already married to him.

It was a blow to Gideon's heart.

Was he an idiot? Had this been Rune's plan all along?

No. Gideon scattered his doubts. *She wouldn't do this.*

He believed that.

But if Rune had kept her part of their bargain—or worse, been *forced* to keep it . . .

"*Gideon!*" whispered Laila. "We need to go *now*."

Laila was right. After Soren's army took the harbor front—which was seconds from happening—they would sweep outward, into the city.

Gideon let her drag him away. Together, they ran.

Behind them, smoke choked the sky as the harbor burned.

FIFTY-TWO

RUNE

CRESSIDA LEFT A TRAIL of destruction in her wake.

The army retreated. The Blood Guard abandoned their stations. The aristocracy fled to their cottages and summer homes outside the city.

The Good Commander was nowhere to be found.

The ones who remained were the people. Those who had nowhere else to go. They hid behind bolted doors and locked shops. Rune saw them peek out from behind window curtains as she passed, only to hide when their eyes met hers.

The witches took the palace easily. It had been abandoned before they arrived, its marble halls quiet as a tomb. As if waiting for its true master to return. All Cressida had to do was walk in and claim it.

In the throne room, Rune stood between Seraphine and Juniper, close to the back wall. Witches filled the great space, watching as Cressida Roseblood walked up the columned promenade. The windows were dark as the night descended. The black lace train of Cressida's dress trailed behind her. Petals from her rose crown fluttered to the ground.

Tears gleamed in her eyes as she stared at the empty thrones ahead.

Cressida ascended the dais steps and approached the middle throne, caressing the black onyx before turning to face them.

"Tonight, we will finish taking the city." Her voice carried across the great room. "Anyone who swears fealty to me will be pardoned of all former transgressions—except for Blood Guard members and Republic officials. These, along with anyone who refuses to make an oath of loyalty to their queen, will be annihilated."

Cressida sat down on her throne.

"Executions begin at dawn."

Silence filled the massive room at her words.

It was broken by a shout: "All hail Queen Cressida!"

All around Rune, others took up the chant.

"Long may she reign!"

One by one, witches fell to their knees like a dark, rolling sea. Beside her, Juniper got down. Seraphine followed.

I helped bring this about, thought Rune.

Soon, she was the only one left standing.

If I hadn't duped Soren, none of this would be happening.

Cressida's eyes narrowed. Her eyes pierced Rune's from across the room, that deadly gaze trying to force her to her knees by sheer strength of will.

Memories flashed through Rune's mind.

Cressida drawing back her whip. The heat of the lashes. Her skin tearing open. The puddle of blood beneath her palms.

Rune's heart pounded, trapped in that moment. The terror turning her into a petrified animal.

It reminded her of the revolution. The night the Blood Guard came for Nan.

She'd been terrified then, too.

Holding Cressida's gaze, Rune lowered to her knees.

"Long may she reign."

PART THREE

We buried her today: our beautiful queen, our beloved sister.

She deserved a grand procession, like the mighty queens before her. Her people should have packed the streets, lighting candles in her honor and throwing flowers at her feet. Saying their goodbyes.

But the Usurper forbade it.

So we took Althea the Good to the temple and built a pyre. Beneath a weeping sky, we spoke the words of parting and pressed holy kisses to her forehead. We anointed her bloodied body, wrapped it in white shrouds, and released her to the Ancients.

And when all that remained of her was ash, we prepared for the worst.

—THE DEATH & BURIAL OF QUEEN ALTHEA,
WRITTEN DOWN BY THE ACOLYTES

THE FIVE DECREES OF CRESSIDA THE VICIOUS

1. A nightly curfew is in effect. Citizens must be in their homes at dusk and remain there until dawn. Anyone in defiance of this order will be shot on sight.

2. Royal Army officers are authorized to raid any household and arrest anyone who does not cooperate with their search. If a traitor is found, every household member will be arrested and brought in for questioning.

3. Titles and holdings belonging to traitors, dead or fled, will be seized and redistributed among citizens who have proven their devotion to Queen Cressida.

4. All citizens who willingly turn in patriots will be well compensated.

5. Those who refuse to swear an Oath of Loyalty will be executed.

Long live the Queen.

FIFTY-THREE

RUNE

SOREN'S ARMY SECURED THE capital. Soldiers swarmed like ants down every street, kicking in doors that wouldn't open for them and dragging the inhabitants out. Those who made oaths of loyalty to the queen of Cascadia were spared; those who refused were shot in front of their families.

Most took the oath.

Anyone connected to the old regime who hadn't escaped the city was brought in and interrogated. Those who refused to talk were tortured. If they still refused, they were executed. Those who talked spared themselves an extra night or two, but once they ran out of information to extract, they were executed, too.

Many witches were happy to hunt down the very people who once hunted them. But at the fringes, Rune detected a growing unease.

"They're afraid," said Seraphine one night, her voice cloaked by a silencing spell, preventing the two witches posted outside Rune's bedroom from listening to their conversation.

Rune was trapped here. Every door and window was sealed with Cressida's magic, and they had encased Rune's hands in witch restraints, taking them off only to let her eat or relieve herself.

All day and night, two witches were posted outside her door, and when Rune *was* let out—for a single hour, at dinner—these guards were her escorts, reporting her every word and action to Cressida.

Rune was like an expensive jewel, locked up tight. If something happened to her, Cressida would lose her only chance of resurrecting Elowyn and Analise.

The only reason Cressida let Seraphine visit was because Seraphine was powerless to help Rune. Everyone was.

"There's a growing number of witches who don't support her but will never stand against her so long as she has an army at her disposal."

Rune couldn't exactly blame them. *She* was terrified of Cressida.

"As long as she has Soren's army, and as long as she succeeds in raising her sisters, no one will speak against her."

"So nothing can be done," said Rune. Her palms itched beneath the iron restraints that fully encased her hands.

"Not nothing," said Seraphine, her eyes glittering in the dim light. "If Cressida could be compromised—if she lost Soren's support, or were weakened in some other way—it would be easier to draw out dissidents."

Rune remembered Gideon's plan: to hunt down and kill the last living Roseblood. It would be a serious blow to Cressida.

"You could dispose of me."

Seraphine made a face. "That's not what I meant."

But it would work.

"I could tell Soren the truth: Cressida is planning to kill me and therefore has no intention of letting me become his wife."

The problem was, she hadn't seen Soren since she and Gideon escaped aboard the *Arcadia*. She knew he was on the island; Cressida had requested he take his soldiers and do a sweep of the countryside surrounding the city, setting up encampments there to ensure the Blood Guard didn't hit them with a surprise attack.

Rune suspected he didn't know his fiancée was here,

imprisoned. That Cressida had made him believe Rune was still kidnapped by witch hunters.

"Cressida would only retaliate," said Seraphine, forcing Rune to recall the whip. The lashes. The blood.

Sweat beaded her hairline. Her chains clinked in her lap as she shifted uncomfortably.

"A better plan would be to destroy Elowyn and Analise's bodies."

"Except no one knows where they are," said Rune.

It was one of Cressida's tightly guarded secrets.

"A spell like that needs constant renewal. Cressida's been away from the island for months; she needs to either replenish it or finally resurrect them. I believe she'll go to them soon. And when she does, she'll take you with her."

Rune nodded. She knew her days were numbered. Cressida wanted her sisters at her side, and Rune was the key to raising them back to life.

She would have tried to escape before now, but the restraints, the spells, the constant watch of her guards made it impossible.

"Soren is due back any day. When he returns, I'll tell him the truth."

If I'm still alive.

Once the prince learned Cressida intended to kill Rune, he would get her to safety.

"And if she's keeping him away to prevent exactly that?" asked Seraphine.

Rune looked to the windows, blackened by the night. She felt close to despairing. Of course that was why Cressida sent him away.

"We can't wait for Soren," said Seraphine.

"Do you have a better plan?" Rune lifted her restraints in the air to demonstrate her prisoner status. "I'm always exactly where she wants me to be. She has two witches following my every move, not to mention spells locking me into my rooms."

"Actually," said Seraphine, "I *do* have a better plan."

CHANDELIERS TWINKLED OVERHEAD AS servants uncorked bottles of wine and poured them into goblets. The banquet hall was awash in golden light as Cressida's court laughed and gossiped at tables, waiting for the show trials to start.

Every evening at dinner, Cressida's enemies were brought before her to beg for their lives.

As Rune glanced around the lavish room, she found witches dressed in finery, eating off gold-rimmed plates. As if Cressida had already won. As if she'd never *not* been queen.

Was it really this easy? Or is this an elaborate show?

If the Blood Guard rallied and came marching in tomorrow, would they stand a chance against her? Or would they be defeated?

Rune didn't want to find out. Her hands fidgeted in her lap as she waited for the sign from Seraphine, ready to set their plan in motion. She tried not to think about the price of getting caught. All she had to do was touch the scars marring her back.

Soon, soldiers brought in their daily captures: Tribunal members, Blood Guard soldiers, anyone who'd worked for the Good Commander or one of his ministries. Each one was forced to their knees before Cressida's table, awaiting their sentence.

Some witches put their forks down to watch; others continued their conversations. They'd barely been here a week, and many were already bored of the nightly entertainment.

It reminded Rune of private purgings, rare events when witches were brought out at dinner parties and killed while the guests enjoyed their after-dinner coffees.

We're still in hell, she thought. *It just has different trappings.*

As prisoners begged for their lives, or the lives of spouses and children, witches sipped their wine and ate their desserts. Unbothered.

Or at least, that's how it appeared.

Like Seraphine, Rune suspected some, maybe even most, *were* bothered—but too scared to show it.

Their theory was substantiated when the next prisoner was dragged in.

The Commander's spymaster.

As they dragged her before Cressida's table, Juniper's hands clenched the tablecloth. Rune looked from Juniper's tight-knuckled grip to her face, which had gone whiter than bone, her gaze fixed on the girl who'd been forced to her knees.

She seemed to recognize the prisoner—whose dark hair was up in a topknot, her left ear missing. Juniper's chair scraped the floor as she shoved it back.

"Excuse me," she said, stumbling away from the table and rushing from the room.

Rune stared after her until a soft snore drew her gaze to the guards seated across the table. Both were asleep. One with her head on her arms, the other with her chin resting on her hand.

Seraphine cleared her throat. "Juniper seems upset, Rune. Perhaps you should go check on her."

Rune glanced at the witch beside her.

Leave your guards to me, Seraphine had told her earlier.

Had she enchanted their drinks?

Was Juniper in on this scheme, too?

Her heart skipped.

Folding her napkin with a calmness she didn't feel, Rune glanced across the room to where Cressida sat at a table with her inner circle of witches. The queen wore a navy blue gown that shone like midnight, and her white hair was braided tightly back. Her attention was fixed on the spymaster kneeling before her. The girl glared at the witch queen, refusing to grovel or beg.

There was something familiar about her.

Rune shook it off, rose from the table, and slipped into the hall.

Without her casting knife, she needed something to draw blood so she could cast *Ghost Walker*. She planned to escape through the kitchens, grab a sharp knife, and then steal a horse from the stable. From there, she would take a train to the north-west side of the island, where she was less likely to be recognized and no one would be on the lookout for witches. Sparsely populated due to its high winds and barren landscape, that part of the island consisted mainly of small fishing towns. She'd find someone to sail her away—or steal a boat and sail herself. And all the while, she'd be hidden by Seraphine's spell, unable to be Seen by any sibyl.

Her plan was cut short by Juniper.

The girl had one hand pressed to the wall and the other pressed to her stomach. From the way her chest heaved, she looked like she was about to throw up.

"Juniper?"

The witch jumped, spinning to face her. Her black hair was braided into a tight crown atop her head, and her dark brown eyes were wide.

She looked like she'd seen a ghost.

"Are you all right?" asked Rune.

"I . . . I know that girl. The one they're calling the spymaster."

Rune frowned. Maybe Juniper *wasn't* in on Seraphine's scheme.

Juniper looked to the banquet hall doors. "My parents said they sold her. They told me she was on the Continent, and that I'd never find her. I followed every lead. I looked *everywhere*."

Rune followed her gaze to the doors she'd just come through, still shut. She could not be standing here the next time those doors opened.

She needed to go.

Now.

She turned to head for the kitchens, when Juniper whispered: "I thought Harrow was dead."

Harrow.

The name jolted Rune. It wasn't a common name. What were the chances the Harrow kneeling before Cressida was Gideon's friend?

"Then the soldiers brought her in, and I . . . Rune, I have to save her."

If Harrow *was* the Commander's spymaster, she would be sent to the interrogation rooms for sure. They would try to break her. She was too valuable for them not to.

Go! Now! Every second you remain here is a risk!

Rune clenched and unclenched her hands, still staring down the hall toward the kitchens.

"I wish I could help you, Juniper. But I can't."

Rune wasn't about to risk her life trying to rescue an enemy who wouldn't do the same if their positions were reversed. Besides: Harrow was as good as dead. There was nothing Rune could do to change that.

An old fear had woken up in her. Like a serpent, it coiled around her heart. Choking off anything that might prevent her survival.

She turned on her heel and started walking away, heading for a door she knew led to the servant quarters.

"You're the Crimson Moth," Juniper called after her. "Saving people is what you *do*."

Not anymore.

"She's friends with the Blood Guard captain," said Juniper, more quietly. "She'll know where Gideon is. If Cressida finds out his location . . ."

That made Rune stop.

Because of course that's what Cressida would use Harrow for.

You think you can protect him from me? Cressida had told her. *Once I have my throne, the first thing I intend to do is hunt Gideon down.*

Rune knew what would happen if Gideon fell into Cressida's hands.

If he's even still alive.

The thought squeezed her heart.

And if he is alive?

"Fine," she growled, spinning to face Juniper. A plan—a stupid, dangerous plan—was forming in her mind. This would be her last rescue. After that, no more.

"I'll save this girl for you." And for Gideon. "But I need something from you in exchange."

Juniper palmed the tears from her cheeks. "Anything."

"When they ask you where I am, you tell them you haven't seen me. You have no idea where I went. Got it?"

Juniper nodded. "Yes," she breathed. "Of course."

Rune stepped back. "Leave the rest to me."

FIFTY-FOUR

RUNE

*T*HE INTERROGATION ROOMS WERE inside the palace prison. Luckily for Rune, she'd seen a prison map two months ago, aided by Alex, when they'd been planning to break Seraphine out. That plan had never come to fruition, but the map was still inside Rune's head. Where it could aid her now.

She couldn't cast *Ghost Walker*. Without her casting knife, or something sharp, she had no way to draw the blood required. Rune was about to make a detour to the kitchens when someone stepped directly in front of her.

"Rune?"

The prince blinked, as if surprised to find her here. He looked disheveled and exhausted.

"Soren?"

Had he ridden here from the front lines?

Rune, who'd been hoping for his return, was suddenly annoyed by it. Now that she'd saved herself, he'd come and planted himself directly in her path.

"Thank the tides you're safe." Soren's voice was quiet. Tired. "I feared the worst . . . how did you get free of that brute?"

As he closed the distance between them, she realized they hadn't seen each other since Gideon's "kidnapping" in the bridal shop.

"Soren, I—"

Before she could fill him in and reveal Cressida's plans, he pulled her against him and planted his mouth on hers.

All of her senses recoiled at once.

No.

Pressing her palms to his chest, she shoved him away.

"Soren." She gasped for breath. "There's something you need to know."

"Come now, darling." He wiped his mouth with the back of his hand. "I had half my army out looking for you. I was worried sick . . ."

He reached for her again, his fingers brushing her cheek.

Rune flinched and turned her face away.

"Stop."

He frowned. "What is this?"

"This," said Rune, motioning between them. "Is over."

His face darkened. "Should I remind you of the deal we made?" He moved toward her. Rune stepped back. "*You*, for all this." He waved at the palace halls around them. "Cressida has her throne, which means you belong to me now."

Anger flickered in Rune's belly.

Why in the world had she believed this man would deliver her from anything?

"Cressida has no intention of letting you have me," she said. "She's using you. She uses everyone. You and I are just pawns in her game. The night we met? You didn't run into me. I planted myself outside of your opera box. I *arranged* our meeting, my lord. Because Cressida needed your army, and she knew you wouldn't be able to resist me."

His nostrils flared. "You little deceiver . . ." Again, he moved toward her. Again, Rune stepped back, keeping just out of reach.

He was backing her toward a corner. She ducked, trying to dart around him, but he grabbed her throat and shoved her hard against the wall. Her back flared with pain as her wounds reopened. Her vision went bright white.

She felt his free hand pawing at her bodice. Felt the fabric tear and the dress loosen around her chest.

"I always get what I'm owed," he said.

The pungent smell of him was everywhere. His touch made her want to curl up into a ball. She felt sick, knowing what he was about to do.

Stop him.

But how? He was bigger, stronger. She had no way to cast a spell.

He's a soldier. He'll be armed.

She glanced at his hip. Sure enough, there was a pistol holstered there.

As more fabric ripped and Soren lost himself to his lust and rage, Rune reached for the gun.

She turned off the safety and cocked it.

Gideon's voice flooded through her, calming her, helping her focus: *If someone tries to hurt you, and there's no other way to stop them, don't think twice. Just shoot. Got it?*

Lifting the gun to Soren's head, Rune fired.

FIFTY-FIVE

RUNE

*T*HE KING OF UMBRIA'S son fell dead at her feet.

Rune stared at him, her entire body quaking with shock. *Good girl,* she could almost hear Gideon say.

She was about to turn and walk away, when the sight of Soren's blood stopped her.

Crouching, she pressed two fingers to the blood dripping from his temple, then used it to draw the symbols for *Ghost Walker* on her forearm. Normally, she'd worry about corruption. But she hadn't killed Soren to cast an Arcana spell; she'd killed him in self-defense, and her magic knew the difference.

It flared inside her. The feel of it, like a current coursing through her, comforted Rune. Her breath came easier, even if her hands still shook.

By the time soldiers came running in their direction, Rune was passing beneath the prison's entrance, undetected beneath the cloak of her spell. Overhead, images of the seven Ancients were impressed into the steel archway.

Up ahead walked Harrow, her hands in manacles, accompanied by two witches.

An iron gate blocked their entry into the prison's first section. Its thick black bars were forged to look like doves in flight, all soaring to the top of the entryway where the engraved words *Mercy Gate* loomed above. At their approach, the gate clinked slowly open.

Noticing a casting knife sheathed at each witch's hip, Rune stepped as close as she dared and carefully slid one out. The witch tilted her head, as if sensing Rune's presence—or perhaps scenting her magic—but the gate swung open, and she immediately turned her attention within, stepping through it with Harrow and the other witch.

Rune's grip tightened on the stolen knife as she slipped in behind them, invisible beneath her spell.

The sour smell hit her first. *Sweat.* And mold. Decades of it, probably. The dampness clung to the cold air.

Normally, interrogations happened at Blood Guard headquarters. But Cressida had blown those up months ago. Now, prisoners brought in to be interrogated were held here, inside the prison's first section.

Two wide bays spanned out from this corridor, curving like wings, out of sight. A prison guard led them down the nearest bay, where doors lined each wall.

Rune followed, her footsteps silent on the stone.

At the end of the cell bay, the guard unlocked a door and held it open. The witches shoved Harrow inside, where she would stay until the interrogator finished her other examinations.

Before the guard shut the door, Rune slipped into the cell. The door locked behind her, plunging her into darkness. It enclosed Rune like a tomb, heavy and suffocating, making her think of Nan awaiting her death in a cell like this one. Imprisoned in total darkness.

"*Fuck*," said Harrow.

The word was followed by the sound of her sliding down the wall as she collapsed to the floor.

Rune's absence had likely been noticed by now. And it was only a matter of minutes before news of Soren's murder reached Cressida. Once it did, she would put two and two together.

Soon, every witch and soldier in the palace would be hunting for Rune.

She needed to get Harrow out quickly.

Rune smudged the spellmark on her arm, then used the stolen casting knife to draw enough blood to cast *Torch*. A white
flame flared above her open palm, forcing Harrow to glance up.

Surprise flashed across her face, but she hid it almost immediately, smoothing her expression to one as blank as stone.

"Looks like someone tried to have their way with you."

Rune looked down to discover her bodice torn almost to her
waist and the shift beneath showing through.

"He tried," said Rune. "Now he's dead."

Harrow's head tilted, studying Rune. As if impressed and
trying not to show it. The chains of her manacles clinked as
she stretched like a cat. Like this was a totally normal conversation under totally normal circumstances, instead of one she
was having while imprisoned in a dark cell. "I assume you want
something from me. Otherwise you wouldn't be here."

Rune stepped forward.

Harrow flinched.

"I won't hurt you." Rune crouched, wetting her fingers with
blood from the cut she'd made. Taking hold of Harrow's manacles, she drew the spellmark for *Picklock*. "I'm going to get you out
of here, but we need to be quick. You won't slow me down, will
you?"

"No, ma'am," said Harrow, studying her beneath the light of
that eerie flame.

"Good," said Rune as the magic rushed out of her, humming
in the air.

The manacles fell open, clanking to the stone floor.

Harrow rubbed at her wrists.

Rune rose to her feet.

"Let's go."

FIFTY-SIX

RUNE

*R*UNE'S SPELLS KEPT THEM concealed as they escaped the prison and avoided the guards frantically running the palace halls, clearly searching for someone. By the time they entered the stables, the chaos was behind them. Between the stalls, dust spiraled in golden shafts of light, and the occasional horse whinny broke through the silence.

"Who are they looking for?" asked Harrow.

"The prince is dead," Rune whispered as a roan mare thrust her head over a stall door to nuzzle her shoulder. *Ghost Walker* didn't work on animals, whose senses were more advanced. "They're looking for his killer."

Harrow fell silent, putting the pieces together.

"Where's Gideon?" Rune asked her.

"Last I heard, the Blood Guard went west. I imagine they took him with them."

"West? Do you know where they're headed?"

Harrow studied her, trying to decide if she was trustworthy. "There's an abandoned fort on the coast. They call it the Rookery. The plan is to rearm there."

If they were bringing Gideon with them, it meant they didn't plan to execute him. With the capital overrun by Soren's army and Cressida sitting on her throne, the Blood Guard needed all the help they could get. Perhaps Gideon was too valuable to dispose of.

Opening the stall door, Rune quickly tacked the mare,

concealing her with *Ghost Walker* before holding the lead out to Harrow. "Take her and get out of the city."

"Where will you go?" she asked, taking it.

"If Cressida catches me, I'm as good as dead." Rune entered the next stall and started drawing the marks for *Ghost Walker* on the horse's rump. "I need to get off this island."

But first, Rune needed to make one last stop: Wintersea House.

If her home was about to be torn apart by war, she too needed to rearm. With Soren dead, it was no longer certain that Cressida would win. If she did, she'd kill Rune. If she didn't and the Good Commander regained power, *he* would kill Rune.

The only thing to do was run.

And if Rune was going to run, she wanted some of Nan's spell books with her. She knew enough spells to get by, but she had no way of learning more. She'd be utterly alone out there.

More importantly: the books were her last link to her grand-mother. If Rune was going to leave everything behind, forever, she wanted a reminder of the woman who'd loved her so much she sacrificed herself so Rune could live.

"I was wrong about you," said Harrow, watching Rune tack the second horse.

It almost sounded like an apology.

WHEN SHE ARRIVED AT Wintersea, it was dark and crawl-ing with Blood Guard soldiers. Four stood in uniform outside the gates, guns at their sides, while more patrolled the grounds.

Wintersea House is the residence of Noah Creed now, Gideon had told her.

Had the Good Commander left soldiers behind to ensure his property wasn't ransacked?

Rune nudged her horse past the ones guarding the entrance. *Ghost Walker* would fade soon. It had been several hours since she'd cast it. She needed to hurry.

Rune was passing the stables when a familiar whinny made her halt her stolen horse.

Lady. Nan's old show horse.

Rune had been forced to leave her behind.

Dismounting, she crept inside the stone stable. It wasn't long before Lady's glossy white head poked over a stall door, staring straight at Rune. As if to say, *What took you so long?*

Rune's heart swelled at the sight of her.

She flung her arms around Lady's neck, giving her a tight hug, then swapped her with the horse she'd stolen. She led Lady from the stable toward the back of the house, stopping next to Nan's labyrinth, which formed one of three entrances to the gardens. The labyrinth was overgrown, its rose hedges in desperate need of pruning. Leaving Lady at its entrance to wait for her, Rune turned to face the back of Wintersea House. Her gaze skimmed up the wall, stopping at the window directly overhead, two stories up: her casting room.

Thick ivy snaked over the stone walls, diverting around glass panes. Rune grabbed the old vines and started to climb, hoping they would hold her weight. Hoping *Ghost Walker* would last long enough for her to find the spell books she needed and get out.

By the time she reached the window and unlocked it, three patrols had walked by beneath her. Swinging the pane quietly open, Rune crawled inside, careful not to land with a thud, in case anyone occupied the rooms below.

She'd been afraid to find her casting room empty, its illegal contents burned. But the room was untouched, exactly as she left it: with crates full of spell books she'd packed before her world turned upside down.

The secret wall was shut tight, suggesting Noah hadn't found it.

Rune moved slowly through the room, letting her eyes adjust to the darkness. Grabbing the matchbox off her desk, she struck a match and lit a candle.

Quickly, Rune searched the room. She found a small purse full of coins, as well as Lady's whistle on the desk. She pocketed them both. Next, she turned to the spell books packed into wooden shipping crates.

There were far too many to take. She'd have to choose three or four. Something manageable.

Wary of her footfalls, Rune pulled out half a dozen books and brought them to the desk. There, she sorted them into two piles: *bringing* and *leaving*.

She pulled one particularly heavy book from the stack, and another slid out with it, falling to the floor.

It landed with a *thud*.

Rune froze. She tilted her head, listening for voices—or footsteps. Some sign the guards in the house were alert to her presence.

But Wintersea was silent.

Swallowing, Rune sat on the floor with the book in her hands, flipping through the pages in the flickering candlelight. It was old, by hundreds of years perhaps, its yellow pages brittle.

She turned to the first spell. A summoning spell. One capable of calling an Ancient from the world beyond this one.

To do what? Rune frowned down at the page.

It seemed silly. If the Ancients existed at all, they'd abandoned this world centuries ago. They could only be summoned in the stories parents told their children at bedtime.

A floorboard creaked outside the room.

Rune's spine straightened. She turned her head to listen.

Maybe it's the house.

Wintersea was over a hundred years old. The slightest bit of wind made its bones creak and groan.

The sound came again. Closer this time. Just beyond the false wall.

Rune's heart began to hammer. She closed the book.

The latch *clicked*.

Rune blew out the candle, plunging the room into darkness.

The wall swung open as she got to her feet.

Someone stepped into the room with her.

FIFTY-SEVEN

GIDEON

"*A*LL WITCHES ARE TO be shot on sight."

Gideon stood against the wall, watching as junior soldiers ran back and forth, packing crates of Noah's belongings to bring from Wintersea to the Rookery, where the army was headed.

"Do not hesitate. Do not give them the benefit of the doubt."

Gideon watched the small council of ministers who'd managed to escape the capital confer with Noah around his dining room table.

Rune's dining room table, he corrected himself.

Gideon rubbed at the manacles chafing his wrists, prompting the soldiers on either side of him to glance his way.

One of them—a young man named Felix—had enlisted when he was just sixteen. He was a scrawny little thing with fiery red hair. No one believed he'd survive the first week of training. Gideon remembered Laila and some of the others placing bets on when he'd pack up and go home.

Gideon had watched as the other recruits beat the boy into the dirt again and again. But Felix always got up, battered and swaying on his feet. Determined to prove them wrong.

So Gideon had taken him aside and trained him himself.

That was a year ago.

Now he's my jailer.

He supposed it could be worse. They could have left him in

that cell for Cressida to find. They could have killed him on the road for his crimes.

Instead, they'd kept him alive. With Cressida on the throne, Gideon was a valuable asset. He knew the witch queen intimately, could predict her behavior—or so they hoped.

But Gideon had *also* proven himself sympathetic to witches. So they couldn't exactly trust him, either.

Hence the chains.

And the guards.

"You need to leave within the hour, sir." Aila Woods, the former minister of public safety, looked haggard from nights spent trying to organize their scattered numbers and get them to a safer location. They'd decided on the Rookery—an old citadel on the island's western coast. It had been abandoned half a century ago, but was still heavily fortified. "Prince Nord's army has ransacked the estates closer to the capital. They'll come for Wintersea any day now."

"Yes, yes, I'm aware." Noah looked equally tired, his face lit by the dim glow of a lantern.

Reports of executions came daily, and morale was lower than ever. They'd lost a lot of soldiers, and the only weapons and ammunition in their possession were what they'd carried out. If they had any hope of stopping what was coming, they needed to regroup, acquire more arms, and launch a counterattack.

Which was why they were retreating to the coast.

"I'll make sure my brother gets out in time," Laila told Aila. She stood to the side, arms crossed as she glanced at the map of the Rookery laid out across the table. "You all should leave *now*. Take the back roads. Soren's soldiers have been spotted twenty miles up the main one."

Thump!

Gideon looked to the ceiling, where the sound had come from. From his previous visits to Wintersea, he knew the bedrooms lay directly above them.

"Did you hear that?" he asked his guards.

They exchanged a look between them.

"Hear what, sir?" said Felix.

Both were younger than him and clearly nervous. He was *Gideon Sharpe*, after all. Former Blood Guard captain, not to mention a hero of the Republic who'd killed two witch queens in the revolt.

Gideon glanced at the emergency meeting happening around the table, but the conversation continued unabated. Neither Noah nor his ministers had heard the sound.

Laila, however, glanced his way.

So I'm not hearing things.

He raised an eyebrow, motioning with his chin toward the ceiling.

Going to check that out?

Perhaps it was a clumsy soldier packing Noah's belongings.

Or perhaps it was something more insidious.

Grabbing a lantern, Laila crossed the room to him. "That noise—did you hear it too?" She looked to the ceiling. But no sounds were forthcoming.

He nodded. "Could be a bandit."

In the aftermath of Cressida's attack, estates had been ransacked, not just by Soren's army but by thieves hoping to fill their pockets with valuables. From the frown creasing her brow, though, Laila wasn't worried about bandits. She was worried about something worse.

"I know this house better than you do," he said. "Take me up with you."

Laila studied Gideon in the glow of her lantern. She might trust him more than the other soldiers, but not by much.

"I'm not going to run off and join Cressida," he told her. "I'd rather drown myself in the sea."

Laila breathed in. "Fine." She turned to Felix and held out her hand. "I'm borrowing the prisoner. Give me his keys."

Since Laila was acting captain, Felix did as she said. He seemed relieved to hand Gideon over, honestly.

After Laila removed his manacles, Gideon followed her out of the room and up the staircase to the second floor. The gaslights were off, plunging the main hallway into darkness.

"I'll start at the far end," said Gideon. "If you start here, we can meet in the middle."

Laila nodded, stepping into the first bedroom and taking her lantern with her.

Gideon strode quietly down the dark hall. On his way to the end, he passed the door to Rune's bedroom.

He'd made the calculation already, downstairs. The *thump* had come from this general area. But stronger than his knowledge of the house's layout was a feeling in the pit of his gut.

A *knowing*.

Gideon stepped inside Rune's bedroom.

It still smelled like her. Like the wind and the sea and the rain. Like something wild and untamable. He breathed it in.

In the moonlight flooding through the windows, he searched the room quickly. The floorboards creaked beneath his weight as he checked closets and the space beneath the bed. But there was no one here.

Gideon was about to turn and leave when he remembered the false wall.

He turned to face it.

Beyond the wall lay Rune's casting room. Discovering it was what had led Gideon to realize she was the Crimson Moth.

Gideon pressed his hands to the wallpaper, feeling for the crack. When he found it, he pushed in, and the latch *clicked*.

The wall swung open.

The smoke of a freshly extinguished candle wafted out.

Gotcha.

Gideon stepped into the room . . .

. . . where a blunt object whacked him over the head.

FIFTY-EIGHT

RUNE

*R*UNE DROPPED THE CANDLEHOLDER and ran. The soldier cursed, then lunged for her. His hands closed around her ankle. Rune fell. The floor rose to meet her elbows, spiking pain up her arms.

They grappled in the dark: him trying to pin her down, Rune struggling to escape him.

She kicked him in the shin. He cursed and let go. The moment he lost his advantage, Rune sat down on top of him, pressing her stolen knife to his throat. Panting with the effort.

He fell immediately still beneath her.

The only way to escape now was to kill him. Before he called for help.

I've killed a man already tonight. What's one more?

But she couldn't bring herself to press down, to slit his throat.

"Well?" he growled. "What are you waiting for? Kill me and be done with it."

Rune froze.

That voice.

It was honey to her soul.

"*Gideon?*" she whispered, nearly bursting into tears at the possibility.

He went rigid beneath her.

He's alive.

"It's me," she said. "Rune."

She withdrew the knife from his throat. The moment she

did, he grabbed it and flipped her onto her back. Rune winced as her wounds tore, pain flooding her anew.

"Prove it." He pressed the knife's cold tip to her heart, ready to plunge it in. "Prove you're her and not some other witch wearing her voice."

His body was tight as a coiled spring.

But this was *Gideon*. Rune wasn't afraid of him. Just the opposite: she wanted to wrap her arms around him and never let go.

It seemed impossible that she had found him. That he was even alive.

What is he doing at Wintersea?

"The last time you saw me," she whispered, "I was stealing apples from your cupboard. You asked me if I'd miss you. I said no."

His breath shuddered.

"Liar." He dropped the blade and lowered his forehead to hers. "You said you'd miss me the way a fox misses a wolf."

"Which is not at all."

She could almost feel him smile in the darkness. He slid his palms over her jaw, taking her face in his hands. His touch was a balm. Rune wanted to wrap her arms around his shoulders and pull him close, but the wounds on her back had reopened, and the longer he pressed her into the floor, the worse it hurt.

The pain made her stiffen.

Gideon felt it and pulled immediately away, misunderstanding her.

She wanted to explain—except that would require telling him what Cressida did. Gideon would want her to show him the scars. And *that* Rune would never do.

She wanted him to remember her as she had been: beautiful, not . . . flayed.

Not *hideous*.

The weight of Gideon lifted as he got to his feet and relit a candle. In the flickering light, Rune remembered her disheveled state and what Soren had done. She sat up and scuttled toward the wall. But it was too late. Gideon saw her torn bodice and the ripped shift beneath.

His eyes blackened.

"Who did this to you?"

Rune glanced at the floor, feeling ashamed without knowing why. She gripped the torn fabric, holding it closed over her chest.

Gideon dropped to his knees in front of her, the heat of his rage rolling off him. But his voice was less of a growl now. He was controlling it, she realized. For her sake. "Rune. Give me his name."

Tears burned in her eyes as she remembered the moment with Soren in the hall. She wanted to tell him, but her throat wouldn't work. The words wouldn't come.

"It doesn't matter," she managed. "I killed him. I took your advice and didn't hesitate."

Gideon studied her in the candlelight, eyes ferocious, brow furrowed. He lifted his hand to tuck her messy hair behind her ear. His hand lingered, then dropped. As if he wasn't sure if she wanted to be touched. "I suppose that saves me the effort of killing him myself."

"I thought they killed *you*," she whispered as they stared at each other. Her fingers itched to trace the lines of his jaw, the bridge of his nose, the stern ridge of his brow. "I thought I'd never see you again." Her voice broke.

He softened. "I thought you were leaving."

"I did leave."

"Then what are you doing here?"

A sound from down the hall made them both jump. Gideon looked to the casting room's open wall.

"There are dozens of Blood Guard soldiers in this house." He rose to his feet. "They've been ordered to shoot you on sight. You have to hide . . ."

He started to cross the room when footsteps echoed from the bedroom beyond. Before Gideon could close the wall, sealing them in, Noah stepped through the opening, with several soldiers flanking him.

They must have heard the noise from Rune and Gideon's scuffle. Laila stumbled in behind them.

At the sight of Rune, they all drew their guns.

Gideon stepped in front of her.

"Take Miss Winters out back and shoot her," Noah told his sister. "I'll deal with the witch's whore."

Something red-hot burst to life in Rune.

How *dare* he call Gideon that.

She grabbed her stolen knife from where Gideon had dropped it and stepped out from behind him, staring down the barrel of Noah's gun. "Gideon has more valor in his thumbnail than you have in your entire being, you piece of—"

"*Rune.*" Gideon's voice was a warning.

But what could Noah do? Shoot her? Laila was going to do that anyway.

"Drop the knife," said Laila, her pistol raised as she stepped closer.

Rune raised both hands, as if to surrender. But instead of dropping the knife, she threw it.

Straight at Noah.

He ducked, but not fast enough. The blade sank into his shoulder and he screamed.

His gun went off. The shot went wide. Rune lunged for him, feeling feral. Like all of her rage and grief and fear suddenly had a target, and if she could just *hit* it, maybe she would feel better. Like herself again.

Laila grabbed her around the waist before she could, while the other soldiers descended on Gideon.

Rune scratched and thrashed like a wildcat. But it was no use. Laila called for backup, and suddenly they were throwing her to the ground and pinning her there. Laila pressed one knee to her flayed back.

Pain exploded through Rune. She fell still.

They bound her wrists and hauled her to her feet.

"No," said Gideon. "No!"

As they dragged her from the room, Rune glanced back to see soldiers restraining him. A wild expression blazed in his eyes as his muscles bunched, struggling against four captors.

"Laila, don't!"

Laila paused. "She put Cressida on the throne, Gideon. *Cressida*, who's executing people as we speak." She glanced back. "That monster killed my father."

Rune remembered it. The way Cressida so casually put a bullet in Nicolas Creed's head. The way he collapsed to the stones, utterly silent and still.

"Like your father killed Kestrel Winters?"

Laila straightened.

"Rune had to watch her grandmother die," said Gideon. "Just as you had to watch your father die."

Laila's nostrils flared. But she said nothing more. Only tightened her grip on Rune's arm and continued walking, leading them out of Rune's bedroom and into the hall, forcing Rune downstairs, out the back door, and into the chilly night.

"Leave us," Laila told the other soldiers. "I'll take it from here."

Alone, she marched Rune into the gardens.

"On your knees."

Rune did as she said. The earth was hard and cold beneath her, and the sky was bright with stars overhead.

With her hands bound in front of her, Rune breathed in the scent of Nan's roses.

This is a good place to die.

The Wintersea gardens were better than a platform surrounded by a bloodthirsty mob. Perhaps they would bury her here, among the roses.

Rune heard a soft *click* as Laila cocked her gun.

At least I got to see Gideon, she thought, remembering his calloused hand against her cheek. *One last time.*

She closed her eyes, breathed in deep, and waited for the shot to come.

FIFTY-NINE

GIDEON

"**Y**OU WOULD HAVE GONE down in history as a hero," said Noah as Felix and the other soldiers wrestled Gideon into his chains. "Instead, you fell in love with a witch."

She was always out of your league, Sharpe.

Gideon suddenly remembered the way Noah used to look at Rune—from across a ballroom, or an opera box. The way his eyes tracked her.

He wanted her, Gideon realized.

He remembered the things Noah had said about Rune at Alex's card game, months ago. Ugly things meant to hurt her reputation.

To punish her for rejecting him.

It all suddenly made sense.

"Is that really what bothers you—that I fell in love with her?" Gideon growled as they tried to lock the manacles around his wrists. "Or is it that she loved me back?"

Noah's mouth twisted in a scowl.

"You don't want her dead because she's a witch," said Gideon, "you want her dead because she didn't want *you*."

Noah stepped closer, raising his gun. Silently telling Gideon to cooperate with his captors. "Soon she won't want you, either, since she'll be six feet underground."

The thought of Rune dead made Gideon's heart turn to stone. But he'd heard no gunshot. That meant she was still alive—for now.

He struggled harder against the soldiers trying to subdue him. But it was four against one, and despite his efforts, the manacles clicked, locking his wrists behind his back.

How was he supposed to get to her, chained as he was, with so many armed soldiers intent on preventing him?

Rune is resilient. She'll find a way to survive.

She had to.

Gideon didn't want to live in a world without her.

He turned his angry gaze on Noah.

"The problem with love is the more you try to destroy it, the stronger it becomes."

Noah sneered.

But not so long ago, Gideon believed the same thing Noah did: that loving Rune made him weak. That trusting her made him a fool.

Nothing could be further from the truth.

"It might look like weakness on the surface. But in truth, it's tougher than steel. Love can't be controlled. Love can't obey unjust laws. Love will always oppose tyrants."

Gideon felt Felix glance at him.

"Love is the real enemy of the regime, and that's why you despise it. It's why Cressida tries to crush it. Because you both know, deep down, it has the power to topple you."

"I'm tempted to shoot you right here if it will end your blathering," said Noah, stepping closer. "But I have something better in store."

Chained, Gideon was little more than a muzzled dog. He posed no threat. Which was precisely why Noah came so close. He wouldn't dare threaten Gideon if they were on equal footing.

The two young men stared each other down.

Looking at Noah was like looking at a younger version of

Nicolas—a man who'd taken Gideon under his wing and treated him like a son. Noah and Nicolas were nothing alike. It made Gideon wonder how a son could fall so short of his father.

Nicolas had fought hard for everything he had; Noah was handed everything on a silver platter. Nicolas was valiant and brave, a natural leader. Noah was a coward and an opportunist who'd seized the position of Good Commander before his father's body was even in the ground.

"I'm going to propose a trade," Noah told him. "*You*, for the prisoners Cressida is executing."

The thought of being handed over to Cressida made Gideon's blood run cold.

"I have a feeling the witch queen will give me whatever I ask for, if it means she gets her whore back." Noah smirked, then turned to Felix. "Bring him downstairs and put him on a horse. We're leaving for the Rookery as soon as the witch is dead."

"Yes, Commander."

Felix and his comrade seized Gideon's arms as Noah strode from the room and into the dark hall. But before following him out, Felix pressed a small object into Gideon's hands. Something cold and hard and slender.

The key to his manacles.

Gideon glanced at Felix, who stared straight ahead as he and the other soldier hauled him through the darkness.

His chest swelled at the gift.

And then he got to work.

In the darkness, Gideon slid the key into the lock. His chains clinked as they moved, masking the sound of his manacles opening.

Gideon shook them off. The chains fell to the floor with a *thud*.

Hearing it, Felix's comrade turned. Gideon grabbed the boy's gun, shoved him out of the way, and took off down the hall.

"Hey! Stop him!"

Gideon heard the soldiers ahead turn, but the hallway was dark, and they couldn't see well. Gideon had the advantage.

He barreled past them, catching up with Noah on the stairs. The Good Commander turned, his eyes widening at the sight of Gideon, who grabbed his coat.

Thrusting him up against the wall, Gideon sent his fist soaring into Noah's face.

He did it again.

And again.

The pain that bloomed in his knuckles was nothing compared to the catharsis. He shook off the sting while Noah slid to the floor, dazed. As much as he'd love to finish him, Rune was in danger. He had to get to her.

Moonlight filtered through the windows here, giving the soldiers behind Gideon a better view. They fired on him as he raced down the steps. Gideon jumped the rail, and their bullets missed.

He shouldered the front door open and bolted outside, hoping he wasn't too late. That Rune was still alive.

Shouts echoed from inside as Noah raised the alarm. By then, Gideon was already rounding the house.

He stopped in his tracks at the sight of Rune on her knees and Laila raising her pistol, about to fire.

"Laila! No!"

Startled by his shout, Laila flinched. The crack of her gun split the night. Gideon looked to Rune, who seemed startled but unharmed.

The shot had gone wide.

Laila drew a second gun and pointed both straight at him.

"Are you out of your damned mind?" she shouted, fury etched across her face.

He lifted his hands to show her he wasn't a threat. "This is not the way we win."

Her chest rose and fell with her unsteady breaths, but her aim remained steady.

"Laila—"

"Shut up, Gideon."

Shouts echoed from the house. Soldiers would swarm them soon, and it would be over. With Rune's hands tied, she couldn't cast any spells. And Gideon was one man against dozens of soldiers—many of whom he'd trained.

Laila glanced over her shoulder, toward the house.

"Laila . . ."

"I said, *shut up*. I'm trying to think." She dropped her arms in an infuriated huff. "I'll give you fifteen seconds, all right?" She nodded to Rune. "You better hope she runs fast."

Gideon wanted to hug her. Instead, he grabbed Rune's arm and hauled her to her feet.

"Thank you."

"Now you owe me double!" she shouted as they ran.

Rune led them past manicured hedges and groves, to the wilder part of the gardens. They were nearly at the garden gate when the bullets started to fly.

Crack! Crack! Crack!

Gideon lifted Rune over the gate, then jumped it, careful to keep his body between her and the soldiers. Shielding her from the gunfire.

They ran through the meadow. With her hands tied, Rune was slower than usual. The first time she stumbled, Gideon helped her up and a bullet lodged in his shoulder. He bit down on a growl as the pain seared through him.

They kept running.

The second time Rune stumbled, another bullet found its

mark—in Gideon's hip this time. So he scooped her into his arms and pressed on, keeping his eyes on the woods up ahead. Rune didn't fight him—which should have been the first sign something was wrong. She simply gave in, pressing her cheek against his chest as she slumped in his arms.

Soon, his shoulder and hip throbbed with heat and pain. He felt himself slowing.

He was losing blood. Too much blood.

Get to the woods.

It was their best chance to lose their pursuers.

When the open meadow gave way to the shelter of trees, Gideon trudged through the undergrowth, driving them deeper in, where the forest was thickest. The back of his jacket was warm and wet now, soaked with blood. His body felt heavy, his mind cloudy, and more than once, his legs didn't do what he wanted, and he stumbled.

With so much blood lost, he was bound to lose consciousness soon. He couldn't continue much further.

But if he told Rune that, she might stay with him and be recaptured.

"We'll have a better chance if we split up," he said. "You go on ahead. I'll double back."

He heard the soldiers in the woods now: their voices, their gunshots, the whinnies of their horses.

Rune turned sharply to face him. "But how will we find each other? There's nowhere safe."

She blurred before him. Gideon pressed his hand to the trunk of a tree, steadying himself against the slow spin of the woods.

"Rune . . . if I don't make it—"

"Why wouldn't you make it?"

Her voice seemed far away. Like he was underwater.

"Gideon?"

His legs were trying to decide whether or not to keep holding him up.

They decided against it.

The earth rushed up to meet him.

"Gideon!"

SIXTY

RUNE

AS GIDEON COLLAPSED TO his hands and knees, Rune caught sight of his coat. Which glistened darkly. Rune frowned, looking closer. *What* . . .

At the sight of the blood, her heart plummeted into her stomach.

"You absolute idiot." She dropped to her knees, her wrists still bound with rope. "Why didn't you tell me they shot you?"

Gideon just shook his head, his eyes going unfocused. "Leave me here. I'm dead weight now."

Rune wanted to grab his shoulders and shout the sense back into him. "If you think I'm leaving you in the woods of Winter-sea to die, you're dumber than a stump."

A horse whinnied close by.

Rune froze, listening.

There were soldiers on horseback everywhere. She needed to get Gideon out of here.

But first, she needed to stop his bleeding.

Remembering the spellmarks Juniper had drawn on her arms to stop *her* bleeding, she touched his soaked jacket. "Gideon? I need your permission."

He glanced up at her. Even in the dark, she sensed his confusion.

"I need your blood."

"Oh." He nodded. "Go ahead."

Another horse whinnied, and Rune paused to listen before turning back to Gideon. Hoping she remembered the spellmarks accurately, she drew them on his skin—a cumbersome task, with her hands tied. When nothing happened, she assumed the spell had failed.

But then: magic rushed, flowing through her like sunlight. It swirled around them, infusing the air.

Gideon breathed in as if inhaling some delicious aroma, then struggled to get to his feet.

Rune came to his side, helping him up. But when his arm came around her shoulders, pressing down, the weight was too much for her flayed back and she clenched her teeth at the pain.

He withdrew his arm. "What's wrong?"

She shook her head. "It's nothing." At the sound of voices in the trees—closer than before—she added: "Can you walk without help?"

That spell would wear off in a few hours. They needed to get somewhere safe before then, so Rune could dig out the bullets and sew him up.

"I . . . think so." He stood, shakily, on his own two feet.

Suddenly, a soft *whuff* came out of the darkness. Much too close.

Beside her, Gideon tensed.

But Rune smiled, recognizing the sound.

"It's all right," she said as the silhouette of a giant horse emerged from the trees several feet ahead. "It's Lady."

Rune had remembered the whistle in her dress pocket while Gideon carried her through the meadow. She'd pulled it out and blown one hard, fierce note—a sound inaudible to human ears. Neither Gideon nor their pursuers would have heard it.

But Lady did.

"She found us."

The horse bobbed her head and whinnied softly.

Rune helped Gideon mount the horse, who in turn grabbed her hand and pulled her up in front of him.

SIXTY-ONE

RUNE

*T*HEY BROKE INTO THE Wentholt family's summer home.

Well, technically, they *walked* in. The back door was unlocked.

After escaping Wintersea, Rune agreed with Gideon it was the safest place at the moment—the cottage was tucked away in the woods, far from the main roads, and likely the family had already fled. With any luck, they'd be able to get supplies and tend his wounds before moving on.

Gideon was eerily quiet as she helped him through the Wentholts' house, searching for first aid supplies. The ashen hue of his face worried Rune, who knew her spell would wear off soon. She could recast it, but what he really needed was someone to dig out the bullets, then sanitize and stitch up the wounds.

In the empty servants' quarters, Rune lowered Gideon into a chair to rest and then rifled through cupboards, trying to find what she needed. *Torch* blazed overhead, the white flame following her as she searched drawers and boxes.

Her body buzzed with panic. There was nothing here. She was about to go look in the kitchens, where she might find a cleaner, sharper knife to dig out the bullets. But then what? She needed to disinfect the wounds somehow. She needed a needle and thread to stitch them closed.

Rune cursed herself for not learning more healing spells. If she got the chance, she would correct that.

She was crossing the room toward Gideon when the sound of voices stopped her in her tracks. Rune smudged the spellmark on her hand, extinguishing *Torch* and plunging them into darkness.

A man laughed—a low, husky sound.

"I don't care," said the other voice. "Let the bastards find us. I'll fight them all off. For you, I'd . . ."

A low groan cut him off, followed by the sound of a belt buckle hitting the floor.

Rune glanced at Gideon in the dark, her face heating.

Were they . . . ?

Was this . . . ?

The gaslights flickered on.

Two young men entered the room—both in the midst of undressing, their hair messy, their lips swollen from kissing—and froze at the sight of intruders.

"*Bart?*" said Rune, staring at the redheaded boy whose unbuttoned shirt gave them a full view of his chest.

"*Rune?*" said Bart, his mouth falling open as he looked from her to Gideon.

Rune drew the gun at Gideon's hip and raised it. "Call for help, and I'll shoot you both."

The young man beside Bart lifted his hands in surrender. He was shorter and stockier than the Wentholt heir, his complexion darker, and unlike Bart—who was wearing a three-piece suit in complete disarray—he wore plain clothes.

"I thought you were dead," said Bart, raising his hands. "Both of you."

Bartholomew Wentholt had always been the silliest boy at every party. His obsession with himself and his constant bragging about his newest purchases—be they shoes or carriages or tea sets—got him easily dismissed. Bart was the heir to a

massive estate, and therefore an excellent catch for any girl looking to increase her station, but his annoying personality put off
most families.

Rune studied Bart from across the room. Perhaps it was his
disheveled state, but she found someone very different from that
empty-headed aristo staring back at her.

"Who else is in the house?" asked Gideon, who hadn't risen
from his chair. Likely because the act of doing so would put him
on the floor.

"My maid, Bess," said Bart. "No one else."

"And who knows you're here?"

Bart shook his head. "No one."

Rune glanced to the young man at his side. He'd been utterly
silent since entering the room. "Who's this?"

"This—"

"Antonio Bastille." The boy interrupted Bart. "I'm a cook
employed by the Wentholts. What's wrong with him?" He nodded toward Gideon, who looked like he was trying very hard
not to fall out of his chair.

"He's been shot. We hoped to find supplies here."

Antonio dropped his hands to his sides. "I'm trained in the
healing arts. I can help him."

His way of speaking was too formal for a cook, and a little
strange. Rune couldn't place it. She tightened her grip on the
gun, unsure if she should trust him. But Gideon needed help—
desperately—and thus far she hadn't been able to provide it.
Hesitantly, she lowered her pistol and stepped aside, nodding
for Antonio to approach.

She kept her finger on the trigger.

"If you hurt him—"

"I took an oath before the Ancients," said Antonio, rolling

up his sleeves as he came forward. "I can't hurt any living thing. Can you help me take off his coat?"

"Antonio was an acolyte," said Bart as Antonio undid Gideon's buttons. "From the Temple of the Ancients."

It was where Rune had tried to summon the Roseblood heir. The same temple that had been destroyed during the revolution and its acolytes either killed or driven underground.

Had Antonio been there the day the Blood Guard stormed the temple? Had he seen the slaughter with his own eyes?

"I'm sorry," she said. "It's horrible, what they did."

Antonio only nodded, silent, as he finished unbuttoning Gideon's coat. Rune helped lean Gideon forward, and together they carefully stripped off the blood-soaked coat. The white shirt underneath was stained red.

"What's this?" Antonio touched Gideon's neck, where Rune had drawn spellmarks to stop his bleeding. He glanced up, staring at her. "You're a witch?"

"Got a problem with that?" growled Gideon.

As if he could do anything about it in his weakened state.

Antonio only nodded in approval. "He would have bled out had you not cast this," he told Rune. "You saved his life."

He sounded genuinely pleased. That pleasure—at her skill and at Gideon being alive—reassured Rune. She took her finger off the trigger and set the gun down on the table. "How can I help?"

"You can help me take off his shirt. Bart, can you boil some water? And fetch a bottle of the strongest spirits we have in the house."

Rune moved to pick up the gun again and tell Bart to stay right where he was, because what was to stop him from sending a message to the Commander—or worse, Cressida? What was to stop him from simply fetching a weapon of his own and killing them both?

But Antonio touched her arm, and the gesture was so gentle, it coaxed Rune's attention back to him.

"We all need to trust each other." He nodded to the empty doorway where Bart had stood a moment ago. "You are in a position to damn him as much as he is to damn you."

Rune assumed he was talking about their relationship, which was obviously far more than master and cook.

"He's tried very hard to put people off him—young eligible women especially—to keep us a secret," explained Antonio.

Rune studied the acolyte, who obviously lacked the two things aristocrats like Bart Wentholt required in a partner: the ability to give him heirs, and the ability to advance his position in society. For this reason, Bart and Antonio could never marry. And if they were found out, the Wentholts would likely force their son to marry some girl against his will. If he refused, they could disown him outright.

"You've just exposed what he's successfully kept hidden for years," said Antonio.

"I see," said Rune.

Had it all been an act, then? Had Bart Wentholt merely pretended to be a shallow, narcissistic airhead to repel courtship attempts?

If so, Rune applauded him. He'd certainly fooled her—and she was a master of pretending to be something she wasn't.

Bart returned a few minutes later with not only boiled water and spirits but a kit of supplies. Inside were tweezers, bandages, and a needle and thread—everything Rune had searched for and failed to find.

Gideon crossed his arms over the table and leaned his head against them as Antonio worked. He clenched his teeth as Antonio dug out the bullets and sanitized the wounds with alcohol. Rune crouched beside Gideon, holding his hand and letting him squeeze as hard as he needed when the pain was too much.

Finally, he was cleaned, stitched, and bandaged. Some color had even returned to his face. While Antonio cleaned the instruments and Rune washed her bloodied hands, Bart poured them all drinks from the bottle of whiskey he'd fetched.

Gideon declined. Rune followed suit, remembering what happened the last time she'd imbibed.

As Antonio pulled up a chair, Rune turned to Bart. "Where's the rest of your family?"

"On the Continent. They sailed two weeks ago, to join my sister in Umbria. She's married to a man from Caelis and begged them to come as soon as she heard rumors of war brewing."

Rune nodded. Bart's mother was a retired witch hunter; she would have been executed.

"Why didn't you go with them?"

"I didn't believe the rumors." He looked at Antonio, eyes glittering in the gaslight. "Or maybe I did, and didn't care."

"I refused to leave," said Antonio, filling in what Bart had left out. "This island is my home."

And if Antonio wouldn't leave, was the unspoken sentiment, *neither would Bart.*

A soft silence settled over them. The gaslights hummed on the walls, but they weren't bright enough to fully light the room, leaving the four of them half in shadow.

"It's only a matter of time before Cressida takes over the countryside," said Rune, breaking the silence. "She'll find this place. She'll find both of you."

Bart shrugged. "Where else are we supposed to go? Her soldiers already ransacked my family's estate. This is all we have left." He swirled his whiskey, then set down his glass. "I was never fond of the Republic, or the Rosebloods. I don't care who wins in the end. I'm tired of hiding and pretending." He glanced at the boy sitting next to him. "Antonio and I have decided to live out the rest of our days—however numbered—the way we've always wanted to: beside each other. No more hiding."

Antonio gazed at him, the corners of his mouth turning up in a sad smile.

"What if they don't have to be numbered?" said Gideon, breaking the silence.

Everyone turned to look at him.

"What if you could live a full life *as you are*, without reper-cussions?"

Bart glanced away. "You're speaking of a fairy tale."

Rune had to agree.

But Antonio set down his drink and said, "I'm listening."

That small encouragement was all Gideon needed.

"This island has known tyranny for too long," he said. "It's time to try something new. A world where we can all live as equals."

"You're being naive," said Rune.

Gideon turned to look at her. "How so?"

"How are you going to bring this new world into existence? You have no army. No support. Meanwhile, Cressida has taken the capital, and the Blood Guard are regrouping, intending to take it back. Neither side wants a world where people like you and I live as equals. Either Cressida will win, or the Blood Guard will. And if it's the former, you'll be killed—or worse." At the thought of what *worse* entailed, she glanced away. "If it's the Blood Guard, I'll be killed. Those are the only possible outcomes."

Which was precisely why Rune intended to get on a train and ride it as far as she could, then pay someone to sail her, or just sail herself, away from here.

Gideon was silent for a long time, studying her in the lamplight. "You're wrong."

She frowned up at him. *What?*

"There's a third possible outcome."

He glanced across the table to the only person in the room eating up his words: Antonio.

"Most of us are sick of the options we've been handed. We don't want to go back to being ruled by a corrupt dynasty of witches, but neither are we okay with the Republic's authoritarian control. Deep down, we're hungry for something else." He glanced at Rune. "Those who say they aren't are too scared to imagine such a world is possible. If they could be convinced, we would stand a chance."

But Rune remembered the bloodthirsty mob cheering on Nan's gruesome death. She remembered the witches in the throne room, all too happy to pledge their loyalty to Cressida, knowing full well what her reign would entail.

Rune could no longer think about Cressida without feeling the whip stripping flesh from her back or remembering the smell of her blood in the air. Or that horrifying moment when she realized Cressida wouldn't stop lashing her until she was dead.

A tide of fear rose in Rune's throat. Threatening to pull her out to a dark sea and drag her down to its depths.

Rune had known this kind of fear only once before: on the night she and Nan realized they couldn't escape the new regime and the only way for Rune to survive was to turn her beloved grandmother in.

Rune pushed her chair out and strode from the room, gulping down air. Reminding herself it had been two years, and being turned in was what Kestrel wanted. That she had forgiven herself for the decisions she'd made in the past.

Besides, Cressida was far away. Rune was safe here.

But for how long?

"Rune."

At the sound of his voice, she squeezed her eyes shut. She didn't want him to see her like this: so scared, she couldn't catch her breath.

Steeling herself, Rune turned to face him.

Gideon had followed her into the hall and stood with his hand planted against the wall, letting it hold him up. His face was haggard in the dim light.

She couldn't leave him yet. It was her fault he'd been shot. So she'd wait. And then she'd do the safest thing for them both: disappear.

"Do you know any witches who might be willing to defy Cressida?" he asked.

She and Seraphine had been speaking of this very thing before she fled the palace. Now that Soren was dead, how many of his soldiers would stay and fight for Cressida? Not all. And those who did would expect payment, not promises.

Without Soren, her position was not as strong as it had been a few days ago.

"I could summon Seraphine." She, at least, might be interested in hearing Gideon out. As for others . . . "I doubt the rest would risk themselves."

Just like I won't risk myself.

If Gideon wanted to get himself and everyone close to him killed, that was his business. Rune wasn't getting involved.

Gideon nodded. "One is better than nothing."

One? Against a legion of witches? Against an army of soldiers?

Had some sort of blood poisoning set in from those bullets, affecting his ability to think clearly?

She turned to face him fully. Perhaps she could talk him out of this.

"Gideon. You and I both know there are only two possible

paths here. One leads to a malevolent witch queen; the other leads to an authoritarian regime. Alex was right: if we want to be free, the only option is to leave and never look back."

"No," said Gideon, pushing away from the wall. She saw what it cost him—the way he swayed; how his jaw clenched. "There's a third path. You're just refusing to consider it."

Rune shook her head. "Trust me, I've considered every option."

"This path doesn't exist yet," he said, stepping in close. "It needs to be forged."

His words were making her teeth hurt.

"By who? You and me? Pitting ourselves against not one, but two armies? Have you gone completely mad?"

"Maybe."

That tide of fear rushed up again, coming to drown her.

"I know you're trying to be noble, but this isn't the time," she said. "You're being foolish, and it's going to get everyone you love killed."

"And you," he said, studying her in the darkness, "are letting your fear rule you."

Rune's hands fisted.

"Fear is the only response in this situation! If you hadn't misplaced your brain somewhere between here and Wintersea, you'd be afraid, too!"

She turned on her heel.

"Cowardice doesn't suit you, Crimson Moth."

Her anger flared like red-hot embers. *A coward, am I?*

"I'd rather be a coward than a fool," she said.

AFTER STORMING OFF, RUNE was still fuming as she paced the rooftop gardens of Bart's summer home, muttering angrily to herself.

Deep down, she knew Gideon was right: she *was* being a coward. But being a coward was the only way to stay alive, which was exactly what Rune intended to do.

Besides, she was also right: Gideon's idea *was* foolish.

Being right did nothing to squash the guilt, however. And since her pride wouldn't let her apologize, Rune did the next best thing: she cast a *Messenger* spell to tell Seraphine where she was. She used the knife she'd stolen from the first aid kit to nick another mark in the back of her calf, letting it join the dozens of silver moths in flight that etched her skin.

I shouldn't have called him a fool.

The shape of a luminescent crow flared to life in front of her, perching on the balustrade. The crow shimmered, bright as starlight.

A hundred years ago, Queen Callidora used magical crows to send her messages. Or so the history books said.

This spell was allegedly one of hers.

The moment Rune breathed the name *Seraphine Oakes* onto the spell, the crow spread its wings and launched into the air, heading east. It would fly to the palace and present Rune's location to Seraphine, at which point it would disintegrate.

Seraphine could decide if she wanted to come here or not.

"Miss Winters?"

Rune turned. An elderly woman in servant livery stood between two lattices creeping with ivy.

"Mr. Wentholt asked me to make up a room for you."

This must be Bess.

The maid led Rune to a bedroom in the guest quarters, where she touched the white nightgown laid out on the bed. "This was Miss Celia's," she said. "You'll find more of her clothes in the armoire. Help yourself to them; she won't mind. My mistress hasn't set foot here since her wedding three years ago."

"Thank you," said Rune, rubbing her arms to keep out the chill. With no fire in the hearth, the room was colder than she was used to. But no one wanted to risk the smell of smoke, which might lead unwanted guests straight to their location.

"Normally I'd invite you to warm up in the bathhouse—it's heated by underground hot springs. But Mister Wentholt only arrived this evening, and I haven't had a chance to get it ready. However, there's a hot spring nearby you can wash in. I can give you directions tomorrow."

"Thank you," said Rune, who looked forward to getting properly cleaned up. "I'd like that very much."

"If there's nothing else, Miss Winters, I'll take my leave."

Rune was about to bid her good night, when she stopped herself.

"There is one more thing." She turned to look at Bess. "Do you happen to know the schedule for the nearest train station?"

"I can fetch it for you. But . . ."

"But?"

"There are rumors, miss. People are saying Westport Station will soon be shut down. The queen doesn't want anyone else escaping."

Rune narrowed her eyes. *Of course she doesn't.*

"In that case . . ." Rune reached into her dress pocket and pulled out the pouch full of coins she'd taken from her casting room. "Could you buy me a ticket for whichever train is going furthest northwest, while it's still in operation?"

Bess blinked as Rune placed the pouch in her hand. "Of course, miss. I'd be happy to."

SIXTY-TWO

GIDEON

GIDEON RETURNED TO THE table where Antonio and Bart were whispering, their expressions serious. Bart was not convinced of this fledgling plan, but with Antonio's encouragement, he began making a list of potential allies, scratching down names of aristocrats who might be sympathetic to their cause.

Gideon sat quiet, unable to focus on the task at hand. His heart remained in the hallway, watching Rune stomp away.

Something was wrong with her, and it was eating him up. She didn't want to talk about it—she'd made that clear by the distance she kept. She flinched at his touch. Avoided his gaze. Walked out halfway through the conversation as if she were weary of his ideas.

Weary of *him*.

He'd seen her torn bodice, leaving her lace shift exposed for anyone to see. Soren had done it—he was certain. But how far had he gone? How badly had he hurt her?

Gideon's mind went to the darkest places—he'd been there himself. He knew those places intimately. The idea of Rune at someone's mercy made his body harden with rage.

I killed him, she'd said. *I took your advice and didn't hesitate.*

But it was no consolation, because Rune was still carrying it with her. He saw it in her eyes whenever he looked at her: anguish and pain and barely controlled fury. She looked like she might break apart at any moment from the effort of holding it all in.

They were in unfamiliar territory, and Gideon had no map to navigate the rocky terrain.

Antonio reached over, touching him lightly on the wrist. Gideon looked up to find Bart gone, taking the list of names with him.

"Where did he go?"

"To bed. I'm heading there in a moment, but I wanted to ask if everything is all right?"

Gideon glanced down, staring at a wet stain on the table from the bottom of Bart's whiskey glass. "I was too harsh with her tonight."

Antonio withdrew his hand, waiting for the rest.

"I think someone broke her."

"Ah," said Antonio, leaning back and folding his hands on the table. "Anything else?"

Gideon glanced up. "I'm afraid I won't be able to put her back together."

"You can't put her back together. Only she can do that."

It wasn't at all what Gideon wanted to hear. He frowned at Antonio's shadowed face. "And if I lose her in the meantime?"

Antonio's eyes softened. "Love is patient, Gideon."

He clenched his fists. "So I should stand back and do nothing?"

Taking the bottle of whiskey, Antonio uncorked it and poured some into the empty glass in front of him. "Not nothing." Taking a sip, he said: "You could start by being less afraid."

It was what Gideon had accused Rune of: being afraid.

"You could try *trust* instead. Trusting not only her, but yourself."

Gideon stared at the former acolyte. "This conversation isn't making me feel better."

Antonio laughed. "Perhaps a sleeping draught, then? We have the ingredients in the kitchen. I can make one for you. It will help ease the pain, at least for tonight."

He meant the pain of Gideon's wounds, but he could easily have meant the ache of Gideon's heart.

"I find a good night's sleep makes me clear-sighted in the morning."

Gideon sighed and pushed out his chair. His tired body groaned in protest as he forced himself to his feet. "Fine. I'll take your sleeping potion."

If he was going to pit himself against two armies—Cressida's *and* the Good Commander's—he would need all the clear-sightedness he could get.

THE NEXT MORNING, GIDEON woke to warm sunlight on his face and the smell of Rune on the pillows. He opened his eyes, reaching for her.

But the bed was empty.

And *cold*.

He glanced at the armchair pulled up to the bedside, but it, too, was vacant.

It was just a dream.

Antonio's draught had worked a little too well. Gideon had slept like a stone, but all night long, his dreams were full of Rune.

They were so vivid, he'd been certain they were real: Rune slipping into his room in the dark and closing the door behind her. Rune sinking into the armchair and leaning forward to brush his hair off his face. He'd woken at her touch—or at least, he had in the dream—and wrapped his fingers around her wrist. Pulled her under the covers. Curled his body around hers like a protective shell, running his palms over her chilled skin to warm her.

He remembered the softness of her thigh beneath his palm. The salt taste of her skin on his lips.

But no. He couldn't. It had been nothing more than a dream.

Gideon couldn't touch Rune; Cressida's curse prevented it.

He banished the images from his mind and got out of bed. After dressing, he descended the stairs to the salon. Halfway down, he heard a familiar voice growl, "I know he's here."

Harrow?

"Tell him I need to speak with him."

Gideon continued down the stairs, stopping at the bottom. Harrow stood at the entrance to the salon—a large open space punctuated by scattered pillars and a massive fireplace. Standing across from her was Antonio.

"If you don't fetch him, I'll . . ." Her golden eyes lit on Gideon. *"Finally."*

"Come to turn me in?" He leaned his uninjured hip against the rail and crossed his arms. "Should I expect a platoon of officers breaking down the doors any moment?"

Harrow flinched at the question. She opened her mouth as if to answer, then changed her mind.

"The Blood Guard are rudderless," she said instead. "With your defection, there's no chance of them making a strong stand against Cressida's forces. We're all sitting ducks."

Gideon frowned. "So you want me to do . . . what, exactly?"

"Come back with me."

As she stepped toward him, he noticed her bruised wrists and the welt on her cheek. His eyes narrowed.

"Soldiers need their captain."

"If I return, Noah will kill me this time. And even if he doesn't . . ." Gideon shook his head. "I'm no longer in the business of slaughtering witches."

Her eyes flashed. "If you don't return, *we* will be slaughtered by the very witches you're suddenly so fond of."

There was a sudden flurry in the hall, coming from the front entrance. Harrow tensed, looking in the direction of the noise.

Had soldiers followed her here? Was this a trap?

Stepping past her, Gideon touched the gun holstered at his hip, ready to draw it if necessary.

"Her spell told me to come here," came a feminine voice. "To this house. Is she all right?"

Gideon watched as Seraphine Oakes entered the salon. At the sight of each other, both witch and witch hunter froze.

Rune did as I asked.

She'd summoned Seraphine.

He dropped his hand from his gun.

"You." Harrow spat the word from beside him. Before he realized what was happening, she'd grabbed his gun and pointed it at Seraphine.

No. Not Seraphine.

There was another girl on Seraphine's heels. One he hadn't seen until now.

"Wait . . ." He stepped toward Harrow. This was the last thing he needed here, where he'd planned to broker peace between enemies, not spark a bloodbath.

"Do you know who this is?" Harrow hissed, darting out of Gideon's reach. She spoke to him without taking her eyes off the girl. "*Juniper Huynh.* Her parents locked me in their cellar and left me to starve. Juniper let them. She left me to *die.*"

Gideon glanced from Harrow to the witch at Seraphine's side. The girl's long dark hair was braided over one shoulder and her brown eyes shone at Harrow.

Juniper. The girl Harrow loved.

"Give me one good reason I shouldn't shoot you right here," Harrow demanded.

Juniper didn't even try to defend herself.

"Harrow." Gideon stepped closer, reaching for his gun.

Harrow drew a knife from her belt and swiped it at him,

forcing him to step back, never lowering the gun, or her gaze, from the quiet witch across the salon. "If Cressida Roseblood were standing across the room, you would take the shot. Don't tell me you wouldn't."

She was right. He would. But . . .

Someone stepped in front of Juniper, cutting her off from Harrow's line of fire. She wore tan riding leathers, and her cheeks were bright pink from the cold. Her strawberry blonde hair was wild, tugged free of its messy braid, as if she'd been galloping straight into the wind.

Rune.

Harrow narrowed her eyes. "Step aside, Crimson Moth."

But Rune stood firm, chin held high, keeping Juniper behind her.

Seeing her on the wrong side of a gun made Gideon's pulse spike. He moved to intervene.

But Rune lifted her hand, silently telling him to stop as she stared Harrow down.

"If it wasn't for Juniper, you'd be dead right now. She all but forced me to break you out of that prison cell."

Gideon raised a brow, glancing to his friend. Harrow had been captured? And Rune had rescued her?

An interesting twist.

"You owe Juniper your life."

"You're lying," said Harrow, still holding her knife aloft and pointed at Gideon with one hand while the other aimed the gun at the witches.

"I wish I were." Rune narrowed her eyes. "Clearly you didn't deserve it."

To Gideon's surprise, Harrow lowered both weapons. But whether it was because she believed Rune or because she was indebted to her, Gideon couldn't tell.

"Well, isn't this pleasant," said Bart, who must have entered during the tense exchange. He stood in a baby blue robe with the crest of his house stitched in silver on the breast pocket. "Why don't you join us for breakfast? Antonio, can we accommodate a few more this morning?"

Antonio was calmly scanning the salon, taking in each person—natural enemies, all—when his gaze fell on Seraphine. At the sight of her, he frowned and tilted his head ever so slightly, as if asking a silent question.

In answer, Seraphine dipped her head. Almost imperceptibly.

"That won't be a problem," said Antonio, tearing his eyes from Seraphine and glancing to Bart. "Why don't you show everyone to the terrace while Bess and I prepare the food." He stepped in front of Harrow and held out both hands, palms up. "No weapons at breakfast, I'm afraid."

Harrow eyed him, then slammed both the gun and the knife hilt into his open hands before following Bart toward the gardens. She didn't look at Juniper.

Gideon hung back, trying to catch Rune's eye as the witches passed, but she was already in conversation with Seraphine, and if she noticed him, she didn't show it. As he took his place behind her, following this strange entourage into the gardens, he noticed a red mark on the back of her neck, peeking up above her leather collar. Like a freshly healed scar.

He frowned, wondering how she'd come by it.

SIXTY-THREE

RUNE

*I*T HAD BEEN UTTERLY stupid to go to Gideon's bed last night.

Rune was certain he'd been too drugged to remember her climbing under his covers and burrowing into him. That wasn't the problem.

The problem was, *she* remembered.

She remembered all of it.

His heat, driving the chill out of her body. The delicious feel of his bare skin against hers. His powerful arms holding her fiercely, tightly. As if she was *his*. As if nothing could hurt her so long as he was there.

It could be like that every night, if you wanted.

And she did want it.

That was the problem.

Rune had woken from a nightmare and found herself alone in the dark. These days, her nightmares were usually about Cressida. But last night, it was Nan who walked her dreams. Blood Guard soldiers dragged her grandmother up the purging platform's steps as she screamed for Rune to help her. But the crowd pressed in from all directions, and the more Rune tried to get to her, the more they forced her back.

Until Nan's screams fell silent.

Rune couldn't sleep after that. Every shadow hid a nightmare. And though it was irrational, she wanted Gideon. In a moment of weakness, she went searching for him.

She found him sleeping in the bedroom across the hall, along with some tincture on his bedside table. Giving it a sniff, Rune recognized the smell of a sleeping draught.

It was a mistake, and she regretted it. She couldn't let it happen again. She needed to tear herself away before Cressida found them. It was only a matter of time.

There were two choices: have Gideon ripped away from her, or leave before he could be.

No, there's a third choice. You can ask him to come with you.

She shook the thought away.

"Sugar?"

Rune glanced up to find Bart Wentholt holding out a mug of coffee in one hand and a sugar bowl in the other.

Rune took the coffee, cupping its warmth. "Please."

It was funny how, now that she was really looking, there was an intelligence in his warm brown eyes she hadn't noticed before. Bart Wentholt had fooled her into thinking him a dolt, and Rune admired him for it—the way one con artist admires another.

Bart dropped a lump of sugar in her mug before moving on to Seraphine, who was already taking her seat at this table on the terrace. Around them, bees droned in the flowers, birds sang in the trees, and sunlight filled the air.

It was strangely peaceful, for an island at war.

Harrow sat on the opposite end of the table from Juniper, who sat on the other side of Rune. Gideon took the seat between Harrow and Bart.

An invisible line had been drawn across the table, separating witches from patriots. The patriots had no reason to believe these witches weren't secretly loyal to Cressida or her causes. And the witches couldn't be sure this wasn't a trap, with Blood Guard soldiers coming to arrest them at any moment.

If this was going to work, they all had to trust each other. But no one had a reason to.

Maybe, once he sees how impossible this mission is, Gideon will give up and come with me.

"Seraphine, Juniper . . ." Gideon glanced from witches to patriots. "This is Bart. And it seems you already know Harrow."

Juniper shifted in her seat but said nothing. Harrow crossed her arms over her chest and scowled.

"Well?" she asked Gideon. "What's your plan, Comrade? The Blood Guard are looking for you. Cressida is looking for you. You can't hide here forever."

"He doesn't have a plan," said Rune.

"*Yet.*" Gideon shot her a withering look. "I don't have a plan *yet.*"

"It's not too late to hand them in." Harrow nodded toward Rune, Seraphine, and Juniper.

"What I do have is a proposition," said Gideon, ignoring her.

He rose from his seat and stood between the table on the terrace and the gardens beyond. Rune stared into her coffee, preparing herself to listen to his nonsense all over again.

"You said yourself the Blood Guard are rudderless, Harrow. And Noah Creed is not his father. If it's true his army is bleeding soldiers, we can draw those soldiers to our side. I know these men and women. I know what they want, and what they'll fight for, and I'm willing to bet there are those on *your* side"—he glanced at Seraphine and Juniper—"who want the same thing: a world where they and their loved ones can be happy and safe. A world without tyranny, violence, or hate. A world where we can live as equals."

Harrow blew out a skeptical breath and sank lower into her chair.

"*You* have been hunting us for years," said Juniper suddenly.

"What reason do we have to trust you?" She glanced at Harrow. "*Any* of you?"

"I just gave you your enemy's weakness," said Gideon. "The Blood Guard are floundering without a strong leader. There's one reason to trust me."

"She's right, though," said Bart. "Even if it were possible to steal the Good Commander's army from under him and then crush Cressida's, why would anyone believe we wouldn't return to hating each other?"

Gideon seemed about to respond when Seraphine's voice cut through the noise.

"Cressida's army is also in shambles," she said, folding her hands on the table. "Half of Soren's soldiers blamed Cressida for the prince's murder and left, taking his ships with them. The other half she pays to keep in her employ—but at some point, the money will run out."

This seemed to surprise Gideon, who glanced at Harrow, as if trying to confirm the information.

"Even now," Seraphine continued, "many witches are deeply troubled by Cressida's tactics, but are afraid to rise against her when disloyalty will cost their lives. They know Cressida is the only thing standing between them and the witch hunters, and for that reason alone, most will remain loyal. She is the lesser of two evils. However: with Soren's army diminished, and without the sisters she badly needs to rule at her side, Cressida will struggle to hold on to her power. If someone were to offer the witches a better deal, they might be persuaded to abandon their queen. Or better yet: turn on her."

This, Rune knew, was exactly what Gideon wanted: fault lines running through both sides.

But was Seraphine truly considering this? Allying herself with Gideon's reckless cause? Very few witches would dare stand against Cressida, knowing how painful her vengeance could be. Rune had the scars on her back to prove it. Witches who hadn't seen Cressida whip her almost to death would have heard the story. It would be a cautionary tale.

Gideon planted his hands on the table, leaning in as his gaze locked with Seraphine's. "If we permanently ensured she can't resurrect Elowyn and Analise, would that help?"

"It would be a start."

"There's a long-lost heir, right?" said Harrow, leaning her chair back so it balanced on only two legs. "A sibling Cressida needs to do the resurrecting? If we found and killed them, it would put an end to her resurrection plans."

Seraphine tensed. Juniper reached for Rune's hand beneath the table.

Rune stared into her coffee, a chill sweeping through her as she remembered Gideon's plans to hunt down the missing Roseblood.

There hadn't been enough time to tell Gideon the truth. And even if there had been, Rune wasn't sure she wanted him to know.

If he knew it was me, what would he think?

Not only had her biological family destroyed his, but Rune was the sister of the girl who'd abused him.

Would he do as Harrow recommended—dispose of her before Cressida could use her?

It would be the smart thing to do, anyone would agree. Her death could prevent the resurrection and upend Cressida's plans for ultimate tyranny.

She watched Gideon run a hand over his rough-shaven cheeks, as if contemplating Harrow's question. Before he could answer it, Juniper interrupted, still squeezing Rune's hand.

"Instead of murdering innocents"—her voice sharpened as

she cut her gaze to Harrow—"I'll return to the capital and learn where Cressida is keeping her sisters' bodies. If we destroy them, they can't be resurrected." Juniper glanced at Gideon. "While I'm there, I could recruit more witches to our cause."

Our cause.

Rune couldn't help but notice the word choice.

"And why should we trust *you*?" The legs of Harrow's chair slammed onto the floor as she leaned across the table, eyes narrowing on Juniper. "You could just as easily give us all away."

There it was again: *us*.

Juniper stared her down. "The same could be said about you."

Our. Us. Despite their squabbling, they spoke as if they were on the same side, even if they didn't know it yet.

"I've never given Cressida reason to believe I'm disloyal. She trusts me." Juniper spoke to Gideon now, ignoring Harrow. "As soon as I learn where Elowyn and Analise are preserved, I'll report back."

"I'll go with her," Harrow cut in. "To ensure she doesn't double-cross us."

Juniper's brows shot up her forehead. "You? You'll be recognized and put to death the moment you set foot in the capital."

"And you care about that?"

Juniper glanced away. From across the table, Harrow couldn't see the shine of tears in Juniper's eyes. Rune squeezed her hand.

"And if this entire plan fails?" Rune demanded, cutting through the argument.

She glanced from Harrow and Juniper to Gideon and Seraphine. "You will be responsible for the slaughter of those you give false hope to. If your barter doesn't pay off, and Cressida wins, she'll torture and kill everyone who stood against her. You know this."

Seraphine studied Rune with her onyx eyes. "You're right. But if there's a chance—"

"You were supposed to be gone," said Gideon from across the table, pinning Rune with his heated gaze. "And yet, here you are."

Anger ignited in her chest. Rune wanted to say she didn't have a choice; Cressida had tortured her and dragged her back. But the thought of Cressida brought back the sting of the whip and that bone-deep fear.

"You want to run away?" he said. "*Go.* No one is stopping you."

The words stung. He glared at her, as if he no longer cared whether she was here or not. As if her doubt annoyed him.

As if *she* annoyed him.

Bess and Antonio shattered the tension by stepping onto the terrace, each one carrying a large, lidded platter.

"Breakfast is ready," sang Antonio, setting his platter down on the table.

"You have some more visitors, Captain Sharpe," said Bess, lowering hers.

Summoned by her words, a ragtag crew of people stepped out onto the terrace. At the sight of them, Gideon rose to his feet.

"Ash? *Abbie?* What are you doing here?"

It wasn't just Ash and Abbie, but the entire group from the *Arcadia.*

Gideon's old comrades.

"I got a strange telegram from Laila," said Ash, rounding the table to pull Gideon into a fierce hug. "All it said was you were in dire straits, and to come if we could. I must say, things are pretty grim out there."

They pulled apart. Gideon stared at his old friend, eyes full of wonder. "And you came all this way to . . . ?"

"To help, of course." It was Abbie who spoke.

Abbie stepped forward and Ash moved away, until it was just her and Gideon, considering each other.

"We're here to support you."

Rune couldn't help but notice the way Abbie looked at Gideon. Like she believed in him. Like she would follow him into hell, if only he asked.

It was *this* that made Rune push away from the table and flee.

SHE WANTED TO LOOK at Gideon like that. Wanted to believe in him like that. To trust he could deliver them from this.

But she didn't believe it. She *couldn't*.

She could only believe in Cressida's cruelty and power and vengeance. She believed Cressida would prevail, and execute them all. She believed Gideon would lead everyone to their deaths.

I can't stay and watch that happen.

She wanted to put the whole world between herself and the scene on the terrace.

Bess had given her directions to the hot spring this morning. It wasn't the other side of the world, but it would give Rune privacy. Not only had she not bathed in days, but there was little chance of someone finding her there and seeing her destroyed body.

It was only a ten-minute ride to the hot spring, situated at the top of a mossy headland. By the time she and Lady arrived, she was a little less upset. Hot water gushed from the source, forming a waterfall as it flowed down to the flat stones beneath.

Rune left Lady to graze further afield, grabbed the towel and the bar of soap she'd put in the saddlebag, and headed for the waterfall. Setting her towel down on a dry rock, she stripped off her clothes and stepped into the steam clouding the air. Its heat caressed her skin.

She drew closer to the waterfall, her feet slapping against wet stone. Already, she was feeling better. More herself.

She saw now how ridiculous it was, the way her chest tightened at the sight of Abbie. And how humiliating, that the look between Abbie and Gideon made her want to run like some small, frightened animal.

She wasn't *that* girl. She didn't trip over silly feelings.

Rune *survived*.

She stepped into the waterfall, letting its heat soak her skin. *This is all I needed. A chance to clear my mind.*

Turning her face into the rushing water, she closed her eyes against the warm droplets . . .

. . . and burst into tears.

SIXTY-FOUR

GIDEON

AFTER THE COMMOTION CAUSED by Gideon's old friends, more chairs were pulled up to the table, and Abbie, Ash, and the others squished in. As Antonio and Bess retreated to the kitchen to cook more food for their unexpected guests, Gideon finally sat back down.

Which was when he noticed the empty seat across the table. "Where's Rune?"

Bess, bringing out more coffee, poured some into Ash's cup and said, "I saw her riding into the headlands. There's a hot spring out there. I told her the heat would do those wounds of hers some good."

Gideon frowned, remembering the scar he'd seen on her neck. "What wounds?"

Bess startled, missing Ash's cup and spilling coffee on the tablecloth. "Oh! I assumed you knew." She shook her head. "I'm sorry. I shouldn't have said anything."

Gideon was about to press her when Juniper said quietly, "Rune's back was flayed to the bone."

His temperature spiked.

"What?"

Bess nodded, clearly relieved to no longer be the only one revealing Rune's secret. "I saw the marks this morning, when she asked for help dressing."

Flayed to the bone?

"Who—"

"Cressida whipped her within an inch of her life," said Juniper.

Everyone turned to stare at her.

"It took all of my skill to stop the bleeding," she added. "She was in and out of consciousness for days. She was in a sickbed for the entire voyage back to the island. She . . . she didn't tell you any of this?"

Gideon's fists clenched beneath the table.

Seraphine frowned at Gideon. "Rune defied Cressida, knowing what would happen. She did it to break your curse."

To break my . . .

He thought of his dream. Of Rune climbing into his bed. Of her softness and warmth, nestled against him.

It wasn't a dream.

"Cressida was going to kill her," said Seraphine. "The only reason she didn't is because I gave her what she wanted: the name of the missing Roseblood heir."

Gideon's head spun.

Cressida knows Rune is her sister.

Who else knew?

Seraphine wouldn't state it outright, not here, because it would put Rune's life at risk. But if Rune ended up back in Cress's hands . . .

He pushed out his chair and rose to his feet.

"Where is this hot spring?"

SIXTY-FIVE

GIDEON

*H*E FOUND HER IN the waterfall, her back to him, her eyes closed as she turned her face into the spray. Her pale, naked form stood out starkly against the dark gray rock.

With her wet hair pulled over one shoulder, Gideon had a full view of the harm done to her.

Vicious red lines crisscrossed her back, from shoulders to hips. Deep, fresh scars. Gideon's stomach clenched at the sight.

At the thought of Rune beneath a whip, his rage swelled.

He would make Cressida pay for this.

Dismounting Bart's horse, he strode out onto the flat, glistening rock.

"Is this why you've avoided me?"

Rune jumped, startled, and turned to face him. Her eyes were red from crying.

"Wh-what are you doing here?" She grabbed a towel resting on a nearby rock, quickly wrapped it around herself—hiding herself from him—and started toward Lady, who was grazing nearby. "You're not supposed to be here."

Gideon moved to intercept her, stepping into her path. "And where am I supposed to be?"

No way was he letting her evade this conversation.

With no answer to give, she padded backward on her bare feet, returning to the spray, which quickly drenched her towel.

"*Rune.* Why didn't you *tell* me?"

At his question, her face crumpled.

Suddenly, her fear made sense. Rune now knew firsthand what it meant to be at Cressida's mercy.

She's terrified.

Gideon stepped toward her, into the falling water. Within seconds, he was as soaked as she was.

"I'm her sister," she said, as if this might repel him.

"I don't care."

Or rather, the only reason he cared was because it put her at risk.

She looked up, startled. "You . . . don't?"

Gideon reached for her wrist so she couldn't bolt, running his thumb gently over the little knot of bone there. "Let me see your back."

She seemed about to refuse, so he took her face in his hands. "Let me see. Please."

Her shoulders slumped and she turned, letting the sodden towel fall to the stone at their feet, leaving her back exposed to him.

He hissed through his teeth at the crisscrossed scars ridging her back, the red lash lines cutting through her pale, smooth skin. Some had healed; others were still raw. It made him want to weep.

"Oh, Rune . . ."

"I know." Her voice cracked on the words and she lifted her hands to her face. "I'm hideous."

"No." The word burst out of him, angry. How could she think that? Gideon stepped closer and locked his arms around her waist. "Not possible."

He lowered his mouth to a scar on her shoulder, kissing the raised skin. A breath escaped her. He kissed another scar, and the tension left her body. "You are the kindest, cleverest, bravest girl I've ever met." He kissed more and more scars, tracing them gently with his mouth. "These scars are only further proof of that."

No pain flared. He was touching her without consequence.

His curse was broken—and here was the cost: Rune in pain; her courage in tatters.

"She could have killed you." Pulling her closer, he pressed his cheek against the crown of her head. "Why would you risk yourself?"

"Because I couldn't stand the thought of her making you suffer." Rune's hand lifted to his arm, skimming down to his hand, where she linked her fingers with his. "And because . . ."

Still facing away from him, she turned her head so her temple grazed his jaw, nuzzling him.

"Because I was stupid enough to fall in love with a witch hunter. Stupid enough to hope he might love me back. And if he did, I wasn't going to let anything come between us again."

She turned into him, forcing his embrace to loosen. As she studied his face, watery rivulets traced down her cheeks and dripped from her chin.

Her hands lifted to the buttons on his shirt, her eyes asking a silent question. Gideon nodded and let her undo them. Let her peel the soaked garment off him and drop it next to her towel.

Rune stared at the brand on his chest, lifting her palm to the scar. As if she didn't believe her sacrifice had worked. As if she were waiting for the pain to flare; for the branded lines to turn ember-red.

But they didn't.

All Gideon felt was pleasure at her warmth, her gentleness.

Rune laid her cheek against the scar.

"I would do it again," she whispered. "Just for this."

I don't deserve this girl. He slid his palms against her cheeks and tilted her head back. *But I want to. I want to be the man who deserves Rune Winters.*

He let his eyes trace the lines of her face before lowering his head to kiss her lips.

Rune's breath shuddered. She slid her fingers into his hair.

"Were you in my bed last night?" he said against her mouth.

"Me? In your bed? You must have been dreaming."

"Hmm."

They were touching, skin to skin, as the water rushed over them. Nothing stood between them anymore. No secrets. No curses. There was nothing to stop them . . .

Rune's arms came around his neck as she arched against him. His grip on her hips tightened.

"Come with me," she whispered, running her hands over him.

Gideon smiled against her mouth. "Where would you like to go?"

"Anywhere," she said, trailing kisses down his throat, nipping gently. "Anywhere other than here. We could sail to the other side of the world. We could *live*, Gideon."

Ah.

They were right back where they started.

He let his hands drop.

"Rune."

She must have heard the answer in his tone, because she stepped back, her face falling.

"If we leave, Cressida wins," he said. "Laila, Harrow, Bart, Antonio . . . every one of them will die. You're asking me to abandon them? To abandon my *home*?"

"Yes," she said, her eyes pleading. "To be with *me*."

He stared at her, feeling torn in half.

Of course he was tempted. A life with Rune? It was worth

everything. Which was precisely why he needed to stay and fight. This was where they both belonged. He wanted to save it—for her, for *them*, more than anyone. Anything less, and he would never be the man she deserved.

Gideon would stand beside her, fight beside her, *die* beside her. But he wouldn't run away with her. Running wouldn't fix anything.

Believe in me, he wanted to say. *Trust me to lead us out of this.*

"I can't stay," she said, defensive. She raised her chin and crossed her arms over her chest. "I don't have a choice. You must see that."

What he saw was the girl he loved, hollowed out by fear.

"This is our home, Rune. Yours, mine. Don't you think that's worthy of fighting for?"

Something flickered in her eyes, but whatever it was, she smothered it. "Home is where you're safe. This island hasn't been safe for a long time."

"Then stand with me and fight for a better one."

She just shook her head sadly and turned, walking to where her clothes lay, pulling them on over her damp body before heading toward Lady.

But Gideon wasn't about to give up on her. Not yet. Somewhere beneath the fear was the girl he loved. A girl who stared down danger with a smile and a knife. His brave, clever Crimson Moth.

He strode after her, intercepting the path to where her horse grazed.

"I know you're scared," he said, walking backward. "I know this is hard. But I need you. Who else can show them the way if not a witch and a witch hunter, fighting side by side?"

He stopped and reached for her arms, bringing her to a stop.

"There is a better world waiting to be born, Rune. A world

that belongs to all of us. But it will never arrive if we don't fight for it."

"And if you're wrong?" she demanded. "What if everything that's broken *can't* be restored?"

"What if it *can*?"

She pulled free of his grasp. "She'll kill us both."

Gideon stared at her. "Then it will be an honor to die at your side."

She made a frustrated sound and shook her head. "Are you even listening to me? I can't watch you fall into her hands again!" She pressed her palms to her eyes, as if trying to grind the nightmarish visions out of her mind. "I could recover from Nan's death, and Alex's. But I won't recover from yours." She glanced up at him. "It will shatter me."

"It won't," he said, closing the gap. Touching his forehead to hers. "You're stronger than that."

"Maybe I was once," she whispered. "I'm not anymore."

He ran his hands up her arms and shoulders, cupping her neck. She started to soften beneath his touch. But when Gideon tried to draw her closer, she stiffened.

"I've made up my mind." She pulled away. "Is this your answer? You won't come with me?"

He shook his head, miserably. "I can't. There are too many lives at stake."

Rune gave a tight, terse nod. She understood, but he was breaking her heart. Her face said it all. "Then this is goodbye."

She turned and continued down the path toward Lady, then mounted her and rode away.

It nearly killed Gideon to let her go.

But he did.

SIXTY-SIX

RUNE

*R*UNE FELT LIKE HER heart was made of clay, and someone had smashed it into a thousand pieces.

She understood why Gideon had refused her. Of course she did. But it didn't make her feel any less broken.

Put it behind you, she told herself as she rode Lady away from the hot spring. *You're leaving. He's staying. That's the end of it.*

Her train departed this evening. Bess had bought her the ticket. She would be gone by sunset.

If she wanted to get to the station in time, she'd have to leave soon.

Rune needed to change into fresh clothes and retrieve her train ticket. She hurried to her bedroom, passing Abbie on the stairs. Recognizing Rune, the girl stopped and turned. As if to say something.

Rune rushed past. She didn't want to face Gideon's old sweetheart—a girl who was now very much free to win him back.

She ran faster up the stairs.

Rune couldn't bear to stay here a moment longer.

SIXTY-SEVEN

GIDEON

GIDEON STOOD AT THE second-floor window overlooking the gates of the Wentholts' cottage. His clothes were still damp from the waterfall, and his hair dripped water down his neck as he watched Rune ride Lady out through the gates.

In that moment, he knew, somehow, that she was not coming back.

Gideon watched until she disappeared into the surrounding woods and lingered long after, his temple pressed to the cool glass, wondering if he'd made the right choice.

"You didn't go with her?"

Rousing himself, Gideon turned to find Harrow behind him, leaning up against the wall, her arms crossed over her chest.

Gideon was so used to seeing Harrow with her dark brown hair pulled up in a topknot, he almost didn't recognize her. She'd let her hair down. Long and straight, it shimmered in the sunlight. Softening her hard edges.

"The girl I love would never respect a man who'd willingly abandon innocents to be slaughtered."

"Perhaps she's no longer that girl."

She is.

Beneath the hurt and fear and anger, she was the same Rune he'd fallen in love with. He believed that. She'd simply forgotten herself—the way he had once forgotten himself.

"If I went with her, she would come to despise me for my

cowardice," he said. And even if she didn't, he would despise himself. Gideon shook his head. "That's not the life I want with her. Nor is it the life *she* wants, deep down." He looked to the window. "She's just too scared to remember that right now."

Harrow stepped up beside him, staring out the same window.

"You should follow her at least, to make sure she's okay."

He glanced at his friend, eyebrow cocked. "Since when are you worried about Rune's safety?"

Harrow ignored him. "Westport Station is swarming with Cressida's soldiers and spies. There are witch-hunting hounds with them, for sniffing out the Crimson Moth."

His stomach dropped. "What?"

"Bess was there early this morning, buying Rune's ticket."

How did Harrow learn that? She'd been here all of two hours.

"At the very least, you should make sure your girl gets safely on her train." Harrow turned her golden eyes on his. "Don't you think?"

"Does that witch of yours have something to do with this change of heart?"

"Juniper is *not* my witch," she snapped, eyes narrowing with warning.

But it was too late. Gideon had glimpsed the crack in her armor. She might not have forgiven Juniper—or him, for that matter—but something was shifting in Harrow.

They considered each other.

"Does this mean you're with me?" he asked her.

She scoffed, turning to walk away. "I'm with whoever pays the most for my services."

"Funny how you never charged me before," he called after her. Which was true. Any information Harrow had given to Gideon, she'd given freely. No strings attached.

"There's always more than one kind of payment," she shot back, her hair swishing across her shoulders.

Gideon didn't know how to answer. In the years she'd worked with him, digging up clues to help him catch and purge witches, had he paid Harrow in some other way?

Perhaps purging witches was the payment.

But if so, what kind of currency was Harrow trading in now?

WESTPORT STATION WAS IN chaos when Gideon arrived.

He wore a brown traveling suit loaned to him by Bart, who'd argued it would help Gideon blend in.

No one would be looking for Captain Gideon Sharpe in a suit.

With Ash's pistol tucked into his belt and an extra box of bullets in his pocket, Gideon took up position against the station's brick wall, making sure the brim of Bart's wool cap kept his face in shadow as he scanned the chaotic crowd pushing toward the only train on the tracks.

He'd quickly learned the source of the chaos: this station was shuttering at sundown, by order of the queen, who was hunting a rogue witch rumored to be the Crimson Moth. By closing down all nearby stations, Cressida hoped to prevent her prey from getting further afield.

The train sitting on the tracks was the last one leaving. Possibly forever, if this war tore their country apart. Which meant Rune needed to be on it if she wanted to get out tonight.

He spotted her almost immediately.

Or rather: he spotted a *version* of her. She'd altered her appearance, like she had on the *Arcadia*. Instead of strawberry blonde, Rune's hair was the pale gold of wheat, braided down her back. And when she glanced around, scanning for danger, Gideon saw her chin was more pointed, and her eyes were blue instead of gray.

If he didn't recognize her illusion from the ship, he might have missed her altogether.

Gideon watched her push through the crush of people desperate to get on the last train—which was nearly full—while the porters tried to keep things under control.

Once she was safely on board, Gideon would turn around and go back. With so many of Cressida's soldiers patrolling the station—many with hunting hounds at their sides—he couldn't afford to linger.

Finally, as the stationmaster announced last call, Rune pushed her way up to the ticket inspector. Gideon had just relaxed, readying himself to leave the moment she stepped onto the train, when a loud bark made him freeze.

He glanced over to see a dog dragging a soldier through the parting crowd, heading in Rune's direction and attracting the attention of several other soldiers nearby.

Even if Rune got on the train, the dog would follow her in.

Where she'd be trapped.

Gideon pushed away from the wall, shoving through the mass of bodies, using his shoulders and elbows to fight his way through. A few yards from where Rune stood with the ticket inspector, he stepped directly in front of the dog.

Pretending to stumble, he threw his weight toward the soldier and forcibly got himself caught in the leash.

"For Mercy's sake," he muttered. "Keep control of your dog, will you?"

The dog barked, trying to drag them both toward the train. But the leash was now looped around Gideon's calf, and he planted himself firmly in place. With Gideon's full height and breadth blocking Rune from view, the soldier no longer saw which direction the dog was heading.

"Step aside, sir, or I'll arrest you for interference."

Gideon's eyebrows shot toward his forehead. "Interference? *You're* standing in *my* way."

Behind them, the train whistled, warning everyone away from the tracks. Gideon quickly glanced over his shoulder to see Rune disappear inside while the porter pulled the steps away from the train.

"Sir, this is your last warning."

The dog snarled and yanked. The leash tightened around Gideon's leg.

"Step aside, or I'm bringing you in."

So long as the train was in the station, soldiers could still board it. Gideon refused to let that happen.

"How am I to step aside," he said, staring down the young man in uniform, "when your dog has ensnared me in its leash?"

Two more soldiers arrived.

"What's the problem here?"

Wanting to keep their attention on him, Gideon said, "The problem"—he shoved the soldier in front of him hard enough to cause a scene—"is *boys* who can't control their mutts."

"Hey now."

Gideon saw a soldier reach for a set of handcuffs.

"That's assault of an officer."

Gideon was about to turn and challenge him, too, when a third voice joined in.

"Captain Sharpe?"

Gideon looked at the new arrival to find a woman with silver casting scars on her cheeks. Her black hair was loose around her shoulders, and her eyes were catlike as they pierced him.

Gideon didn't recognize the witch, but she clearly recognized him.

He glanced at the train, which was groaning as it slowly pulled away from the tracks.

At least Rune is safe.

"Leave him to me," the witch said, lifting her casting knife to Gideon's throat, ensuring he didn't try anything.

She seemed to outrank them, because the soldier released the tangled leash, loosening its viselike hold on Gideon's leg. The hunting hound bolted after the train.

But it was too late. The train was leaving the station. If they wanted to catch her, they'd have to beat it to the next one—an impossibility on foot or horseback.

As the soldiers chased the dog, the witch found the gun tucked into Gideon's belt. She slid it out, pressing the barrel between his shoulder blades.

"My orders are to bring you in, dead or alive." She prodded him toward the tracks. "Now *move.*"

SIXTY-EIGHT

RUNE

*R*UNE PUSHED HER WAY down the overcrowded aisle, looking for an empty seat.

People crammed the train car. Rosy-cheeked children sat on their parents' laps—sometimes two or three per lap—while adults stood in the aisle, stepping aside only to let Rune pass. Either the ticket inspectors had taken pity on half these people or they'd been bribed to let more on than the train had capacity for.

Either way, Rune didn't care.

She'd made it.

As she found her seat, the tension in her body evaporated. She sat and turned her face to the window, her breath whooshing out of her. On the other side of the glass, people waved money at the porters, desperate to get on the train even as the steps disappeared from the doors, while others cried as they bid goodbye to loved ones inside the cars.

"I didn't think we'd make it," said a passenger across the aisle—a woman with a toddler in her lap. "What's going to happen now?"

Her husband leaned over and kissed her head. "I don't know," he said, reaching for her hand and gripping it tight. "But we're together. That's what matters most."

Rune looked away, blinking back tears.

The train whistled again.

The desperate crowd beyond the window dimmed as she

caught sight of her reflection in the glass. It wasn't the girl she'd illusioned herself to look like; it was her real self. Magic didn't work on windows, after all.

As she studied the face in the glass, that unnerving question resurfaced.

Who am I?

Who is the real Rune Winters?

No matter how hard she searched for a trace of Nan in her features, there was nothing of Kestrel Winters in Rune. Which made sense; she and her adoptive grandmother weren't related by blood. But neither could Rune find any hint of her half sisters. There was nothing of Cressida. Or Elowyn. Or Analise.

But as Rune studied her reflection, she realized she had seen the shade of her hair somewhere else. And the color of her eyes. And the shape of her jaw.

She'd seen it in three other people, in fact. Very recently.

Something wild and bright flickered inside her, like a freshly lit candle.

No.

She tried to snuff it out. She couldn't wander down that path. She'd already decided: *this* was her path.

I'm leaving.

The engine chugged, pulling them slowly forward. Rune leaned her temple against the cold glass. Soon, she'd be out of Cressida's grasp. Soon, she'd escape the Blood Guard for good.

Soon, she thought as the train left the crowded platform behind, *I'll be free.*

Nothing could make her turn back now.

SIXTY-NINE

GIDEON

G IDEON STUMBLED ONTO THE empty track, shoved there by the witch at his back. Behind them lay the station's platform.

The train was gone.

Rune was gone.

He tried not to think about that. Tried instead to think about why this witch was taking him into the rail yard instead of putting him on a horse and sending him straight to Cressida.

Perhaps he should be grateful.

"Cressida sends her regards, Captain Sharpe."

"Cressida can go fuck herself."

"I'll pass on the message when I hand her your bleeding heart." She pressed the barrel of Gideon's loaded gun harder between his shoulder blades.

He had no idea how strong she was, or what spells she had up her sleeve. But one thing he was sure of: if he tried anything, she would shoot to kill.

"It's a little sad, don't you think?" He was trying to stall. Trying to concoct an escape as he stepped over the iron rails. But all he had on him was a box of bullets in his pocket. *She* had his gun. "Cressida couldn't keep my heart with her winning personality, so she sent *you* to cut it out of my corpse. Will she put it in a box, I wonder? Keep it beneath her pillow?"

She dug the gun harder into his back. "Keep blaspheming

the queen, and I'll tie you to these tracks so you can watch your death coming a mile away."

She could, if she wanted to. There would be other trains still running. Supply trains bringing food, coal, and other necessities to the capital. Cressida would need them if she wanted to win this war.

Defiance burned through him. "Cressida Roseblood will never be my queen."

"You'll choke on those words."

"So be it. Kill me. A hundred others will rise up to replace me."

"And they'll be slaughtered, too," she growled. "Get on your knees."

In the distance, a train whistled.

Gideon glanced toward the sound as he dropped to the ground. But there was no train in sight.

He expected her to step back, preferring to put a bullet in his head. But she drew her casting knife and pressed its sharp edge to his throat.

The steel was cold. He shivered, waiting for death.

"Too bad you won't live to see your precious Republic crushed into the dirt," she whispered at his ear. "Sweet dreams, dear—"

BANG!

Gideon flinched, his ears ringing with the gunshot.

But no pain exploded through him. No bullet pierced him.

The witch dropped her knife. A second later, she toppled, hitting the ground beside him with a *thump*.

BANG!

Still on his knees, Gideon spun, falling back onto his hands.

BANG! BANG! BANG!

Someone stood behind him, pointing her gun at the dead

witch. She fired until the chamber clicked, clicked, clicked. Out of bullets.

Her gaze lifted to Gideon.

Rune's illusion was gone. In the light of the setting sun, the wind whipped her red-gold hair free of its braid, and her eyes were thunderous as she lowered the smoking pistol. Her cheeks were red, her skin shone with sweat, and her chest heaved, as if she'd run hard, all the way here. Desperate to get to him in time.

He'd never seen a more beautiful sight.

Or a more furious one.

"What the *hell*, Gideon?"

SEVENTY

RUNE

*I*T WAS AS THE train was pulling away from the platform that Rune saw him out there in the railyard: Gideon,
dressed in a fancy riding suit, the brim of a wool cap shadowing
his face . . .

And a gun pressed between his shoulder blades.

Something ferocious roared to life inside her.

But the train was leaving the station, and with it, her last
chance to get out. Rune knew what it would cost her to get off.
And suddenly, it didn't matter.

None of it mattered except this.

She had to shove past the passengers blocking her way down
the aisle, and then screamed like a lunatic until the staff opened
the door for her.

And then she jumped.

From a moving train.

Onto the platform.

She felt her world collapsing in on itself as the train left the
station and she ran across the rail yard, not knowing if she'd get
to him in time. She'd run harder than she'd ever run in her life.
Ran until her lungs burned and her legs screamed, and then ran
even harder.

And now here he was: sprawled across the train tracks, his
hands in the dirt, that ridiculous wool cap knocked from his head.

Alive.

It made Rune want to fall to her knees and weep with relief.

If she hadn't glanced out the train window one more time before the platform disappeared, he'd be dead. And she would be riding away from the station, oblivious.

A fist squeezed her heart.

"What are you doing here?" she demanded, gripping the pistol in her hand, anger spiking through her. She'd stolen it off a soldier in the station.

"Me?" he said, pushing himself to his feet. "What are *you* doing here?"

Rune pointed to the dead witch at her feet. "Saving your *life*!"

She glanced at the distant train. The one she was supposed to be on.

"You've ruined everything!" She threw down the pistol. With its empty chamber, the gun was useless to her. "That was my last chance to escape!"

His face darkened. "Then you should have taken it!"

"And let her kill you?"

"That's why I came: to make sure you were safely on board when it left."

A dog barked in the distance, interrupting them. Gideon looked over Rune's shoulder. Whatever he saw there made his face blanch. He grabbed the pistol she'd thrown to the ground and shoved it into his belt. "We have to go. *Now.*"

Rune glanced back to see a group of soldiers and several hunting hounds cross the rail yard, moving swiftly toward them. Guns drawn.

Damn it.

Gideon grabbed her hand, pulling her after him, further out into the yard. But there was nowhere to go. Just tracks for miles, and every so often, parked train cars.

Barking and gunshots drowned out a distant train's rumble.

Luckily for Rune and Gideon, the soldiers were a good ways behind and were firing as they ran, making their aim unsteady.

Another rumble—like thunder—followed by a loud whistle made Rune glance down the tracks.

It wasn't *her* train making that sound. It was another train coming through, traveling down the furthest set of tracks in the yard.

And Gideon was heading straight for it.

"You're kidding," Rune wheezed, pumping her legs as hard as she could.

"It has to decrease its speed." He spoke through labored breaths. "Once it enters the yard, it won't stop . . . but it'll slow."

Rune glanced back. The dogs were gaining on them.

It wasn't a choice. They would have to jump on.

Long before she was ready, the train pulled up beside them, engine chugging. Its wheels screeched on the tracks as it braked, slowing only barely. The sound was so loud, it drowned out the dogs and the gunshots.

Rune and Gideon pumped their legs faster.

Most of the cars had windows, meaning this wasn't a supply train. But there were no people aboard either. Not that she could see, anyway.

Gideon's hand tightened on hers, as if to say, *Ready?*

Rune wasn't ready. The train was going way too fast. What if she jumped and missed? What if she fell under the wheels?

But the dogs were right there, snarling behind them. And Rune's legs were tiring. *Slowing.*

And already, the train was passing them by. Only three more cars, and it would be gone.

"I thought you said it has to slow down!"

Gideon didn't answer. Just let go of her hand, preparing to jump. He sped up beside her. She watched him time it just right:

waiting until the second-to-last car was beside him and launching himself at the platform's rail.

He grabbed hold, the toes of his boots landing on the platform's edge. He pulled himself over the rail.

"Show-off," she growled.

Gideon turned back to wait for her.

But it was too late—the car passed her by. She lost sight of Gideon as the next car—the end of the train—pulled up beside her.

This was it.

Her last chance.

She had to jump, or she'd be left behind.

The dogs snapped at her heels. Bullets whizzed past her head. She should give in. Give up. It was useless to try.

No.

Something sparked inside her. An old feeling. A familiar feeling. Like she was back in the midst of a heist, outwitting a certain Blood Guard captain, risking everything for the possibility of saving one more witch from the purge.

She'd forgotten the thrill of it. How it made her feel untouchable.

Invincible.

I am the Crimson Moth.

It was the answer to her oldest question.

You are the kindest, cleverest, bravest girl I've ever met.

This was Rune Winters. This girl. In this moment.

Rune fixed her gaze on the last car's platform, knowing it was now or never.

And then she jumped, soaring toward it.

Seconds before the train pulled out of reach, her fingers caught the railing and locked around it. Her knees banged against the cold steel, sending pain flickering through her.

Rune held on.

Ignoring the bullets bouncing off the train car and the snarling dogs below, she pulled herself up and over the rail.

This is what I've been running from. Not Cressida. Not the Blood Guard.

Rune was running from herself. From what she wanted most deeply, and feared she couldn't have.

The door of the car swung open. Gideon stepped out, pistol raised, shooting at the soldiers. Firing until he was out of bullets, then reloading and firing again. Never lowering the gun until the train left the rail yard, picking up speed and carrying them out of range.

SEVENTY-ONE

RUNE

TOGETHER, THEY STUMBLED INTO the dark car, windswept and breathing hard. The train rattled and clinked. Rune pressed her palm to the wall of the cramped hallway as it lurched on its tracks, trying to keep her balance. Trying to catch her breath.

When she glanced at Gideon, she found him leaning against the opposite wall, staring at her. Through the windows, the sun was almost below the horizon.

Rune gazed at this mountain of a boy. The one who'd risked his life alongside her. A boy who'd proven, again and again, they were better together than apart.

Why in the world had she left him?

Because I'm afraid of losing him.

Except running away *meant* losing him. Voluntarily.

What had she been thinking?

Rune never should have asked him to leave with her. In doing so, she'd asked him to go against his conscience. His *goodness*. She knew perfectly well what it would have cost Gideon to accept her offer. And she'd asked him anyway.

It was like Rune had changed places with Alex, who'd begged her to run away, and in doing so, proven he hadn't really known her at all.

"Are you all right?" he asked, breaking the silence.

Rune barely heard his question. She was remembering the

other train pulling out of the station, remembering her reflection in the glass.

"You asked me once if I wanted children," she said.

He tilted his head, as if this was the last thing he'd expected her to say.

"I want three."

Rune had seen them that day in the yellow house, while bullets whizzed over her and Gideon's heads: three little ones laughing as they ran through a field of wildflowers.

She had known immediately they were Gideon's. But this evening, while studying her reflection in the train window, she realized they were also *hers*. She'd seen their features in her face.

Rune was scared to even hope for it: a family of her own. People to belong to. She didn't know if it was a true vision, or fanciful thinking. All she knew was she wanted it. Wanted *them*.

But in order to have them, she had to stay.

Gideon ran a hand through his dark hair, glancing to the window.

"This train is going south," he said. "That means the next station is a few hours away. We can get off in that yard, and I can help you hop another one. Or we can find a harbor that hasn't been infiltrated and get you on a boat."

She frowned.

That wasn't exactly the response she'd hoped for.

"Gideon, I just said—"

"You want a family one day." He dragged his attention away from the window, fixing it on her. The look on his face seemed . . . sad. "I understand. It's why you want to escape."

"No." Rune stepped toward him, shaking her head. "I mean, *yes*. But . . ." She reached for his lapels, gripping them with both hands, anchoring herself to him against the train's jolt. "I'm offering you terms, Gideon."

He frowned at her, confused.

"Do you still want me to stay?"

Lifting a hand to her hair, he tucked a wild strand behind her ear. "More than anything."

"There's something I want, too. Something that would make me stay."

He was watching her closely now. "I'm listening."

She lowered her gaze to his throat, suddenly feeling uncertain. What if he didn't want the same thing?

"Sometimes," she said, staring hard at the collar of his jacket, "I fantasize about being your wife."

His eyebrows shot toward his forehead. "Really?" He grinned, clearly pleased. "Your fantasies are a *lot* more wholesome than . . ." The grin slid away. "Wait. What are you saying?"

He pressed his thumb to her chin, forcing her gaze back to his.

"I want to be your wife, Gideon."

The pulse in his throat kicked. "And these children you also want . . . they're *our* children?"

"I'm pretty sure that's how it works, yes." More quietly, she said: "Is that all right?"

Gideon plunged his fingers into her hair. "All right?" He pressed his forehead to hers. "Rune. Being married to you would be the honor of my life. You're saying you'll stay and fight, if I marry you?"

"More or less." She ran a hand up his chest to rest against his heart. "Is that extortion?"

His mouth curved. "I'll happily be extorted by you."

Tugging off his riding gloves, he dropped them one by one to the floor. Lifting his bare hands to her face, he slid his palms along her jaw, tender but firm. The feel of his bare skin against hers filled Rune with a yearning so powerful, she feared she might die of its absence.

His eyes were downcast, staring at her mouth.

"Do you remember on the *Arcadia*, when I woke you from that dream?"

A blush crept up her neck.

Merciful Ancients. He couldn't just forget about that?

"You never told me what it was about."

Her entire body prickled with embarrassment. "You really can't drop this?"

He shook his head and bent to press his lips against her neck.

"Maybe we can talk about it later?" she said.

"It'll be hours until we reach the next station," he murmured, his lips a soft graze.

Rune clenched her fists as he kissed down her throat, remembering the dream all too vividly. The steam from the boilers. The heat of their growing anger. The press of his—

"We were . . ."

She swallowed.

"You were . . . touching me."

"Touching you?" Gideon glanced up with a sly smile. "Like this?" He ran a hand slowly down her arm, raising the hairs there. Rune shivered, but shook her head.

"Show me."

"Why is this so important to you?"

"The way you said my name that night . . ." He ran the backs of his fingers up the buttons of her blouse. Rune's stomach pinched with desire as he stopped to undo the uppermost one. "I want to hear you say it like that again."

The words made her flush.

"Gideon—"

His fingers undid the next button while his dark eyes locked with hers, like a dare. She knew what those hands could do, and that mouth. He'd shown her before.

And because she couldn't resist him—or a challenge—Rune stared him down as she untucked her blouse from her pants.

She felt the pulse in his wrist quicken as she took his hand in hers, sliding it under the silk, pressing his calloused palm against her stomach. His pupils dilated as she showed him exactly what she wanted: guiding his hand to her breast and cupping the soft curve with his palm, the way he did in her dream.

His thumb stroked, making her hum with pleasure.

"What else?" His voice was low as he nudged her temple with his.

Rune glanced around. But there was no one on this train except them—and, presumably, the conductor at the other end.

She undid the buttons of her pants, and took his other hand. Pressing his palm between her hip bones, she guided his fingers down between her thighs. His breath shuddered. The air crackled between them as his hand pressed into her soft warmth.

She did not take her eyes away from his face.

Gideon needed no instruction this time. They stared at each other as his hand moved against her, fingers stroking, warming. He slid one inside her and Rune clenched around him, gasping.

"This is what you dreamed of that night?" He sounded breathless. "This?"

She nodded, her body temperature rising along with the pleasure he was stoking. Her hands slid up the hard planes of his chest. Looping her arms around his neck, she pushed up on her toes and dug her fingers into his hair, sealing his mouth with hers.

Kissing Gideon was like coming home. A steadying force, reminding her of who she was, and where she belonged.

"Rune . . ."

The way he breathed her name set her blood on fire.

His fingers plunged inside her, deep and insistent. Like he knew exactly what he was doing.

Rune arched against his hand.

"Gideon."

But instead of finishing, he pulled away.

The loss of him unbalanced Rune. "Wh-what are you doing?"

Glancing to the doors in this hallway, he stepped toward one and opened it, revealing an empty storage room. "This is a passenger train."

"So?" Annoyed by his lack of attention, of *devotion*, Rune tried to drag his eyes back to her by tugging off her blouse and dropping it on the floor.

Gideon's gaze zipped to the strap of her bralette.

"So . . ." he said, stepping toward her. "Passenger trains have sleeper cars."

His arms locked around her waist as he pulled her against him. Rune tugged his mouth back to hers, kissing him as he walked her backward, toward the door between this car and the next. He opened it, still kissing her, and a rush of icy wind came howling in.

Rune yelped in surprise. Gideon ran his hands down her bare arms, which had erupted in goose bumps. Trying to warm her.

The wind whipped through their hair and clothes. It was twilight, and the stars were freckling the black sky overhead.

"Ready?" he called over the howling wind and rattling train, holding out his hand to her.

"This is madness!" she laughed, grabbing his hand and following him from one platform to the next.

When he opened the next door, Rune stepped inside another storage car.

"Let's just stay here," she said, pushing him up against the wall and peeling off his jacket.

"Tempting," he said as the train lurched. "But no."

He started toward the next door, kissing and caressing and coaxing her along with him. Rune unbuttoned his shirt as they went, pushing it off and pressing her mouth to the scar on his chest. Exploring him with her lips, tasting him with her tongue.

Gideon pressed a hand to the wall, his breath hitching. For a moment, he seemed about to give in to her. But he rallied and pulled open the door, dragging her to the next car.

Several more cars strewn with several more pieces of clothing later, they found what they were looking for: the sleeper car.

It was full night by then, and only the moon's light flooded in through the windows. Gideon chose a room and pulled her inside, stripping off their undergarments as he guided her to the bunk.

"Tell me what you like," she whispered in the darkness, her hands wandering over him as he laid her down in the crisp sheets.

"I like you," he murmured into her hair, kneeling between her legs. About to finish what he'd started several train cars ago.

She shook her head. That wasn't good enough.

The last time they'd done this, Gideon had known exactly how to please her. As if Rune was a locked door and he had the only key to open her.

Rune wanted to be that for him.

He lowered himself on top of her—gently, so as not to aggravate the fresh scars on her back—and started tracing a line down her body with his mouth.

"When you're alone," she said, undeterred, pushing herself up on her elbows, "and you think about us, together, what are we doing?"

He glanced up from where his lips were pressed to her thigh. "Do *you* think about that?"

She looked away, smiling. "Answer the question, Gideon."

He seemed about to protest, but instead reached up into her hair, still bound in a messy braid.

"I think about doing this."

He tugged it loose, so it fell over her shoulder.

"And this."

He rolled onto his back and pulled her on top of him. Rune laughed as she straddled his hips.

"And . . . this."

Sitting up, he cupped her neck, bringing her mouth to his. Rune hummed low in her throat as he kissed her hungrily. His arm slid around her waist, sealing them together as he slowly rocked against her. Showing her what he wanted.

The fire in her belly grew hotter and brighter with every rocking thrust.

Grabbing hold of the bunk overhead, Rune rolled her hips to meet him. Paying attention to his breath, his pulse, the way he groaned when she did something he really liked, and then did more of that. Until they found their perfect rhythm.

She marveled at the magic of it. Like there was something far bigger than themselves binding them together. Working like a fiery spell.

"Rune." He spoke her name like an incantation. *"Rune."* His fingers plunged into her hair. "If you don't slow down, I'm going to—"

She cradled his face in her hands. "I want you to, my love."

His eyes gazed up at her, tender, defiant. Trying to resist. To hold off and wait for her.

Rune narrowed her eyes at him, determined to win, until he laughed aloud. It was his laugh that did her in—the sound of his love and delight. She lost herself in it. Pressing her forehead to his, she let the fire overtake her, too.

They made love like it was the last time. Like they wouldn't survive tomorrow.

Just in case they didn't.

SEVENTY-TWO

GIDEON

WHEN THE TRAIN SLOWED at the next rail yard, they retrieved their clothes, dressed, and jumped off. The yard was deep in the countryside, wheat fields on one side, rye on the other. They found two horses grazing in a pasture close by and borrowed them. Rune left her pouch full of coins behind to compensate the owners before they returned them.

They rode for the Wentholt cottage, keeping to the woods and following the rivers as much as possible to avoid the main roads. When Wintersea came into view, they ventured close to see if it was abandoned. The horses were gone. No guards patrolled. The house appeared to be empty.

Carefully, they ventured inside so Rune could fetch the spell books she'd failed to steal last time, which might come in useful in their stand against Cressida and the Good Commander. The empty marble halls echoed with their footsteps. Paintings had been smashed and tables overturned, but whether it was the Blood Guard who'd done it, or bandits, or Cressida's hired soldiers, they couldn't tell.

As they walked the vandalized halls, Gideon was transported to the first time he'd ever set foot in this house: the night Blood Guard soldiers dragged Kestrel Winters away to be purged while he kept a close eye on the old witch's granddaughter.

He remembered Rune standing there, letting it happen, her face stoic as a statue. Gideon took her hand and squeezed it firmly, hating that he'd played a part in the most horrible night of her life.

I can't change the past, he thought as they walked, taking in the damage. *But together, maybe we can change the future.*

When they started up the staircase, Rune rested her free hand on the mahogany railing. Her voice rang with certainty as she said, "One day, this will be my home again."

Gideon stood watch outside her bedroom while she collected the things she needed. He paced quietly, listening for any sound of danger, stopping at the window near the end of the hall and scanning the grounds to look for signs of intruders.

But all was still at Wintersea. No one was out there.

He was about to turn away from the window when he heard a sound. Like metal striking metal.

It was so faint, he assumed it was coming from outside.

But then he heard it again.

Clang!

He looked to the floor at his feet.

Clang! Clang!

He frowned.

It's coming from beneath us.

"Do you hear that?" whispered Rune, poking her head outside the bedroom. She held a dusty leather-bound spell book in her hands, and her hair was a tangle of red-gold in the candlelight.

Unholstering his gun, he headed for the stairs. "Shut yourself into the casting room, and don't come out until I return."

Gideon didn't wait for her to do as he said, knowing she would listen to him only if she wanted to. Instead, he descended to the main floor. By the time he reached the servants' quarters, the sound had stopped. Rune hadn't followed. He waited, listening.

It came again.

Clang! Clang!

It wasn't mechanical, and the silence between each clang seemed sporadic. Sometimes the sound was harsher, sometimes softer, as if someone was striking something angrily, then despairingly.

It was louder now. Coming from directly below him.

The basement.

Gideon searched the servant quarters until he found a set of cramped stairs in the kitchen, leading down. He took them.

The basement was damp as a cellar. The walls and floors were made of rough-hewn stone. And with no windows to let the light in, it was too dark to see. He had to go back for a lamp.

CLANG! CLANG! CLANG!

His footsteps quickened until he arrived at a door, certain the sound was coming from behind it.

CLANG!

Gideon took the safety off his pistol.

CLANG!

He turned the doorknob.

CLANG!

He opened the door.

The room was pitch-dark. The moment the door swung in, the sound abruptly stopped. Lifting his lamp, Gideon shone the light inside.

It was the boiler room. Warmer than the hall beyond, the space was full of iron pipes pumping water to the house's upper levels.

Inside the room, wearing her red uniform, stood Laila.

Her wrists were manacled to the pipe beside her, and in her grip was a wrench—which she was striking against the pipe.

"Gideon?" Her dark hair curled in the humidity, and her eyes were ringed with shadows.

"Laila?" He stepped into the room, staring at her. "You're supposed to be at the Rookery. What are you doing . . . here?" He glanced around the boiler room.

"I'm being punished for letting you and Rune escape."

He stared at her, not comprehending. It was one thing for Noah to be angry at his sister's defiance, but leaving her for dead?

"Noah demanded I hunt you down and bring you back—to prove my loyalty. When I refused, he locked me in here for Cressida's mercenaries to find."

A tide of anger swept through Gideon.

"Does he not know what soldiers do to women in wartime?" he said through gritted teeth.

"On the contrary," said Laila, glancing away. "That's why he left me here." She stared at the wrench in her hands. "I had to decide: starve to death, or be discovered by the wrong type of soldier." Her gaze lifted to Gideon. "Luckily, the right one walked in."

He heard the relief in her voice. She'd been expecting a very different fate.

Gideon crossed the room and pulled her into a hug. She leaned her head against his shoulder, a shaky breath escaping.

"You have no idea how glad I am to see you."

For the briefest of moments, he was thankful they were at war. In war, rules of civility were altered. If Gideon ever came face-to-face with Noah, he could shoot him with a clean conscience.

"And the other soldiers? They left you here, like this?"

She shook her head. "They didn't know. Noah sent them ahead before ordering his guards to lock me up. They likely arrived at the Rookery thinking I was a day behind them."

Gideon reached for the chains of her manacles, looking for the lock.

"Noah took the key with him."

He dropped the chains and studied the pipes. They were welded together. He doubted an axe—should he even be able to find one—would do much damage.

How was he going to get her out of here?

"I can help."

The voice came from behind them. Gideon spun as Laila's gaze sliced toward the open doorway, where Rune stood in the shadows. A pale white flame flickered in the air above her outstretched hand. Slung over her shoulder was a leather satchel stuffed with books.

"As I'm sure you remember"—the corner of her mouth lifted in a half smile—"I have a spell for picking locks."

SEVENTY-THREE

RUNE

*A*FTER FREEING LAILA, THEY all rode for the Wentholt cottage, arriving shortly before sundown. They had to split two horses between the three of them, so Rune rode with Gideon.

It was Rune who sighted the red uniforms through the trees—Blood Guard officers. A dozen or so, patrolling the grounds.

They halted their horses.

How many more were inside?

It doesn't matter, thought Rune, her eyes narrowing on the red coats. She'd gotten out of stickier situations. And her friends were inside that cottage.

She dismounted the horse, leaving Gideon in the saddle, and headed straight for it.

"*Rune,*" Gideon whispered. But before he could stop her, six soldiers emerged from the trees, guns pointed right at them.

Gideon and Laila immediately raised their hands while Rune contemplated grabbing Gideon's holstered pistol—or the knife sheathed at her calf—when a surprised voice called out.

"Hold!"

A young soldier with copper hair lowered his rifle, motioning for the others to do the same.

"It's Sharpe and Creed."

Rune frowned, glancing to Gideon and Laila, who looked relieved as they dismounted their horses.

"*Felix?* What are you doing here?" Gideon strode toward the red-haired soldier, and they clasped hands.

"The Commander sent us to hunt you down," said Felix.

Gideon froze, his hand falling to his side. "You're here to arrest us?"

"No, sir." Felix glanced at his comrades, who all stood at attention. "We're here for our orders."

Gideon cocked an eyebrow. "Orders?"

"Yes, sir."

He looked to Laila, as if hoping she'd explain it.

"Well, Captain?" She crossed her arms over her chest. "What *are* your orders?"

～～～

WHILE GIDEON, LAILA, ASH, Abbie, and a platoon of Blood Guard soldiers filled Bart Wentholt's parlor, strategizing about what to do next, a message arrived from Harrow. She and Juniper had acquired the information they needed.

Gideon—

The bodies of Analise and Elowyn are hidden at the Crossroads. Cressida is planning to travel there before the new moon. The spell preserving them is fading, and if it fades entirely, their bodies will decay. She needs to strengthen it before that happens.

—Harrow

The Crossroads was the meeting place of three major rivers, all colliding in a dangerous gorge. The force of its crashing currents created a deadly whirlpool.

"She says nothing else?" asked Gideon, taking the note from Rune and turning it over, looking for more. There was nothing about Juniper's attempt to recruit witches to their cause. Nor did Harrow say if they planned to remain in the capital, or return.

"It's a renewal spell," said Seraphine, who'd been reading over Rune's shoulder. "It must be performed on a new moon. If it isn't, she'll have to wait until the next one."

"It sounds like that will be too late," said Rune.

Cressida wouldn't miss her window.

"Do you have a map of the island?"

Bart produced one for him. They spread it out across the table, measuring the distance from their location to the Crossroads.

"Looks like a three-day ride to the Crossroads from here," said Gideon.

"The new moon is four days away," said Seraphine.

"If we get there before her," said Rune, "we could find and destroy the bodies, eliminating any chance of resurrecting them." This would—*hopefully*—embolden more witches to turn against the witch queen.

Her gaze met Gideon's. They had to try.

It was decided that Rune, Gideon, and Seraphine would travel to the Crossroads ahead of Cressida. Bart and Antonio would remain behind to wait for Harrow and Juniper, along with any other witches they recruited. Meanwhile Laila, Ash, Abbie, and the other soldiers would head for the Rookery—to take it from Noah by force, with help from allies inside.

But even if Rune located the bodies of her half sisters, she'd need the counterspell to break the enchantment protecting them. The magic preserving Analise and Elowyn might be weakened, but that didn't mean it wasn't still strong enough to repel Rune's attempts to burn the bodies.

Determined, she went to search the spell books she'd brought back from Wintersea, hoping an answer to her problem lay within their pages.

RUNE SAT ON THE floor of the study encircled by candles, their flames dancing in the darkness. Spell books were scattered across the floorboards around her.

She'd searched each one and hadn't found a counterspell.

When the floorboards creaked, Rune glanced up. Antonio stood framed in the doorway, holding a lamp.

"Everything all right?" he asked, shining light into the room.

Rune sighed, pulling her toes toward her and hugging her knees to her chest.

"I need a spell to break the one protecting Analise and Elowyn," she said, glancing to the spellmarks on the pages before her. "But it's not in any of these books."

Perhaps she could create such a spell. She'd done it before. *Ghost Walker* was her invention.

But it took me months to get that casting right.

She didn't have months.

Hopefully Cressida's preservation spell had weakened enough for them to destroy the bodies without interference—that's why the witch queen was traveling to the Crossroads. The fading magic made her sisters' corpses vulnerable.

And if not . . .

We could take them with us to destroy later.

The idea of kidnapping corpses made her feel ill. But Rune would do whatever was necessary to strike a blow against Cressida.

Antonio entered the room and lowered himself to the floor beside her, sitting cross-legged inside her ring of candles. The smell of sugar and cinnamon came with him, likely fused to his hair and clothes from a day spent with Bess in the kitchens.

He opened a spell book. As he leaned over it, studying the marks on its pages, a tiny medallion swung out from beneath his collar, catching the light. Etched in its surface was a spectacled woman with an owl perched on her shoulder.

Wisdom.

The Ancient.

"Is that who you were consecrated to?" asked Rune, reaching to touch the silver oval dangling in the air. It was no bigger than the pad of her thumb.

Seeing what she meant, Antonio tugged the loop of cord over his head, and handed her the medallion. "Wisdom. Yes."

Studying the face impressed into the silver, Rune remembered the spell she'd come across while gathering spell books in her casting room: a spell for summoning an Ancient.

Absently, she said, "You don't think it's really possible to summon one, do you?"

Antonio went quiet. "Queen Althea did."

She glanced up into his face. "You believe that?"

It was from the stories Nan used to tell her as a child: Wisdom was Queen Althea's closest advisor, and this was why Cascadia flourished for decades under her rule.

"It's a fact," he said, taking back the cord and medallion and pulling it over his head. "Near the end of Althea's reign, shifting loyalties resulted in strong support for her cousin, Winoa Roseblood. Althea refused to enforce what Winoa and her followers believed to be true: that given the lack of magic in their blood, non-witches were subservient to witches. But Winoa's propaganda had already infected the court, and a plot to dethrone Althea was gaining traction."

Rune had never been given this history lesson. She listened with rapt attention.

"Althea called on the Ancients to advise her," Antonio continued. "This was centuries after the Resurrection Wars, when the Seven Sisters had sworn never again to intervene in mortal affairs. But Wisdom took pity on Althea and allowed herself to be summoned.

"Althea wanted to denounce Winoa's dangerous ideology, declare her a traitor to Cascadia, strip her of her titles, and exile her. This, Wisdom knew, would lead to a civil war that would tear the country apart and leave many dead. She advised Althea to call a council, one that would draw Winoa's supporters and their idea of witch supremacy out of the darkness, bringing it into the light, where everyone could see it for what it was: a heresy."

Rune frowned. "Did it work?"

He shook his head. "No. Winoa, with the backing of Althea's advisors, betrayed her cousin in the very chamber where Althea hoped to root out her court's corruption. Instead of a council, there was a slaughter: Althea and her supporters were stabbed to death, and from their blood, Winoa forged a new rule—the Roseblood Dynasty—ushering in a reign of tyranny and bloodshed that would last for decades."

The candle flames flickered as Antonio fell silent. Rune stared at him, stunned.

This was not in any of the stories Nan had told her. Though Rune could understand why: it would have given her nightmares.

"And Wisdom just let it happen?"

"The Ancient found Althea lying in a pool of her own blood, her body as cold as the stones beneath her. Realizing her advice had caused a terrible tragedy, Wisdom bound herself in human form to Cascadia, until she corrected her error. Only then would she rejoin her sisters in the world beyond this one."

Rune studied Antonio, who obviously believed the historical account. It was a nice idea: Wisdom as a kind of sentinel, waiting for the right moment to set the world to rights. But obviously it was a myth.

If it were true, it would mean she's still here. Walking among us.

It made more sense that Althea had come up with the idea to hold a council on her own, and historians wrote Wisdom in later.

Antonio nodded to the book lying open in his lap. "Arcana spells were outlawed. Why would your grandmother have a spell book full of them?"

"I don't know," said Rune, glancing down at the spell in question.

RESURRECTION OF THE DEAD, the inscription read.

Rune had come across it in her search and set it aside to study later. But Antonio was poring over it now in the glow of his lamp.

RESURRECTION OF THE DEAD
CLASSIFICATION: ARCANA

A close kin must be sacrificed in the casting of this spell. Nothing less than a parent, child, or sibling will suffice. To resurrect the dead, the following steps must be taken:

To begin, cut the sacrifice and use their fresh blood to draw the required spellmarks on the bodies of the dead. Once all the spellmarks are complete, use your casting knife to pierce the heart of your sacrifice. The magic in the marks will draw the life force from the victim, infusing the deceased, resulting in their resurrection. For this reason, the sacrifice must be living when the spell begins, and only after the spellmarks are drawn can they be killed. A dead victim will not work, even if the blood is fresh. The victim's life must be taken in the process of casting the spell, or it will fail.

An addendum had been written near the bottom of the page:

This spell is forbidden under the laws of Cascadia. If for some terrible reason it must be used, be warned: the sacrifice will die, and the witch who undertakes it will corrupt herself beyond redemption. Proceed at your own risk.

Rune shivered.

If people knew she was Analise and Elowyn's sister, it would be in everyone's best interest to kill her, permanently preventing Cressida from using her to bring their sisters back.

Antonio closed the book and shoved it away from him.

"What changed your mind?" he said. "You seemed so set on leaving."

Rune thought of Gideon's belief in a better world, and his willingness to die for it. She thought of their future children running through a field, full of laughter and joy.

"I realized he's right," she said. "You get the world you're willing to fight for."

She glanced at the medallion hanging from Antonio's neck.

"Can acolytes officiate weddings?"

"In certain circumstances, yes." Antonio cocked his head at her. "Why do you ask?"

"Could you marry us, when this is over?"

If he noticed she said *when*, not *if*, he didn't point it out. Only smiled.

"It would be an honor."

Stringed instruments hummed from beneath the floorboards, breaking her concentration. Rune and Antonio frowned at each other, confusion etched into their foreheads at the sound.

Music?

They went to investigate, the music growing louder the closer they came to the ground floor. In the room where they'd left Gideon, Laila, and the others to finish their strategizing, they found what could only be described as a revel.

The furniture had been pushed against the walls, and two fiddlers, still in Blood Guard uniforms, stood in the middle of the room, furiously slashing their bows against their strings. Everyone else danced around them. As if they weren't in the midst of a war, but an after-party.

Several more people had arrived while Rune was upstairs searching through spell books. She recognized a good number of them: aristocrats who'd run in her social circles when she was still pretending to be a vapid socialite and hiding her witchy nature.

Bart danced up to them with flushed cheeks.

"Is that Charlotte Gong?" Rune asked him, catching sight of the girl. Charlotte was talking with a group of soldiers at the outskirts of the dancing while her fiancé embraced Laila. "And . . . Elias Creed?"

The brother of Noah and Laila, he worked for the Ministry of Public Safety—the bureaucratic office that oversaw witch purges, among other things.

Rune had always suspected Charlotte of secretly sympathizing with witches. Perhaps that explained his change of heart?

Or perhaps Elias had been a sympathizer all along.

"They had nowhere else to go," said Bart, turning to watch the revelry. "Cressida's soldiers have seized or ransacked every home within fifty miles of the capital. Those who didn't run were taken captive. *These*"—he nodded to the group—"were lucky to escape with their lives."

Antonio motioned to the dancing, his eyes alight. "And what's this?"

Bart smiled, fox-like, in the gaslight.

"One last party," he said, grabbing Antonio's hands and pulling him toward the dancers. "If we're going to die, darling, let's die happy."

Rune smiled, watching them disappear into the frenzy. Leaning against the wall, she scanned the room, noticing neither Harrow nor Juniper was present. Had they remained in the capital? Or were they traveling back even as music rang in her ears? What would they think when they walked in on a raucous party?

Her gaze found Gideon through the dancers. He stood in the same group as Charlotte, listening to whatever she was saying. The moment she sighted him, he looked up, as if sensing her attention.

Excusing himself from the conversation, he started toward her. His jaw was dark with stubble from days without shaving, and the sleeves of his shirt were rolled to his elbows. He looked tired but resolved.

Rune swallowed as he approached, remembering what they'd done on the train. His gaze bored into hers, as if he was remembering it, too.

"You owe me a dance," he said, loud enough for her to hear over the music.

Her brows arched. "Excuse me?"

"I once dared you to accompany me to an *actual* party, or don't you remember?"

There will be no ball gowns. No hired musicians. No songs with ridiculous steps, he'd told her a lifetime ago, in the halls of Wintersea, describing exactly *this* kind of party.

Name the date, and I'll be there.

Careful, Miss Winters, or I might call your bluff.

He stopped directly before her. Rune leaned harder against the wall, her gaze trailing up his chest until her head tipped back to meet his eyes. The merriment beyond—the music, the laughter, the dancing—fell quiet. As if they were the only two people in the room.

"You accused me of . . . what was it?" she said, feeling weirdly breathless. "Not wanting to be caught dead with 'riffraff in disreputable locales'?"

"Prove me wrong, then." He trailed his knuckles across her cheekbone.

She wanted to wind his fingers through hers, to pull him upstairs and into a bed. But she stood her ground, running her gaze down him. Sizing him up. "I'm not sure you're sufficiently disreputable, Gideon Sharpe. I'd better wait for more scandalous riffraff."

He growled low. Grabbing her around the waist, he buried his face in her neck, nipping gently with his teeth. "I can be scandalous."

Rune laughed and let him drag her into the fray.

He led her in a dance she wasn't used to, and as her heart beat wildly in time with the song, her face flushing and her hair sticking to her sweaty skin, Rune looked at the people around her, spinning and stomping across the floor as if this were the last song they'd ever hear.

Even if we can't bring down Cressida, Rune realized, *the world we want to forge already exists.*

It was right here in this room.

It was a world where enemies could be not just allies, but lovers and friends, and most of all, equals. It was a world where no one needed to hide who they really were.

She wished Alex were here to see it.

As the song ended and cheers rang out, Gideon grinned down at her, sweaty and breathless. Cupping her face in his hands, he kissed her hard on the mouth.

Rune marveled. A witch being adored by a Blood Guard captain in plain view of everyone? Only a week ago, it would have been absurd. *Impossible.*

But they were standing on the cusp of something new. Fragile and shimmering, like a butterfly emerging from a chrysalis. Who knew if it would survive longer than tonight?

Rune kissed Gideon back, determined to remember this moment, just in case it didn't. Because for the first time in her life, she was completely herself.

And that was worth everything.

Even dying for.

SEVENTY-FOUR

RUNE

*I*T TOOK THREE DAYS of hard riding to get to the Crossroads.

Halfway, the group split up. Laila took the soldiers and headed for the Rookery, hoping to seize it by force, with the help of a substantial number of Blood Guard soldiers on the inside who were waiting for Laila's command. If Rune and Gideon were successful at the Crossroads, they would soon join her.

Bart remained at the Wentholt cottage, in case Harrow and Juniper returned with more witches for their ranks. Charlotte Gong, Elias Creed, and the other exiled aristocrats remained with Bart, organizing search parties of the homes and towns invaded by Cressida's army, hoping to find survivors.

Gideon and Rune continued to the Crossroads, accompanied by Seraphine and Antonio. Antonio had volunteered at the last moment, surprising Rune.

"Bart doesn't mind being parted from you?" she asked him.

"Sometimes our paths must diverge from those we love," Antonio said as they rode, side by side, scanning the surrounding mountains. "But if love is the highest power, our paths will converge again—if not in this world, then the next."

The words felt like a premonition, making her shiver.

"You believe that?" she asked. "That love is the highest power?"

He glanced at her like she'd asked him if water was wet. "Don't you?"

At sundown, they heard the thunderous roar of the Crossroads before they saw it: the gorge opening up and the hungry white whirlpool below. Its currents swirled angrily, like water down a giant's drain.

In the center was a rocky island maybe twenty paces across. A rickety rope bridge connected the island to the gorge's bank. It jerked and swayed, beholden to the strong winds surrounding them.

Rune knew in her gut that small island was where she needed to go. It's exactly where Cressida would hide her half sisters: in the center of a whirlpool.

She glanced at Seraphine, finding her eyes also focused there, as if she sensed the same.

"Gideon and I will go look," said Rune, adjusting the strap of her satchel containing the necessary spell book. "If I need you, Seraphine, I'll wave."

Seraphine nodded as Antonio continued scanning the mountainous hills around them. The moon was a pale sliver against a red sky, reminding them that Cressida would arrive soon. The new moon was tomorrow. Best to find Rune's half sisters and get out.

Gideon went first, testing the bridge. He'd strapped a shovel to his back—in case they had to dig the bodies up—and sheathed a pistol at his hip. The bridge swayed beneath his weight, making Rune's heart lodge in her throat. But his grasp on the rope never slipped, and he quickly pulled himself forward. When he finally reached the other side, he nodded to her.

Rune stepped onto the bridge.

Spray dampened her clothes and hair. The ropes—slippery with water—chafed at her stiff hands until the skin broke. More than once, her foot slipped, and she nearly went down.

She wouldn't survive a fall into those currents. The whirlpool would drag her under, and even if she managed to come up for air, the water would smash her body against the rocks, snuffing the life from her.

Rune righted herself, checked that her satchel was secure, and continued.

Gideon's gaze never left her. She felt him watching her every move, felt him tense every time she stumbled. When she was within reach, he held his hand out.

Rune grabbed it, holding tight.

He pulled her to safety.

They split up, checking for signs: upturned earth, or an unnatural pattern in the rocks. Cressida would have buried them here two years ago, returning at least a few times to renew her spell.

But Rune didn't find them in the ground.

She found them lying in a still pool, hidden by reeds. It was the glow that alerted her to it. When the tall grass shifted and the pale light shone through, Rune caught sight of a white casting signature: a rose and crescent moon.

Rune waded through the reeds until she stood at the pool's edge. The water was crystal clear. Beneath the pale glow of Cressida's signature, she saw them: two young women lying peacefully under the surface, as if asleep.

Silver-white hair framed Elowyn and Analise's faces. Long, pale eyelashes rested against their fair cheeks. And there was a gaping hole in each of their foreheads where a bullet had gone in, dealing a killing blow.

Rune's breath froze in her lungs.

My sisters.

She swallowed, not wanting to step into this place in which they rested, waiting for Cressida to bring them back to life. But in order to check the strength of the magic preserving them, in order to *destroy* them, she'd have to drag them out.

Drawing a deep breath, Rune walked into the shallow pool. As soon as her boot touched the water, the pool blackened. A force like lightning exploded outward, striking Rune. It turned her vision bright white and threw her backward, into the reeds.

She landed on her rump, pain flickering through her.

Rune winced and sat up, staring at the pool, its black waters still rippling from her disruption.

The spell was obviously still intact.

So why did Harrow's note say it's fading?

Without the counterspell, they couldn't break it. And if she couldn't enter the pool to drag them out . . .

"What happened?" Rushing over, Gideon crouched next to her. "Are you all right?" Catching sight of Elowyn and Analise beneath the water, his eyes darkened.

"The spell won't let me near them," said Rune. "Maybe Seraphine will have a solution."

But as he helped her up and they turned toward the bridge, Rune realized an unbreakable spell was the least of her problems.

Across the roaring whirlpool, Seraphine and Antonio were on their knees, a gun pressed to each of their heads. Beyond them, a hundred or more soldiers ringed the gorge.

Among them were witches. Dozens of witches. Their casting knives shimmered in the last light of the setting sun.

Juniper was with them. Her eyes were red from weeping, her hands were bound in front her, and at her back stood Cressida—with a knife to Juniper's throat.

Harrow, too, was restrained. A soldier gripped the spymaster's hair as they forced her to her knees.

We've failed, thought Rune.

"I'm sorry, Comrade!" Harrow's anguished voice echoed over the water. "She made me choose!"

Rune remembered Harrow's note from three nights ago, telling them Cressida was traveling to the Crossroads.

It was a setup.

Rune's thoughts spun faster than the whirlpool.

This was why the pair hadn't returned. Why Gideon had received only one brief message from Harrow. Juniper had gone to recruit witches to their cause, and someone had ratted her out to the witch queen, further using her to compromise Harrow.

"She had to choose between betraying you or watching Juniper die," Rune realized aloud. She glanced at Gideon, whose expression was a mixture of shock and anger. "Cressida would have threatened to kill Juniper unless Harrow led us into a trap."

Deep down, Rune thought, *she still loves her.*

"Cress will kill them both as soon as her goals here are accomplished," Gideon growled.

"Then let's ensure they aren't accomplished," said Rune.

At some point, Gideon had drawn his gun, pointing it at the soldiers on the other side. But he only had so many bullets, and every soldier *also* had a gun—most of which were pointed right back.

Cressida would have ordered Rune to not be harmed; she needed her alive.

Would she have ordered the same for Gideon?

No, she thought, remembering the witch who'd nearly killed him on the train tracks. Remembering Cressida pointing her gun at Gideon's chest and firing—only to be thwarted by Alex.

Gideon was disposable.

Rune reached for his free hand, lacing their fingers tight as she scanned the gorge.

We are completely surrounded.

Laila and their soldiers were leagues away, heading for

the Rookery. Their allies here—Seraphine, Antonio, Juniper, Harrow—were hostages. It was only Gideon and Rune, surrounded by a deadly whirlpool, and on the other side: enemy soldiers. All of whom had their guns aimed directly at them.

Her breath hitched sharply. Cressida was now crossing the bridge, followed by several witches.

"Thank you for doing my work for me!" The witch queen moved confidently along the ropes. She'd discarded her traveling cape, and her casting knife shone at her hip. "You couldn't possibly have made this any easier."

BANG!

Gideon fired on Cressida and the witches with her. The bullet ricocheted off some invisible shield surrounding them and flew into the night.

BANG! BANG!

More bullets flew, only to bounce off again.

"*Gideon*," Rune warned, seeing the soldiers surrounding them lift their guns, aiming straight at him. Waiting for Cressida's command.

Gideon wasn't listening. Rune felt his desperation with every shot of his pistol. Saw it in the unsteadiness of his hand as he reloaded. He was not going down without a fight.

Except the fight's over, Rune realized as Cressida and her witches stepped off the bridge.

Their allies were all taken hostage. Their only weapons were Gideon's gun—clearly useless against Cressida—and Rune's spellbook. But any spell Rune tried would only be deflected by those magic shields. There was no point even attempting to cast one; by the time she drew the spellmarks, Cressida and her witches would be on them.

And Gideon would be dead from a hundred bullets.

BANG!

Cressida was ten paces away. She'd be here in seconds. The other witches were fanning out, preparing to surround Gideon and Rune. Beyond them, the soldiers cocked their guns.

Cressida raised her arm, about to give the command to fire. To end Gideon.

And suddenly Rune knew there was only one way left to beat her.

She thought of *Everlasting.* A spell with no end.

Rune could keep Gideon safe forever with that spell.

She thought of everyone who called this island home. People who deserved to be safe.

Rune could keep them safe with her life—by giving it up before Cressida could steal it from her.

She remembered her dream at the summoning stones: her and Gideon, face to face, in the dark and the rain. *It wasn't rain,* she realized now as the mist of the whirlpool soaked them.

It wasn't a dream.

Her eyes burned with the realization.

BANG!

The gunshot brought her back to the gorge. Rune turned to Gideon, whose eyes were dark with fear.

"Try to reach the bridge," he said, still firing. "If I keep shooting at them, maybe—"

He was in denial. Refusing to see what was right in front of him. Rune wouldn't even make it to the bridge. And if by some miracle she did, more witches were waiting beyond it, not to mention the soldiers.

"Gideon."

He didn't seem to hear her.

Cressida was seconds away. Any moment now, soldiers would shoot him dead, forcing Rune to watch him die. And then Cressida would kill Rune, too, resurrecting their sisters and cementing her reign of terror.

If Rune didn't act now, the world she'd glimpsed last night would be snuffed out in the blink of an eye.

She couldn't let that happen.

BANG!

"If you can get to Seraphine," said Gideon, "maybe you can—"

Before he wasted the last bullet in the chamber, Rune grabbed the hot barrel and forced it down.

"Gideon."

He jerked his head toward her, studying her for a moment. Droplets of spray shone in his hair, making it look darker than usual.

"Let go of the gun."

He frowned, his eyes wild with confusion.

Swallowing down her fear, she said, "Do you trust me?"

It seemed to take all of his strength to do it, but he let her take his pistol.

The sacrifice must be living when the spell begins.

She was going to die. That was certain. And in light of that certainty, there was only one choice before her. Only one move left to make.

A dead victim will not work, even if the blood is fresh.

With trembling hands, Rune turned Gideon toward her. Away from the horror a few steps away.

The victim's life must be taken in the process of casting the spell, or it will fail.

"Look at me." She made sure the pistol was cocked. Just like he taught her.

Her hands shook harder, making her realize she couldn't do this herself. She was going to need his help.

Tearing his eyes from Cressida, Gideon fixed them on Rune.

Placing her hand over his heart, she said, "I want you to know I am so grateful, so *lucky*, to have loved you." Her voice wobbled. "Even if it was only for a little while."

Gideon's jaw clenched. "What are—"

Rune shook her head. The tears prickling her eyes made the sight of him blur.

"If I have to die, I want to die like this." Rune took his hand and wrapped it around the pistol as she pressed the barrel against her heart. "Right here. With you."

Gideon stared down in horror at the gun. At his finger on the trigger.

"No," he said, trying to step away. "*Rune.* You can't ask me—"

"You *must.*" She grabbed a fistful of his shirt, keeping him with her. Her throat heated. Tears trailed down her cheeks. "It's the only way now. You know what will happen if you don't."

He looked away in disgust, his grip limp on the gun in her hand, pointed at her chest.

"If you don't do it, she will." Rune glanced over his shoulder, to see Cressida grinning. Like something out of a nightmare. So close. Almost here. About to rip them away from each other forever. "There's no third option. She'll kill me and use my death to bring about a much bigger nightmare."

When she looked back into his face, his eyes shone with tears.

"It's either you or her," she said. "Don't let it be her. If you love me, you won't let it be her. Gideon, *please.*"

Her voice broke on that plea.

His grip on the gun tightened, so Rune let go. Taking his face in her hands, she pushed up on her toes and kissed him.

Hot tears spilled down both their cheeks.

"It's been an honor, Captain," she whispered against his lips.

Gideon let out a soft cry, but he didn't fail her.

Pulling the trigger, he sent a bullet straight into her heart.

SEVENTY-FIVE

RUNE

*T*HE *BANG* DEAFENED HER.

Gunpowder burned in her nose. Pain and heat flooded her chest. Just before Rune's legs gave out, Cressida's enraged scream shattered the air.

Gideon's arms encircled Rune as he caught her, lowering them both to the ground. The strength of him was everywhere, surrounding her like a comforting blanket as the blood gushed from the cavity in her chest.

It surprised her, even now, how both gentleness and strength could be bound up together in one man. She was in his lap, some part of her realized, and the warmth against her cold cheek was his chest, the steady beat beneath, his heart.

I'm going miss the sound of your heart, she thought.

"What have I done," Gideon cried, his entire body trembling. *"What have I done?"*

"You spared me," Rune whispered, touching her blood-soaked fingers to both of his cheeks, drawing a mark on each one. Gideon was so consumed by grief, he didn't notice. "You spared all of us."

Cressida needed Rune's life to resurrect their sisters, and Gideon had stolen it from her.

The cold started in her fingers and toes, the chill spreading inward slowly, to her core, until Rune knew she'd never be warm again.

She closed her eyes, saying a silent goodbye to him and to

the life they might have had together. Saying goodbye to those three joyful children she'd never get to meet.

In mere steps, Cressida would be upon them. Rune smiled, remembering the last symbol she'd drawn on the floor of Larkmont, after the whipping, as she collapsed in a pool of her own blood.

I didn't just break your curse, she wanted to tell him. *I reversed it. Forever. Cressida can't touch you.*

But she was fading too quickly, and the words wouldn't come.

Sensing Cressida's proximity, Gideon's arms tightened on Rune. His tears splashed onto her face.

"I love you," he whispered into her hair. "I should have told you so much sooner. *I love you, Rune Winters.*"

Death was pressing in. As its shadow slid over Rune, Antonio's words echoed inside her:

Sometimes our paths must diverge from those we love. But if love is the highest power, our paths will converge again—if not in this world, then the next.

Pressing her hand to Gideon's heart, Rune whispered: "Come find me in the next world."

And then Death found her.

SEVENTY-SIX

GIDEON

IDEON THOUGHT HE'D ALREADY seen rock bottom.

How wrong he'd been.

The moment she stopped breathing, he knew it. As her body went limp in his blood-soaked hands, all he could do was stare at her, disbelieving.

She's gone.

As the sobs crawled up his throat, Gideon dropped his forehead to hers.

Cressida was shrieking somewhere behind him. Cursing his name. Her presence like an imminent hurricane.

He didn't care. The world beyond him was nothing but a blur.

Let her come.

Gideon was still cradling Rune in his arms when the witch queen's shadow slid over him.

"You have no idea, the ways I'll make you suffer for this."

He tore his gaze from Rune's face and looked up at her.

Spellmarks were inked in blood down her bare arms and rage contorted her face. Her hair billowed in the wind as if she were a storm incarnate.

Her presence was a deafening thunder.

As she spoke, she smeared more blood onto her arms, forming symbols. The air sparked with magic. Her fingers crackled with lightning.

Cressida flung out her hands, hurling the bolt at Gideon.

The air sizzled and cracked. The immense power should have knocked him flat on his back—instead, it ricocheted off him, as if hitting some unseen armor, and struck Cressida instead.

She landed flat on her back.

What the hell?

Still cradling Rune, Gideon watched Cressida roll over, groaning with pain. She shook her head and pushed herself to standing. Beyond her, the witches who'd crossed the bridge hung back, glancing uneasily from their queen to Gideon.

Spinning to face him, Cressida's eyes narrowed to slits. Pulling the gun holstered at her hip, she raised it and fired.

The bullet should have been a direct hit; she was only a few strides from him. But again, Gideon felt it rebound, flying straight for Cressida, missing her face by a hair.

He remembered the enchantment Rune had once cast on his jacket.

It's for repelling harm, she'd told him. *Like armor, the spellmarks will deflect a knife aimed at your chest, or make bullets bounce off you.*

He glanced down at the girl in his arms, her eyes closed forever.

Had Rune done this? Cast one last spell of protection, somehow?

One thing was clear: Cressida couldn't harm him.

Setting his beloved down gently, Gideon rose to his feet.

Cressida fired four more rounds. Each one ricocheted off him.

She stumbled back.

Cressida screamed, slicing her arm, making more spellmarks with the blood gushing out. The wind picked up, howling in Gideon's ears. The whirlpool churned faster, the water rising like a hurricane, swirling around them. Cressida lifted her hand, flinging her arm toward Gideon, hurling the whirlpool at him.

Several tons of water descended on Gideon. He braced himself for the crush, ready to be swept out into a watery vortex and dashed against the rocks.

Only it never hit.

The water crashed, slamming against Rune's invisible dome-like shield, falling around him and Rune like a waterfall before rushing back toward the whirlpool, nearly sweeping Cressida out with it.

Leaving him completely dry.

When the witch queen regained her footing and saw he was still standing, utterly untouched, her eyes blazed with fury. She drew more spellmarks, readying a new spell.

The casting knives of every witch standing on the shore flew upward, out of their sheaths. Like arrows, they shot in unison toward Gideon, glittering in the vanishing sunlight, their lethal edges aimed at his throat.

But they, too, failed to meet their mark.

One by one, they came up against Rune's spell, their tips bending, chipping, then clattering to the stones around him.

This time, Cressida's eyes widened in fear.

"Fire, you imbeciles!" she screamed at the soldiers standing on the bank. "Shoot him!"

Their bullets soared like comets. Coming straight for Gideon.

Every single shot bounced off.

Gideon thought of his Crimson Moth and smiled through his sorrow.

Even in death, my love, you are a wonder.

The gunfire abruptly stopped as soldiers took cover from the rebounding bullets. In the chaos, Gideon saw Juniper knock her captor to the ground and steal her gun. His heart thrilled further as Harrow wrapped her restraints around an enemy soldier's neck until he passed out beside her. She grabbed his gun and started firing.

BANG! BANG! BANG!

The witches who'd crossed the bridge were backing away, returning the way they'd come, trying to escape the line of fire.

Gideon stared down Cressida.

The wind whipped around them. It was only the two of them now.

"My brother showed you mercy once," Gideon shouted over the whirlpool's roar. "I won't make the same mistake." He closed the gap between them. "On your knees."

Cressida slashed her casting knife at him. "Never."

Gideon huffed a laugh. "You can't hurt me anymore, Cress. You'll never hurt me again."

Rune had done that: reduced this powerful queen to a pathetic creature when met by Gideon Sharpe.

He grabbed the wrist of her hand—the one that wielded the knife—as she tried to cut him down. His hand tightened, crushing, until her grip loosened.

It fell to the ground.

Grabbing her throat with both hands, Gideon squeezed, forcing Cressida to her knees and into the dirt. "If there's a hell, I hope you burn in it."

"Go on, then." Her eyes glittered black as she stared up at him. "Send me to hell."

His hands tightened.

"I'll never stop haunting you, Gideon. I will always—"

"Wait!"

Seraphine was stepping off the bridge, coming swiftly toward them, with Antonio on her heels. A white spell flame floated over their heads, lighting their way in the twilight. Across the whirlpool, Juniper and Harrow blocked access to the bridge. With them stood a dozen witches, forming a wall of defense.

Seraphine was right, he realized.

More and more were defecting. With no way to resurrect Elowyn and Analise, with Cressida at the utter mercy of Gideon, they had far less to lose and were coming to join the line forming between the witch queen and those trying to aid her.

Seraphine crouched next to Cressida; Antonio joined her a few seconds later. In his arms was Rune, and on his back was her leather satchel. He lay Rune carefully down on the other side of Seraphine, then pulled back the satchel's flap and withdrew a spell book.

The white flame hovering in the air cast an eerie glow over them all.

"Any moment, witches are going to break through that barricade," Gideon told Seraphine, his hands tightening around Cressida's throat, choking off her breath. "I need to put this dog down."

"Not yet." Seraphine touched his arm. "Trust me."

So Gideon loosened his grip on the witch queen's neck.

Seraphine seized the knife sheathed at Rune's leg while Antonio opened the spell book to a page marked with a ribbon, holding it up for her to read.

Catching sight of the spell, Cressida laughed.

"An *Arcana*? We both know you won't risk corrupting yourself, Seraphine."

Gideon saw the movement too late: Cressida snatching her moon-curved casting knife and lunging for the witch beside her.

It was Antonio who grabbed her wrist, holding her back.

"Little queen," laughed Seraphine, "I am incorruptible."

Cressida frowned, her gaze flickering over Seraphine's face.

"My name is *Wisdom*." Her voice rang like a drawn blade. "And I've waited a long time for this."

The witch queen's face paled, and she tried to rise. Gideon slammed her down, pinning her beneath his knees, his hands tightening around her throat.

Seraphine . . . is Wisdom? The Ancient?

She didn't look like a being who'd created the world. She looked like a mortal woman, barely older than twenty.

Wisdom's dark eyes flickered, then glowed bright white as she sliced Cressida's arm, Antonio holding it steady. The blood gushed, thick and red, and Wisdom dipped her fingers in the stream. She used it to draw seven spellmarks across Rune's lifeless body: on each of her open palms, at the base of her throat, across her lips and forehead, and then, after instructing Antonio to take off Rune's boots, she drew two more on the soles of her feet.

When she finished, a coppery smell bled through the air, mingling with something else. Something older than these mountains. Something far more primal than the murderous currents crashing around them.

Magic.

Ancient and powerful.

Wisdom turned to the witch queen trapped beneath Gideon, with no hope of escape. Antonio pinned Cressida's arms to the ground above her head, allowing Gideon to let go of her throat and lean back, restraining only her lower body. Cressida writhed and squirmed, but they held her fast.

With Rune's knife in both her hands, the Ancient lifted the blade high in the air.

"The queens and commanders of this world may think they know something of power," she said. "But true power is divine, and her judgment is final."

She plunged the knife straight into Cressida's heart.

The witch queen gasped and the symbols on Rune's skin glowed moon-white. As if joining in with the breath she took, coming alive as Wisdom's magic stole Cressida's life force and poured it into Rune.

Magic flared, disorienting Gideon and making his teeth ache. Building and building until it caused a pressure in his head so painful, it felt like it would explode.

And then: Cressida fell still.

The tension lifted.

Rune inhaled a sharp breath.

SEVENTY-SEVEN

RUNE

COMING ALIVE WAS LIKE waking up to the world's wonders.

When Rune opened her eyes, it was dark. But not the darkness of death. This dark was different. Trapped in the black web above her were tiny pricks of light.

Stars, she realized.

All her life, she'd taken them for granted. Why hadn't she stopped to admire their beauty more often? She should have spent every night staring up at the sky, filled with awe. Knowing that one day, the stars would shine no more.

Rune inhaled. Breath filled her lungs, expanding her chest. It, too, was wondrous. She pushed it out again, into the world, then sucked it back in.

Why hadn't she known what a precious gift it was, this breath, flowing in and out, over and over, every day?

"Rune?"

Her breath faltered.

Gideon.

His voice poured warmth back into her, melting away the last of Death's icy hold. She sat up and found him staring at her.

Her Gideon. She wanted to trace every stern line of his face. Wanted to run her fingers through his tangled hair. Wanted to feel the roughness of his cheeks beneath her palms.

The bloody symbols—one for *Witch's Armor,* the other for *Everlasting*—still lingered on his cheeks.

"Alex loves you," she blurted, wondering where the words had come from. "The day he died, he made me promise to tell you. But I . . . I never did."

She felt Alex now, all around her, in the way a dream sometimes lingers in the moments after you wake.

Gideon leaned forward on his knees and cupped the back of her head with his hand. As his forehead touched hers, a shaky laugh escaped him.

"Did he remind you of that just now?" His smile was in his voice.

"I . . . I don't know," she whispered, wrapping her arms around his neck, breathing him in, hugging him close. "Maybe."

Over Gideon's shoulder, she saw Seraphine and Antonio kneeling over Cressida's dead body. Seraphine was whispering something while Antonio held Rune's spell book aloft for her to read.

Cressida's corpse burst into black flames. Rune watched them devour the witch queen. Her *sister*.

Gideon's arms came around her as she hugged him harder.

When the fire burned out, only a heap of ash remained. Next, Seraphine called up a wind, scattering the ashes into the whirlpool. Washing all remnants of Cressida Roseblood away.

"The other two?" Antonio asked, glancing toward the pool where the corpses of Elowyn and Analise lay beneath the surface. With Cressida dead, her casting signature had disappeared.

The spell protecting them was broken.

"We'll burn them, too," said Seraphine, getting to her feet to help drag the sisters out of the water. "Just to be safe."

Gideon gave Rune a squeeze before letting her go and rising to help them.

When it was done, and all three former witch queens were nothing but ash on the wind, Seraphine glanced at something in the distance.

Rune stood and turned to look. Gideon and Antonio stepped up beside her, watching as six figures appeared at the water's edge. Each one shaped like a woman, glowing faintly. As if they were made of moonlight.

Rune stared with her mouth agape.

"Is that . . . ?"

Seraphine walked slowly toward them, her humanity receding with every step she took, until she, too, was as bright as the moon.

But she didn't join them. Not yet. Pausing, she turned to face Rune. The lines of her face were the same, and her hair still billowed like a cloud around her head. But she was flesh and blood no longer; she was something else.

"Goodbye, Rune Winters."

Her voice was still Seraphine's, but not Seraphine's. It was like the wind, howling through a tunnel in the rock. It was the sea in a hurricane. Fierce, mighty.

She touched Rune's cheek, the pads of her fingers soft as a butterfly's wings. "Kestrel would be proud."

And then she was gone. Turning away to join her ancient sisters.

When they were together once more, they disappeared like the stars at dawn. Retreating to the world beyond this one.

SEVENTY-EIGHT

*L*AILA CREED STRODE THROUGH the stone halls of the Rookery, the sounds inside waking with the dawn. Sunlight filtered in through the windows as the sky flared pink over the sea. The soldiers behind her dragged their hostage down to the mess hall, where a platoon of Blood Guard officers was enjoying breakfast.

The Cascadian Army—what Laila and her soldiers had started calling themselves on the journey here—had snuck into the heavily fortified citadel last night, through the servants' quarters, where Blood Guard officers loyal to Gideon Sharpe had let them in, given them arms, and now padded out their ranks.

"Laila . . . Laila, *please.*"

"Shut him up," she barked, shoving open the double doors leading into the mess hall.

The Cascadian Army filed in behind her, lining up against the walls, marching through the aisles between tables, armed with the weapons belonging to the men and women currently eating.

Laila halted. Every head bobbed up to stare at her.

"Listen here!" She shouted so her voice would be heard across the mess hall. "As of now, you have new orders."

The two soldiers behind her stepped forward with the hostage, shoving him to his knees. Along with his wrists being bound behind his back, Noah Creed's mouth was now gagged.

As every soldier in the hall stared in shock at their Good Commander, he lowered his gaze to the floor.

"Effective immediately, no one is to be hunted or harmed for being a witch, and all purgings are outlawed."

"Says who?" shouted some wiseass three tables over.

Laila glanced over to find four of her soldiers already dealing with him.

"Says Commander Gideon Sharpe," she growled.

At Gideon's name, a hush fell over the hall.

"You have three choices before you." She held up her index finger. "You can enlist in the Cascadian Army and begin reporting to Commander Sharpe." She held up another finger. "You can hand over your uniform and go home." She held up a third. "You can be hauled off to prison, where you will spend the rest of your days rotting in a cell next to this piece of shit." She nodded to her brother, cowering on the floor, and shoved him with her foot. "Anyone unclear about any of that?"

No one raised their hands.

"Perfect. Enjoy your breakfast. Afterward, every one of you will report to the courtyard, where you'll receive new instructions or be dismissed."

Amidst nervous whispering, the former Blood Guard officers went back to eating, the watchful gazes of Laila's armed battalion looming over them.

EPILOGUE

THREE MONTHS LATER

RUNE STARED OUT THROUGH the front windows, her attention fixed on the parked carriages lined up outside Wintersea House. A full moon shone from the blue-black sky as guests dressed in glittering finery trickled in through the front doors.

Rune clasped her hands to stop them from shaking.

I can't do this.

Lifting the hem of her evening gown, she spun on her heel and marched past the stairs leading down to her ballroom—which was decorated for tonight's celebration, not to mention full of chattering guests. She glimpsed Bart Wentholt's coppery hair and heard Juniper's bright laugh. But her friends only strengthened her conviction.

I can't go down there.

Rune slipped into her bedchamber, where all was quiet and still. The lights were turned down for the evening, and the door to her casting room stood ajar.

She swung it open and went inside, heading straight for the window, where she opened the latch and pushed out the pane.

A warm breeze flowed in.

Rune paused for a second to close her eyes and breathe it in, remembering how lucky she was. How never again would she take anything for granted. Not the breeze on her face. Not the moon or the sky. And certainly not this island she called home.

It was that in-between time when summer transitioned to

fall. The trees were changing color, and the winds were getting rougher. The temperature could be hotter than the height of summer one day, and so cold it might as well snow the next.

Tonight was closer to the former. Warm and breezy.

Rune hiked up the skirts of her dress and climbed into the windowsill, planning to scale the ivy and escape through the gardens.

"Where the hell are you going?"

The voice made her freeze.

Rune stared toward the fields, where a path carved through the wildflowers, leading into the woods and down to the sea.

"Just . . . um . . . checking the gardens."

She ducked back inside, resenting the blush blooming up her face, and spun to face the intruder. Gideon Sharpe leaned against the door frame, arms crossed over his broad chest, staring at her with an amused expression.

"I asked Lizbeth to make sure the paths were lit"—she avoided his gaze, letting her eyes scan the shelves full of spell books—"so the guests can stroll there. I want to make sure she didn't forget."

"You can't go out the back door, like a normal person?"

Rune glanced longingly to the window. To the moonlit path through the fields.

Gideon pushed away from the door and came toward her. "What were you actually doing?"

Rune's gaze snagged on his militia-styled tailcoat, its rust-red shade complementing her turquoise evening gown. Gideon would have been a gentlemanly vision of perfect style had it not been for his cravat. Which he'd completely botched.

He couldn't go downstairs like that.

"It's the perfect night for a swim, don't you think?" she said, closing the distance between them, her fingers itching to fix the cravat.

"A *swim?*"

"Mmm." She reached for the white silk around his neck and started untying it. "Just think . . . you and me. *Naked.* In the sea. No one will even notice we're missing."

He raised an eyebrow. "I think people will notice that their new parliamentarian—who they're here to celebrate tonight, and whose house they're all gathered in—is nowhere to be found."

Rune made a face as she tugged the white silk free of his neck, lifted his collar, then tied it again. "We can be fashionably late."

As in, so late, we arrive when everyone else is drunk and leaving.

Ever since the election results were announced, Rune had been like a jumpy horse in a cramped stall. She'd been chosen to represent her district in the House of Commons, the heart of Cascadia's new government. Thirteen officials had been elected, with each one having a seat in parliament. Six seats had gone to witches; seven to non-witches.

Rune crossed Gideon's cravat over itself twice, then pulled it through, tying the knot and tucking it into his waistcoat.

Perfect.

"Antonio spent a week making the cake."

"So he says," she murmured, running her hands up Gideon's chest and looping her arms around his neck. If she couldn't convince him with words, there were other ways to win him over . . .

"There are a hundred people downstairs waiting to—"

Rune pressed her lips against his throat.

He fell silent. She continued kissing, moving slowly upward. She felt the change in him—the stiffening of desire. His hand moved to her hip, then slid to the small of her back. Drawing her closer.

"What are you doing?"

"Kissing my husband?" She slid her fingers into his hair and pushed up onto her toes, only to find his mouth waiting for hers.

Their hips collided as he pulled her flush against him.

Rune suddenly regretted retying his cravat. She should have left it off. Should have unbuttoned his coat and then moved on to his shirt . . .

As Gideon dragged her bottom lip between his teeth, Rune's fingers moved to the buttons of his tailcoat, undoing them. When he realized, he grabbed her wrists, stopping her.

"*Rune.*" Her name was a frustrated growl. "You're not going to seduce me into running away from your party with you."

She pouted as he stepped back.

"These people want to *celebrate* you."

Those words pinched her with guilt. Rune glanced away.

"What is this really about?" Gideon reached for her hand, running the pad of his thumb over the thin scar at the base of her ring finger. "There's nothing to fear anymore. All you have to do is be yourself."

That's what I'm afraid of.

"What if I disappoint them?" she whispered, avoiding his gaze. "What if they don't like the real Rune Winters?"

He laughed.

"Beloved." He took her chin between his fingers, trying to drag her gaze up to him. "That's not possible."

She tugged her chin free and started to retreat, but he grabbed her around the waist and pulled her back, nipping her bare shoulder, then kissing the edge of a scar peeking up above her dress.

"You're the opposite of disappointing."

"What if I fail them?" She weaved her fingers back into his hair. "What if none of this works?"

"Then we keep trying and fixing it until it *does* work." Releasing her waist, he grabbed her hand again, lifted it, and kissed the ring-like scar banded around her second smallest finger. "Just like everything else."

Rune glanced at the matching scar banded around his finger.

They were casting scars formed from the spells she'd performed during their wedding, which Antonio officiated, keeping his promise. While speaking their vows as their friends bore witness, Rune had cast two spells: one for speaking the truth, and the other binding them to their words.

So now, instead of wedding bands, they wore wedding scars.

"You have to start somewhere," he said. "And *this* is where we're starting."

Winding his fingers through hers, Gideon tugged her from the casting room. She resisted a little, but eventually gave in, letting him pull her to the staircase leading down to the ballroom. Where their guests waited.

Rune paused at the top of the stairs. The chandelier winked overhead. Her pulse stumbled as more and more people turned to look up at the Crimson Moth and her army commander.

She glanced wistfully back in the direction of her casting room and the open window.

Noticing, Gideon leaned in and whispered against her cheek, "How about this: when these aristos are gone, you and I will reconvene. *Naked.* In the sea. Deal?"

Rune bit down on her smile. "Deal."

Gideon tucked her arm through his as they faced their friends.

"It's time to make a new world, Rune. Are you ready?"

ACKNOWLEDGMENTS

Thank you Danielle Burby, for everything you do, but most of all, for believing in me. I'm so glad we found each other.

Thank you Vicki Lame, for letting me write the books that make me feel most alive. I love that I get to keep working with you!

Thank you to everyone at Wednesday Books for sending my stories into the world with a bang: Vanessa Aguirre, Sara Goodman, Eileen Rothschild, Alexis Neuville, Brant Janeway, Alyssa Gammello, Kerri Resnick, Olga Grlic, Eric Meyer, Chris Leonowicz, Cassie Gutman, and Martha Cipolla.

Thank you to Taryn Fagerness and my foreign editors, translators, and publishing teams. Seeing my stories in languages other than my own never ceases to blow my mind.

Thank you to the indie bookstores and booksellers who championed this story and recommended it to readers. (With extra special thanks to Thistle Bookshop and Words Worth Books!)

Thank you to Canada Council for the Arts, for helping me keep the lights on and the roof over my family's head while working on this duology.

Thank you to my family, for watching my sparkly princess child so I could get more words written.

Thank you Joe, for never doubting me. I'm not sure how I got so lucky, but I'm grateful every day that I did.

Last of all, thank you *readers*. To those of you who've been here since *The Last Namsara*, and to those of you just finding my books now. Please believe me when I say that it is such an incredible privilege to entertain you. (Unless you're *not* entertained and are hate-reading these acknowledgments, in which case: carry on.) Getting to write stories for a living is a tiny miracle and I do not for a second take it for granted. I would not be here without you.

For what it's worth, *The Crimson Moth* was my "fuck it" project. When I first sat down to write this story, I'd just had a baby and was very much in survival mode. I did not care what anyone thought about this book screaming to get out of me because I didn't have room to care. I only had room to write, and because time was of the essence, I couldn't waste it on anything but the story *I wanted*. If my agent or editor needed to pull me back from the brink once it was written, so be it. But I wasn't going to hold myself back. I couldn't have if I wanted to. I was in primal, new mother, burn-everything-unnecessary-to-the-ground mode.

And then *The Crimson Moth* came out . . . and sold out across retailers its first week.

And then it debuted on the *New York Times* bestseller list.

I was floored. I definitely hadn't set out to write a bestselling story; I just wanted to write *this* story. I suppose if there's a lesson here, it's something like: follow that *fuck it* feeling.

That is my hope for you, dear reader. It's the same hope I had for Rune at the beginning of her story. (And for myself, in a way.) I hope you stop caring so much about the opinions of others and allow yourself to *live*. I hope you find the courage to be unapologetically yourself and start making your life—and maybe even the world—what you and the ones you love need it to be.